DEADLY DUTY

Joshua Travers, DA Adventure Series

By

Martin C. Brhel, Jr., Esq.

Disclaimer

This entire tome is fictional; ergo described as the first novel in my planned *Joshua Travers, DA Adventure Series*. The events herein described, and each of them, are imaginary, aka: Fantasy. Make-believe. Made-up. Unreal. Invented. Pretend. Imagined. Fictional.

Each and every one of the characters, as well as any other entities, whether private or public, are fictitious and not intended to represent specific persons, living or dead, or any type of enterprises.

Incidents portrayed as taking place are fully fictitious, even when settings are referred to by what appear to be true and correct names. The reader should not infer that the events so set ever happened.

Dedication

Deadly Duty is dedicated to the late Tommy Deen Morris, and his family, including his heartbroken widow, Donna, and their still grieving children. Alphabetically, they are:

- David Lynn Morris
- Kelli Grimes Morris
- Melissa Ann Morris, aka *Missy*
- Steven Wayne Morris.

When Donna learned her soulmate had been fatally wounded, while attempting to perform what should have been a routine repossession of yet another debtor's pickup truck, she expected TD's killer would be arrested and prosecuted for murder.

On my watch, that would happen, even in so-called *liberal* California.

Instead, an 1880's Texas law, Penal Code §9.41, combined with the killer falsely claiming he thought TD was stealing his truck, led the grand jury to not indict. Donna rejected this, and sought her own brand of justice.

Donna, your valiant struggle to honor TD's memory inspired me to write *Deadly Duty*. Could I really ignore the hurt in your eyes? May God bless you, and keep you and your family safe. With every fiber of my being, I salute you.

A reserved spot will remain in my heart, even longer than I linger here.

Special thanks to longtime, revered friend, Bill Kasal. We met when you videotaped one of my Crime Control Foundation events, in the '90's, doing it for FREE. You did 10 years, as the Palm Springs PD Reserve Captain, too.

Now, you've formatted *Deadly Duty*, creating its beautiful covers and spine, again doing so for free. Trust me, my brother, when I say a reserved spot awaits you one day, near the Pearly Gates.

Please note that Bill is also a fellow writer. Go to Amazon.com, and Google his name, Bill Kasal, so you can find his delightfully entertaining books. You will love him just as much as Mary and I do. I promise!

Joshua Travers, DA Adventure Series ©

(The Inside Scoop)

To my esteemed readers:

On the front cover of every book I write, immediately below my name, whether it's a *Joshua Travers, DA Adventure Series* novel, commencing with *Deadly Duty*, a biography, or one of my Courtroom Survival books, you will find the phrase **A Copper Bible Book**. I'll explain why in a bit.

Although www.CourtroomSurvival.com remains under reconstruction, I invite you to visit my **Books & Law Enforcement Teaching** page, et al, to obtain updates on my many books, whether they are in progress, or already completed, as well as other useful information.

Due to a recent hacking incident, I've temporarily disabled the **Comment** form on each website page. But, when time permits, I will restore each. Once I've done that, you can conveniently contact me at my site, by posting your question or comment, at the bottom of any page.

I began writing books, way back in the 1980's, and decided to self-publish, creating **Copper Bible Book Company** as my home publishing business. My first two books were written for law enforcement officers, aka LEOs. LEOs are informally known as cops or coppers.

Therefore, the first two words of its name, Copper Bible, were born. I saw my books as good books for cops, aka *copper bibles*. Still do. Now, every book I write will carry that designation, right on the front cover. And, that's true, whether it's one of my 5-star -rated *Joshua Travers, DA Adventure Series* novels, a griping biography, or an instructional Courtroom Survival book.

My own **CBBC** will publish them all. And, here's a heads-up. Each and every *Joshua Travers, DA Adventure Series* novel will be replete with both false and true clues, vis-a-vis any future plot(s).

Question? Will the true clues actually be true? Or, will they be as fabricated as the false ones? JT knows. But, do you? So, what's my game plan? Publish a new novel every six months, until my entire series is complete.

Like any other self-respecting novelist, I don't claim to be terribly original. In fact, I'm not. And, having said the aforesaid, as we trial lawyers tend to say, I write fiction, by drawing inspiration from real life events.

So, if you have any suggestions for future *JT, DA Adventure Series* plots, please contact me. If I use your own tall tale(s) in any future tome(s), I will list you, by name inside. And, as long as I have your delivery address, I will send you a personalized, complimentary book, each time we do that, just as soon as that one is in print.

Although I do most of my communicating via the 'net, you can snail mail me at **PO Box 6068 Laguna Niguel, CA 92607**. And, while I cannot defy the laws of physics, any more than you, I am faithful to incoming E-mail, generally responding within 24-hours. Reach me at mbrheljr@aol.com.

Like JT, I, too, possess a moniker: *drug czar of the desert*, thanks to one of my former dope cops. Yes, I treasure it. From the bottom of my heart, thank you for being here. Please *ask a friend to tell a friend*. And, when you do that, ask them to pass your information forward.

Table of Contents

PROLOGUE

For those of you who don't know me yet, I suppose I should introduce myself. I'm Joshua Edward Travers; District Attorney of what is now Solita County, California. My surname's first syllable sounds like *a*venue, not *a*viation.

You probably don't know this, but I became my county's DA without even getting elected. How did I do that? That's an interesting tale; probably as interesting as how Solita County actually became a county. But, the story I'm trying to share here isn't about me or my domicile. Thus, I'll just add this so we can move on. Here goes.

The incumbent DA died in office. The number two guy wanted to be a judge. I wanted to be DA. I suppose you can say it's all about location and timing. That hits the nail right on the head. But, let's save it for later. Ditto with how the eastern halves of Riverside and San Bernardino counties ultimately uncoupled to fashion Solita County.

Like I just said, this isn't my story. *Deadly Duty*, my first published book, is about the courageous, never-ending struggle of a young Houston widow trying to find justice for her slain husband. Here's how I got involved.

A bunch of boxes unexpectedly arrived at my office from Texas one day. These mystery packages were all addressed to me from the same sender. Someone I didn't even recognize…someone named Dawn O'Mara. I could have stood on top of all the documents and seen Russia. It was that tall.

What in holy hell? Without even trying, this woman flat bowled me over. This interloper also wanted me to sue some car dealership she claimed had hired her husband to do the repossession that killed him. Sure, this got my attention. Homicides generally do that. But, first of all, I'm not a civil lawyer. Ain't my bag. Besides, civil bores me to tears. Second? I'm a brand new DA and have important work to do here. Third? Solita County's my jurisdiction, not Texas. I both live and work in southern California. I'm a big fan of Texas. Sure, it's a great state and all. But, once again, it's not my turf.

This woman also hinted I should empanel a new grand jury to do the job the first one didn't do. I'm supposed to indict a guy named Johnny Walker that she says murdered Tommy Deen O'Mara? How? I'm not a Texas special prosecutor. Hell, I'm not even a Texas lawyer!

Chapter 1

We need to gab about me for just a bit so this whole thing makes sense. Being the DA means I'm Solita County's top cop. For whatever it's worth, I love being the guy who drives this particular bus. Having this privilege is truly a blessing and an honor. I was born to be the DA. And, I thank God each and every day for Him not disagreeing.

Folks who share stories, reciting verbatim everything said by whomever said it, drive me bonkers. I'm referring to the ones who have to share, word-for-word, everything said by whoever said it, instead of just giving you a Readers Digest version. Why don't they just tape record stuff? Since we don't know each other well enough yet, I'm going to err on the side of caution and assume you don't appreciate such literal verbiage any more than I do. And, even if you do, no offense, but I'm still not inclined to go there. Therefore, I'll work hard to keep quoted dialogue to an absolute minimum.

I've only been the actual District Attorney for a few months now. And, it seems, no sooner did I get this job, than I received the aforedescribed package from Mrs. O'Mara. She still hasn't said why she contacted me. Nor, have I found it necessary to ask. All I know is that she did. I mean, one day she wasn't here and the next day she was. Simple as that.

I summarily dismissed her idea as nothing short of basic garden variety lunacy. Wrong state. Wrong job. Wrong everything. But, I also learned something. I discovered the requesting party, as in Mrs. O'Mara, was quite persistent. Akin to mi esposa.

Let's face it. She just isn't one to give up. I don't necessarily have a problem with stubborn. I mean, I'm stubborn myself. Stubborn can be a good thing. That's fine except, at the time, I was getting paid to do other stuff. I had a brand new constituency counting on me to protect them. They still are and I'm still doing that. But, she got me to thinking.

Her massive container of unsolicited documents pretty much laid out the entire case. Frankly, I found myself shocked at how much information she provided. How did she even obtain some of it? I suspect this gal has some pretty solid sources. But, it still doesn't explain how she got this material. We are talking about some rather sensitive information. Keep something in mind. I have a respectable circle of sources and am not sure I could have gotten my hands on some of this material. Read between the lines.

A cacophony of voices began speaking to me. No, I wasn't hallucinating. They came from several audio and video tapes she sent. As you may have already figured out, my sense of humor occasionally leans toward the dry side. At least, that's what I've been told. I'm not trying to influence your opinion, however. Think what you wish.

I've always prided myself on having impeccable sources of information. Any self-respecting cop or prosecutor should. That's like drag racers calling themselves quick. It goes with the turf. But, Dawn O'Mara continues to open my eyes. As a rule of thumb, civilians simply don't dig up this sort of information. Okay, I don't mean to beat this to death, so let's move on.

It quickly became clear that Lady O'Mara just might be the exception to the general rule. It made me wonder what she did for a living. She appeared to be patient. A person has to be, in order to locate everything she sent me. Who knows? Maybe she's part bloodhound. Or, former CIA spook? I wasn't really sure. What I did know was that something was surely extraordinary.

A cover letter was at the top of the stack of O'Mara's documents. Considering I would eventually learn this stranger is a layperson, I found she wrote it rather well. At least I didn't find any misspellings or punctuation issues. Let me put it this way. It was better than what I've seen other lawyers do. And, I tend to be more than just a bit nit-picky about such stuff.

My job is to string words together into meaningful sentences. That's what I do. That's what all lawyers are supposed to do. This is true, irrespective of what area of law we practice. Some folks say we talk funny. That's not correct. We are verbally precise. We must be, in order to persuade others, and we are, if we expect to get paid for our services. A good lawyer is a wordsmith. Call me mercenary, but I like to eat.

Dawn asked me to phone her once I'd reviewed everything. She obviously assumed I would. Importunate lass, isn't she? This could spell trouble. But, she also made me think. Her letter introduced me to her late husband. It was evident how much she loved this guy she affectionately called TD.

Reading her letter prompted me to review the rest of what she sent. Initially, I was only going to skim the first few documents so I could tell her I wasn't interested or was too busy or something. Whatever. All I knew was that I didn't want to get involved and the sooner I could tell her that, the better. As I would learn, however, all this would soon change. And somehow, I found time to review everything, even though it took me nearly two long weeks of nearly daily attention to do so. I read, viewed and listened before and after work each week day, as well as almost all of each involved weekend. That was time I should have been investing in learning my new job, making me a bit resentful.

My normally sweet wife, Molly, the one with the great disposition, got more than a little cranky in the process. I even found myself listening to tape recordings while driving. By the time I was done with my assessment, I didn't know it, but I was already hooked. I hate telephones. And yet, I found myself phoning O'Mara.

Chapter 2

As I've already said, Dawn shared a lot of information with me, providing me lots and lots of particulars. She even told me how she and her late husband fell in love with one another. Her cover letter and the enclosed documents completed the picture. Once we spoke, I felt I knew everything I needed to know about her entire life with Tommy Deen O'Mara. I now knew each of them.

Glancing at the clock, I realized we'd been on the phone more than three hours. That shocked me. Remember? I'm the guy who hates telephones. Generally, I find them a complete and total waste of my time. They are just so damned invasive. But, it was still easier than flying all the way to Houston. By the time we hung up, my left ear felt like Mike Tyson tried to eat it. My right ear didn't feel a bit better either. As I tried rubbing circulation back into them, I wondered if my health insurance covered restorative plastic surgery. And, I still didn't know why she had chosen me. Texas had to have its own flock of lawyers. It's a big place.

Dawn omitted no details. Talk about verbatim accounts. I learned when, how and where they met, and, once again, how much they loved each other. She said the hole in her heart would never heal. I believed her. During our conversation, she even reiterated her letter to me at least once. It was almost as if she had taken the time to memorize it. Suddenly, it dawned on me that Dawn was speaking. Apparently, I was sidetracked, as I tend to do, and was mulling something over that she said when we were on the phone.

"I was running. I knew I was running," she began. "I could feel it in every pore of my body. At least, I thought I was. But, what was really goin' on? Was I awake? Was I asleep? Was I dreamin'? Either way, I knew I was moving as fast as my little old legs could carry me. But, I just could not close the gap. I could not get close."

Dawn said she felt herself starting to hyperventilate. She forced herself to breathe rhythmically. She shared that she even took the quantum leap of coaching herself to relax by breathing in a certain manner. I listened to her rendition as patiently as I knew how. Marginally so. Telephones. Phones and schedules. Patient, I'm not.

Have I mentioned yet I am not patient? Anyhow, she said she glanced over her shoulder at her car. The big black Lincoln Town Car wasn't a mirage. She could see it. There it sat, plain as day, haphazardly parked at the side of the potholed road. It was right where she left it. She knew her car, and even nicknamed it *Black Beauty*.

Dawn didn't know exactly where she was, even if she thought she'd been here before. She looked at her enormous Lincoln again. The driver's door was still open. Its window was partially open. This sure didn't sound like a dream to me. Much too vivid.

"Too many details," she said. "Couldn't be a dream. Was it the real McCoy?"

How should I know? So far, she had me totally puzzled. I'm not even good at crossword puzzles. I'm short on patience, remember? Dawn debated for an instant whether to stop. Should she go back and close the door? Should she roll up her window? Should I get an unlisted phone number? On top of everything else, I really had to pee. But, this isn't something you can tell a stranger. Especially a woman, particularly when you're a tight ass like me.

"My God," she said, looking around. "This is not a good neighborhood."

The lanky blonde spotted TD's little red wrecker tilted precariously in the ditch. It practically beckoned her. She maintained her frenetic race toward it. Suddenly she stopped, as she approached bright yellow crime scene tape.

Been there, done that. Difference for me is that whenever I see crime scene tape, I start looking to see who the uniform is with clipboard duty, so I can sign in and get to work on yet another homicide callout. I don't have to do callouts anymore, as the DA. But, I've put myself in the rotation so I don't get rusty. And yes, I like to stay on top of what's going on.

Crime scenes for civilians are a whole different story.

She debated whether to jump over or duck under it. Dawn vacillated for a brief instant. She touched the shiny plastic ribbon. Then, she heard a voice. Someone was calling her name. She glanced over her shoulder.

A uniformed Houston patrol officer was reaching for her. She didn't recognize him and pressed forward, trying valiantly to stay ahead of him. Dawn was bound and determined to reach her destination. She was going to do that. She wasn't going to let a law enforcement officer deter her. Not this time. O'Mara was a woman on a mission.

One way or the other, she was getting inside the tape. I could hear it in her voice.

"Dawn!" She repeated to me what the disembodied voice said. "Dawn? Baby doll? Are you okay?"

"How does he know my name?" she pondered.

Dawn looked around again, wondering how he knew her well enough to know her name. And, to call her *baby doll?* Now, that was getting way too personal. She desperately searched for Tommy Deen's face. No one was allowed to talk to her like that. Not even cops. She was a lady. Tommy Deen was very protective of Dawn and she knew it. In fact, she applauded it. She enjoyed the fact he did that. Quite independent, she nonetheless appreciated his devotion. After all, she was still his woman and he was her man. Dawn told me she normally just called her husband TD. But, that wasn't unusual. So did everybody else who knew him. He was the sort of person who instantly made you feel you'd known him forever. He was the All American kid who grew up just like everyone who loved him figured he would.

Dawn heard the voice again. Where in the world was she? This time, it was louder. And, more clear. Distinctly more clear. The sound jolted her awake. She sat straight up in bed, trying to orient herself. Dawn realized she was panicking again. Her nightgown was soaking wet. Her heart was pounding like a drum. Her stomach felt queasy. Rivulets of sweat ran between her breasts. Her chest was heaving. She could feel the perspiration. It already was pooling in her navel and trickling downward. She blinked, as she looked around. The repo wife still wasn't sure where she was.

Her vision slowly came into focus. She saw her husband. It was TD. He was staring at her. His face seemed to mirror unease, but he was also smiling. Was he alive? Or, was he an angel now? She heard his voice. It, too, epitomized anxiety. He gently held her face in his hands. Somehow, his doing this made her feel weak. He uttered his favorite term of endearment to her.

"Baby cakes, you okay?"

"Oh, TD. Thank God. I *was* only dreamin'. It wasn't real."

"It wasn't real, babe? What wasn't real?"

Dawn began to sob. She then shared what she'd just dreamt. She told TD about the phone call and her wild drive to his wrecker. She described dealing with the cop and wrestling with the crime scene tape. Or, more correctly, she shared her dream about fantasizing she was doing that. As she tried, she couldn't shake the amused look TD had on his face.

TD grinned, as she told him this. He asked her to take a sip of water and go back to sleep. She protested, but he was firm. TD assured her no dream could ever hurt either of them. Dawn wasn't sure she agreed. Considering what I knew, I wasn't so sure I did either at this point. I don't claim to begin to have even a fraction of the answers I thought I had when I was still a snotty-nosed twenty year old college student, misbelieving I knew far more than I really did. And, one of these is whether dreams have any significance. In the meantime, Dawn concluded with TD's final remark. She said she didn't know whether to breathe a sigh of relief or be upset. Why was he patronizing her?

"I got work to do. See?" he said, playfully touching her cheek with his fingertips.

Chapter 3

Some of the cops I serve with have given me a number of different nicknames: *Josh, Trav, JT* and *JET* are included in this mélange. The last one is an acronym from the first initials of my full name, first, middle and surname, rather than a comment on how fast I can still run or how fast I drive. I should probably invoke the 5th on that one, although I doubt I really still have the need for speed that once drew me to race motocross.

Somehow I've also acquired the moniker *Truth*. Not to be outdone, I'm told a handful of petty defense attorneys have added a few anatomically descriptive ones we won't talk about. Just sore losers, I suspect. Much to their credit, they don't share those particular ones with me face-to-face. I'm not a violent guy. But, I also am not one of those turn the other cheek kind of folks, especially when it comes to being disrespected. It's not about me. But, I'll be damned if anyone is going to get away with disrespecting my office.

In the meantime, let's get back to our introductions, so we can get on with what I am satisfied is a fascinating story about Dawn. My role as District Attorney has been an E-ticket ride, all the way. In short, it's anything but monotonous. Let me put it like this. It's anything but boring. That's good, considering how quickly I become jaded. And, if my hunches are right, it looks like my life is going to get a whole lot more irregular. You've probably already figured out where I'm going with this observation. If not, please listen. Cops have lots of expressions. Pardon my language, but one of them is *shit magnet*. An example? Visualize the cop who innocently begins his shift and runs smack into the middle of an armed robbery in progress. Somehow, I am similarly magnetized. When I was younger, there were actually days I felt a certain kinship with that little kid in the newspaper comics who walked around with the black cloud hanging over his head.

Don't misunderstand that observation to mean I'm saying I am not blessed or that I am unfortunate. Let me clear that up right now. I *am* blessed. And, I have the best damned job any lawyer could have. No amount of money could convince me to exchange it for another one. That call is strictly up to the voters of Solita County. But, for some reason, I also can't say that there is a perpetual sea of calm around me either. Go figure.

Solita County is a pretty conservative place. I'm talking old school. Real old school. I mean Ozzie and Harriet Nelson-style traditional. Lots of American flags fly here. And, many U.S. Marine Corps flags wave daily atop front yard poles. Us residents park our vehicles and unabashedly display little American flags whenever Marine convoys pass through our town's main drag on their way to wherever they are being deployed.

We each flash our vehicle's headlights and blow our horns, if we meet each other on the road. We wave. They wave back. I generally also get a salute. I'll explain that in a bit. Doing all that is more my wife's idea, than mine. Some of these kids may not survive active duty. We know this. Molly and I do, that is. I suspect some of them do too. Life isn't always fair. Molly and I pray for their safety at the start of every day. Let's just say I've buried too many friends and leave it at that.

Sometimes, I get a bit cynical and have to ask God if He is really paying attention. Then, I realize I am but a mere mortal who doesn't have all the answers. But, it doesn't diminish my anger whenever the boys and girls who keep America safe from foreign bad guys don't come home alive. This sort of patriotic fervor shouldn't be terribly surprising. An enormous Marine base resides nearby. Its official name is the Marine Corps Air Ground Combat Center-Twentynine Palms. Semper Fi and all that good stuff.

In case you're wondering, yes, I, too, did time there. We live in Yucca Valley, the biggest town in the Morongo Basin which is about 20 miles west of there. Lots of friendly people live here. It's a family-oriented place. Lots of young parents. Lots of little kids. But, the age range covers the field. Some folks way up into their eighth decade of life and beyond call it home. And, more than a few are Twentynine Palms graduates just like me.

Many active duty and retired military and law enforcement live here. Many have served in both of these entities, gravitating from military to law enforcement. A goodly number did time as military police officers. Word on the streets is to stay out of certain neighborhoods, especially if you're a bad guy. Rumors swirl about lead poisoning being bad for one's health. We chuckle, but do nothing to dispel this. Why would we? Whatever works to keep good guys safe and sound.

Granted, we're not very friendly to criminals. But, that's of no moment to me or any other law-abiding resident. We're not the felony welcome wagon. Good riddance, we say. This appears to be the shared consensus of our community. Let the bleeding hearts in places like San Francisco keep their career criminals warm and fuzzy. We don't.

But, most locals hold doors open for strangers at area businesses. It doesn't matter what your gender is. Folks just do that for each other. And, we say hi to each other and try to be polite drivers. Up here, you find lots of decent folks. We work hard, believe in God, obey the law and pay our taxes. We also vote. And, most of us vote for conservative candidates. In other words, we're pretty much like you, hopefully. It's almost as if our area collectively decided to stop the clock somewhere back in the 1950's. If you pause for a moment and listen, folks swear you can hear Richie Vallens or the Big Bopper singing. It's my kind of town. Also helps explain my protective stance.

Twentynine Palms is where I completed active duty. I was still a JAG lawyer. That's JAG, as in Judge Advocate General. I began Marine Corps life as a Second Lieutenant and retired from active duty as a Colonel. Now, I'm a reservist. Molly still thinks I'll be a General. Who knows? That is out of my hands. And, I love being the DA even more than I love being a Marine. Hard to imagine, huh? God couldn't have written a better job description. Actually, I guess He did write it. And, military service clearly prepared me for public service and all the clear-headed decision making that goes with this particular job.

You can call this experience the privilege of continuing to serve. The pay ain't bad. Nice benefits. There's always plenty of excitement afoot. And, the best part? Just like any other American prosecutor, constituents pay me to do the right thing. My job is to convict the guilty, acquit the innocent and seek a fair disposition on each and every case I touch. This isn't just my inclination. It's my ethical duty. In other words, I dispense justice. I do the right thing. Nice fit.

All prosecutors are supposed to do this. That's our job. Dispensing justice is done for both victim and defendant. In case you're wondering where I'm going with all this, I'm not off on same irrelevant tangent. All this ties directly into the reason for Dawn's request. She didn't believe any justice was afforded her family by her own DA. She could well be right. Being one occasionally means dispensing justice in far more substantial quantities than a defendant may prefer. Translation: we rearrange housing accommodations for bad guys. The kind of hotels we fill are the grey bar variety. Easy entry. Difficult exit.

As I take this impromptu trip down Memory Lane, it finally hits me. I now grasp what's happening. A grieving widow has just thrown me a curve ball. And, it hangs there, threatening to dump every ounce of my 185 plus pounds right square on my fanny. A voice deep inside tells me I have an important job to do in Solita County and should simply tell Dawn O'Mara I am not the guy she needs to avenge whatever happened to TD. Sure I'll pray for the man, but, at this point, I'm not quite sure what I'll tell her. Maybe I'll just direct her to her county's bar association and suggest she see if the folks there can give her guidance on what local lawyer she should hire, right there in Houston.

Sitting at my desk, I slowly reread her letter again. It's been days since we spoke but I can still hear the sound of her voice. And, amazingly, I continue to feel her pain. I now carry that letter with me everywhere I go, so I can peek at it as needed. As I weigh her missive for the umpteenth time, I realize I'm talking to myself...again. I'm becoming fixated. Is this bonkers or what? Or, am I just going nuts?

"This is bizarre," I mutter, far louder than I meant to do.

At first I don't realize I was actually speaking audibly. I look up. My next-in-command is standing in front of my desk. Stealth's nickname is well deserved. He's slippery, like Teflon. An enemy combatant wouldn't stand a chance. In years past, some didn't. Better them than him. Or me. I'm glad he's on my side. Newly minted Assistant DA Benjamin (pronounced Beng-ha-meen) Armendariz has just stolen into my office like a damned sneak thief or something. Bennie is good at that. And, I mean real good. One moment he isn't there and suddenly, ta da, there he is. As a helpful aside, the only person I know who can get away with calling him *Benjamin*, pronouncing it as if it's a Spanish word, is his own mother. I'm serious. Don't even try. In fact, don't even think about it.

Bennie and I go back many years. We served together in the Corps. And, don't you dare pronounce it *corpse*. When I was Staff Judge Advocate, Ben was one of my best prosecutors. Actually, he was probably the best. What am I saying? He was the best of the best. When I joined the DA's office, I was delighted when he followed me here to Solita.

"You're mumbling to yourself," he repeats himself.

Initially, I debate whether to tell him about Dawn's request. However, the reality of our sharing Desert Storm duty in the early '90's quickly puts that issue to rest, once and for all. After all, we've been a team for a long time. If it ain't broke, don't fix it. I quickly decide that I must tell him. And, I do.

"Yeah, whatever," I grumble. "Ben, listen up. This is confidential sh-- ...stuff."

In case you're wondering what my verbal sensitivity is all about, Molly has been riding my ass...uh, I mean my butt. She says I cuss too much. Cuss too much? I'm a Marine and a DA for crissakes. It's almost genetically inbred. But, to avoid familial conflict, I'm trying to clean up my act. She's probably right. Doing so won't kill me, assuming I don't just up and pansy myself to death. But, old habits are also damned hard to break.

Back to my conversation with ADA Armendariz.

"This letter is from a Houston widow named Dawn O'Mara. She wants me to come to Texas to prosecute the guy who killed her husband."

"She what? Wait. Just hold on, JT. Start at the beginning, please."

I explain.

"And, she even wants me to sue a bunch of folks, once I get there. Absent law school, I barely know a tort from a tart. I've been the actual District Attorney for what...two...three months now? And, this woman is asking me to drop what I'm doing and go to..."

"Eighty-four days."

"What?"

"Eighty-four days you've been the DA."

"Whatever. That's not my point, Captain Precision. Any thoughts?"

"Prosecute? Sue? In Texas? Wow, that is off the charts. How you gonna do that?"

I throw my hands into the air, signaling stormy conditions could be brewing soon.

"Wait. I've got it. Why don't ya just ask the California Legislature to annex Texas? We can declare Houston part of Solita County. However, that might not go over big with the Board or your own constituents. Texans might not like it much either."

At first, I thought he was being serious. I should've known better. Obviously he wasn't. Bennie has never run away from an opportunity to make a joke. I shake my head and simultaneously scrunch my brow. Bennie grins one of his 1,000 watt smiles. His mind's sharp as a tack. Unfortunately, he's also a committed smart ass. Oh well. So am I. How in hell can you be upset at a guy who can smile one of those kinds of smiles?

Bennie also remains quite the ladies' man. I no longer am. That's fine. He's still single. I'm now happily married. BA and I once were quite the dating tag-team. No watering hole on any cocktail circuit was off limits. Bennie's motto? *No muff too tough.* He assures me God was thinking of us when He invented women.

He also mentions something about statutes of limitation, but I ignore him. In court, BA gets away with mischief most other lawyers wouldn't dream of trying to imitate. Frankly, folks are wise to not walk in his moccasins. They wouldn't survive. Predictably, some folks envy him. But, you can't help but smile when he does. He smiles. I smile. Bennie the Magic Man.

During our single days, I called him Bennie the Bad Boy, or, Bad Boy Bennie. But, don't misunderstand me. Ben is a consummate professional. If he wasn't, there is no way in hell he would be part of my team, and he's been that for a long time. Even so, BA remains a bit of a bad boy at heart. Long live statutes of limitations and the Fifth Amendment after all? Probably. Whenever he turns on his boyish charm, I still laugh. I do now. But, I quickly get serious again, so I can explain the situation. So does Bennie. He knows me. As a prosecutor, he's learned to quickly shift gears. Any prosecutor who can't multi-task, and do it efficiently, will get run over by the rest of the thundering herd. It goes with the turf. If you're going to run with a buffalo herd, be at the front. The view is better, as is the smell. I explain what's going on.

"Bennie, Dawn O'Mara claims the guy who killed her husband also beat the rap before a Harris County grand jury. They no billed him. He basically admitted to the cops he did it. And, she claims the police didn't put the case together right. Says the DA wimped out…blah, blah, blah. You know? The usual Monday morning quarterback analysis you hear from an amateur."

His tongue makes a clucking sound. He contemplatively strokes his chin. I continue. And, I'm feeling better and better to get this off my chest. Sure, I already talked to Molly about it. But, Ben's a lawyer. As my professional next-in-command, I highly value his opinion. I should. I'm the one who hired him.

I needed another sounding board. And, it needed to be a legal sounding board. I also needed a bit more objectivity than Molly provides on this issue. She usually gives great advice. Always has. But, she's still miffed I'm tied up with all this. Can you blame her? I don't.

"You're right. She's probably just another Monday morning General who doesn't know what she's talking about," Armendariz observes. "Another arm chair quarterback," he adds, as he mixes metaphors.

Bennie does that on occasion. He continues. I say nothing.

"Thinks she can second-guess law enforcement? And, probably doesn't know a jury box from the release button for the shotgun. We're used to dealing with these kinds of critics, Trav."

"I'm still reviewing what she sent me."

Without warning, I suddenly laugh. He looks puzzled.

"What?"

"Can't you picture my new business cards, BA?"

"Huh?"

"Joshua Edward Travers. Solita County DA. Prosecutor for hire. Motivated *and* mobile. Frequent flier miles included. You dial. I file."

"That rhymes. How poetic! Ferris Bueller, you're my hero," he chides.

"Hey, do I claim to be flipping Shakespeare? Do I, Stealth?"

I frown. Bennie doesn't even bat an eyelash. He transitions smoothly.

"Harris County? Isn't that where Houston's at?" he asks.

"You just ended a sentence with a preposition."

Hmmm? First mixed metaphors? Now, dangling prepositions or whatever the hell they are? Now, it's Ben's turn to get snippy. But, surprisingly, he says nothing and just stares at me. I didn't expect that. He usually has a quick retort.

"I guess. Never been there. Why in hell would I go there? Crissakes, Bennie. I've got enough headaches here without taking on some out-of-state murder case. And, yes, you hit the nail on the head."

I gesticulate with both hands flailing up in the air again.

"How would I even have jurisdiction to prosecute a crime committed in another state? Remember, if a murder occurred, it was likely committed by one of that state's residents against another of that state's residents. Do me a favor."

"Yeah?"

"When I'm done reviewing what she sent, I'm going to bang out a skeletal brief. Once I do that, I need you to read it, chew on it, digest it, and give me your thoughts. I need to know what you would do, if you were me. No third party eyes or ears, though. Okay? And, BA?"

"Yeah?"

"No damned sugar-coating. I need the unvarnished truth, whether I agree with it or not. Read me?"

"Gotcha, Truth."

BA disappears out my door and into the hallway. Like a ghost, he's gone.

Chapter 4

Tommy Deen O'Mara had been in the repossession business for nearly 25 years. Prior to this, the long tall Texan held a number of different jobs; many associated with the automobile business. He even owned his own used car lot for a while.

One day, a friend told TD just how lucrative repossessing motor vehicles could be. This pleasantly surprised him. And, he learned there was very little overhead compared to the inventory needed to run a car store. Sure, there was an element of danger. He knew that. TD heard all the stories. They all did.

The financial rewards that some hard work could generate for Tommy Deen and his loved ones easily outweighed any risks. He was too smart to get hurt. Tommy was a thinker. He was a planner. Sure, he worked hard. But, he also understood that working smart always took first place over mere sweat or brawn. As Dawn shared TD's earlier history with me, she said facing the hazards made sense to them, as long as they took adequate precautions.

Risks are part of many businesses. They aren't limited to just repos. People need to do whatever it takes to survive. TD O'Mara wanted to get ahead financially. So did Dawn. A debtor might be in arrears. And, vehicles were how they got to work. Motorcars helped keep proverbial wolves away from their door. They had done that previously and would continue to occupy the same role.

Having your own transportation is something America's working class still depends on. Unlike students and those many others label as poor, buses just don't cut it, especially if you don't live close enough to any bus lines to make it feasible. And, working folks haven't got the bucks to pay some fancy chauffeur to drive them around either. So, the most viable option is to have your own car or truck. After all, isn't this still the land of apple pie, motherhood and Chevrolet? It all began with Henry Ford and the iconic Model T and simply took off from there. Americans love our cars and trucks. We even loved the old German made VW Beetle when it arrived at our eastern shores in the 1950's. We're not European. But, even though the Bug was from Europe, it was plain and simple, made of hardy stock like Americans are. Most of us don't want to ride buses. We don't ride Eurail, not unless you're a student or tend to think like Europeans do. And, neither do Texans. This is the USA. Not Europe, with all of its teeny, tiny countries smaller than many of our own states, and a county or two.

We ain't one of those namby-pamby foreign countries where too many folks eat those little slimy things cluttering up sidewalks after a good rain or other stuff with names just too hard to pronounce. Haven't they heard of

Bugetta or whatever that stuff is that kills snails? Works fine here on this side of the pond. And, haven't they ever heard of good food? How 'bout some Tex-Mex? Ain't they ever heard of carne asada? Frijoles? Arroz? Salsa? Chili con carne? That's what workin' folks like. Lots of Texans are workers. Hard workers. Decent, honest workers. And, ones that aren't afraid of a little sweat either.

We salute Detroit here. Not Paris or Rome. Or, that fog-infested little island called Great Britain. Many workers here live from paycheck to paycheck, unlike ones in those foreign welfare nations that coddle folks from cradle to grave. Unlike there, welfare isn't meant to be worn like a badge of honor. Not in the USA. And, when you're counting on yourself to make your own way, rather than sucking on one of government's artificial teats, sudden separation from your one and only vehicle can take a tenuous situation from bad to worse in a heartbeat.

Dawn shared some examples of the dangers. She said it didn't take TD long to discover, first-hand, how touchy, even dangerous, desperate people can be. He learned survival of the fittest was more than a cliché some bearded guy named Darwin created. O'Mara also learned a correlation existed between the degree of desperation someone experiences and the raw depth of danger this presents. A hungry man can be a deadly animal. The hungrier one is, the more jeopardy is at hand. Wielded weapons include guns, knives, baseball bats, rocks, vehicles and virtually anything else not bolted or tied down. Arsenals even include saliva, feet, fists, knees, forearms, elbows and foreheads.

Although Tommy Deen had not been seriously injured on the job so far, it wasn't for lack of someone else trying. TD never shared his daunting on-the-job experiences with Dawn until the last few weeks of his life. Had he done so earlier, I believe Dawn just might have convinced him to retire. So did she. Unfortunately, by the time his wife knew, it was too late for her to do anything about it. The barn door had been flung wide open and the horse was halfway to the next town. Closing the door at that point wasn't going to accomplish much of substance, other than keeping the fugitive equine outside.

TD spoke of the time he was trying to repossess a car in one of Houston's rougher neighborhoods. As he backed his tow truck up to a targeted vehicle's back bumper, he heard a profane shout. Looking in the direction of the booming voice, he saw the biggest, angriest black man he'd ever encountered in his entire life. The guy's hands were like a pair of ham hocks, connected to tree trunk-like arms. This none too gentle giant had to stand at least six feet six inches and weigh close to three hundred fifty pounds of solid muscle. His catcher's mitt of a right hand was wrapped securely around the entire breach/trigger area of a double-barreled, sawed-off shotgun, with his left hand securing the barrels from underneath. The man's right forefinger was on the trigger. And, the 12 gauge was pointing right at TD's head and chest area; one squeeze and he knew he was a goner. He didn't need to be told to skedaddle twice and leapt behind the steering wheel, fired the engine to life, then quickly crammed his shifter into drive and stomped the accelerator right to the floorboard. The blast blew out his rear window. Fortunately, as he roared away, it only peppered him with glass fragments causing minor lacerations.

He initially told Dawn someone had thrown a rock. TD finally told her the truth a few weeks before his death. He said this was an up close and personal reality check. Tommy knew this was a battle for human survival, not racial superiority. He confided to her that he was toying with retiring from the repo game. Dawn told him she wholeheartedly supported that decision, just like she supported the one that got him into the business in the first place. It was a reality check for both of them. In any event, this particular jolt was more than what he needed to fully grasp the dangers accompanying his turf as a repo man. He understood the risks. But, the monetary rewards motivated TD to continue doing a job lesser men would never have the backbone to tackle in the first place. As I was quickly learning, it was one most folks could never do, neither for love nor money.

Dawn shared a conversation he had with a longtime friend. TD told him of the ambivalent feelings he was wrestling with about his considering leaving a job that paid him more than twenty thousand dollars a month. His friend asked if TD planned to be the richest man in the graveyard. Tommy observed the man but said nothing. He didn't have to. The ice cold glint from the man's eyes spoke volumes.

Dawn said her man lovingly stroked her hair before he began easing out of their bedroom to go elsewhere. In his mind, he'd done his job as her husband. He was confident he had sufficiently calmed her down following the premonition she hoped and prayed was just a bad dream. But, she was anything but placid. Her steady breathing told TD she was falling asleep. Dawn kept her hair long. She knew her long, flowing tresses reminded him of how she looked when they met. As he'd done many times before, he told her again how truly beautiful she was, as he stood by her side.

Dawn said TD regularly told her this. And, she never tired of hearing him tell her. After they met, he told her the instant he laid eyes on her that he knew she was the woman he would marry. And, this committed bachelor generally got what he wanted. Little did he know, like most other men, that women may let the man do the chasing. But, it's generally permitted only until the man is snagged, hook, line and sinker.

Chapter 5

According to Dawn, back in the day, TD was a footloose and fancy-free bachelor. She described him as far more concerned with mapping out his next planned date, than investing the time and energy needed for a long term relationship. I found nothing unusual about that. Sounded like a typical unattached male to me. At the time, TD didn't care if anyone else knew that. In fact, like many single guys, he wore it like a badge of honor, more for bragging rights than for any other purpose. Dawn laughed as she told me how they met. And, I mean she really laughed.

She said TD was driving a shiny black Corvette convertible. She was driving her bright red Mustang in the adjacent lane. Once he spotted her, he tried to flirt with her at a number of successive intersections, as they waited for traffic lights to turn green. But, true to form, Dawn pretty much ignored him. She went so far as to turn up the volume on her stereo so she couldn't hear him. She said the only reason she didn't also roll up her window was because the weather was too nice. But, TD was persistent. He actually enlisted the services of an on-duty cop he knew to vouch for him as a good guy. The officer was someone he had known for a long time.

As soon as she let her defenses slip, she agreed to join him for breakfast at a nearby Denny's and experience one of their signature dishes. She had never eaten at a Denny's before and once he had tantalized her taste buds, she had to sample her first Grand Slam. Following the officer's intervention, for the first time since they met and she learned what his name was, Dawn smiled. She was still guarded, but the smile was genuine. And, as she was to soon learn, no one had ever called her baby-cakes before either. In fact, no one had ever called her anything even close to that.

"Ain'tcha ever been to a Denny's, baby-cakes?" he pointedly asked her. Not waiting for an answer, he proceeded to describe what a Grand Slam breakfast was; his face displayed a big grin.

She shook her head from side-to-side, as she replied "uh, uh. Can't say I have."

"That's some right quality chow. Tall stack of pancakes, drippin' with your own choice of thick, sweet syrup? Eggs, any way you like 'em, scrambled, over easy, with bacon, sausage or ham? Toast, biscuits, English muffins, jam, jelly or honey? We're talkin' some mighty good eatin' there, pretty lady. You up for it, beautiful woman whose name I still don't know?"

"I'm Dawn."

"Dawn what?"

"For the time being, just Dawn is fine."

"Well, *just* Dawn," he joked. "I am honored to make your acquaintance."

Chapter 6

You need some additional background to better grasp how I fit into this particular puzzle palace, as we peer through the O'Mara looking glass. In other words, I'm not done introducing myself yet. Please be patient. We'll get back to Dawn and TD real soon.

Think of this as the sort of texture you might add to drywall to make it look nicer. Some who know me say I'm a bit mercurial. I don't think so, but reasonable minds can certainly differ on that, just like any other issue. Personally, I see myself to be steady as the Rock of Gibraltar. But, yeah, I do have a slightly short fuse and am the first to say so.

It's said that some folks describe me as an overgrown Boy Scout...one who drives too fast...cusses too much...smokes too many stogies...and occasionally enjoys a few too many adult beverages. Reputations apparently die hard, passage of time or not.

Actually, this far better describes me when I was much younger. I'm still growing up, just like the next guy. But, I've grown up a whole lot from those days. If this means I'm human, mea culpa. I'm working on correcting bits and pieces of what critics call personal peccadilloes. And, I'm having mixed results. Sure, I'm growing. But, I'm no magician. I don't control the laws of physics. That's the job for the Almighty. Not some simple country lawyer like me.

I'm just not old enough yet to relinquish every vice I still enjoy. Truth be told, I'm also too anally retentive about certain things. This includes my sworn duties. I'm paid decent money to do what I do. Voters expect me to unfailingly serve them. And, I hope I am doing just that. Bennie and Molly are my closest critics. And, they both tell me I'm doing okay. If anyone can factually criticize me, they can. And, they do. I'm not suggesting either is a fanny-kisser who is shy about providing critiques. They're not.

I have absolutely no patience or sympathy for criminals. Punitive potty training stories bore me. If you did the crime, get ready to do the time, whatever the law says that means. That's why I became a DA. When my duty to be a good citizen started regularly trumping my ethical responsibilities to my more challenging clients, I knew I was on the wrong side of counsel table. So, I moved, all the way to the other side.

Even though I was a defense attorney at the beginning of my civilian legal career, I have even less tolerance for a very small handful of some of them than for the clients they represent. Most lawyers are honorable. But, for the ones who aren't? Call me sleazebag-phobic. When a prosecutor tells you

you're too honest for your own good, as a defense attorney in the middle of a landmark murder trial, need I say more? It's time to move on. I squeezed that short tour of duty into my time between the Corps and the DA's office. It was instructive, if nothing else. I view defense counsel the way I do because I know where most of the bodies are buried. They do too. Sadly, some even have the picks and shovels to prove it. They know most of the tricks. I pulled some of them myself in years past.

This isn't something I'm particularly proud to admit. But, it is how the game is played by what cops call *the dark side*. That's because defense counsel is ethically duty bound to zealously represent their client. What does this *really* mean? You have to be ready, willing and able to make a hard-working cop look like a fool or a liar to a judge or a jury if this is what it takes to get your client acquitted. As long as you aren't *suborning perjury* or *perpetrating a fraud on the court*, you are doing your job, if you are trying to free your client. Those terms mean you can't encourage or allow a witness to tell a lie under oath about a material fact. Nor, can you get away with bamboozling the judge. Other than that, however, everything else is fair game. Doesn't matter if you know your client is guilty as sin. Same ground rules apply. Sucks, huh? Maybe you have to be on the dark side first in order to better appreciate the prosecutorial light.

My so-called Golden State has lots of statutes. We call them Codes. Alphabetically, major ones are Business & Professions, Civil, Civil Procedure, Evidence, Government, Health & Safety, Penal, Vehicle, Welfare & Institutions, and so on, with a bunch more in-between. And, California criminal lawyers speak a weird language. We talk in numbers. But, that's true in most other states too. This is true, whether we're DA's or defense attorneys. Ditto for cops and judges. If private investigators and law clerks want to sound cool, they do too. It's all about being numerical. And, I'm not kidding either. A quick trip to any California criminal courtroom will confirm what I am telling you. This is true in any part of my state. The numbers refer to the various code sections we veteranos have generally committed to memory from overuse. For example, robbery is a 211 (two-eleven), burglary is a 459 (four-five-nine), vehicle theft is a 10851 (ten-eight-five-one).

A helpful suggestion? Never call robbery a two-*one-one*, burglary a four-*fifty*-nine or vehicle theft a *one-zero*-eight-five-one. I don't know why. Just don't do it. It's not correct. If you do so, folks will know you're terminally amateurish. Fair enough?

A favorite for California cops is Evidence Code 1035 (*ten-thirty-five*, never *one-zero-three-five or any other combination*). Why does the law enforcement team genuflect at the altar of this particular section? We invoke 1035 to thwart defense counsel from obtaining the identity of confidential informants, or anything else we deem hush-hush. It's not like we are playing some silly-assed form of real life chess. This is done in order to protect public safety from bad guys who don't play by any rules, except their own once in a while. We call confidential informants CI's, pronounced See-Eyes. The initials speak for themselves. Some informants are called CRI's, i.e., confidential *reliable* informants. I've never understood the need for such distinctions. Does it make sense to use an informant that isn't reliable? Be that as it may, I'm sure appellate courts can tell us why. Counsel may suggest I'm not bright enough to understand dissimilarities as subtle as these. But, this old farm boy has never been able to tell a partly pregnant cow from a fully pregnant one either. Pregnant is pregnant, right?

Defense attorneys dismissively call CI's and CRI's *snitches*. They're pissed off that their client recklessly blabbed to an informant and got popped. Maybe it's easier for the dark side to paste negative labels on things they don't fathom. Sort of like how left-wingers criticize conservatives for identifying conspiracies. Does this also mean you are paranoid just because you correctly observe someone is following you? As a DA, I've learned that defense counsel go to seminars. And, I can always tell when, as they try their new stuff out the next time one of them tries a case against me.

This includes doing things like falsely accusing the DA of committing what's called *prosecutorial misconduct*, just to interrupt the prosecution's momentum. Perhaps they are just sore losers. For some odd reason, they remind me of the folks on the opposite side of my own political spectrum. I won't say what that is. But, I'll give you a hint. A local defense attorney once told a newspaper reporter I was so conservative I probably thought some guy named Rush Limbaugh was liberal.

Dammit! I think I just let the cat out of the bag. Maybe leftists go to seminars for reasons similar to those of defense counsel. Maybe they do it to learn how to falsely accuse their rivals of seeing conspiracies that really do exist. If I call a counsel table in the courtroom a Lamborghini Countach, does this mean it'll grow tires and wheels and drive away? I've prosecuted enough conspiracy cases to know what a conspiracy is. And, if a passel of liberals are falsely claiming there are no conspiracies afloat, this sure sounds to me like a rudimentary conspiracy. All it takes is two people joining together for the same purpose, in order to commit a crime. Hmmm?

Over the years, I've heard lots of confidential stuff from cops. These are the boys and girls whom I'm privileged to serve alongside. Somehow, someone apparently decided I'm supposed to be the de facto father-confessor for our troops. A collarless padre of sorts. I'm not sure that really suits me. But, it's not something I'll waste energy fighting, either. As my former boss said, it ain't the hill I need to die on. So, now I'm Dear Abby? Actually, that's fine. I get bored easily and love to hear good stories. I'm also curious. Okay, you win. Maybe I'm just plain nosy. Either way, I like to keep my finger on the pulse of what's happening. Cops are great CRI's. You think you've heard good stories? If you haven't heard some really good ones from the cops I work with, trust me, you haven't heard anything yet, especially if it starts with "this is 10-35."

I've already told you, depending on the subject, I can be a bit of a tight ass. But, if you think I get uptight, watch a cop go ballistic when someone asks for the identity of one of their informants. This is why 10-35 is a cop favorite. Actually, it's from the 10 Code, and is 10-36, not 10-35.

Whenever any peace officer strolls into my office, looks around conspiratorially, and whispers "this is 10-35," I know I better be ready to take something to my grave. And, it'll almost certainly be entertaining. Usually is. Cops are wonderful story tellers. But, I already told you that. I just thought it deserved repeating.

Needless to say, a number of my conversations commence with this unique caveat. Expect to learn something interesting. I've gleaned information from cops they won't even tell their beat partners, spouses, or clergy. And, they especially won't share such information with their supervisors. Gleaned. Now, isn't that just a wonderful word? It means gathered, scraped together, and so on. And, I don't hear many people using it. So, I try to use it every once in a while to gauge the reaction I get from folks who don't use it themselves. They practically dive for the nearest Funk & Wagnalls. Being obnoxious every once in a while is good for the soul. It is for mine, at least.

Cops say they view me differently from most other DA's. I suspect it's because they know I keep my mouth shut. Maybe there's more. Perchance it's our shared choir practices? Perhaps I laugh at their jokes or can tell good ones myself every so often? I'm not sure. But, I'd be a liar if I told you I'm not flattered. 'Cuz, I am.

"You're one of us" is one of their favorite expressions. Mine too. They're talking to me whenever they say that. I love it! This may also explain why the former Assistant District Attorney, aka ADA, rode me like a Bactrian racing camel before she finally agreed to file her own retirement papers. That event, if I may, was the best thing to ever happen to public safety. What in the hell was she thinking? Did she think we were conspiring against bad guys? Actually, we were. We still are. We team up to protect public safety by rearranging the housing accommodations for bad guys. We don't break any laws to do that. Predictably, she was never privy to any real 10-35 stuff, even though she thought she was in the loop because she was the top DA in the desert. She wasn't privy. You can take that to the bank, too. We called her the Chief Chick, the Ice Maiden, and other stuff I won't repeat here.

"You're too close to the cops," she warned me, not long after I was hired. I was puzzled and asked what she meant. She advised I went on "too many *police* ride-alongs." Were there actually other ride-alongs I'd consider doing?

Maybe she was subtly suggesting I should go hitch a ride on the Bookmobile. Either way, in her mind, even one ride-along was one too many. Forget the team concept our Government Code and appellate cases dictate.

Did she think sharing the front seat of a police car means you're part of some secret coven? I mean, come on already. We're not talking about blood oaths here. Where and why did she develop such an intense dislike for or disinterest in police officers? Maybe one of the young studs broke her young heart many years ago. I do remember hearing she was married to a probation officer long before I came to the desert.

Might explain why I never saw her at any local cop funerals as I stood there blubbering like a baby, as I buried yet another friend. If nothing else, the woman is terminally naïve, with prior convictions. That's another cop-ism. Felony stupid is another one LEO's use a lot. In case you're wondering, they mean the same thing. Ironically, after all the flack I caught from her on this issue, the DA later directed all the troops, *including her*, to begin going on ride-alongs. His unwanted motivation was a true Hobson's choice. And, I could not have been happier. Sad to say, I actually gloated. Yeah, I know, I should've been a bigger man. But, I wasn't. I enjoyed it immensely.

Here's what happened. One of my colleagues declared his own candidacy for an upcoming election. He, too, wanted to be the elected DA. As soon as the incumbent's challenger began sucking up the support of most local police officer associations, the DA asked why they were backing his underling. POA brass told him he didn't seem to care about their members' welfare. And, as their reasoning went, if he didn't care about the front line troops, he didn't care about public safety. Therefore, they didn't like him either. Seems logical. The incumbent had no choice but to acquiesce. Actually, surrender is a closer description. But, I'm trying to be kinder and gentler here. Molly's counting on me.

No sooner had the cops collectively decided to back his opponent, than he began asking what he could do to change their perception of him. His prosecutors needed to go on ride-alongs, they said, just like I'd been doing on my own all this time. He very grudgingly agreed to order this be done. The DA quickly authorized up to 16 hours of monthly compensatory time off for any participating prosecutor. I learned I would have earned more than 200 hours of comp time each year since I'd been there, had this new policy existed when I joined the office. But, it wasn't going to be retroactive.

That's five weeks of paid vacation per year. This is not a paltry sum. Vacation time is like currency. You can use it or just sell it back. I don't go on ride-alongs so I can get extra money. I do it to learn what cops do for a paycheck. But, come on. Fair is fair. His game plan, on the other hand, was duplicitous at best. Lots of carrots. No sticks. Typical politician. Prosecutors who chose to go on ride-alongs could now fatten themselves further with tax dollars. Slackers faced no penalties, hiding behind their Memorandum of Understanding, as a bar to punishment. His bark lacked any teeth. Therefore, any barking was not followed up by even the threat of any bites.

Mandatory ride-alongs ended just as abruptly as they began. Why? The DA got reelected. The coppers saw through his pathetic charade and immediately began grumbling again. Lucky for Marvin, it was his last election. His ticker did him a favor. Had his heart not killed him? Well, I'm not suggesting anyone was gunning for him. Not really. All that was coveted was his job, not his hide.

The many cops I work with provide all the daily inspiration I need. So, if they admire and respect me, how can this be anything short of mutual admiration? They've earned my respect and admiration the old-fashioned way. They have done it with professionalism and hard work. Period.

Molly often shares their comments with me. This happens whenever she runs into them, usually when she's out and about doing her professional thing, working rooms and such. She's great at remembering what she hears. She can repeat verbiage verbatim. Mol claims cops say stuff like "…I just love that guy…" Naturally, being inquisitive, I ask her to match names with comments. Sorry, I also have an ego. Mea culpa. Maybe even mea maxima culpa. Or, maybe I'm just as insecure as the next guy. Whatever.

Irrespective of what any underlying issue is, Dr. Freud, she generally isn't very helpful there. Why? Molly isn't real good at remembering names. I ask why. She says it's because I know too many people. I suggest she should write names down. She retorts that she isn't a newspaper reporter or a receptionist, usually followed up by something in Spanish that isn't printable. Well, it is. Just not here. This is supposed to be language I offer for family reading.

Mi esposa doesn't find my proposal terribly convincing. In fact, as noted, she even makes a rare and inappropriate suggestion. I respectfully decline. As another quick aside, Molly is bilingual. In her free time, she teaches me something she calls *Spanglish*. She tells me to be patient as this is transitional and it takes time. I tell her my high school Spanish teacher didn't even use the word Spanglish. Molly reminds me I am not fluent in Spanish, whether it involves speaking, reading or writing. She's called my bluff. And, I decide it's time to shut up.

Spanglish isn't really a separate language. The word Spanglish combines the first part of *Span*ish and the last half of En*glish* into a new word: Spanglish. It's colloquial. Spanglish is the use of Spanish and English words or phrases in the same sentences. Throw terms, like *veterano* or *esposa*, into a sentence full of English words, and voila, you have Spanglish. As you can see, I'm not the only teacher in our household. Far from it, in fact.

Chapter 7

My corazon, like me, also works outside the home. Amalia Gonzales Travers is Chief of Staff for our local State Senator. But, since this is not her story any more than it's mine, I'll save her career info for some other time and place. But, I will make this observation. I doubt I've ever met another human being who is as extremely talented, in so many different areas, as she is. Molly's great at just about everything I can imagine. This includes cooking, writing, photography, gardening, arts and crafts and probably even more pursuits I haven't thought to include here. Some I simply won't. Too private.

The list is nearly endless. And, as you already know, she's bilingual. She also has a very green thumb. We now have our own nursery as a sideline business. We didn't plan for it. It just happened. Some folks rescue animals. Molly rescues cacti. Our nursery business began with her rescuing one cactus attacked by some damnable rodent. I don't recall if it was a gopher, a squirrel or some other herbivore with fur and big teeth. Anyhow, Molly literally brought it back from the brink of death. That led to a second rescue. Then, a third, which slowly but surely led to a cactus garden. You get the picture.

But, to get more into Molly's cacti, it would also mean getting off track and into a discussion involving where we live. Hacienda Del Sol is our high desert ten acres just this side of heaven. It's our sanctum sanctorum where we decompress. Everybody has their own hidey-hole where they can recharge. HDS is our private place. More on that, some other time, too. But, I do know this much, without any hesitancy. Molly is an amazing woman and I thank God every day she's my wife. This helps me understand Dawn better. Basically, Molly hears the same stuff from the cops I do. It's nice to have a reliable second opinion. In the courtroom, we call that corroboration.

She's my own CRI. Or, should I just say CI? Maybe I'm being inadvertently redundant. Kind of like saying VIN number. Nonetheless, life is good. Actually, it appears I just let the cat out of the bag again. So, even though Molly remains reliable, to be technically precise, I can no longer call her a confidential informant. You now know who she is and what her role is. Her proverbial cover has been blown.

Chapter 8

When I was still Deputy-in-Charge of my office's Major Narcotic Violator Program, my duties required me to constantly juggle more balls than Enrico Rastelli. Now, with my added duties as the actual DA, the congestion has increased.

I try to balance my professional time between supervising subordinates, media relations, endless meetings, case reviews and court appearances, jaw-jacking with defense counsel, hanging with cops and serving constituents. This includes comforting victims and witnesses. Time consuming? Yes. But, it truly is a genuine labor of love. Maybe the key to staying on top of everything is to get up early enough. And, I do.

The original MNVP designation was a misnomer. I renamed it, officially changing its name in our Policy Manual. For reasons I'll never grasp, Marvin, or maybe one of his predecessors, titled it Major Narcotic *Vendor* Program. What's this vending stuff? That notion offends me on several levels.

First of all, not everyone who makes money from the illicit dope trade *vends*. Sure, some sell. But, others grow, cook, transport, or may merely be hired help doing whatever they are told to do in order to obtain their paycheck. The latter are not what you might call the big dogs. These minor players' tasks include cleaning up meth labs immediately following a cook, obtaining supplies, buying food and performing other menial tasks. Therefore, vend is inaccurate. It's overly inclusive. However, everybody plays a role. I will never attach any air of legitimacy to an illegitimate enterprise. Produce sellers *vend*. Those in the dope business *offend*. Therefore, as soon as I was sworn in as DA, one of my first official acts was to change the name. That's because they all violate.

I still do MNVP duty. I do it because I choose to do so. I will probably never lose my love of prosecuting major dope cases. Keep in mind a few of Marvin's hand-picked slackers are still here. I haven't figured out how to fire them yet, without buying my county a wrongful termination lawsuit or two. If I am nothing else, I am terminally cheap. I don't waste my own money and sure as hell will not knowingly throw away the precious Solita County tax dollars I am entrusted to spend wisely.

In the meantime, I will not turn MNVP over to any of these freeloaders. Solita County public safety deserves better. Don't worry. I will get rid of them. I just need to carefully document their malfeasance so I can do this right and make sure they don't come back. There are enough nuisance suits flying around jamming up the courts. I don't need to add to the problem by giving hungry lawyers a reason to file legitimate lawsuits. My predecessor and my successor both gave the MNVP store away. I remember. So do my dope cops. The narcs were ready to mutiny. We aren't going down that road again. Not ever. This is why I'll proceed slowly and evaluate who I want to head up this most important position, once the dead wood is gone. In the meantime, I handle MNVP myself. Ignorant people call dope cases victimless crimes. They could *not* be more wrong. Addicts commit a daily shopping list of significant crimes, i.e., misdemeanors and felonies, to get the money to get their dope.

That reminds me. I need to share something. I like learning new things daily and I suspect you do too. Book readers tend to be pretty smart folks. Smart people understand the importance of erudition. I, too, enjoy reading. But, that's beside the point. I'm not claiming I'm some sort of flaming genius. Sure, like you, I realize I'm no dummy either. But, I do keep my finger on the pulse of what's going on, in my community and elsewhere. And, therefore, here's my morning tidbit. Every pound of dope seized means 20,000 less addicts will get high that day. And, when I say dope, I don't mean marijuana. I'm talking addictive stuff like heroin, cocaine or methamphetamine. Next time you hear someone whining about local narcs *only* seizing mere kilograms of dope, please educate them. That's 44,000 addicts per kilo. And, remember to tell the skeptics that a kilo is 2.2 pounds. Do the math. Just one kilo is enough dope to get an entire medium-size city high. Affected addicts are out there, right now, robbing, cheating and stealing whatever they can trade for their next fix. Even one kilo is a lot of chemical body additive. We all have to do our part. Ignorance has no excuse. There's a good reason why it's called dope.

Hopefully, by now, you see why handling this MNVP assignment properly requires having a certain amount of fire in the belly. And, I don't mean gas. When I'm sure I've found the right person, I'll step aside. But, not before that happens. In the meantime, defense attorneys continue complaining I'm still being unreasonable. For some reason, that still makes me smile a lot. Sure, I really don't have to handle these major narcotic cases. After all, now that I'm the DA, I can do whatever I want, subject to the blessings of my constituents. But, I promised the dope cops I'd never allow another slacker to handle dope cases again. And, I won't. I didn't ask to be nicknamed Truth. But, I won't dishonor it with prevarication, especially on public safety issues.

As the District Attorney, I have plenty of other stuff to do. However, I also know my old MNVP assignment was more screwed up than a poorly planned fire drill, ever since I got involuntarily transferred by the Ice Maiden into the homicide unit several years ago. Ice Maiden, as mentioned before, is one of Sally Boulder's nicknames. Her other monikers are Chief Chick, as I've already mentioned, and the Ice Bitch. I do not claim authorship rights, but know the intellectual property owner of each of these pet names. Their secrets are safe with me. And, I salute each and every one of them for their ingenuity.

In case you haven't figured this out yet, Ms. Boulders is not well liked, even by her own merry band of sycophants who have trouble breathing through their own noses for reasons I don't need to explain here.

I grew tired of hearing complaints from dope cops about how much they missed the good old days when I still had the assignment full time. I've already admitted I enjoy applause. For God's sake, how could I not like working dope cases? I am such a sucker for compliments. Dope cops are a rather experienced lot. My own dope cops are absolutely as good as they come. Pardon my bluntness. But, they kick ass and take names. May God bless and protect each of them. These guys put such air tight cases together, every time I waltz into court, I look like a rock star. And, I'm serious about that. I try to credit them at every media interview. Thanks to them, I'm the guy who falls on the football in the end zone after my one of my teammates carries it all the way from our own one yard line. They do all the work and I dance in the end zone. Try beating that.

Cops write the tunes to accompany the bad guy's lyrics. I play the piano. As good as they are, it could just as easily be a player piano. I mean this. It really could play itself. Visualize a piano on autopilot. They could even make a pedestrian prosecutor look good.

We knew we had a job to do. So, we rolled our sleeves up and went to work at the beginning of my tour of duty handling major dope cases. By the end of our first year, 150 years' worth of state prison sentences had been generously doled out by various judges to dope smugglers, street level dealers and meth lab operators. Our entire team celebrated. Frankly, that was no easy feat, considering my lazy predecessor had conditioned all of them that probation was the proper sentence. That's easy to do when your MO is to duck doing jury trials, in return for soft sentences.

Critics called us lucky. One nervy defense attorney actually called us Nazis. Nazis! Can you believe it? Why? Because his clients all went to prison, instead of getting probation like my predecessor would have given them? Nazis don't take oaths to protect and defend the U.S. Constitution. But, I did. Frankly, the SOB is indeed lucky I didn't punch him right in the mouth. The weekend in jail would have been well worth it. Yeah, I know. I'm the top cop and am supposed to be mature enough to put up with such mindless insults. Well, I did, didn't I? I never punched the mope. I'm just saying doing so would have given me great pleasure. A decision to not behave like that shouldn't stop me from toying with taking the law into my own hands when such situations arise. Besides, the First Amendment is meant to be used, not abused. That obnoxious scumbag was doing the legal equivalent of yelling fire in a crowded theater. For whatever it's worth, the U.S. Supreme Court agrees with me on that issue. And, the late Associate Justice who wrote that particular opinion was one very liberal guy, unlike me.

Last I heard my predecessor is now a deputy County Counsel somewhere up north. Good riddance. Now, she can continue avoiding the courthouse. Rumor has it deputy county counsels don't work hard. I know a few. And, I'd have to say that sounds about right. Let me put it this way. From first-hand experience, I don't recall ever seeing a deputy County Counsel handling a jury trial. Res ipsa loquitur.

Lawyerly laziness aside, dope cases are a strange breed. My critics say that's why I fit in so well. Whatever. All I know is that this is an assignment you either love or hate. Sort of like the New York Yankees. Critics say my beloved Yanks buy World Series titles. Whatever. If their competition was as good as they are, they could too. So, yeah, I love the Bronx Bombers and I love working dope. Go Yankees! Go MNVP!

Chapter 9

When you've practiced law as long as I have, you begin accumulating singular experiences. Some are your own doing. Others are events you're merely privileged to witness up close and personal. Either way, most should be shared with others. Some is the stuff of legends. Court appearances include the usual stuff…routine arraignments…pre-trial appearances…and all the contested proceedings. The latter include preliminary hearings, pre-trial and post-trial motions, jury trials, sentencing hearings and last, but certainly not least, violations of probation hearings.

I sat stewing in court one morning, during my inaugural tour of duty in MNVP. I was pissed off and anxiously awaiting the arrival of a specific defense counsel. One who was routinely late, I should add. And, I had already run out of patience. Someone was both wasting my time and precious tax dollars by forcing me to just sit, twiddle my thumbs and wait for him. I was not a damned bit happy about this. The court calendar listed only one appearance for me the entire day. Lots of other work beckoned. A pile of untouched files was still on my desk. Not surprisingly, the cops had more search warrants ready for my review. One LEO had already stuck one warrant under my nose for my purview. Eight different investigative teams constantly vied for my attention.

We all worked so well together, we ran like a well-oiled machine. Dead time in the dope suppression business is nothing short of anathema. Cagey defense attorneys know this. And, they routinely subpoena more dope cops than relevant for search and seizure motion hearings. They do so for tactical reasons hoping the prosecutor will blink first and offer them a deal. Never worked for them on my watch. Far from it. In fact, it just pissed me off and made me dig my heels in and prepare for yet another fight.

As usual, I also had to return an endless procession of phone calls, as well as respond to mostly spurious defense motions. If I didn't do it, it wasn't getting done. A quick peek at the court calendar conclusively identified who the AWOL mouthpiece was. In case you're curious, it was none other than a practicing jackass commonly called *Chucky*. I honestly cannot think of a more annoying waste of time than him. He really chafes me. How he ever got his license to practice law remains a mystery. Arrogance and incompetence are never a good combination.

My only scheduled court appearance the entire day was with the one attorney I absolutely despise. Could it really be *Charles Arthur DeNova aka "Chucky," aka My Cousin Vinnie?* Unfortunately, yes, it was. I felt like beating my head on the floor, or worse. I said a quick prayer that included this line, "…Lord, keep me away from sharp objects…" If you're the sort of person who is averse to going to a dentist, you are getting the idea how much fun Chucky is to deal with.

His nickname comes from the movie by the same name starring Joe Pesci and the lovely Marisa Tomei. Just like Pesci's supercilious character, Vincent LaGuardia Gambini, Chucky also took the bar exam six times before he finally passed it. Or, so I'm told. Actually, come to think of it, he told me that himself. Can you believe it? Six fricking times? Let me put it this way, I've never actually seen his bar license. So, saying he really is a lawyer, in and of itself, is an article of faith.

Assuming he is, this may speak volumes for grit and stubbornness. But, it speaks even louder to his professional competency, or lack thereof. I chewed him out once for a stunt he pulled. Instead of realizing I was chiding him, he thought I was applauding his moxie. I wasn't. But, don't get me wrong. I am not singling this guy out for disparate treatment. Let's just say I am not alone. My dislike of DeNova is shared by every prosecutor in my office, whether they have personally dealt with him or not. And, I am not responsible for the group disliking of him. It just sort of grew of its own accord.

I don't mean to get off track bitching about some defense attorney who should probably be taken outside and shot. Yes, I know I have a story to tell about Dawn and TD. But, venting sure makes me feel better. A lot better. Akin to a good digestive system readjustment. Plus, all these side trips eventually all fit together somehow.

Chucky's notoriety precedes him. This line of foes doesn't just stop at the door to the DA's office. In fact, I can't think of anyone who knows DeNova that doesn't also find him to be an absolute horse's ass. And, he also has the typical short man's syndrome. This long list includes my colleagues, defense attorneys, judges and the usual smattering of courtroom personnel: clerks, court reporters, foreign language interpreters and bailiffs. The in-custody defendants openly laugh at him during his court appearances.

Oh yeah, speaking of defendants in jury boxes. That's where all the in-custodies are seated by Sheriff Court Services' deputies for their pre-trial court appearances. Vinnie has even gotten in trouble for going into the box, not for the purpose of talking to existing clients, but so he can troll for new ones. The man has the balls of a brass monkey. I'll say that for him.

I won't bore you now with all the Vinnie stories. I'll save those for some other time. And, I'm certainly not saying this one isn't a great story. It is. Too many folks applaud tall tales about Vinnie for it not to be. There are actually several DeNova stories more than worth sharing. But, some other time, okay? Let it suffice to say, on this particular occasion, DeNova was late again, causing me to cool my jets for more than an hour. So, what did this mope do when he finally showed up that morning? When he showed up, the first words out of his mouth were "…I need a continuance…" Not *good morning* or *I'm sorry*. I wanted to wring his neck. Actually, I almost did. Him and his client. I'm almost beginning to wonder if much more dealing with defense attorneys will require me to begin attending anger management classes.

The reason for his requested prolongation? His client had hepatitis. *Hepatitis?* Upon learning this, I immediately kicked his client out of the courtroom. I informed the judge what I had done. He cleared the courtroom and did some quick medical research, in order to determine if Vinnie's client had infected his courtroom, including his Honor. This particular judge tends to be…how can I say this delicately? He's delicate. He's the sort of person who might read a story about some brand new disease. And, guess what? He begins suffering from all the symptoms. Okay, he's a hypochondriac. That's the word I was looking for. Hypochondriac.

So, the judge parked himself back in his chambers for what seemed like forever, before he graced us with his presence again, in order to make his grand announcement. Meanwhile, all the lawyers are doing slow burns, impatiently waiting for the judge to start calling the calendar again. Strangely, they weren't pissed off at me. Just Vinny. However, it turned out DeNova's client did not have the super infectious kind of hepatitis I feared he had. Thus, we disrupted virtually an entire morning's calendar for nothing. Better safe than sorry. And, a good time was had by all. Maybe Chucky will be on time next appearance.

Chapter 10

As I drove home the afternoon Dawn and I spoke for the first time, I pondered her comments about sharing her nightmare with her best friend, Janie Wells. I often use drive time to cogitate and was glad I could do so during this trip. Dawn told Wells how real her dream seemed. In fact, she said she told Janie the same thing she told me, including receiving the phone call, driving wildly to the scene, running and seeing what she called *TD's little red wrecker* in the ditch near DPS.

"Janie, I kept runnin' and runnin'. I could see TD's little red wrecker. But, I couldn't get any closer. I ran and ran. It was like bein' on a conveyor belt movin' the wrong way."

She was so vivid, I could picture myself right there soaking up the whole thing. Dawn began to cry. Janie took her hand and gently patted the back of it. O'Mara told Wells she knew it was more than just a dream, or even a nightmare. It had to be. Dawn was sure it was a premonition. Janie listened patiently but said nothing.

"Like I told you, Mr. Travers. It was like a preview of somethin' to come. Somethin' was really gonna happen. I thought so, anyways. I don't know. This had never happened to me before. Really. I mean, first I get the phone call from the police sayin' TD was shot. Then, I jump into my car and was there…like, instantly. Then, I…"

Dawn and Janie had been best friends since high school. They shared information with one another they generally wouldn't give to other people. Sounded 10-35-like to me. She told Wells she had also shared her dream with TD.

For the first time, Tommy confided to her that he was considering retiring from the repo business. She said this surprised her. Dawn knew how stubborn he could be. She'd previously broached the subject, but found no traction.

"Let's talk about it next month," he reasoned.

TD just smiled one of his award-winning smiles and reached down to hug her. Dawn was not a short woman, standing nearly five feet eight inches. But, TD was that much taller that he had to do that, every time he gave her one of those hugs. That was the end of their discussion. Wells asked her what they were going to do. Dawn said she wasn't sure and mentioned she prayed about it a lot. She suggested Dawn sit down with TD so they could make an actual decision. Dawn told me she agonized over not being more assertive. Janie reminded her TD was not a mind reader.

"You have to speak your mind, honey."

"Mr. Travers," Dawn commiserated. "I should have jumped on this. Like immediately. The instant I first felt like that. TD might still be alive. Instead, as Janie said that, I just stared off into the distance. I didn't say nothin'."

Chapter 11

Before I realized it, I was home, in front of our solar-powered main gate, as my car's engine gently burbled. I still love to hear my 911 Carrera 4 idle, almost as much as I love to hear it accelerate. I am not that materialistic, all in all. But, I adore this motorcar. Considering how many years it's taken me to buy it, it goes without saying how much I cherish it. I've named it Quick Silver.

Yeah, I know. It's goofy to name a car, isn't it? So what? First of all, the name seems to fit. It's silver in color. GT Silver, to be exact, according to the manufacturer. Why GT? Who knows? You're going to have to ask the folks at Porsche that question. And, it's also faster than jet stink. Ergo, Quick Silver. Its model name is Carrera. This hot rod has all-wheel drive. That's where the 4, after Carrera, comes from. And, surging from its rear-mounted engine are 385 fire-breathing horses. Four-wheel traction is more than mere exotica up here. Clean air and 4,000 feet also means snow in the winter. Four wheel drive means staying mobile. Plus, with all four wheels pulling, it puts its horsepower to use. Unlike two-wheel drive models, it never feels like the front and back ends are trying to swap positions. That's called increased safety.

As I walked through our kitchen door, Molly was wiping her hands on a kitchen towel. She took her apron off and hung it over the back of one of the bar stools at our breakfast counter, before following me outside. I needed to talk to her about Dawn O'Mara's request that I go to Texas for a short spell to sue and prosecute some people I couldn't even identify from a lineup. And, even if I could, my jurisdiction in Texas was still nothing more than zilch. I was in desperate need of a sounding board. Rarely do I ever need anyone's guidance. But, I always knew I could take what Molly said to the bank. She was bright, loaded with common sense and not shy about sharing her knowledge. Frankly, Molly and Ben were the only two I ever relied on for direction. Him for the legal stuff and her for the feet-on-the-ground common sense input.

"Your thoughts, corazon?" I began.

"My amor," she began. "You've been a prosecutor for a long time. You're still a Marine. My sources say you'll retire as a General when your days as a reservist are through. You've done private practice. Look what you've accomplished so far. You've been Deputy-in-Charge of just about everything at the DA's office. You've successfully tried so many cases. And now, you're the DA; the HMFIC."

That last bit put me back. I'm not used to hearing my wife swear, even if it's using an acronym that includes profanity, such as head motherf…well, you get the idea of who or what she was describing as the person in charge. But, that aside, at the risk of sounding hypercritical, this told me absolutely nothing I didn't already know or couldn't at least surmise on my own. So, I tried again.

"What about Texas?"

"Texas?" She laughed. "You failed to mention this damned assignment is in Texas."

All I could say was "…ah…didn't I?"

She caught me off guard on two points. She was right about Texas. I forgot to include that. And, as I just explained, it was out of character for Molly to curse. Let's just say she's much closer to sainthood than I am. I try to be good. I really do. But, a willing spirit just isn't enough on most occasions. And, I knew unequivocally that I have a bit of room for improvement before it's time to ring the bell at the Pearly Gates.

I said nothing at first. I didn't laugh. After a pause, I spoke again. Molly frowned. We strolled through the cactus garden, now covering nearly two complete acres. As we walked, I gently redirected the conversation back to Texas.

Molly asked how I planned to choreograph all this. Frankly, at the moment, I really didn't have a plan. In fact, I didn't even have a clue. But, like any other issue, I knew there had to be a solution hiding in there somewhere. And, don't ask me to explain this but helping O'Mara just felt like the right thing to do.

Chapter 12

During our next conversation, Dawn reminded me how TD was hired to do what ultimately became his last repo. TD didn't trust the dealership, specifically Deals on Wheels' manager, Jake Crenshaw, so he secretly tape-recorded their meeting.

After his murder, Dawn found the cassette where he usually kept important items in their home office. As she figured, it was in the top drawer of the filing cabinet closest to their desk, in the folder labeled Deals on Wheels. Substantively, this audiotape is a valuable piece of evidence. But, how can I convince a judge that it's admissible? For starters, does it violate any wire-tapping laws? I wasn't sure and needed to research Texas law. Even if admissible and legal, it might nonetheless be limited to impeachment. But, I wasn't going to look a gift horse in the mouth. I'd been a lawyer long enough to know I probably could get it admitted into evidence. If not, the worst any judge could tell me was no.

But, another wrinkle exists. I still haven't decided if I'm going to get involved. For one thing, I'm a fairly new DA and have a lot on my plate. Besides, I don't know if I can turn my official duties over to anyone else, without drawing Board or constituent disapproval. Even though the Board isn't an entity that tells me how to do my job directly, as my only bosses are the voters, indirectly, the Sups do play a role in that they must approve my budget requests. And, it's not wise to bite the hand that feeds you.

Privately, I lecture myself for not telling Dawn no. This is not the sort of work District Attorneys do. Not the civil stuff anyhow. That sort of mild litigation with burdens of proof far below beyond a reasonable doubt is usually what Attorney Generals do. But, neither of them is going to another state to convene a grand jury. My God, am I losing my mind? However, this case intrigues me, perhaps even more than most other new challenges I face daily. To put it mildly, it was inexplicable. At my request, Dawn sent me a copy of the tape. TD was in the manager's office at the used car lot talking to Crenshaw. The clarity was good. I later learned they refer to their vehicles as previously owned, not used. But, isn't that a bit like calling a jackass a donkey and feeling smug about it? The quality of the tape was nothing short of exceptional. I've listened to many tape recordings of undercover police operations, over a span of many years, and was prepared for the worst. Some are bad enough to be maddening. To my pleasant surprise, it was just like being there with each of them.

There was no static; no muffled voices. No coughing over the sound of someone speaking. No slurring or sounding like someone was in a rain barrel.

It was as close to perfect as one can get. Good work, TD! And, thank you Sony. I pushed the rewind button so I could listen to it again. The tape stopped spinning and I hit the play button again.

"So, Jake the Snake, what's the scoop with this repo here?" he asked. "Y'all honestly tellin' me, and I mean *really* tellin' me, this one is fresh? A veritable virgin, you say?"

"TD, this baby's such a virgin it still gots a hymen. Intact. Never been used. Never been abused," the used car manager promised him with an evasive grin.

"So, what's the skinny?"

"Some damn drunk loser. Lives in one of them shotgun shacks over near the Department of Public Safety. Ain't makin' his payments. So, we need his truck back. Hard to believe," he added, "that civilized folks would even live in that ghetto."

Crenshaw quickly added "but, maybe I'm makin' too many assumptions here."

"DPS? High rent district, huh?" noted the veteran repo man. He joined in the chuckling. As usual, Jake's bout of hilarity ended with something that was halfway between a snuffle and a cackle.

"Yeah. Wanna know how bad this mope's credit is? It's so-o-o-o bad our little old iron lot here made him agree to weekly payments. Weekly! Can you believe that shit?"

Crenshaw laughed again. TD said nothing and just continued looking at him.

Jake described the debtor as a non-violent drunk. He'd been arrested for DUI's, public intoxications and "one or two" for spousal abuse, according to Jake. He called the guy's wife a nagging shrew who provoked each confrontation.

"She asked for a major tune-up," as the car man put it, "each and every time."

TD would never learn that Crenshaw's statement was untrue, due to his tragic death. Having dealt with many such cases myself, that didn't ring any warning bells with me either. Most DV cases I've prosecuted have had drunk, stoned and mouthy spouses riling one another up. Therefore, beating up one's spouse didn't necessarily mean the abuser would ever be violent toward others. In fact, I personally found most husbands prosecuted for DV would never be brave enough to confront another man. However, doing so from a cowardly nighttime ambush isn't exactly being confrontational.

But, now that I knew this guy shot and killed O'Mara during the attempted repo, the tape's relevance began speaking for itself, confrontation or no confrontation. That act, signifying an abandoned and malignant heart changed the playing field forever. Crenshaw falsely assured TD he was the only repo man assigned to this account. To someone who doesn't understand the intricacies of the repo biz, that may not seem terribly significant. But, it is, and here's why. Part of the reason Tommy Deen O'Mara was murdered was because another repo man inadvertently awakened the shooter. Otherwise, he might have slept completely through TD's repo. Alcohol tends to be a rather effective sleep aid. According to Dawn, absent this, TD would have been in and out in mere seconds and on his way back to Deals on Wheels with another repo.

"Quick like a bunny," she explained.

I could hear the shuffling of paperwork in the background. Dawn told me a former dealership employee confidentially told her Jake kept all his repo folders at his desk. He didn't show any repo man more than they needed to see, in order to complete their deal. Crenshaw never showed them more than he needed.

"Here 'tis…the whole kit 'n caboodle," he brazenly lied.

"So, when can I grab his wheels?"

"I've got that spelled out in the paperwork, TD. His weekly payment was due last Friday, so he's already fair game. Up to you, now, my friend. It's all up to you. It's your show and only your show."

Chapter 13

Dawn told me about a talk Tommy had with her, talking about the funny feeling he had in the pit of his gut. After his meeting with Crenshaw, he said he couldn't put the sensation into words. It was more instinctive than anything else. TD didn't trust Crenshaw. He couldn't verbalize it. He said it was deeper than mere waffle. Abstractly, this somehow reminded me of the Supreme Court justice who once remarked he couldn't define obscenity but would know it if he saw it. Irrespective of anything else, the repo man said he could sense something. He could feel something looming. It felt like impending doom. Instead, he chalked up the strange feelings in his gut to Dawn's bizarre dream about him getting shot.

Per Dawn, Tommy was generally pretty faithful about listening to his instincts. But, this time, he apparently had ambivalence. TD was a logical man. Could there be any other rational explanation? She had finally done it. Dawn asked him to quit the repo business. He promised he would think about it. Maybe he'd even do this soon.

In fact, he hinted, this one just might be his last rodeo. Her man still had some free time before he left. TD decided to check and double-check the minutiae he never took for granted, choosing, as usual, to err on the side of caution. According to Dawn, his routine never varied. Dawn knew what he was doing, based on what the time was when he was doing it. Tommy was that predictable. O'Mara had done this job for so long and in so many different settings, he bragged he could do it in his sleep. I suspect he could. Per Dawn, TD always inventoried all his supplies first. Tom would confirm he had everything he needed, including his reading glasses and a second pair.

Next, he'd test both the rechargeable flashlight and its battery-powered backup. He counted out extra batteries. According to Dawn, TD left nothing to chance. After that, he would designate three 16 ounce bottles of drinking water. Thermos of coffee. Traveling mug. Sweatshirt. Coat. Pens. Extra pens. All the paperwork for each repo. Everything had to be in order. If he was a lawyer, I'm sure he'd have made a decent prosecutor. Document by document, TD inspected each page to verify that each and every relevant detail was in place. This included his working copies of each and every repossession contract.

If anything took a sideways turn, he was always ready with a backup plan. As he put it, he needed to assuage *Johnny Law* that each and every repossession was legitimate.

He wasn't out there stealing vehicles. And, he didn't need anyone thinking he was. This was especially true if he was on someone else's property, particularly in the nighttime. Tommy Deen knew the applicable law. He had to know it. And, he'd discussed it at length with Dawn, tutoring her as he dutifully explained everything he knew. Such attention to detail impacted what he did for a paycheck. It impacted the quality of their lives. They were decent people. Each of them deserved a good life.

One of these laws was an arcane one; a circa-1880's Texas law. To this very day, Texas Penal Code §9.41, et seq, still permits property owners to shoot any intruder they catch on their property in the nighttime. In fact, this law still legally shields anyone protecting their property. Period. No other reason need be given. It's my property. It's nighttime. You're on it. You're trying to harm my property or take something I own. I have a gun. It's loaded. I know how to use it. I'm willing to use it. I'm using it. Bang! You're dead! For good reason, TD paid particular attention to this one. He told Dawn he would occasionally feel an indescribable pinging in his gut. It wasn't so much a sound or a feeling as much as it was this unmistakable sensation he could neither shake nor define. Sort of like that judge. Rather than even trying to deal with it right now, however, he decided to ignore it and concentrate on his pre-repossession drill. It had become so standard a part of his working life, he called it his doing prepossessions. TD had to make sure he was really ready. This was familiar turf. It gave him comfort. It took his mind off other things.

TD knew such fastidiousness would prepare him for any situation. And, Dawn always made a point of looking at all of TD's repo paperwork before he left. Doing so gave her an idea of how long he might be gone. And, it reduced any chance of mistakes. This allowed her the luxury of being able to go back to sleep. Thumbing through the paperwork, she perused the names of each of his intended targets. She read the names. Last on tonight's list, but certainly not least, was an interesting one: Johnny Walker. Just like the whiskey. Other than that, his name meant nothing to her. Dawn didn't ask but assumed TD scheduled tonight's repos alphabetically. She could find no other determining factor. However, she knew her man had a solid reason for everything he did.

"Okay," he told her, "now that I know the players, let's be sure we know the game plan."

Chapter 14

TD pulled out his paperwork for the first planned repo of the night and spread it on their kitchen table in front of them. He walked over to the coffee pot and poured himself a cup of strong black coffee. He didn't pour Dawn any. He needed to stay awake and she needed to sleep. Instead, she sipped some steaming herbal tea, sweetened with agave nectar. Tom knew it was Chamomile Mint, but couldn't remember the brand. He recognized the aroma. Pulling out a copy of the title and registration, he set them next to one another. First, O'Mara compared the vehicle identification numbers on each document with one another. Pulling out the repo document itself, he made the same comparison. Everything was in order. Next, he repeated the same exact procedure with the others. So did Dawn.

"Yep," he noted. "VINs match. So do license plate numbers. Same with registered owners, physical addresses and vehicle descriptions."

The paperwork had to identify the right vehicle and its owner, registered owner that is. Deals on Wheels was still the legal owner and would remain that until the outstanding balance on that vehicle was paid in full. If the RO could adequately assure the LO they deserved another chance to make the payoff, then they would be selected. If not, then a new name would take their place on the paperwork, after their former vehicle was resold. TD looked at Dawn. She nodded her approval. She was as much a part of his routine as he was. If everything went smoothly, he could conceivably do all of these repos that same evening.

His personal lawyer taught him something many years ago. He called it *habit and custom*. Or, maybe he called it *custom and usage*. TD couldn't recall which he said it was. In any event, he knew it was some sort of legal expression. Dawn remembered it too. She was with him at the lawyer's office when the tutorial took place. He explained how it works.

"Assume," the mouthpiece said, "you do a certain task in your line of work. Assume further you do it the same exact way each and every time you do it. If you ever testify about it in court, like anything else, you must do so under oath. What if you can't recall details about a given event?"

The lawyer said that was why this issue was so critically important. Doing it, you can show a judge or a jury you probably acted properly because it's how you always do that. *Circumstantial evidence of habit and custom.*

"Yup, everything checks out," said TD. "We are good to go."

Dawn liked such certainty. TD took another gulp of coffee. It was now starting to get cold. He made a face. TD noticed the strange pinging had returned, but said nothing.

She described seeing "…that strange look on his face…"

"What, babe?" she asked.

"It's nothing. Well, time to go to work."

Loading his duffle bag, he grabbed his coat and set everything down. They headed toward the master bedroom, with Dawn guided by TD. He did this by gently resting his hands where her upper arms joined her shoulders.

"Time for you to go back to sleep, baby-cakes. And, time for me to make us more money. More moola. Mas dinero."

As she crawled into bed, he bent down to give her a kiss like he always did, before he left to begin another evening round of repos. She stretched feline-like and smiled at him, as her eyes slowly closed. She wondered if she should go with him this time. She opened her eyes, but he stopped her in mid-thought.

"Uh-uh. Close your peepers. Bye, baby-cakes. See you in a few," he grinned.

"Please be careful TD. I love you, baby."

"Love you too," he said as he disappeared out the door.

Back at the kitchen table, he gathered up his duffle and jacket. Dawn knew his routine. He would take a final sip of cold coffee, empty the cup, rinse it in the sink, walk out the door and head toward his wrecker, which was parked in front of their garage.

As she began to doze, Dawn could hear water running in the sink. TD was rinsing his cup. Outside, he opened the driver's door and threw his coat and bag on the seat; coat on top of bag as usual. He climbed in and slid behind the steering wheel, inserting the key into the ignition. Dawn watched him do this many times. Habit and custom. He absent-mindedly turned the key. This time, however, he heard nothing. He saw nothing. No sound came from the radio. No dashboard lights glowed or flickered. No lights on the radio's display panel shone. He remembered the dome light didn't turn on either when he opened the door. TD rarely cursed. But, this time, he made a one word exception. He had five separate repossessions to make. This constituted a lot of money to either make or lose. And, he knew it wasn't uncommon for other repo guys to go rogue and bag one or two they weren't entitled to have in situations just like this.

Grabbing his jacket and duffle, he muttered a second expletive as he climbed out and walked to the kitchen door. Dropping his items onto the table, he went outside to his workshop in the garage so he could find his battery charger. There would be no repos tonight. He'd go to his mechanic in the morning, so a repeat of this would not occur.

Chapter 15

Dawn O'Mara gave me a lot of information. For a lay person, her thoroughness continued to impress me. By the time I was done reading, watching, and listening to everything, I knew a lot about all the relevant players, including one Johnny Walker. I knew his truck payments were in arrears. He was laid off from his last job two weeks prior to killing TD. He told Elaine he injured his back on the job. His wife knew Johnny and correctly suspected this was just another of his alcohol-fueled lies.

The true version? His boss fired him, after smelling booze on his breath, again. But, he lied to his wife and said he was applying for Workers Compensation, due to a work-related injury. In reality, the only things hurting him were his head and liver. Even while he was working, his meager income barely covered his cheap liquor, many daily cigarettes, disposable lighters, weekly truck payments, insurance and gasoline. They had no house payment. His grandmother let them live in her next door rental house free of charge.

Now unemployed, their only cash flow was Elaine's modest salary. Johnny didn't qualify for unemployment insurance. He never worked long enough to meet the requirements. He drank vodka because he incorrectly believed it was odorless. It isn't. While it doesn't smell like darker beverages, such as scotch or bourbon, it still contains alcohol. Even when he worked, he could only afford the cheapest stuff he could find. Walker's fondness for vodka was legendary. Those who knew him whispered that his last name should be Smirnoff. Or, maybe Stolichnaya. That's because Johnny believed people would respect him more, if they thought either of these was his real drink of choice. That wasn't true. A stumble bum is still a stumble bum. It's not the fuel that makes the man. It's the man. But, even if Johnny were sober enough, long enough, to grasp this, he was simply not one of the brighter bulbs on the back porch. He just wouldn't get it. Others couldn't care less what he drank. In their minds, a drunk is still a drunk. Perversely, Johnny ignorantly believed the cheap vodka he could barely afford tasted better if he poured it from a bottle manufactured for one of the more expensive brands. He swore up and down that they used a special type of glass that captured the essence of their grain alcohol and would make cheaper booze poured from one of their containers taste better.

A long time ago, he saved until he could actually buy a fifth of Stoli. He declined the counter clerk's offer to put his purchase in a paper bag. Johnny wanted people to see exactly what he had just bought. And, when he got home, he savored every single drop of it. At the end, he held the bottle upside down so long to drain it completely that his shoulder and elbow were sore. He had to rub them with liniment he could ill afford for nearly an entire week. And, when it was finally empty, he kept the bottle to pour the rot gut he usually drank into it so he could impress people with his choice of an alleged quality beverage. Considering all the grain alcohol he'd ingested, starting around the age of twelve, he was lucky he could still remember his own name. Chronic boozing and nicotine addiction made his weather-beaten face look closer to sixty-five than his actual age of 35.

By now, I knew Walker well enough that I could comfortably grill him in court, if I had to do that. He dropped out of school in the ninth grade and drifted from one unskilled job to another. In his mind, anything was better than the broken home he escaped from. Somewhere along the way, Johnny learned how to repair motor vehicles. But, to him, it was merely a way to provide for his vices. He hated work. And, Walker didn't respond well to authority either. Besides, his daily hangovers made getting out of bed increasingly more difficult.

By the time Johnny was twelve, he found himself growing fonder of hard liquor. It quickly reached the point of early addiction. Little did he realize what destiny's ultimate plans held in store for him. Eventually, his chronic shoplifting got him arrested one time too many and the judge finally sentenced him to juvenile hall for an extended period of confinement. Once he was out of custody, he briefly returned home. He couldn't remember if he left or got kicked out by his mama's latest boyfriend. Johnny began drinking store bought hard liquor again, instead of the pruno he sucked down while in custody. He wasn't 21 yet, but the tricks he learned while inside the hall also made it easy for him to obtain a fake ID card. Along with his forged driver's license, he now could purchase adult beverages, even if he couldn't afford them without occasional shoplifting and other crimes to provide him needed seed money.

Walker started working, but spent a disproportionate amount of wages on booze. Johnny soon discovered the cheapest buzz he could get came from vodka. He called the half pints he guzzled *shooters* and could polish them off without even taking a breath.

Chapter 16

From Dawn's own investigative work, I learned Jake Crenshaw had been the manager at Deals on Wheels for nearly three years. The dealership was but one of many new and used vehicle dealerships owned by Reginald Baron. Born dirt poor, Reggie's gift of gab and his unquenchable penchant for hard work and long hours steadily improved his pecuniary landscape. Hard work and ever-developing persuasive skills securely molded his growing new and used car and light truck empire.

After thirty-three years of growth, he now presided over a sales and service empire worth close to two billion dollars. Reggie's many businesses now spread through three different states: Texas, Oklahoma and Arkansas. Baron's Houston used car lot was ruled by Crenshaw with an iron fist and located only a half mile down the road from the private repair garage where Walker was recently fired.

Those in the trade labeled Deals on Wheels an *iron lot*. Initially, I didn't know what this meant. As part of her instruction of me, Dawn explained an iron lot sells used vehicles. But, others in the industry claim they are worth little more than their value as scrap iron. This is a polite way of calling them junkyards. Critics claim iron lots sell nothing but junk. Maybe so.

President Ben Brawley oversaw the sales and service of Baron's new and used passenger cars and light trucks. But, before selecting him, Reggie first installed himself as Chairman of the Board. He did this immediately after his lawyers drafted articles of incorporation. By operation of law, he vested himself with unfettered discretion to call the shots for as long as he saw fit. Brawley might be the President, but Baron pulled all of his strings.

Reggie's role was to decide when and where his proverbial ship would sail. And, he did. Gentle Ben was the man who decided at which ports this vehicular juggernaut stopped, providing Reggie approved. It's not clear how he acquired this particular nickname. For someone as clearly ruthless as Baron himself, it certainly didn't seem to fit. Birds of a feather and all that.

Brawley tended the day-to-day details for Baron who insisted on accountability at every level throughout his entire enterprise. He ordered Brawley to make sure any delegation he personally approved flowed downward from level to level, top to bottom. Ben faithfully obeyed. Reggie insisted each boss assign appropriate responsibility to the next subordinate who answered directly to them. Every person was answerable to someone else. Baron insisted his self-created chain of command had no weak links. And, it had none. Each pointed toward him.

President Brawley answered to Chairman Baron. The general manager of each dealership answered to Ben. Each new and used car manager answered to their general manager. And, so on. Everyone had a boss. Each boss had a boss, except Reggie Baron.

Initially, Crenshaw knew of Walker. But, Johnny was merely a name on one of the many conditional sales contracts for the marginal vehicles sold by the iron lot called Deals on Wheels. Baron arbitrarily decided none of his used car lots would sell what others in the trade called *used* cars. Sure, they were still used cars and rather well used at that. It wasn't so much what they were. It was what Baron chose to call them. Reggie believed he could more easily sway ignorant purchasers, if he labeled his inventory *previously owned motorcars*. With a simple swipe of his pen, Reggie Baron's used cars were now previously owned motorcars. That didn't mean they ran any better. But, this sure sounded nicer. At least Reggie thought so. Apparently many of his customers agreed. They eagerly bought them. Walker became the owner of one of those previously owned motorcars, even though it was actually a well-worn pickup truck. He made weekly payments. And, he now was unemployed again for being caught drunk on the job.

A perfect storm was brewing.

In contrast, a lifelong teetotaler, thanks to his alcoholic parents, Baron's philosophy made his company policy a rather simple one. Get caught stealing or get caught with liquor on your breath at work? You're fired on the spot and immediately ordered off the premises. All in all, if nothing else, Baron was an orderly person. Of average height and weight, he took pride in everything he did, including his physical appearance. The only anomaly was the way he combed his hair over his bald head, from one side to the other, in order to hide this natural phenomenon that ran through his mother's side of his family, characteristic of all the adult males on that side.

Even though the private garage where Walker worked was not owned by Baron, the same rules applied to those employees. The owners of many other local businesses had a straightforward philosophy. If it worked for Reggie Baron, it worked. Period. The man was that influential. Reggie freely admitted he appreciated other business owners possessing the same kind of common sense he said the good Lord blessed him with.

Such a viewpoint meant no drinking on the job. No coming to work with booze on your breath. No coming to work drunk. No getting drunk on the job. Johnny had broken every one of these prohibitions repeatedly. He'd only been caught once. But now, he paid the cumulative price. Crenshaw didn't know why Walker wasn't making payments on his beat-up fifteen year old half ton Ford. He didn't care. Johnny was in arrears not even one week, and now faced repossession of his pickup with its terminally fading paint.

Nothing else mattered, according to the terms of the adhesion contract Johnny signed. I learned all about adhesion contracts in law school. He was stuck. Fair or not, Walker missed a payment and had already forfeited his right to possess his truck. He signed it. He was an adult at the time. And, he would face those consequences.

Now, Deals on Wheels could legally repossess it and resell it to another loser, assuming he couldn't cure the existing default. Since he was behind in his payments, broke and unemployed, the proverbial handwriting was on the wall. Soon, he'd also be without his truck. This long-time used car man was a man of action. Jake didn't like the expression *less is more*. He called it *nothing more than pure unadulterated bullshit*.

I learned Crenshaw regularly hired multiple repo men for the same jobs. He said manifold assignments worked. He'd gotten away with this for years. No matter how good a repo man was, Jake knew mistakes happened. And, he hated mistakes. So did Reggie. He would never miss the opportunity to grab Walker's wheels because some repo man miscalculated. They needed to bag it, tag it and get it ready for resale. Crenshaw faithfully subscribed to redundancy. If it meant a few more bucks, it worked. Cash was king.

If nothing else, he was terminally greedy. Jake had only met Baron one time, at an annual business meeting. It was obvious from his brief but intense monologue Reggie despised mistakes even more than Jake. TD was there and shared what he heard with Dawn. She, in turn, briefed me. O'Mara was present because of his longtime business relationship with Baron. He knew Jake feared Baron. Reggie's redundancy and Crenshaw's reaction said it all. It appeared TD read the situation quite accurately. That reminded me of sharks. Blood in the water.

Meeting the boss taught Crenshaw something. Until that moment, when he confided to Tommy, he didn't think anybody could hate screw-ups more than he did. And, he was not going to let a missed repo slow his cash flow or kill his career.

So, whether it was considered proper or not, Crenshaw almost always severally assigned repos. This he did not share with O'Mara or any other repo men he hired. It was not an acceptable practice in the industry. Any insider knew this. Screw the competition and screw his critics, opined Crenshaw. As long as Reggie Baron was pleased, Jake was happy as a clam at high tide. TD didn't sign his paychecks. No repo man did. He wasn't going to mess with the momentum. No one was, including TD.

"What they don't know *can't* hurt me!" he chuckled mischievously, as he picked up the phone to call TD.

Crenshaw knew numerous assignments were dangerous. He later admitted this in the deposition I used to grill him. It wasn't easy. Like pulling teeth. But, I knew the key to obtaining the information was to wear him down. And, I did, eventually. Otherwise, however, he claimed such a practice was perfectly safe because he'd been doing it for so long. *Time-tested*, he called it. I asked him why he didn't alert his repo men to this practice. Calling his answers duplicitous would be a compliment.

I lost my cool and called him a pathological liar. Needless to say, his lawyer and I got into a dust up. We had words, first on the record. Then off. First in the hearing room. Then outside. Amazingly, no punches were thrown. It still wasn't pleasant. I'm no saint. But, I sure as hell wasn't going to let a liar get away with that sort of nonsense either.

Jake arrogantly espoused his own version of the golden rule. *He who holds the gold rules!* By over-assigning people to repossess the same vehicle, he knew it increased the possibility various repo men might simultaneously arrive at the same location. But, he didn't care. The passage of time would make that prophesy self-fulfilling. Assigning compound repossessors also increases the likelihood repo men might believe others are poaching. Slowly but surely, I was learning a lot about the repo business.

Thank you Dawn! She was proving to be a very capable mentor. I knew it was a highly competitive business. Makes practicing law look altar boy-tame, by comparison. It sure doesn't need the Jake Crenshaw's of the world pouring rocket fuel on those particular flames. He knew how many times repo men nearly came to blows at the car lot when one of them believed another was trying to sneak their way up the established rotation. Competition was that fierce. Two-faced Jake always denied doing various assignments. But, that didn't mean money isn't money.

TD told Dawn Jake didn't mind repo guys taking him out for dinner or drinks. Nor, did he mind them slipping him a bottle of his favorite scotch, in return for favored treatment. He didn't see this as bribery. Jake called it one hand washing the other. Quid pro quo; this for that. One good old boy helping another was how Jake described it. Crenshaw knew the general manager would have his job if he ever got caught. He winked, as he told Tommy this. Jake was one treacherously greedy bastard.

He knew all too well how to play the game of the overworked executive who merely made innocent scheduling errors, should something untoward happen. All he had to do was claim he had the wrong date or wrong account.

Jake's biggest concern was not pissing off the boss or even his own repo men. Instead, the prospect of riling up a repossession target rattled him far more. He knew this would be a guy down on his luck and in a bad mood to begin with. Such a guy either had no control over financial issues or didn't know how to maintain them properly.

A repo just might put him over the edge. While Jake considered himself adventurous, he was not a brave man. And, he knew it. The last thing he wanted to deal with was some lunatic ranting and raving because his previously owned *motorcar* was now missing in action.

Chapter 17

An anonymous Deals on Wheels employee confided something to Dawn in an almost conspiratorial fashion. Meanwhile, Crenshaw retrieved Walker's repossession documents to review them again. He really did know who Johnny Walker was, despite his protestations to the contrary. This particular employee worked there long enough to know Jake's MO. Inside and out. Before he was done blabbing, Crenshaw answered a shopping list of questions to this mysterious person. Sleeping with the boss had its own unique rewards. Unlike the heart, the way to a man's brain is not necessarily through his stomach.

Jake couldn't remember how many repo men he'd hired. Was it three? Maybe four? Or, was it five? He honestly couldn't remember. A quick review of the file refreshed his recollection. Above all, he needed to be sure he hired enough repossessors to quickly complete the Walker repo. He didn't want them banging and bumping into each other in the dark on the same repo. Not with this nut job, at large. Not with all his threats. Crenshaw gave each man at least four other repos to decrease the odds they would all show up simultaneously at Walkers. If they did, he'd just lie and claim he made a mistake.

"C'mon," he chided Will Brooklyn, as his finance manager was leaving his office for the day.

Little did Jake realize taking an employee into his confidence, as he had done for too long, would have such dire consequences. He mockingly called Brooklyn his *Girl Friday*, Jake was on tenuous ground with both his bedmate and with Brooklyn. Had he known she was fond of both Dawn and TD, and couldn't care less about him, he would have been far more circumspect. Jake didn't know she and Will were also confidantes.

"What are the odds that's gonna happen, Wilbur? I've been doin' this stuff for a long, long time, and nothing like you're suggestin' has ever happened before. Not on my watch, anyhow. And, it ain't gonna happen either. Bet your sweet ass on that."

Brooklyn's first name was not Wilbur. It was William. He asked everyone to "...please, call me Will..." William was too formal. He didn't like Bill either. Crenshaw knew calling him Wilbur infuriated him. And, he did that simply because he could.

Jake told Brooklyn his smile reminded him of that talking TV horse with the owner named Wilbur. And, to be sure his grating humor wasn't missed, he routinely mimicked the horse's trembling "…Wiiilllbuuurrr…" to be sure Will understood.

Since Jake outranked him, Will knew he had to put up with such mistreatment. This wasn't a very smart tactic for a guy who bragged he had an overabundance of raw intelligence. In short, Crenshaw's people skills were lacking. And, he really wasn't that smart. His paramour didn't like this either. She viewed Will fondly and remarked that a decent, hard-working guy like him should be treated better. Resentment had been building for a long time. She was tired of being treated like a piece of meat. Hell hath no fury.

I began reading the statement she gave Dawn concerning Johnny Walker's violent side. At a minimum, TD deserved to know this, prior to repossessing the man's truck. Hiding such information would prove costly in more ways than one. Still water runs deep. She told Dawn "I heard that drunken bully. He came into the dealership shootin' his mouth off about what he would do if anyone ever tried to repo him. Me, the cashier and that big old customer all heard him. Ever hear a Murphy's Law? Trust me. It works." Not surprisingly, I learned Dawn's anger intensified, when her source also shared the pre-repo conversation between Crenshaw and Brooklyn. Like her informational sources, Dawn also liked Brooklyn who sometimes had dinner with her and TD.

"Aw, that's just an old wife's tale, Wilbur," said Crenshaw.

If he was a bit more perceptive, Jake might have heard pinging just like TD did. He explained to his F&I man why he believed it was safe to assign multiple repossessors to the same accounts. He said he was playing the odds. F&I? I didn't know what that meant. Dawn explained that's auto dealer shorthand for Finance & Insurance. Her source studiously eavesdropped, fairly regularly, as she pretended to nonchalantly place folders in Crenshaw's filing cabinet.

When she spoke, Dawn paid rapt attention. Among other things, she learned Jake derisively lectured Will to "…just stick to your numbers and let me do the heavy mental lifting…"

Dawn doesn't like condescending folks any more than I do. Neither does her source. And, then again, I don't find that terribly surprising. How do you react to such impudence? Crenshaw arranged the planned repossession so none of the men involved, he thought, would be at Walker's place at the same time. He foolishly believed the operation would be flawless. Dawn thought of Murphy's Law. So did I. And, it appeared, so did fate. What Jake failed to factor into the equation were some simple unexpected events. As he would learn later, consequences have a way of deservedly biting unsuspecting people right on their keesters. And, they also impact innocent folks.

The dead battery in TD's wrecker delayed his attempted repossession until the following night. Due to scheduling issues, the other repo guys didn't tackle this particular repo as scheduled the previous night either. The storm was brewing. Little did Jake realize his deceit would instead cause nearly the entire group to end up at the same work site on the same night. Amazing what a lawyer can learn during discovery, no? So much for all of Crenshaw's planning, preparation and practiced perfidy.

A simple ninety second repo by an experienced hand like TD, with other men doing repossessions elsewhere, was quickly replaced by a convergence of four separate paths inexorably linking up with impending disaster.

Chapter 18

The next morning, TD was wide awake around day break. So was Dawn. Considering how many years he was out and about working during the wee hours of the night, he surprised himself being up this early. Dawn agreed to accompany him into town. He always enjoyed her doing that.

"So," he joked, "this is daylight. I nearly forgot what it looks like."

They took the wrecker to their mechanic for a quick inspection. Once there, TD and Dawn would go to breakfast. After last night's battery incident, he was leaving nothing to chance. The wrecker's motor turned over on his first attempt. This meant the charge he gave it last night was still holding. But, exercising caution, he decided to go to his mechanic. TD wanted to be sure his work truck was fully operational. Pulling into Ryan's Auto Repair, they got out and ambled over to the owner.

"Hey, Philly Cheese Steak!" he yelled.

As soon as he heard the familiar voice, big Phil Ryan turned and broke into a big grin. TD was the only person who called him that silly nickname. And, he was the only one who could get away with doing it. Its impetus? Ryan's healthy appetite.

"TD, what in hell's a practicing vampire like you doin' out here in the sunlight?"

Ryan smiled, making the shape of a cross with his forefingers as he spoke.

"Thought I'd better get to work on my tan. Never can tell how long it's going to be before I see the sun again."

"And, Dawn darlin', I swear you get lovelier every time I see you."

She smiled but said nothing.

"So, what brings you both here today?"

"I need you to sweep my entire rig. Front bumper to back bumper. Dead battery last night. Can't afford to have it broke down. Y'all know I can't make any money sittin' around drinkin' coffee."

"Why don't we have Smitty inspect it while *you* buy *us* breakfast over at Steaks 'n Stacks?"

Neither O'Mara knew who Smitty was. This was the first time they saw the new mechanic. They didn't realize he replaced Walker, after Johnny got fired by Ryan last week. As a rule of thumb, their wrecker didn't require a lot of time in the shop.

They didn't know Walker either. He and Smith were not working at Ryan's the last time they were there. Unlike Smitty, Johnny didn't hold jobs very long. Ryan's Auto Repair was no exception to his spotty work history. Smitty, on the other hand planned to be there a while. Ironically, if Walker held any job as long as he could hold a vodka bottle upside down, he'd already be a raving success.

Hey Smitty!" Ryan called out. "Drop what you're doin'. I need you to check out TD's little red wrecker. Do the whole enchilada, okay? Electrics. Fluid levels. Belts. Tire pressure. All that shit. Make sure it's ready to rumble when you're done. Okay?"

Ryan grinned conspiratorially at TD and Dawn.

"We'll be over at Steaks 'n S…"

"Phillip Ryan!" Dawn scolded. His face reddened. "Y'all know I don't cotton to such language. And, 'specially in my presence."

"I meant check *everything*. We'll be havin' ourselves some grub over there," he said gesturing toward the restaurant next door. If you need us for anything, just holler, *before* you cost Mr. O'Mara any money. So, set aside what you're workin' on and get hoppin' with this one right now. Read me?"

Smith nodded toward his boss and promptly got to work, as ordered. After a leisurely breakfast, the three strolled back to Ryan's business. Phil patted his more than generous gut. Otherwise, strangely enough, he was quite normally proportioned. Those who didn't know the man would say he had a beer belly. Ryan was just an eater and appropriately, ingested calories never got far from the scene of the crime.

"Whooee! That was some mighty fine eatin', TD. Yessiree, Bob…mighty fine. You do realize that inspection Smitty's givin' your truck ain't gonna cost you nothin'. That is, so long as no parts need replacin'. Them, you'll have to pay for."

Tommy Deen snorted.

"Well, that's a good thing. Considerin' how much food your fat belly is now digestin', I ain't got no money left, anyhow. No way. No how."

O'Mara grinned as he said this.

"Shit, TD. If I had even half of your money, I'd burn every red cent I've ever earned."

"Gimme a break, Philly. You still have the very first dollar you ever earned. I've seen it myself over your cash register up on the office wall. And, in its own frame, no less. You're so damned cheap you could squeeze a nickel and make the buffalo jump clean off it."

"Well, at least I admit to bein' cheap. Guys like you try to sugar coat it and say you're *frugal*. Crissakes, all anybody's got to do is to look up the word *cheap* in the dictionary and find your picture next to it. Case closed. End of discussion."

Dawn rolled her eyes, but chose to say nothing. When Smitty was done, the only recommendation he made was to replace the battery. According to his voltmeter, two of its cells were a bit low and he couldn't promise it wouldn't go dead again. So, he replaced it with a brand new Interstate. The O'Mara's drove home after paying their bill.

Chapter 19

You already know I've been a trial lawyer for a long time. Attention to detail is my turf; my stock in trade. My life blood requires this. I don't expect similar scrutiny from lay people. I don't mean to keep beating on this. But, Dawn's attention to detail deserves its own attention. She also has a proclivity for getting other women to confide in her. That's a gift. So far, she's been a trusted intimate to at least two others. One is a former employee at the car lot whose name I have yet to learn. All Dawn would provide were her initials.

The other indirect contact, quite surprisingly, was with Elaine Walker. As a longtime student of human nature, I'm not so much surprised she spoke to Dawn as I am at the depth and breadth of her information. Somehow O'Mara found the sweet spot and tapped into it. This is particularly puzzling considering their respective histories. Hell hath no fury. Thursday night arrived at the Walker residence. Jobless Johnny sat around his house drinking vodka and smoking cigarettes most of the day. The house stunk. By the time his wife got home from work, he was staggering drunk. And, he was in a bad mood. Walker was a mean drunk. He was angry for several reasons. He was unwaged. He hadn't been able to make his truck payment the previous Friday. He still owed money on his tired old truck. And, his stomach hurt. Self-inflicted wounds didn't seem to resonate with him.

Johnny knew the car lot vultures might try to take his truck tonight. So, he decided to sleep in the front room. If he did, he'd be on the couch. Walker considered himself a light sleeper, even when stone drunk. He would attempt to listen for any strange sounds. At first, Johnny told Elaine he was on the couch due to stomach flu. Later, he claimed he was listening for burglars. Much later, he admitted he was looking for repo men. Elaine slowly shook her head, lowered it and wearily headed toward the bedroom, and the unused marital bed.

Walker had no idea how big or how tough the repossessor might be. So, he hid his loaded 30-30 rifle behind the couch for security. Let anyone try to take his truck. He was more than ready for any uninvited company. Another shooter of vodka and his nerves would be steady enough for any contingency. I enjoy adult beverages as much as the next man, but this guy's consumptive capacity was phenomenal.

The obvious immediate problem? Alcohol is a central nervous system depressant. If you consume enough, it slows your system down to the point where you eventually become unconscious. Johnny was no more immune to the laws of nature than anyone else, perceived light sleeper or not.

He once immaturely prided himself on how much alcohol he could consume. Like legendary imbiber W.C. Fields, Walker no longer drank for medicinal reasons. His alcohol consumption had finally become a necessity.

The drunken debtor would never be a physically impressive man. He barely stood five foot seven inches tall and weighed less than 140 pounds soaking wet and dressed for extremely cold weather. Had he not consumed the amount of alcohol he'd guzzled daily for the past twenty plus years, judging by bone structure, he probably would weigh less than 120. Alcohol comes with its own calories.

Walker figured he could keep himself awake if he turned the television up loud enough. But, he didn't want to telegraph the fact anyone was home. So, he left the lights off. He hoped to lull any visitor into a false sense of security. Keep the lights off so no one thinks you're home. But, turn the TV up loud enough to wake Rip Van Winkle? The light was off and nobody was home. Call it drunken logic.

In his stupor, he devised what he thought was a viable plan. He would scare the bejeezus out of whoever might arrive, by running out the front door and pointing his deer rifle at them, while bellowing like a mad man. He toyed with simply shooting them. Johnny thought if he did this once, it would scare any repo man enough to not try it a second time. I'm not sure if his lack of judgment was due to the onset of alcohol poisoning or simply because he was not one of the sharper tools in the shed. Perhaps the fact he was a mental dullard was the result of too much chronic alcohol abuse. Whatever the reason, the totality of factors added together soon created the perfect environment for sleep. In due course, Walker was sound asleep. In fact, he almost slept right through a successful repossession.

The first repo man stepped on a steel rake, lying teeth up in Walker's yard. His weight caused the upright prongs to promptly rotate to a position parallel with the dirt. In turn, the laws of physics being what they are, the wooden handle immediately pointed perpendicular to the ground, first snapping to attention, then striking his head so hard he cried out in pain. He screamed so loudly he roused Johnny from his near comatose state. The man later required several stitches.

Somehow, Walker was able to stumble out his front door. Little did he realize he was not the only person this racket awakened. It also woke up repo man number two, parked quietly up the darkened street, snoozing with a pair of binoculars around his neck.

Number two was waiting for number one to leave so he could hook up Johnny's tired old truck, take it to Deals on Wheels and get paid. But, he had dozed off. The sudden commotion convinced him he didn't need the money that badly, nearly strangling himself with the heavy field glasses.

Number two was awake the instant the screen door flew open and hit the house with a loud bang. It sounded just like a gunshot. The light from the TV illuminated Walker on the porch holding a long gun. Elaine heard Johnny shouting curses.

"Get outta here, you sumbitch! Get the fuck off my property before I blow your fuckin' head off, your rotten, lousy motherfucker!" Walker irrationally ranted and raved, while waving the gun.

"I'm gonna give y'all to the count of three to git outta here and then I'm gonna start shootin'. One…two…".

By the time 3 a.m. had rolled around, a still drunken Walker had been visited by at least two repo men. He'd lost count. Maybe it was three. All he remembered was scaring each of them away. He was also furious and getting more enraged by the minute. He hadn't been able to sleep all night, after being awakened. Neither had Elaine. Every time he began to slumber, he was startled awake by yet another sound. He vowed he'd be ready for the next one. More than ready, in fact.

Chapter 20

Dawn later pieced the next several hours together from a number of sources, including TD's repo paperwork, their business' books and other documents. Tonight had been extremely productive. And, it was barely 2:45 a.m. TD had already repossessed three vehicles. He delivered them to Deals on Wheels over on Shepherd Street. TD secured each repo in the small fenced yard at the rear of the dealership, unlocking then locking the padlock on the gate. He did this each time he drove through, using the key Jake gave him.

Dawn said this was part of their standard operating procedure. Habit and custom. The yard, surrounded by an eight foot high chain link fence topped with concertina wire, was specifically designed for repossessions. Each time O'Mara arrived, he unlocked the padlock and opened the gate. Each time he left, he closed the gate and relocked the padlock. Dawn had seen TD do this. And, she had also done it herself. Each repetition mimicked the previous ones. Habit and custom.

He debated whether to try for one more repo or to just call it a night. Dawn knew TD's style. She'd been with him several times when he pondered whether to quit for the night or try for one last repo. She could almost hear him doing the same thing this time. Part of him would simply say enough was enough. Call it quits. He needed to go home and catch some well needed shut eye to recharge his energy reserves. However, his pecuniary side told him he should be buying lotto tickets tonight. Habit and custom.

His luck had really been *that* good. But, it usually was. Every repo was right where it was supposed to be. And, no one had interfered with him doing his job. Basically, it was business as usual. Dawn once kidded TD that his nickname should be Lucky. It wasn't actually luck. TD's success was the end result of his meticulous preparation meeting opportunity. Isn't that the definition of luck? *When preparation meets opportunity!* Even if it was just dumb luck, as she would learn, a person's luck doesn't always hold.

Dawn could visualize him now, having a private conversation with himself. TD drove past DPS. He didn't see any activity in its immediate area. Like a patrol officer, his driver's window was down. He listened for any telltale warning sounds. Dawn knew some of these neighborhoods were not safe places, especially in the middle of the night. Among other things, drug addiction made people do crazy things. But, she knew TD was extremely cautious, especially in the face of performing decidedly deadly duty.

"Sure hope nobody ever needs a cop in this neighborhood. Someone could end up in a ditch and not be found until these folks come to work in the morning. It's so doggoned quiet here tonight, it's like a cemetery," he mused.

TD was focused. He was so busy looking for the Walker address he drove right past the street where they lived. He had to double back, make a U-turn, then turn down Berwyn to drive past their house. He pulled into an empty driveway. As he did, he tried to ignore the resumed pinging. Dawn knew all about TD's pinging. Jokingly, he tried to pawn the sound off as his own personal radar he custom made in his workshop. Tonight, it had helped him make three quick and easy repos so far. He told Dawn many times about his so-called pinging radar. Dawn knew Tommy would follow his usual routine. She knew him so well. He was such a creature of habit. She knew where Berwyn was. He slowly drove down the darkened street.

The first pass allowed him to eyeball the residence. He looked for anything unusual. O'Mara dealt frequently with the deceptively simple task of locating a residence. It's how he got paid. Dawn joked she could set her watch by him. And, sometimes she did. Over the years, TD told Dawn a number of things he'd learned about the repo business. Targets of repossessions generally have other economic problems as well. These include lawsuits and other issues, such as previous or pending bankruptcies. Some may have criminal records. Others may even have outstanding arrest warrants.

Therefore, many of them don't go out of their way to let strangers know where they reside. One way for a debtor to stay off the radar screen is to remove or obscure the numbers which identify the physical location of their residence. Combine that with missing or defective street lights? Locating a residence becomes even more difficult to accomplish. Add to that the challenge of being stealthy enough to locate a residence without alerting the debtor.

TD continued creeping down the unlit street. His first order of business was to identify the Walker residence. Would the targeted vehicle be visible? Could he physically repossess it in his normal fashion? As he contemplated all this, Tom scanned the area for any signs of danger. Can't multi-task? Don't even think of being a repo man.

Locating a residence means categorizing a number of relevant characteristics. First of all, what type of structure is it? Is it a single family dwelling in a residential neighborhood? A unit in an apartment building? A trailer park? A duplex?

Or does the deadbeat debtor live in an extra room or a guest house on someone else's premises? Should they do so, does this also mean there are other people a repo man needs to concern himself with? If they're in a trailer park, is there one main numerical address for the entire place or does each individual residence have its own street number? If the debtor's residence is a guest house, does it have a separate street address? If so, is it primarily accessible from the street or from a more restricted alleyway? In addition to being accessible, where is the actual vehicle? Is it in the open? Is it even visible?

In other words, can you see it? Or, is it concealed? Is it in a garage? A barn? Maybe it's a motorhome. And, if so, does the debtor live in it? If it's at a residence, is that structure accessible from the street? Can you get to it from an alleyway?

What if it's sitting behind something? Is it obstructed or obscured by a fence? How about some other physical barrier? Assume the intended repossession is visible and not protected by any palisade. Does anything have to be moved in order to access it?

Is another vehicle in the way? Perhaps the obstacle is a trailer? How about personal safety? Long ago, TD told Dawn he learned to look and listen for signs of any trouble. Like a cop, he has always driven with his window down, weather permitting.

Are any lights on inside the house? Does this mean someone is still awake? Or, were they left on as a ruse to confuse burglars? How about motion sensors? If so, do any of these offer false clues of any sort? What about outside lights? A long time ago, TD learned some people turn on their outside lights when they are away from their residence after dark. But, some people leave them on at night for other reasons. What does the big picture really tell him?

Chapter 21

Several years ago, TD was chewing the fat with a patrol officer he'd known for a long time. Somehow, the discussion turned to outside lights. The law enforcement officer, or by its acronym, LEO, told him experienced burglars look for such seeming subtleties. What does it really mean? The cop explained the significance of leaving outside lights on. To a burglar's practiced eyes, they are like neon signs. It may likely mean the resident isn't home and the place is vulnerable for illegal entry. Same is true with issues such as piled up newspapers or a lawn well overdue for mowing.

Although Tommy Deen's occupation was not law enforcement, he nonetheless relied on the same indicators. As a dedicated student of life, TD concluded, if it worked for a LEO, it would work for him too. Both are lawful professions. And, each requires on-the-job training in order for the participants to become accomplished observers. Personal safety, unlike many other occupations, is a high priority issue that requires attention to details like these.

"Lit outside lights? A dead giveaway. Lights on. Nobody's probably home. Might as well put a sign out front to that effect," he once told Dawn.

TD looked for other signs. He told Dawn it was worth paying attention to lights activated by motion detectors. They usually have higher wattage bulbs and turn nightfall into near daylight for short periods of time. Although the extra lighting might otherwise be helpful to a repo man, it also tells the vehicle owner they need to determine what is causing the lights to illuminate. It might be an animal. Then again, it might be a human intruder, like a repo man. TD said he might as well arrive with flashing lights and siren. Dawn knew he didn't like motion detectors. And, he carefully explained why.

Another immediate safety issue is dogs. Dogs bark. That's their job. They bark at strangers, including working repo men, and alert their owners. But, aside from the issue of unneeded noise, dogs also bite. Dogs are meat eaters. Their teeth are made for tearing flesh and muscle from skeletons. Favorite biting targets? Try thieves, mail carriers, cops and repo men. Although TD had never been bitten, he had more than his share of close calls. He appreciatively thanked his trusty sneakers more than once. If dogs are present, how many are there? One barking dog may be enough to wake up a sleeping debtor.

But, a pack of dogs makes far more noise. And, multiple canines present an even bigger concern. A single dog may bark, but not bite. Like humans, dogs occasionally lack adequate bravery for a given situation. A handful of dogs, on the other hand, tend to embolden each other. Daring dogs may be brave enough to bite. If one bites, others may follow suit. That's how wolf packs hunt and kill their prey. Sometimes multifarious dogs do things single dogs don't have the courage to do. Like biting a repo man. Pack mentality impacts both man and animals. Thanks to Dawn, I continued learning the repo biz.

The houses on Berwyn are nearly identical-looking shotgun houses; quickly thrown together cheap shacks. They are so called because they are cheap and put together quickly, almost as if a blast from a shotgun created them. This area has no street lights.

To TD, that was good, but also bad. He liked working under the cover of darkness. Dark meant not seeing easily. But, it meant the other guy couldn't see you either. This sort of thing is a double-edged sword. It means a person can easily see something in the daytime and find it difficult to identify in blackness. Such objects include street numbers, license plate numbers and dashboard VIN plates. Not VIN numbers. Just VINs. VIN *number* is redundant and incorrect

Tommy's prior daytime reconnaissance proved helpful. Earlier, he located the Walker residence by simply driving past during daylight hours. He meticulously recorded information in the log he kept in his truck's cab.

He had surreptitiously cruised down Berwyn in his low profile wrecker, appreciating its covertness. If other people saw him driving by, they might mistake his vehicle for a regular pickup truck. In fact, many folks did, including unsuspecting debtors. Innocuous lettering on its doors was inconspicuous. No flashing lights or other accoutrements were visible. The lettering practically blended into the faded paint. Frankly, a glance from unobservant eyes would espy just another tired old truck.

Inside the bed were all the necessary tools of the trade, including the winch, cable and hook; all folded flat when not in use. When operational, they secured the vehicle to be repossessed, allowing TD to make a quick getaway. Unless the harness was up and in use, an untrained eye wouldn't even know they were looking at a sling truck. I found myself gaining even more knowledge about a subject I previously knew nothing about.

Up until now, I assumed all tow trucks had flashing amber lights on their roofs and stood out like sore thumbs. I was learning the repo business. The word stealth was an integral part of the vocabulary. And, I was also learning something else. Before I met Dawn, I knew nothing about repos. I didn't know that. Now, I do. I also continue to learn that every time a person thinks they've learned enough, it's merely an opportunity to learn even more. Every day, there's another kernel of knowledge for any student of life. Somehow the University of Life has more depth than mere classrooms can ever offer.

If you saw TD's little red wrecker driving by, you'd probably say it looked like a regular, run-of-the-mill, older pickup truck with faded red paint. The powerful engine was relatively well masked by an efficient muffler and exhaust system. Tommy knew the 396 cubic inch Chevy motor provided all the power and torque he needed to tow away yet another vehicle, quickly and effortlessly. TD kept his work vehicle as well maintained as any race car. And, he did most of the routine stuff himself. This included regular tune-ups, oil changes, tire rotation and balancing, regular brake jobs, and periodic inspections by one of Phil Ryan's mechanics, just to make sure he'd missed nothing. TD said the expense of doing this was just part of the price of doing business.

If you were a debtor, what you saw wasn't necessarily what you got. But, that didn't stop it from being the thing that got you. The old paint was a nice cover. It reminds me of the dictator's plain, tired-looking, sedan in *Moon over Parador*. Stealthy is healthy.

Although Tommy Deen might know he located the right place, he would still drive slowly past. He said the key to success was finding something just as easily in the dark as during daytime. He remembered the Walker residence had a garage, with a boat sitting right in front of it. TD didn't know why they didn't park the truck in it, but he was relieved Walker didn't do that. Entering to do a repo was a breach of the peace. This would subject him to a residential burglary charge, since it was attached to Walker's house. TD drove by one more time, just to be certain.

As O'Mara did this, he reflected on the advice from his lawyer about habit and custom. This allowed him to truthfully tell anybody in any courtroom, anywhere, at any time, and under oath, what he probably had done, should things turn to crud, even if he couldn't actually remember doing it that particular time. Habit and custom.

TD drove past the house and turned the corner from Berwyn onto Canino. He would drive around the block and pull past Walker's place one final time. He chose to do this rather than back down Walker's driveway and do the repossession. Not just yet. Timing. The repo was contingent on a number of ifs. *If* he hadn't seen any lights on. *If* he hadn't heard any dogs barking. *If* he didn't hear any electronic devices, such as radios, stereos or televisions. And, *if* the coast was as clear as it was going to get.

Reviewing all these contingencies made me glad I did something as uncomplicated as being a trial lawyer for a living. Being a repo man was sounding more and more difficult the more I studied its job specs.

TD turned onto the 8000 block of Berwyn again. The pinging resumed. He approached 8013 Berwyn. Tommy slowed to a stop at the dividing line between the Walker house and the one next door, on the side opposite where the grandmother lived. It was another of those shotgun shanties, looking the same as any of the others. Somewhere, he heard that one was owned by Johnny's uncle. He gave the place another visual once over. His driver's door window was already open. Everything remained quiet. Nothing detectible by any of his senses gave him cause for concern.

Tommy released the clutch. His wrecker slowly began rolling forward. TD next positioned it so he could back straight down Walker's driveway, hook up his target and leave as quickly as possible. Once he completed this one, he was done for the night. Then, and only then, would he go home and get some much needed sleep. O'Mara glanced at his watch. It was 3:25 a.m. He had already flipped the toggle switch to prevent his taillights from illuminating. TD selected reverse and slowly began releasing the clutch pedal. He began backing up. He didn't get far.

Chapter 22

As I proceeded apace further into my review of Dawn's immense pile of information, events continued unveiling themselves to me. It was like being right there. I could almost hear the distinct crack of a rifle interrupting the nighttime silence. This was beyond eerie. TD's red wrecker quickly pulled out of the driveway, leaving wide, black, tire acceleration marks in its wake. Walker's truck remained behind. Later, the silence was interrupted by another sound in a large house on the other side of town.

A telephone was ringing. Dawn's voice trembled as she walked me through that auspicious call. She sounded like she was going to cry. She paused for a few seconds. Only then, did she resume her presentation to me virtually verbatim.

"What? Yes, this is she," she said. "What's going on? What? When? Where?"

Dawn asked questions faster than they could be answered. She began to thank her caller. Her politeness was ingrained. But, inexplicably, she let the phone drop, as it hung there, slowly twisting at the other end of its own spiral cord. A panicky look appeared as she scurried about looking for clothing. She rushed toward the garage.

"It was like déjà vu, all over again" she told me.

"So, here I am, drivin' to the same place all over again. I'm seein' the same crime scene tape. And, I'm seein' TD's little red wrecker again. Please God, am I dreamin' again? Or what? Can I be havin' the same awful dream twice? I asked myself that. It was spooky, like I was playing a rewound video tape or..."

She didn't finish the sentence before beginning a new one.

"...I parked my car and got out, leavin' the driver's door wide open. I ran toward the bright yellow tape. Its bold black capital letters, on that background, said it all: **POLICE-----CRIME SCENE-----DO NOT CROSS**! That's still vividly etched in my head. Burned right into my very brain. If I live to be a hundred, I'll never forget it."

Dawn paused, took a breath and shared more.

"I paid that no never mind, debatin' whether to bend down, as I approached it. No matter what, I was goin' underneath it. Or, I was goin' over it. But, I was goin' in. I was gettin' past that darned keep-out tape. I could even hear my own breathing. I could feel my own heartbeat. Kathump. Kathump, it went."

I mentally replayed what Dawn told me. This time, it was a bit different than the earlier dream. At the edge of the actual crime scene, no imaginary voices were yelling at her to stop this time. At least, she said she didn't hear any. Was this the real thing? Emboldened, she pushed underneath the tape. She ran straight toward the red sling truck. It rested at an unusual angle in the ditch. Dawn knew TD didn't park like this, even in emergencies. The sign in front of DPS read *Driver Licensing Division*.

The ditch was between the roadway and DPS, located at 411 W. Canino. Dawn was suddenly in an even greater degree of panic. She didn't know if she was experiencing reality or not. Was she once again in the exhausting throes of that haunting nightmare? She decided to yell as loudly as she could to see if she was asleep. If so, maybe she could wake herself up, in case she really was asleep. What if she was actually at the scene of TD's wrecker? What if he really had been shot?

If all this was true, she didn't care if people heard her screaming. Let them frown. Let them tell her to be quiet. She opened her mouth to yell, but no sound escaped. Dawn was in a fog and not entirely sure if she was awake or asleep. In a panic, she surveyed the scene. She desperately looked for TD and their red sling truck.

Chapter 23

Dawn was right. Tom O'Mara really was a committed creature of habit, and a perfectionist to boot. Why do I say this? Let's analyze it. He stopped at Walker's driveway and unconsciously shifted his wrecker into reverse. He began backing down its slope, first positioning his wrecker so it backed right to his target's rear bumper. TD didn't realize he was even doing this. He was operating at a subconscious level. It was as if he was on autopilot. But, nonetheless, he did it just as efficiently as if he'd done it on this very same driveway a thousand previous times, instead of doing it, on his one and only attempt.

Tommy would quickly hook up Johnny's truck and make a fast getaway. He prepared to activate the mechanism in the bed. Once fully functional, it would lift the rear portion of Walker's old truck off the ground so he could tow it to the lot over on North Shepherd. As he approached his target, he awaited both the sound and the feel of the slight contact he always anticipated. This would tell him the wheel lift was in place. Once it was beneath the Ford's rear bumper, the lift would raise its rear tires off the ground. Then, he could rapidly tow it away.

Johnny had drunkenly driven in and parked, with the front bumper facing the front of the house. He usually backed down the driveway. Lucky for TD, this exposed the rear end of Walker's rear wheel drive truck. This meant Tom could effortlessly lift the rear tires off the ground and scoot; no need for wasted mental gymnastics. Ironically, Walker was so drunk he also left the keys in the ignition. Had TD known this, he could possibly have avoided even entering the driveway with his wrecker and simply driven it away. But, that would have required a second person on scene, like Dawn, to drive their wrecker to Deals on Wheels so they could drop the repo off and head home.

The wheel lift's job was to quickly raise the selected end off the ground. TD could secure his intended quarry and make his getaway. He had done this so many times muscle memory had already taken over. TD waited for vehicle-to-vehicle contact. Unexpectedly, Tommy felt a searing hot pain, as Walker's rifle simultaneously emitted a loud bark. TD didn't even have time to cry out. Contrary to public misconception, real life shootings are not like they're portrayed on some of the more uninspiring TV shows.

I researched Texas Penal Code 9.41, including related cases and other statutes. They judiciously focus on the right of property owners to use deadly force to protect their property. The lawful authority of a repossessor to do their job appears largely ignored. O'Mara was dealing with what laypeople might innocently call a *legal loophole*. This was one large hole. We're talking

Kenworth or Peterbilt-size. He had legal authority to repossess the vehicle Deals on Wheels sold to Walker. But, TD was sadly learning, Texas didn't mean for this to be a repo-friendly statute. Nor was Texas a repo-friendly state.

Sure, Johnny was mere days late making his mandatory $11.80 weekly payment. But, it didn't matter. Walker's sales contract clearly spelled out the rights and responsibilities of the respective parties. He had to make his payments timely and Deals on Wheels had the right to repossess, if he failed to do that. Adhesion contracts are aptly named. Johnny was stuck.

Baron, or his designee, had the unmitigated right to take immediate possession of the vehicle, even if Johnny was a single payment late. The default could be for as little as one twenty-four hour day. Legally, Walker couldn't complain. He was an adult and had signed the contract. He was adhered to Deals on Wheels. TD could legally repossess such a vehicle any time of the day or night, as long as he didn't breach the peace. Since he didn't have to enter Walker's garage or house to get the truck, one would be hard pressed to legitimately argue any such act had occurred.

O'Mara's survival instincts kicked in. He knew he'd just been shot. And, he was in shock. TD felt faint. He immediately crammed the shifter into first gear and floored the accelerator as he popped the clutch. His life hung in the balance. The unencumbered wrecker burned rubber up the driveway, fishtailing onto Berwyn, as he headed toward Canino. He lacked a pre-cellular phone clear escape plan. I suspect he simply didn't want to get shot again. Swerving around the corner, he felt himself getting weaker.

TD grew fainter. He kept getting woozier. I tried to put myself in his shoes. O'Mara had to concentrate. Where was he? Where was he going? And, what did he need to do? Was the shooter following him? Tommy was quickly losing control, as he continued bleeding profusely. He was fading in and out of consciousness. He saw stars, followed by black. His wrecker left the pavement and augured into the adjacent ditch, nose-first, right in front of DPS. The crime scene photos told the tale. Points of both impact and rest were a palpably short distance from where Johnny Walker lived.

Tommy Deen left no skid marks whatsoever at the place where he died. This told me he failed to apply the brake pedal or steer defensively. This is not consistent with an experienced driver having such a driving emergency. And, TD was indeed experienced. My first reaction would be to hit the brakes and turn the wheel, assuming I was conscious. It was also a pretty clear indicator he was likely not awake, as he left the pavement and slammed into the ditch somewhat parallel with Canino.

The time was now 3:31 a.m. Tommy Deen's life was slowly slipping away.

Chapter 24

Dawn barely felt her knees buckle. She dropped the phone and slumped to the kitchen floor. It landed with a sharp thud, as she began wailing plaintively. The long-corded phone took a lucky bounce. Somehow, it struck the tile floor but didn't break, before it careened back upward toward its cradle. For every action, there is an equal but opposite reaction. She didn't even attempt to hang up. All she recalled was doing was grabbing her clutch and rummaging inside it for car keys. As she fished around inside her leather handbag, she finally found what she was looking for. But, this brought her no joy.

Grief-stricken, she grabbed the keys and her shoulder bag and began running toward the door leading into the garage. As the Lincoln's engine roared to life, she barely gave the rolling door enough time to fully open. Somehow, she managed to not strike its bottom edge. Dawn crammed the shifter into reverse and accelerated, nearly clipping its bottom with the rear edge of her car's roof.

As she backed down the driveway, spinning tires left a distinct black stripe on its cement surface; not a non-slip differential. She failed to come to a complete stop where the driveway met the street before lurching forward. The transmission and suspension protested violently as did the horn of the vehicle she barely avoided striking, angering its driver.

At the moment, she really didn't care. Dawn continued driving aberrantly careless, while roaring away in a cloud of white tire smoke, nearly mimicking the burnout now common for winning NASCAR drivers. The newly-minted widow didn't even remember her trip to the crime scene, she told me later. Barely pushing her driver's door open, Dawn sprang from her seat, not quite releasing her seatbelt. Frustration overcame her. She began crying again, struggling to free herself from the unexpected limitation by the mechanical restraints. She didn't even recall fastening her seat belt before departure from home. All she knew was she was impeded from getting to where she needed to be. Muscle memory. Dawn approached the bright yellow crime scene tape. Squinting through tears, she saw the same ominous words all over again. **POLICE----CRIME SCENE----DO NOT CROSS!** No sooner did she breach the perimeter than a voice called out. *Not again*, she thought.

"Ma'am! Hold it ma'am. You can't be in here."

"But, that's our little red wrecker. Over there. Right over there. Over there in the ditch!" she insisted. "My TD was drivin' it. He's been shot."

The uniformed officer held up his right hand. "I'm sorry ma'am. But, it's still a crime scene and you're not allowed inside it. Authorized personnel only."

"But…" she began. "TD! TD!" she shrieked. "Oh, my God! Oh, my God! Oh, my God! No, please don't let this be!"

Dawn attempted to duck underneath the tape surrounding the area where the wrecker now precariously sat, tilting in the ditch separating DPS property from the roadway. She felt someone grab her arm.

"Ma'am, I'm sorry," the same voice firmly repeated. "I've already told you once. This is a crime scene. I'm sorry it's your husband. I truly am. But, if you ain't authorized, you can't be here. It's that simple."

"But…" she pleaded again. "My husband is in there. He's a repo man. And, he's been shot. I need to see him. I need to help him. I need to see what I can do. Please!" she insisted. "Let me see my TD. He needs me. I'm his best friend!"

"Once again, ma'am. No! Look, I feel your pain. I really do. But, we've got a job to do here. And, if we start lettin' any outside folks inside the tape, we cannot function. We can't do our jobs. Husband or no husband, I'm sorry. You can't come in."

This distraught woman was in no mood to be denied. Dawn now knew her husband had been shot. There was little to no doubt about that now. She knew this couldn't be another dream. There were too many already. How many would this one make? One? Two? More? She'd lost count.

The grieving woman didn't know TD had already bled to death. Dawn told me later she was regularly reminded of the risks TD faced every time he hit the streets. And, he didn't share with her every experience the job brought him. TD didn't want to frighten her any more than necessary. If he forced her hand, she might insist he find another line of work. They both enjoyed the bountiful money repos brought. And, TD enjoyed the incredible adrenaline rush it provided just as much as the money it generated. Dawn already knew this. She had spoken with enough other people in the industry to ever harbor any doubts on that particular issue. And, the material comforts provided by their repo business were self-evident. The house, the furnishings, and the money. Lots and lots of money. Not quite sure she was now a widow; Dawn still knew danger came in many forms. Repo men like TD had been yelled at, physically chased, pushed, shoved, punched, kicked, spat at, swung at, shot at, and threatened with a variety of weapons. Assaultive devices included firearms, knives, baseball bats, jack handles, screwdrivers, wrenches, and motor vehicles; even debtors' bodies.

Targets of repossessions seem to demonstrate just how strong a human being's sense of personal survival really is, even if it's only fiscal survival. If someone needs to buy groceries, they need money to do it and working people need a paycheck to make that happen. In order to get paid, they need transportation to get to work. That's true even if their vehicle is a tired and broken down old truck that probably should be retired.

It wasn't as if Dawn never voiced her concerns to TD. She did this many times. But, most of the time, he would simply smile at her like a kindly and patient uncle. And, every time, he'd promise to come home alive at the end of every working day.

Dawn continued struggling with the officer at the forbidding tape. Thoughts swirled around inside her head. Suddenly, she paused to scream, doing so loudly enough to startle the man in uniform. To anyone nearby, the sound was utterly bloodcurdling. She didn't see the vehicle arrive from the Coroner's office. She didn't have to see it. Instinctively, she knew TD wasn't coming home.

"Dammit, TD. Y'all didn't come home! You didn't come home this time! You promised. You prom..."

Sinking to her knees, she began to shake. Then, she uncontrollably sobbed. A female officer nearby squatted down in front of her and gently hugged her.

"There, there, honey," the stranger soothed, as she softly rubbed Dawn's back with both hands the way only a mother can. As she did this, Dawn stared but didn't see the Coroner's van. Mercifully, her abundant tears prevented her from seeing it.

She didn't realize the initial officer, on scene, had already pronounced her mortally-wounded husband dead and elected to request the crew from the morgue, instead of rescue personnel. Akin to Search-Rescue operations with unhappy endings, this would not be a rescue, but, rather a mere recovery. This discretionary exercise, performed countless times daily in American communities by law enforcement professionals, determines whether the Coroner, instead of emergency rescue personnel, comes to the scene of unattended deaths.

No ambulance would arrive at this particular crime scene. For Dawn, that reality was just beginning to emerge. For Tommy Deen, it was the end and a recovery.

Chapter 25

I continued mentally reconstructing this irresistible conundrum. It was drawing me like a moth to a flame. For some reason, I still did not fully comprehend its undeniable attraction. It was seductively mesmerizing. And, I still hadn't decided what I was going to do. My prosecutorial duties beckoned, distracting me further. But, was TD's murder winning this tug-of-war? I knew I had constituents and employees counting on me to perform my official duties in Solita County. But, for some reason, I wasn't having any luck shaking this thing loose. It kept pulling at me. Tugging and tugging. And, I kept considering and reconsidering.

Immediately following the shooting, TD's assailant slunk back inside his own residence. Two high-powered rifle shots, fired in rapid succession, fractured the early morning quiet. They startled Johnny's wife from a more or less otherwise sound sleep. She had fallen asleep again, following the prior noisy outburst between the repo man who swore he was attacked by the rake and their front door slamming open against their house.

Her grand jury testimony would contradict his claim he meant to only scare TD.

"Dear Lord!" she exclaimed, wiping sleep from her eyes. "What was that?"

"Nothin'!" he slurred. "Jus' go back ta sleep, woman."

"I heard gu…" she began, before realizing he was still holding the rifle. She froze.

"What are you doing with that rifle?" she asked, eying the 30-30 Winchester he had just leaned against the kitchen wall.

"Dammit!" he snarled. "I already told ya. 'S none o' yer fuckin' business. Now, go back ta bed, bitch!"

Elaine didn't even bother to ask him to not call her names anymore.

"Wha--wha--what were you shooting at?" she nervously asked, as she sidled up and gingerly touched the gun's still hot barrel.

"I ain't gonna tell ya twice. I've already shot one guy today. Wanna try for two?" As he verbally threatened her, Johnny tried to step toward Elaine, but nearly fell.

"I'm callin' the cops," she said.

"Yeah? You just do that. Why don'tcha just tell 'em I shot the guy? I don't even know why I'm still married to you, you worthless fucking cunt."

Elaine knew why, but sensibly chose to say nothing. The only steady paycheck in the Walker household was hers. Elaine's alcoholic husband had never held what he could honestly call a steady job. He probably never would. She again declined to respond to his newest insult, not even knowing he'd just lost yet another job. Her testimony was illustrative. Their marriage was emotionally over long ago. She debated whether to call the police. Her husband frightened her. Doing the right thing quickly moved to second place. She understood instinctively that her own survival came first.

Johnny had verbally and physically abused her for a long time, occasionally leaving visible bruises. Often, he inflicted psychic wounds. His unprovoked physical attacks were generally limited to pushing, shoving and shaking Elaine, along with occasional open-handed slaps to her face. Jake had lied.

She was justifiably frightened, especially when *Stoli* was drunk. It was not a nickname she used. If he was telling the truth tonight, he apparently had just shot a human being. At last, he'd finally escalated his ongoing threats to a new and different place. His alcohol abuse had been a daily fact of life for as long as she had known him. He was passed out under a table in a bar when they met. She somehow thought he was cute. And, being a typical woman, figured she could repair him. She couldn't. She had long since given up trying to stop his drinking. Maybe it was time to finally end their sham of a marriage too. The soon to be ex-Mrs. Walker knew she should phone the police. After all, it was the decent thing to do. She ventured outside into the front yard to search for any wounded strangers, as Johnny stumbled toward the kitchen searching for more distilled spirits so he could sleep.

She knew someone might be in need of life-saving medical aid. But, her own instinct for survival was her dominant motivation at the moment. A call by her might provoke an immediate and violent reaction of the worst possible kind. Elaine silently debated with herself. She decided to postpone any phone calls. If she phoned, she would call from work. They had no home telephone. And, she didn't trust his grandmother next door to keep her mouth shut, if she used her phone.

A queasy feeling in the pit of her gut told her this was going to be "…a whole 'nuther chapter…"

Chapter 26

Comfortably ensconced on my own turf, I was determined to do something…anything…not dealing with Texas, at the moment. It's not that I dislike Texas. Actually, I'm a big fan of how Texans conduct business, especially when it comes to how they handle death penalty cases. But, I needed to think. So, I went to court.

I also have a promise to keep. Earlier, I declared I'd tell you how I got saddled with my newest moniker: *Truth*. Here's how. A bunch of cops and I were jaw-jacking one morning in the courthouse hallway. Brent Marvin's name came up. People often joked he was a heart attack just waiting to happen. Why? Chronic overeating. Too much booze. No exercise.

Main topic? The former DA's more than episodic drinking and driving. Don't get me wrong. I'm not without my own assortment of faults. Sometimes, I cuss like a proverbial sailor who has been at sea too long, at least according to Molly. And, other folks say these outbursts tend to happen, whether I'm calm, upset, or simply telling a war story. Mea culpa. Okay? I admit my language is occasionally salty. Facts are facts.

I'm not calling anyone a liar. And, I keep promising Molly I'll clean up my circumlocution. But, I haven't quite got there yet. I'm trying. Yes, I do allow little things to get under my skin. It's true I am no stranger to adult beverages. I drink, okay? Not what anyone could call *to excess*. But, I drink. And I enjoy my cigars; especially with adult beverages.

Some folks tell me I view the maximum speed limit as more of a suggestion than a legal mandate. It's true I found past comfort in triple digit neighborhoods. But, stories aside, my testing of speed limits happened when I was much younger. Today, I try to set an example. Perhaps a somewhat contemporary rollover has something to do with that.

Here is where I absolutely draw a very distinct line, and did so even when I was still driving like I had the Indy 500 checkered flag in view. When it comes to mixing the consumption of alcoholic beverages with the operation of a motor vehicle? I don't do it. Period. End of conversation. And, I don't condone others doing it either.

Don't even try it in Solita County. My reasoning is rather basic. I've been present at too many alcohol-related vehicular homicides, including some really sad ones with minor victims. Little dead kids covered with gore rips your heart right out of your chest.

So, as I headed to court, I stopped to say hi to some of the boys. Actually, I had a funny joke to tell. No, I won't repeat it. It had something to do with an odoriferous drunk waking up to find a very unhappy wife and the immediate need for some laundering of his own undergarments.

The conversation about the pathetic jocular drunk quickly turned to Marvin and his exploits. Predictably, even mention of his name immediately led to stories of him driving under the influence, aka DUI. He'd tested the patience of too many patrol cops for that to not happen. In California, we also call this offense deuce, for short. That's because the Vehicle Code section outlawing them still ends in a two, as in *deuce*. It embarrassed me to have a boss who did this without consequences. If you enforce the law, enforce the law. Don't wink at it and laugh it away because you can. This fired me up. Are you thinking I hired on there so I could clean the place up? Nope. I didn't know Marvin was a drunk until I was hired. By then, I loved the job too much, and decided to stay.

"It's pretty simple, boys and girls," I pontificated. "You guys find deuces. You hook 'em and book 'em. My part of the team prosecutes 'em. Some of these sad sacks get probation. Others go to jail. Some even land in prison. These can be life-changing events for them, dammit, and, for anyone they injure or kill. Indirectly, they also injure their victim's loved ones."

I frowned and continued. My face reddened. I could feel it. I was commencing yet another of my celebrated rants. "Oh Lord," I prayed, "help me before I foam at the mouth again." I didn't really do that. But, it sounds good, doesn't it? I continued.

"And, yet, a guy like Marvin sees zero wrong with getting a snoot full at his favorite watering hole? His drunken ass sits there for hours on end, while his mouth sucks down the sauce? And, he expects any one of you swingin' dicks or dickettes to give him a ride home, like you're fu…uh…frigging taxi drivers or something?"

A Court Services deputy poked his head into the hallway from the next door courtroom. He saw me, scrunched his eyebrows and gave me a withering look, with his forefinger to his lips. He quietly closed the door. I paused for a moment. Then, I continued. I wasn't trying to be disrespectful. But, dammit, he interrupted my tirade.

"That's horse shit! You know it and I know it. But, his brain is too stinking soused for him to even give a rat's ass. Either way, that's the fucking truth!"

"So, instead of kissing his ass and apologetically driving him home from now on, every time you guys catch him, I suggest you folks grow a pair, hook him and begin taking his ass to jail, right where it belongs. I couldn't care less if he's the elected DA. He's the captain of the law enforcement team for this entire county. He should start acting like it, by setting a better example. He's an embarrassment to the rest of us. Period. End of conversation."

"Fucking truth, huh?" someone asked. That was met by laughter.

"Hey, you tell 'em, Truth!" one of the assembled shouted.

The rest resounded with mirth, as the deputy returned to scold us anew. I didn't care. I'd made my point. I heard a handful of *amens* and at least one *halleluiah*. What could I do besides laugh? Nothing really, so I grinned, then chortled too. Ditto for the deputy. He just looked at me and slowly shook his head. But, this time, he was smiling when he disappeared back into his courtroom. And, there it was. My new nickname, whether I asked for it or not: *Truth*.

Chapter 27

Back home again, I read even more of Dawn's material. Then, I listened anew to the tape recorded interview of Johnny Walker by the Houston Police Department. Like lots of other prosecutors, I've reviewed many suspects being interviewed over the years.

This one was unremarkable. It appeared to be standard police operating procedure. Tape recorder was turned on. Date, time and place were listed. Everyone was identified. Then, Houston PD Detective Carlton Larson began the interrogation.

"Today's date is Monday, March 7, 1994. The time is 0815 hours. We're at the Houston Police Department. I'm Det. Larson. Also present is Detective Archer of the Houston Police Department and Mr. Johnny Walker."

I noticed one of the two had what some might call a Texas accent. The other one sounded like he could have been raised anywhere in the USA. As I listened, I absentmindedly tried to visualize what each man looked like. What color was their hair? Was it worn long or short? Maybe military-style, high and tight? Facial hair? Did either of them wear glasses? If so, were they just reading glasses or prescription ones they wore all the time?

What was their height? Their weight? Were they wearing suits and ties? Or, did they wear Hawaiian shirts, like many of the detectives in southern California do? I made a mental note. Today's young cops seem far more preoccupied with staying trim than their predecessors did. Were these two in good enough shape to still hop backyard fences during foot pursuits? I turned the tape back on, wishing the interview was an audio-video tape.

"Mr. Walker, right before I turned on the tape recorder, I explained to you I would tape record this interview, correct?" Larson asked.

"Yeah."

"And, you told me that was okay, right?"

"Yes sir."

"You understand you are not in custody?"

"I do."

"And, you realize you are free to stop this interview and leave at any time, right?"

"Yup."

"For the record, since a tape recorder can't pick this up, you are not mechanically restrained in any fashion, are you?

"Huh?"

"You're not handcuffed?"

"No."

"And, you aren't in leg shackles or waist chains, right?"

"Nope."

"Wait. Hold on. Are you saying 'no, I'm not'? Or, 'no, I don't agree with what you just said'? Please be clear."

I immediately discerned the confusion was caused by the manner in which Larson phrased his last question. The detective needed to be more clear, not the suspect. It wasn't surprising Walker seemed confused. It was unintelligible; legally objectionable. But, since it was water already under the bridge, there was nothing I could do about that.

"Can y'all ask that again?"

"Are you in leg shackles?"

"No."

"Are you in waist chains?"

"No."

"Not restrained in any fashion? No one is physically holding you?"

"Nope and nope."

In court, again, I would object. Those back-to-back questions were legally objectionable, compound, and confusing. A questioner isn't allowed to ask more than one question at a time in any courtroom, if the judge is doing their job. He reminded me of some of those TV talking heads. Their own multiple questions sound more like orations. By the time they are done asking the last one, how can the listener even begin to remember what the first question was? TV talking heads should be trained better, as to how they should question their guests.

"You're here today of your own free will and have agreed to talk with us, without any coercion from me or anyone else, correct?"

"That's right."

"What's your address?"

"It's 8013 Berwyn."

"City?"

"Houston. Actually, that's our mailing address. The house is in the county, just outside town. You know? Houston city limits."

"Were you residing at the listed address on February 26, 1994?

"Yep."

"Alone or with someone else?"

"With the wife,"

"And, what's her name?"

"Elaine…Elaine Walker."

"Own any vehicles?"

"She owns some foreign piece of crap. Had it when we met. Me? Ford pickup truck," he proudly noted. "All I've ever driven is American vehicles. Ford trucks."

"Did y'all possess the truck on that date?"

"Whatcha mean *possess*?"

"Was it yours?"

"Yup. "Though not quite paid for yet," he added.

Archer read its license plate number, as Larson asked him the next question.

"Did you hear what Detective Archer just read to you? Was that pickup at your residence that date? In other words, same make, model, year, license number and VIN?"

"VIN?"

"Vehicle identification number."

"Have no idea 'bout no VIN."

"Show him the registration again."

Larson spoke again.

"See the registration Detective Archer just showed you? That your truck?"

"Yup."

I was beginning to perceive Walker as a man of economic verbosity. And, he seemed rather unencumbered upstairs too. He just didn't strike me as one who would provide a rocket scientist any competition. There was a discernible dullness to his voice. I'm a DA. Let's just say I've heard this kind of person being interviewed before. No risk of his ever being confused with any Rhodes scholars.

"Did something unusual happen around 3:30 that morning?"

"Yep."

"Describe that, please?"

"Sumbitch was stealin' my truck."

"What do you mean?"

"Heard a noise out front. Looked out my front window. Saw somebody backing down my driveway."

"Where was your truck?"

"Right there."

"Where?"

"Driveway."

"Your driveway?"

"Yup."

"What happened next?"

"Grabbed my rifle. Went out front."

"You grabbed it?"

"Uh huh."

"And?"

"Fired a warning shot. Mebbe two. Don't really recall."

"What happened next?"

"Scared 'im off. Burned rubber. Bastard took off. Left like a scalded ape."

"Did you see him again?"

"Nope."

"You realize our ballistics folks have already compared a round from the decedent's body? They tell me it was fired from your 30-30 rifle."

Walker appeared rattled. He watched TV. He knew all about local events.

"Di-di-didn't know that," he lied. "Not 'til right now. Hold on. What's a…? That word? Dee something? Decent. That the one?"

"Decedent. D-e-c-e-d-e-n-t. Means *dead guy*. You killed him. You shot him. He bled to death."

"Di-di-didn't shoot nobody."

"Trust me, Mr. Walker. He's dead. Very dead. And, your rifle fired the shot that killed him."

"Didn't mean to shoot no one. Just tryin' ta scare 'im a little. Stealin' my truck. Ain't a man got the right to protect his property? From thieves?"

"He is…*was*…a repo man. He was there to *repossess* your truck."

"But, on my property. Stealin' my truck."

"Mr. Walker, where were you when you first heard this man?"

"Livin' room."

"What were you doing there, that time of the night? Or, maybe I should say that time of the morning?"

"Couldn't sleep. Stomach problems. Bad stomach. On the couch. Didn't want to bother the missus," he lied.

"Okay."

"So, what's gonna happen?"

"I need to send everything to the DA."

"What's that mean?"

"I'll write a report. Send it to the District Attorney, including a copy of this taped interview. They'll review it. Probably send it to the grand jury, either with or without charges."

"I don't get it."

"Don't get what? Charges?"

It seemed to me like Walker's way of talking was rubbing off on Larson.

"Yeah."

"If the DA sends it with charges, it means the grand jury will almost certainly return an indictment. If they don't, then they probably return a no bill."

"What's that mean?"

"An indictment means you'll be prosecuted for killin' this man. If it's a conviction for murder, you'll be in prison for the rest of your life, unless it's a death penalty case. If so?"

He didn't finish the sentence.

"A no bill means you walk. Get it? No prosecution?"

"Do I need a lawyer?"

"Can't help you there. Don't know what to tell y'all. Keep something in mind. If the case goes to the grand jury and you have to testify, a lawyer can't go with you into the hearing room anyhow. But, that's gotta be your call, not mine. I don't give legal advice."

"Okay."

"A few more questions. Did anyone dial 911?"

"Not me. Don't know if the wife did or dint. Ain't got no phone."

"So, you didn't?"

"Nope. Like I said, mebbe the ol' lady did. I just went back to sleep."

"Maybe I better talk with your wife too."

"So, am I going to be arrested or somethin'?"

Larson turned off the tape recorder, before answering.

"No, not right now anyhow. As a Texas resident, you're in the driver's seat, if you get my drift."

"What's that s'posed ta mean?"

"There's an old law that's still on our books. Real old law. Goes back to about 1880 or so. Keep in mind, I still ain't givin' legal advice. Just thinkin' out loud."

"You said somethin' 'bout me bein' in the driver's seat?

"It's that law I'm talkin' about."

"What does it say?"

"Basically, it says if you catch someone on your property, in the nighttime, you can shoot them in order to protect your property."

Walker already knew this. Chronic debtors keep their ears open. Like other deadbeats, so did Johnny who couldn't recall when or where he heard this. But, he knew a man with a gun had the right to shoot a nighttime thief on his property. Real or not.

"So, I'm in the clear?"

"No, that's not what I said. That particular call is up to the DA and the grand jury, not us. We're just the investigators. They are the legal experts, not us. We're just cops."

Larson made a mental note to contact Walker's wife, after he turned the recorder back on.

"Any more questions? Detective Archer?

"No."

"Mr. Walker?"

"Nope."

"Then, we are off the record. The time is…"

Chapter 28

Dawn also sent me several Houston-area newspaper clippings. Many stories were done by Gene "Scoop" Wrightwood, a veteran reporter for the Houston Chronicle. He covered TD's killing and did related follow-up stories. Although he repeatedly referred to a shield law protecting his sources, he also testified before the grand jury after Elaine admitted they had spoken and dissolved the shield. His testimony reluctantly corroborated hers. The shield law didn't apply.

Why? Scoop identified and quoted her at length in at least one of his articles. Amazingly, Dawn even included a copy of the recorded interview of Elaine by Wrightwood. Don't ask me how. I don't know and don't even want to know. But, I eagerly listened to it.

Prior to their interview, Wrightwood explained to Elaine how he wrote his articles. He said he always made sure anyone he interviewed was corroborated by at least one other source. Otherwise, there'd be no story. He did seem thorough and methodical. Once he was satisfied she understood, Wrightwood turned on the recorder. His interview was much like any done by police officers. He identified himself, listing the time, date, location, her full name and the reason for the interview. Pretty standard stuff.

Elaine's lawyer later argued most of the interview was invalid because no one advised her of the marital communication privilege. I failed to see the relevance. The privilege applied to a spouse's privilege to not testify, not to discussions with media. Walker's version of what happened mirrored what she told HPD. She told Scoop what she and Johnny discussed the morning of the shooting. When they were done, Wrightwood thanked her and asked if she had any questions. She said no.

He reminded her to not discuss anything they had talked about to anyone else without his permission and turned the recorder off. Scoop needed assurance she was as protective of the shield law's confidentiality privilege as he was, whether it applied or not. If there's one thing I've learned as a lawyer, this is a very good example of why laypersons should not practice law and why most trial lawyers should not work on their own motorcars.

Chapter 29

This heart-wrenching tale continued unfolding as I perused new facts. TD's lifeless body was lifted into the Coroner's van to be transported to the morgue. I've read a lot of incident reports, but this one was more than just a little bit beyond the pale.

Once his remains arrived, I knew they would await an autopsy, prior to final disposition. A deputy Coroner arrived on scene. He believed he was speaking privately, with a Harris County Sheriff's deputy standing nearby.

Little did the two lawmen realize that Chronicle reporter Wrightwood's directional microphone picked up their entire conversation. They were discussing the cause of death. Scoop misinterpreted the speculating deputy Coroner.

He incorrectly surmised the cause of death was failure of first responders to arrive in time to prevent TD O'Mara from bleeding to death. Sensing potential Pulitzer material in the making, Wrightwood quickly made a couple of notes and left to find a phone.

He planned to contact the local watch commander as quickly as possible. He needed to beat any other enterprising investigative reporters to the punch. Scoop would not be scooped.

Chapter 30

Quintessentially thorough Dawn somehow even provided me with the gist of a telephone conversation between HPD Sgt. Beck Jacobs and Wrightwood. At this point, I still wasn't inclined to ask questions or look any gift horses in the mouth. My primary motivation was to soak up as much information as possible. Whimsically, I toyed with suggesting Dawn rename herself Hoover, after the vacuum cleaner, not the late, allegedly cross-dressing, FBI Director. Intel continued to flow from her to me, like the mighty Brazos River.

Wrightwood asked Sgt. Jacobs for his spin on the purported failure to respond to Walker's 911 call in a timely manner. He needed confirmation of what he believed the Coroner said. He assumed the call had, in fact, been made. Dangerous assumption. That's why you don't assume. Were we in court, his question would have produced yet another reason to object. It either called for speculation, if not factually based, or assumed facts not in evidence, if he didn't correctly hear the Coroner.

Either way, Scoop was whistling in the wind. Jacobs denied any such knowledge.

As a lawyer, I've learned many things over this particular journey. This is true above all, in my role as a prosecutor. One of the things I've learned is to never accept an allegation just because someone has given it a label. Therefore, until I am appropriately convinced, any purported failure remains just that, i.e., *purported*. The call, however, led Sgt. Jacobs to brief his lieutenant on his conversation with Wrightwood. And, that, in turn, led to a follow-up interview of Elaine Walker by HPD detective Larson to determine if she really made any calls the morning of the murder.

Chapter 31

Elaine Walker agreed to be interviewed by Larson. But, when she hung up, she was uncertain if she'd done the right thing. Something in her gut told her she shouldn't have done that. After all, didn't he tell her she could refuse to talk with them? Later that day, she opened her front door and nervously invited the two officers inside who had previously interviewed Johnny.

Larson appeared to be in charge. Archer, as before, was the other detective. Larson's partner seemed to be along for the ride. As I listened to the interview, I heard the recorder being activated. Next, I heard Larson's voice. I recognized it from his interview of Johnny Walker, and remembered him introducing himself.

"Mind if I record our conversation? Prevents confusion."

"No, I s'pose not."

Larson provided the same exact admonishment he'd previously given her husband. He then proceeded with the interview. Except for names, dates, times and locations, I've heard this same sort of nonsense, ad nauseum. Interrogation is interrogation is interrogation.

"Ma'am, I understand you witnessed a shooting by your husband."

"I didn't see nothin'."

"No ma'am. That's not what I mean. Let me explain. There's an expression us cops use: *eyeball witness* or *eye witness*. That's actually a little misleading. A witness is anyone who perceives an event through any of their senses. That depends on the situation."

"Uh huh?"

"In other words, we use our senses. We smell, see, hear, touch, taste and feel. A percipient witness is someone who witnesses an event with one or more of their senses."

"Okay."

"So, let me ask that again. Did you witness the shooting your husband did on February 26, 1994?"

"I understand now. Yeah, I did. I heard somethin'."

"And, what was that?"

"At first, I thought it was a firecracker. Loud. I was sound asleep in our bedroom and it just went and woke me right up. At first, I didn't know if I was dreamin'. Or, was it for real? Know what I mean?"

"Uh-uh."

"Like I said, it woke me up. That's when I heard the second bang. I knew, right then and there, it was a gunshot."

"Could you tell what kind it was?"

Larson figured this question might be a waste of time, but asked it anyhow.

"Yep. Rifle. Big caliber. I know Johnny has a 30-30. Figured that's what it was when I came into the kitchen."

"Why do you say that?" asked Larson.

"Couple of reasons. First of all, I saw him leanin' it up against the wall. Touched the barrel. Still hot. But, I could also hear him movin' around after I went to bed, yellin' and cussin'. Slammin' doors. I suspect this same guy had been here earlier the same night too. And, 'sides, I know what a 30-30 sounds like."

Archer looked at her, but said nothing. He quickly scribbled something.

"Why do you say that?"

"Which?"

"About the yelling and cussing?"

"He…he was yellin' stuff about repo men."

"What was he saying?"

"Like I said, he was cussin'. I don't talk like that myself."

"What did he say?"

She paused, and then blushed.

"He was usin' the F-word a lot. Also, the mother-F-word."

Larson nodded.

"So, wait a minute, Ms. Walker. Are you saying the sound you heard was a 30-30? Or, are you saying you knew the gun you saw when you came into the kitchen was a 30-30?"

"Both. I know the gun by sound. And, I know it by sight."

"Okay. So another question or two, if you don't mind?"

"Sure."

"Did your husband say anything to you, after you heard the gunshots?"

"Yeah, understand somethin' first. He was drunk. Not like that's anything new. He's always drunk. He…"

"Why do you say he was drunk?"

"The usual."

"Huh?"

"If you was married to him, and saw him drunk as many times as I have, you'd know he was drunk when he's drunk. That's all there is to it."

"What I'm looking for, ma'am, is what it was about him that told you he was drunk."

"He was awake, okay?"

"No, that's not what I mean."

"I don't follow."

Larson explained what objective symptoms of alcohol intoxication are. Once he did so, he asked her if she understood.

"Okay, I get it now. So, you need to know more than the fact I simply know this man to be drunk when he's awake, right?"

"Yes."

She explained, providing details about how he spoke, walked, appeared and acted.

"Anybody call 911?"

"I…uh…yeah, I d-d-did. Actually, I was so rattled, I don't remember if I dialed 911 or the regular number."

"Ma'am?"

"I was nervous. And, I was scared, okay? I was discombobulated. Listen, one minute I was sound asleep and the next? Boom! Wide awake. All because my idiot husband has to be the great white hunter. He even threatened me."

"What do you mean? You mean he scared you?"

"Sure, I was scared. But, I mean he *threatened* me. That's why I said threatened. He said: '…I already shot one guy tonight. Wanna be number two?' Somethin' like that."

"Why'd he say that?"

"You serious? 'Cuz he's mean. He's a bully. He's a drunk. And, he *was* drunk. I actually had the nerve to ask the *lord of the castle* questions, 'steada just bein' the dutiful little housewife. He don't cotton to me talkin' none, most of the time, less'n I'm offerin' to get him a beer or some food, or give him a..."

She didn't finish her sentence and simply blushed again.

"He'd probably been better off gettin' a damn dog. Suspect he'd treat it better 'n me."

"So, you're saying he threatened to shoot you?"

"Uh huh."

"And, you felt threatened by what he said?"

"I mean, yeah, he was drunk. Runs his mouth real mean, 'specially when he's hittin' the bottle. But, yeah, I felt threatened, 'cuz he threatened me. Like I said."

"What does he drink?"

"You mean, like, alcohol?"

The detective merely nodded.

"Usually vodka. Cheap vodka. He ain't all that particular. If it'll get him drunk, he'll drink it. He'd drink shoe polish if it got him drunk."

"Anything further?" Larson asked.

"Wanna know his nickname?"

"Nickname?"

"Yeah, it's *Stoli*."

"Stoli? Like the Russian vodka?"

"What do you think?"

"Anything further?"

"Nope."

The interview was concluded. Someone turned off the recorder.

Chapter 32

As the newly-widowed woman was making funeral arrangements, detectives were completing reports they would present to the DA's office for a filing decision. Any veteran cop soon learns their ability to take a suspect off the street is no greater than a prosecutor's willingness to indict or a judge's readiness to imprison the same deserving defendant. Some substances roll downhill faster than others, and rapidly gather speed.

I next learned of another thought-provoking tête-à-tête. Larson was speaking to a filing deputy at the DA's office. As a lawyer, I've always tried to place myself in the other guy's shoes, in order to best absorb what they may be thinking. It appeared to me Elaine Walker might not be telling the truth about the 911 call. I don't allow outsiders to be privy to any conversation I ever have with any of the cops I serve with. Somewhere, it appeared a breach of security had occurred. And, if there had been, how?

The law calls the accumulation of this sort of information *attorney work product*. And, I always expect any competent prosecutor to function accordingly. No proficient prosecutor should expect any less. Somehow, Dawn had obtained privileged information. I'm not suggesting she did anything wrong herself. For the moment, let's not delve beyond that. Sleeping dogs and all that razzmatazz.

If it were my case and I believed Mrs. Walker was lying about the 911 call, I'd fashion a way to hold her legally accountable. Penalties could range from a simple misdemeanor, commonly called interfering with a peace officer, to a fairly heavy duty felony: *perjury*. The facts and law would dictate what charge might be appropriate. There are a couple of standard routes. At the lenient end, she could face interfering with HPD's investigation of the O'Mara homicide.

The problem with that, however, is she can't be forced to testify against herself because of the 5th Amendment. She could also keep Johnny from testifying against her because they are married to one another. Ditto for any testimony by Elaine against him. Don't blame me. With the exception of the one law I personally wrote and a couple of others that never got to the Governor's desk, I don't write them. I just enforce them.

This particular privilege is called the *marital communication privilege*. And since this one's only a crummy little misdemeanor, this means no real consequences. With no prior record, the typical defendant will get probation with no custody; maybe just a small fine. Therefore, it would make more sense to be patient and let her testify before the grand jury. That's what I'd do anyhow. If her testimony is consistent with the lie she apparently told HPD about the 911 call, at that point, she probably would commit perjury. Since she can't have a lawyer in the grand jury room with her, and, technically, isn't a suspect yet, it's not likely she would invoke the 5th and *not* testify, figuring she's just doing what she's told. As noted, perjury's a felony. Now, we're getting somewhere. Upon conviction, that would also translate to revocation of her right to vote, and so on.

"Visualize me, as a Harris County DA, talking to Larson," I told Dawn.

"Okay. But, first, how do you prove she lied?"

I explained. Dawn seemed to fully grasp what I was saying. I compared the difference between being mistaken as to which agency Elaine claimed to have contacted verses not calling anyone and claiming she had really done so.

I suggested Dawn keep the pot stirred up, so the investigation wouldn't simply die on the vine. It appeared to me no one was aggressively investigating Walker for killing her late husband. This puzzled and disappointed me. Miss Dawn could make a big difference in getting this investigation down to the real nitty-gritty. I asked her to determine the status of the pending prosecution of her husband's slayer. For starters, was Walker going to be arrested? I suggested she try to find out. Lighting fires under fannies can be quite productive, if properly stoked. I know telephonic inquiries aren't guaranteed to produce results. Visualize a roulette wheel. Spinning it doesn't necessarily tell you where it will stop. But, since the worst thing anyone can usually be told is no, I'd consider those pretty decent odds. I recommended she keep the heat turned up.

As I tried to picture such a conversation, I believed Dawn O'Mara would be inquisitive. No doubt, she would demand Walker be prosecuted for murder. However, on the other end of the phone line, I'd expect Larson to educate her about the parameters of Texas Penal Code 9.41. As part of my review, I'd already read and digested it. Section 9.41 allows any Texas resident to use deadly force in the nighttime to protect their property. The obvious issue here? What was Walker's state of mind when he fired the fatal rounds? Did he really believe a thief was trying to steal his truck? If so, 9.41 gave him full legal authority to pull the trigger with utter impunity. It was dark and he had the weaponry. He could literally kill TD and get away with it. In legal parlance, that's known as an *excusable homicide*.

In other words, although Walker killed O'Mara, he wouldn't face any criminal consequences. It wouldn't matter that he was drunk. And, it also wouldn't matter if he was mistaken or was flat out wrong in believing O'Mara was trying to steal his truck.

So far, what had Walker said? He claimed he thought a thief was attempting to steal his truck at 3:30 in the morning. But, I know his protestations of innocence are meaningless, without adequate corroboration. In other words, was there additional evidence to back his play? Or, was he flying solo? As a member of the law enforcement team, I know you don't automatically take a person's word at face value, especially when you are attempting to determine if they are telling the truth.

You have to carefully examine the totality of the available evidence. But, unlike TV cops and robbers shows, I know what you see is not always what you get. Sometimes, you have to dig through all kinds of evidence. Other times, you only obtain a portion of relevant information. When this occurs, you do the best you can with what you have. Up to this point, it appears to me this killing is looking far more inexcusable than excusable. Either way, it certainly wasn't justifiable.

As I keep digging, I've learned the supervising prosecutor in Harris County is a guy named Riley Montgomery. But, that could be academic. I'm still not sure if I'm going to get involved in this matter. Decisions. Decisions. Damn it to hell!

On the one hand, it's crazy for a brand new DA, like me, to think he can set aside his official duties to take on something this time consuming, this far away from home, and totally unrelated to my official duties. But, having said that, I continue to be intrigued. So, I'll keep digging until I have an answer.

Chapter 33

Since I wasn't willing to tip my hand just yet, I decided to let Dawn be the needed conduit. I called to tell her she needed to light a motivational fire under Montgomery. I even outlined what she should ask him. Then, and only then, could I make a decision, and told her so in no uncertain terms. Pussy-footing around isn't my bag. Never has been. Never will be. I asked her to brief me afterwards. Once they spoke, she called me and said Monty, as his friends called him, sounded annoyed at being interrupted. Lest we forget, Dawn doesn't sugar coat things either. The DA was probably staring at a mountain of paperwork he had been trying to mow through all morning.

I know that drill all too well. Been there. Done that. He's a prosecutor. I know the routine. Doesn't matter what state he serves in. He could be quite busy, and just not getting any traction. If he's anything like me, every time he gains momentum, the phone will almost certainly ring again. And, unlike home, it's never a wrong number. No such luck.

As a rule of thumb, a clean prosecutorial desk isn't in the cards. Prosecutors just generate a lot of paperwork. And, that adds to desk clutter. At least, mine's never neat and tidy. This has nothing to do with that old expression about clean desks and sick minds. It's merely a scheduling issue. Laws of physics can only be ignored so far.

Dawn told me she told Montgomery why she was calling. She took copious notes and was able to tell me later, practically verbatim, what they discussed. Frankly, I doubt I could have reviewed more words, even if Dawn illicitly tape recorded the conversation. Maybe she did. I can't say one way or the other. When I spoke with her, I got quite an earful. Dawn told Montgomery, almost immediately, that she got his private number from Larson who suggested she call him. I visualized Montgomery's thoughts wafting through steam pouring out of his ears.

I suspect Larson purposely dumped Dawn into the DA's lap. If so, this guy is an accomplished buck passer. Apparently, he isn't interested in obtaining any favorable future filing decisions from Montgomery. Lifers don't care about stuff like that. I had one cop do that to me a longtime ago. He never did that again. Enough said about that. But, if there's one thing any self-respecting prosecutor despises, it's learning one of the cops you serve with has dumped a problem onto you which they should solve themselves, especially if you're solving other problems and don't need yet another interruption.

Dawn shared relevant parts of their conversation. It went like this.

"Mrs.?...I'm sorry...did you say O'Mara? Is that 'M,' like Mary?" he asked her.

"It's M...like...MY husband was shot to death just tryin' to do his job. Shot down like a dog by a 'M', as in *murderin'* piece of white trash."

She slowly spelled her surname: O-*apostrophe*-M-A-R-A!

"Thank you, ma'am. I know my words and thoughts can't bring your loved one back. But, having said that, I'm sorry for your loss. Truly sorry."

"Thank you for saying that," Dawn remarked, as she began to weep again. "I'm sorry. But, my emotions are still so raw...so bare...so right up on the surface. It's like somebody ripped my very skin right off my body."

"Don't you worry, Mrs. O'Mara, I've been doing this for a long, long time."

"So," she snuffled, "when is my husband's killer going to prison?"

"Please understand something, ma'am. These things aren't on automatic pilot. Killings don't automatically merit an indictment. There's a process we must follow."

"Please explain."

"Here's what I mean. Just like with anything else in life, there's a procedure. Let me give you an example. Are you a baker?"

"Yes, I am."

"Okay then. Follow my hypothetical. You don't just take all your ingredients and dump them into a cake pan and expect to have a cake, right?"

"No."

"In other words, you measure, mix and stir, adding this and that, according to some written directions, depending on what you're baking, don't you?"

"Yes."

"Then, you bake the ingredients in a pre-heated oven for a set amount of time, correct?"

"Yes."

"Probably even use a timer so you don't bake it too long or too little?"

"Uh huh."

"Same thing here. First, I have to read all the police reports prepared by all the officers involved in a given case. Those are my written directions, if you will."

"Okay."

"Then, I have to see if I believe the information I've read establishes all the elements of each crime the suspect is accused of committing. Like you, following those directions. You still with me?"

"Uh huh."

"After I've done this, if I'm convinced all the elements are there, I…"

"Wait a minute. Elements? What are elements?"

"Crimes contain elements, sort of like pieces to a jigsaw picture puzzle or ingredients to that cake you're baking. If they aren't all there, then there's no provable crime any more than you would have an edible cake."

"I don't follow."

"The Latin phrase that covers this is known as the *corpus delicti* rule, or *body of the crime* rule. Take the crime of murder. First, we have to show a human being was killed by another human being. Got it?"

"Yes."

"Fine. That's called a homicide. As opposed to a person killing themselves or being killed by a wild animal, let's say. Homicide just means one person killed another person. It doesn't get into how it happened."

"Okay, I understand now."

"Good. I have a suggestion Mrs. O'Mara. You got a pen and paper with you?"

"Yes. Why?"

"This will be far easier for you, if you make notes on any questions you have and ask me for answers later. I've got a lot of work to do and if you keep interrupting me with irrelevant questions, this will take forever."

"I'm sorry."

Dawn began to cry again.

"I'm sorry," she repeated.

After a pause, he asked "you okay, ma'am? Can we continue?"

"Yes."

"Good. Once we've determined a death is a homicide, at that point we have other determinations to make."

"Okay."

"Keep in mind, *homicide* is the killing of one human being by another. In order for it to be *murder*, the statute requires it must be an *unlawful* killing. This means it must be done with *malice aforethought*. How did it happen? *Intentional? Unintentional?* Is it *murder?* If so, is it *first degree? Second degree?* If not, is it *manslaughter? Voluntary? Involuntary? Vehicular? Excusable? Justifiable?*"

"Whoa," she interrupted. "I know you said no questions, but what does all this mean?"

"No ma'am. I said no *irrelevant* questions. What you just asked *is* relevant."

"I don't understand the difference."

"Relevant means *germane*."

"Germane?"

At this point, Dawn interrupted what she was telling me, in order to make an observation.

"From the tone of his voice, I could tell he was gettin' real impatient with me. It was almost as if he didn't think I was very smart or something. Practically condescending."

After explaining that, she continued with Montgomery's explanation.

"Relevant. You know? Does it have anything to do with the price of eggs? The price of tea in China? That's what *relevant* means."

"Okay, I get it. Please proceed."

"*Intentional* means the perpetrator meant to do it. *Unintentional* means it was *accidental*. If so, was it the result of *negligence* or *gross negligence*?"

"What about murder?"

"First or second degree? *First degree* must be *deliberate* and *premeditated*. If not, it's second degree."

"What does all that mean?"

"Deliberate basically means the killer must have *thought about doing it beforehand*. Premeditated means he *planned to do it*."

"You also mentioned manslaughter."

"Yes, manslaughter can be either *voluntary* or *involuntary*."

"Okay."

"Voluntary is any killing done in the *heat of passion*. Let's say a husband comes home and finds his wife in flagrante delicto with another man, or vice-versa, and kills one or both of them. Or, for example, someone is killed during a *sudden quarrel*, like a drunker bar fight."

"Okay."

"Involuntary is a bit more involved. That can result from any unlawful act not amounting to a felony."

"Yes?"

"Or, by committing a lawful act that might produce death in an unlawful manner, or without due caution and circumspection."

"Uh huh…what?"

"You know? Without thinking carefully enough first."

"You mentioned something about vehicles?"

"Irrelevant."

"But, my husband was in his wrecker when he was murdered."

"First of all, Ms. O'Mara, we don't know legally or factually yet, if it even is murder. And, the fact your husband was in a vehicle doesn't make it a vehicular manslaughter. Now, you're confusing *me*, ma'am."

"I'm sorry," she said for the third time.

"Okay, let's continue. *Justifiable* or *excusable* means the killer has a *valid legal defense*," he emphasized.

"Like how?"

"Justifiable would be, for example, *self-defense* or *defending the life of another person*."

"Excusable?"

"In Texas, *protecting one's property in the nighttime*."

"What?!!"

Dawn said she could hear Montgomery take a deep breath before explaining Texas Penal Code 9.41 to her. He provided an example of a property owner using a weapon in the nighttime to protect their property and a suspected thief dies as a result.

Dawn countered that TD was a repo man, not a thief. The prosecutor explained he was being hypothetical and stressed he wasn't calling him a thief, adding he hadn't even read the reports yet.

"Ma'am, I'm duty bound to follow the law and apply it to whatever the facts of this case are, just like with any other case I am duty bound to prosecute.

Dawn remarked "wow, that's a lot to digest."

"Ma'am," replied Montgomery, "what you just got was a cram course in criminal law, focusing on homicides."

"But…"

"Please, let me finish. All of this is hypothetical at this point. As I said, I haven't even read the file involving your husband's death. So, let me get back to my explanation, okay? I have other work to do. Please, ma'am?"

"Sure, please do."

Montgomery completed his explanation of his role and that of his office in any potential homicide prosecution.

"So, you're sayin' TD's case isn't a sure bet?"

"TD?"

"My murdered husband. Tommy Deen."

"Oh? Sure…right. Ma'am, I won't know any more until I begin reading the reports. Why don't we do this?"

"What's that?"

Montgomery asked Dawn for her phone number and promised to call her as soon as he had reviewed everything to apprise her of his decision. She tried to pin him down specifically when he would do that. But he was vague. He told her he would be done when he was done. He added he was prosecuting at least eight active homicide cases. Two were capital matters, or death penalty cases. And, he was also supervising other prosecutors. At this juncture, he might as well have been saying blah, blah, blah.

He explained his case load required court appearances, speaking with witnesses and defense attorneys, and also conferring daily with other prosecutors and cops. Dawn said, when she described TD's death as a murder, he reminded her it would not be officially called that until the grand jury said it was.

She thanked him, hung up, and phoned me. As usual, with her prior knowledge and consent, I recorded our conversation. Later, I played it back to make sure I hadn't gotten distracted and missed anything.

Please don't misunderstand what I'm about to say. I'm not egotistical. At least, I don't think I am. Molly says I'm not. But, I know good lawyering from bad lawyering. I've seen enough of both to know the difference. This Montgomery guy was good. Real good. He actually did make their conversation sound like a criminal law tutorial. Hell, he'd probably be able to give any other prosecutor a run for their money, including me.

Chapter 34

By the time the interview was over, Larson believed he could prove Elaine Walker committed perjury. But, she had to say the same thing under oath she had just told him. If she did, she was as good as convicted. I had to agree with his assessment. She claimed she made two separate phone calls to report the fatal shooting of TD O'Mara. According to her, the first call was from the house next door, shortly after 3:30 a.m. And, the second call was purportedly made between 6:30 and 7:00 a.m. from work.

In my opinion, her story had more holes than a piece of aged Swiss cheese. She made neither call. Larson first interviewed HPD's dispatch supervisor. They carefully sifted through departmental records. No calls from Elaine Walker were found. And, Johnny's grandmother confirmed no calls were made that morning from her house. Her phone records corroborated that.

Larson did the same follow-up with their sister agency, Harris County Sheriff. His interview of their dispatch supervisor and the same methodical review of their records also produced the same result. Again, no calls from Mrs. Walker. A review of her work place's telephone records also showed no calls to either agency.

The Walkers lived just outside the city limits of Houston. Therefore, the only two likely police departments would be either Harris County Sheriff or Houston PD. I'm not suggesting she couldn't have physically phoned other agencies. But, calling any others simply made no sense. Larson was thorough. I cannot deny that. Walker claimed she had called one or the other; either HPD or HCSO. When asked, she emphatically denied calling any other departments. The proof of the pudding is in the eating, as the old saying goes. She was cooking her own goose.

"Why would I call any of them?" she asked, when Larson offered the names of several other agencies in the greater Houston area.

Larson even suggested other departments, including the communities of Bellaire, Galena Park and South Houston. Her answer to each was an ardent no. The latter was geographically too far away for her to call. But, Larson decided to be extra cautious and ask. He then followed up by checking each of their phone records, just as he did with HPD and HCSO.

This appeared to be a typical police investigation. Larson first tried to prove she committed no crime. He did this to show how he determined she was guilty. I agreed with this methodology. It was orderly, logical and standard operating procedure. Why wasn't he this thorough with Johnny?

Like Larson, I also do my homework. Like me, he wasn't some snotty-nosed rookie. Like most other cops, he learned the job the hard way. Some folks, including cops, give the expression *reasonable doubt* a lot more meaning than what the law requires. As a rule of thumb, most police officers I know are pretty meticulous. I've known more than a few who do their own research. When they are done, they know as much about a given subject as some so-called experts they routinely interview.

In fact, one particular officer I know actually went to the local law library to get a textbook definition of reasonable doubt so he would conclusively know what it meant. He found a dusty copy of Black's Law Dictionary, Revised Fourth Edition. He located the heading **DOUBT**, with **REASONABLE DOUBT** underneath, then photocopied it. He now takes this with him whenever he goes to trial, just in case a prosecutor needs it. The definition reads as follows:

"Reasonable Doubt: *This is a term used, probably pretty well understood, but not easily defined. It does not mean a mere possible doubt, because everything relating to human affairs, and depending on moral evidence is open to some possible or imaginary doubt. It is that state of the case which, after the entire comparison and consideration of all the evidence, leaves the minds of jurors in that condition that they cannot say they feel an abiding conviction to a moral certainty of the truth of the charge."*

He compared those words with the written jury instruction a judge might read in court and couldn't find any meaningful difference, with one exception. Unlike Black's, some current courtroom definitions, including my own state, no longer include the phrase *to a moral certainty*.

It appeared to that officer the language was nearly identical otherwise. He couldn't understand why judges and prosecutors disregard the definition of reasonable doubt found in a legal dictionary.

There it was right on the cover, **Black's Law Dictionary**. People relied on various incantations of Webster's dictionary whenever they were looking for the meaning of other words. Therefore, he couldn't understand why Black's was being ignored. Why, he asked himself, was Black's being so disrespected by judges and lawyers alike? If the language in Black's was even more descriptive than the jury instructions, why not save some paper and ink, and just refer to it? Or, as he later complained to me, *if Black's wasn't followed, what was the point of any law library even buying copies of it?* How do you rebut that? I unconvincingly explained that appellate courts aren't necessarily logical.

Being a typical cop, he thought lawyers and judges overcomplicated everything. Maybe so. Maybe we do. His research may seem like overkill to you. But, this is the attention to detail I find repeatedly in the work of the cops with whom I serve. That's dedication. Just because an appellate court says it's right, doesn't mean it is. Call that my own hunch. These folks may not be relying on their own training and experience on a regular basis. Perhaps folks residing in glass houses shouldn't throw stones. If a perjury case was filed, Elaine would have to do one of two things: (a) take the witness stand and testify in her own defense, or, (b) assert her 5th Amendment right and keep her mouth shut. Diametrically opposite choices.

In my opinion, she had to testify. She needed to explain she'd made a mistake, rather than lying about a material fact. But, considering Larson's seemingly dogged investigation of the facts, I suspected a jury would not buy her story. Facts are facts.

Chapter 35

Any veteran cop will tell you the questions they ask during any investigation will never be answered, until they are actually answered. That may sound trite, but it's true. If a suspect elects to not answer a cop's question, it will remain unanswered. They don't have to, unless they wish to do so, freely, knowingly, and intelligently. For that, we can thank *Miranda v. Arizona* and a host of other federal appellate cases. It's the judicial branch's way of correcting what they perceive to be overstepping by law enforcement professionals when we deal with bad guys.

Whether you agree or disagree with that analysis, it's true. In real life, real law enforcement personnel can't do it like how you see it done on TV. We can't tell the jury what we *think* the answer should be. Any cop or prosecutor knows this. But, it's a view not generally held by uninformed people who don't work in the criminal justice system. Substituting televised versions of cops and DA's from real ones may be deemed sexier by civilians. However, it's certainly far from being instructive. Ignorance might be considered blissful in the eyes of the ignorant. But, as any self-respecting LE pro knows, this philosophy is never helpful to prove a crime occurred.

Uninformed lay people place a far higher expectation of performance on the shoulders of any peace officer than is merited. Experienced prosecutors know, or, at least should know, cops make mistakes, no matter how good they are. And, the same is true with prosecutors, judges, doctors, and any other working stiff on the planet. This is unadulterated fact, irrespective of whether you're talking about blue or white collar workers. Again, facts are facts. And, humans are human.

By that, I mean, we err. I believe we err in order to learn. I joke that I intentionally make mistakes daily, to assure myself I'm still alive. But, that's also why I make mistakes. There's a longtime private joke among lawyers. It's called *the practice of law*. Lawyers practice law just like doctors practice medicine, dentists practice dentistry and psychiatrists practice psychiatry. Each profession apparently practices their craft with the hope they will one day learn how to do it. And, somewhat hypocritically, lawyers criticize LEO's even though what we do is called *practicing* law.

Every occupation has a learning curve. The length and steepness are dependent upon the task to be mastered and the person seeking to master it, in order for us to adequately take care of business. Some jobs have longer learning curves than others. But, the end result is the same. Regardless of what someone does for a paycheck, a period of learning is essential in order to properly perform. Every job requires a set methodology unique to its own particular field.

Lawyers and cops operate precisely the same in one particular area. And, this is true whether the lawyer is a prosecutor or a defense attorney. Irrespective of job description, it's the same drill. Lawyers and cops must rely on facts and apply the law. Any competent judge will insist this be done. Despite what any member of the public may misbelieve, brilliance has little to do with success in the courtroom. Quite frankly, it all boils down to good old-fashioned hard work.

A cop's job is far from done when they snap the handcuffs on a suspect and take that guy to jail. Such wrong-headed thinking is both stupid and delusional, based solely on sheer and utter unmitigated ignorance. Chrome bracelets merely commence the journey. The booking sheet and incident report are but mere roadmaps. Why? Every person accused of a crime in America has certain inalienable rights, guaranteed by the United States Constitution. The Bill of Rights lists our precious Constitution's first ten amendments. Included therein are:

- freedom of speech and religion (1st Amendment)
- freedom from unreasonable searches and seizures (4th Amendment)
- the right to Due Process and privilege against self-incrimination (5th Amendment)
- the right to a speedy and public trial by a fair and impartial jury, the right to confront and cross-examine one's accusers, and the right to counsel (6th Amendment)
- prohibition against cruel and unusual punishment (8th Amendment)

Are you a cop who doesn't believe these impact what you do for a paycheck? Then, you obviously haven't been in a courtroom. Ethical prosecutors don't determine whether they can convict a defendant merely from the facts listed in police reports. We prosecutors must also decide if any of a suspect's constitutional rights have been violated. If they have, then we must determine if we are duty bound to reject such a filing request.

A long-standing U.S. Supreme Court case, Brady v. Maryland, mandates every prosecutor, from sea-to-shining sea in this great land, must voluntarily provide the defense any information tending to show the defendant, i.e., their client, is not guilty. This must be done voluntarily. The defense doesn't even have to lift a finger. They have no duty to even make such a request. The prosecutor must do this on each and every case they touch. That's because we represent *all* the People, including the Defendant. And, the key word is *voluntarily*. If we wait for a defense request for such information, then we have waited too long. That means we have committed a *Brady* violation and are in hot water.

Chapter 36

There is a fundamental distinction between the role of a prosecutor verses the zone where a defense attorney roams. Each side is required to maintain a different set of ethical standards. And, different they are, just as night is from daytime.

Every American prosecutor is duty-bound to dispense justice. This means we only convict the guilty. We must seek a fair disposition in each and every case we touch, and shall always acquit the innocent. On the other side of the aisle, defense counsel's marching orders take them in a totally different professional direction. They must zealously represent each and every one of their clients, within the bounds of the law. While this indeed sounds lofty, it's actual far more down to earth.

Here's what it means to the lawyer, to their client, and to the cop who ends up in that particular set of crosshairs in any of America's busy criminal courtrooms. No lawyer can ethically suborn perjury or perpetrate a fraud on the court. But, beyond that, everything else is essentially fair game, including wrongly accusing any involved officers of being liars or fools. To that extent, the truth isn't that important. A lawyer cannot knowingly encourage or permit a witness to lie under oath to any material fact. That is known as suborning perjury.

Are you asking what a material fact is? That particular key unlocks the door behind which the relevant answer lies. Here's a pair of illustrative hypothetical examples. Keep something in mind. Legal stuff will always lean far more toward having shades of gray than distinct black and white. Why? I'm not sure I have an answer to that. I suspect it's because the legal system is chock full of human beings. And, humans, being what we are, it's really tough to stick any of us into neatly defined pigeon holes. Be that as it may, here is an example or two.

Example #1: A defendant is charged with robbery. His lawyer questions him during their initial interview. Depending on what is said, this may allow them to establish an alibi defense. If it's viable, this, in turn, may convince the jury the defendant was really elsewhere at the time of the charged crime, and may be factually innocent.

If the alibi is believed by the trier(s) of fact, it will show the accused is not guilty. Innocent, actually. To the uninitiated, the word alibi has a pejorative ring to it, sounding almost sinister. But, alibi merely means someone was legitimately elsewhere and not involved in the crime.

Assume, in our hypothetical example, the lawyer knows the alibi for his client is bogus. How? He knows this because his investigator has already interviewed the girlfriend and she said the defendant never showed up at her home, as he claimed. The investigator so informs the attorney. And, when the investigator asked the girlfriend if she knew where the defendant was, she shrieked "…how should I know? The bastard stood me up. For all I know, he could have been fucking his old girlfriend or robbing a damned liquor store…" *(Side note: witness stand profanity happens daily. Get used to it.)*

Ironically, that's precisely what he is accused of doing. Therefore, if the lawyer knows this, but permits his client to testify to an obviously false alibi, he is allowing him to knowingly testify falsely to a material fact. In so doing, he allows his client to commit perjury and, therefore, the lawyer suborns perjury. Sadly, I am not aware of a single perjury or subornation of perjury case any prosecuting attorney's office ever filed for such contemptuous behavior, until I became DA. More on that later. By doing what he did, the lawyer allowed his client to commit a felony and committed one himself.

By contrast, hypothetical #2 uses the same facts as in the previous example, but with a slightly different twist. Here's the dissimilarity. This defendant, in fact, does go to his girlfriend's house to socialize. He does this during the same time frame within which he is accused of robbing the liquor store. The lawyer knows the alibi is legitimate. Defense attorneys call this the SODDI defense. SODDI is a longtime acronym for *Some Other Dude Did It*. But, if factually supported, it's also a legitimate defense. Hypothetical #2 lawyer's investigator has interviewed the girlfriend. She corroborates the defendant's story. He was with her and isn't guilty. He is innocent. Such an alibi would be legitimate, even if the defendant snuck out of his girlfriend's house to actually commit the robbery, but did so without anyone's knowledge; particularly his girlfriend or anyone on the defense team.

Let's say this lawyer actually goes a step further than he is ethically required and has a qualified polygrapher administer a polygraph, or lie detector test, to the girlfriend. She passes it. This indicates she's telling the truth, even if the results of the test are not admissible in court, due to the *Kelly-Frye* line of cases.

However, the wrinkle in the fabric of this set of facts? Both boyfriend and girlfriend used illegal drugs that night at her house. Defense counsel knows this because it came out during the polygraph, protected by the attorney work product privilege. In fact, the girlfriend had to take the poly twice. She failed it the first time due to her nervousness over the drug usage issue. The defendant is on parole. Use of any illicit drugs will violate his parole terms. The prosecutor knows this. So does defense counsel.

Let's say I'm the prosecutor. I know the defendant is a drug addict. I've reviewed the defendant's rap sheet. I know he has previously been convicted of being under the influence of heroin and for possession of it. Over defense counsel's objections, the judge allows me to question the defendant on this issue to discredit his direct testimony by showing he engaged in an illegal act. But, the defendant falsely testifies he did not use drugs with his girlfriend that evening.

Defense counsel does nothing and permits this lie to remain in the trial record. At first blush, it would appear the defendant committed perjury. If so, defense counsel may have suborned perjury, by knowingly allowing his client to testify falsely under oath. Right? However, as an equally compelling argument, one can say the lawyer did nothing wrong and no perjury occurred.

That's because the testimony, while false, did not necessarily pertain to a material fact. Therefore, if no perjury occurred, then no subornation could take place either. Real life courtrooms are not like TV lawyering. And, they are rarely black and white environments. Remember? Shades of gray.

Chapter 37

Riley Montgomery finally found the time he needed to review the O'Mara homicide. He'd been employed by the Harris County District Attorney's office for nearly twenty-five years, joining the office shortly after passing the Texas bar exam. Houston is Harris County's major population center and has approximately 2.25 million residents. Harris County is just a tad over 3.6 million people. The DA's office is a constantly busy place. Bad guys are equal opportunity criminals. They victimize both good guys and other bad guys daily.

Riley estimated he had handled a total of more than 20,000 misdemeanor and felony cases, by the time the O'Mara case arrived on his desk. He previously had tried more than two dozen homicides and had more still pending his attention. Like any prosecutor, Monty quickly learned to develop a routine, getting into a rhythm. Doing this is wise. If you don't, the job simply gobbles you up. Supervising Deputy DA Montgomery developed his own personal cadence, a long time ago. The object of this particular prosecutorial exercise is learning how to properly multi-task. In lay terms, this is known as walking and chewing gum at the same time. Multi-tasking means shifting lots of gears; handling uphills, downhills, curves, and so on. And, doing so all at the same time.

A trial prosecutor must combine research and courtroom preparation with telephone time and court appearances. Sandwiched in between are search warrants, filing request reviews and, at times, seemingly endless meetings. Depending on the office, and the type of cases a prosecutor handles, this may also require interaction with media. It matters not where a prosecutor is or their title. The drill is the same. A public prosecutor meets with colleagues, management, law clerks and defense attorneys. Last, but certainly not least, are daily meetings with cops. Any person who has not attended such a meeting naively views them as an opportunity to goof off. Not true.

Even routine court appearances shouldn't be written off as dead time. Only a rookie will go to court and not take other work with them, if they can. You sit in court, waiting for your cases to be called. If you don't bring other work, wasted time will just slip away. This is time you don't recapture. And, somewhere around the edges of all this, a diligent prosecutor nonetheless tries to find quality time for family, rest, and relaxation. Any veteran DA cannot stress enough the importance of doing this.

Those who find such time also find the energy needed to maintain a healthy family life. But, those who fail in this quest frequently find their crumbling marriages replaced by a succession of one night stands, TV dinners, and cheap booze. Such scenarios almost certainly are accompanied by loneliness and varying degrees of despair. Monty knew friends who had already been down that particular side road twice. He prayed he wouldn't repeat any of their earlier mistakes. Although not all that common, suicides are an occasional reminder of the importance of staying on top of this sort of distraction. Staying mentally in the driver's seat is the key.

Chapter 38

Reggie Baron and Jake Crenshaw were secluded in a hush-hush conference with Baron's corporate lawyer, W. Charles Owens, Esquire, at his own law office. And, they quickly learned he was not the least bit happy. It appeared to be far more than just a bad mood. Reggie hoped he didn't talk like this in court. The survival of the dealership might well depend on the success of the strategy they were now attempting to implement. All three of them knew this. A red-faced Owens spoke first.

"Gentlemen, this is one sorry-assed, fucked up situation."

"How's that, Chip?"

"Dammit, how many times have I've told you, Crenshaw? My name's Charlie, not Chip. Makes me sound like some goddamned East Coast preppy or something. Ain't even my name. Why in hell's name do you do that?"

"Whatcha mean, *Charlie*?" he asked, placing sarcastic emphasis on Owens' nickname.

Owens proceeded to read both Crenshaw and Baron the proverbial riot act. He explained, in painstaking detail, how Crenshaw's decision to assign multiple repo men created liability and why it threatened to destroy Baron's many years of hard work. At first, the Chairman took great umbrage. His attorney was blunt and used an assortment of colorfully descriptive words not quite tame enough to comfortably fit into most polite dinner conversations.

However, Baron was successful because he was objective. And, as he listened, it became clear to Reggie that Owens was absolutely right. Charlie informed them of civil and maybe even criminal consequences concerning the wrongful death of TD O'Mara.

The longtime car dealer knew Charlie was a former prosecutor, so he knew his lawyer wasn't just blowing smoke. Reginald Baron was a thoughtful man. Reggie was also sorting out what he was hearing. And, it was making him practically feel queasy. He contemplated Owens' input. After doing so, he realized the pleonasm was directed more at the situation than at anyone in particular. And, he understood, even if this bombast was directed at anyone, it was not aimed at him. Crenshaw was suspect #1.

"You mentioned something about crimes?" Baron asked.

"Yeah, Reggie. I did. For example, try involuntary manslaughter and conspiracy to commit that particular felony."

Baron's face blanched.

"Manslaughter? Conspiracy? You make it sound like we're criminals or somethin'."

"Well, do y'all even know what a criminal is?"

"I dunno. A robber? A burglar? A car thief?"

"How about anybody I used to prosecute because they were accused of committin' crimes? Any crimes. Any idea how many idiots I prosecuted for killin' other folks with their cars? That's what's called vehicular manslaughter. Here, only difference is, you used somebody else's vehicle to kill a man. Technically, that would never happen. But, sometimes it doesn't take much to rile up a jury. All for a lousy nickel dick repo."

"How in hell did we commit a vehicle manslaughter?"

"Vehicular."

"Whatever. So, how'd we do it? We wasn't even driving the damn thing."

"Didn't say you committed vehicular manslaughter. Wanna know what the evidence shows me...*so far*?"

"Isn't that why we hired you?"

The lawyer just sat and stared. For a moment or two, he said nothing. The room got so quiet you could almost hear each of them breathing. Owens scratched his head. He rubbed his temples. He deliberately cleared his throat before continuing.

"Let's analyze this from both a civil and criminal point of view. Okay?"

Baron nodded.

"Sure. Okay."

"Criminal law has a much higher burden of proof than civil. Reasonable doubt, instead of just a mere preponderance of the evidence, or clear and convincing proof. In criminal, all twelve jurors must unanimously agree. Otherwise, there's no verdict."

Baron appeared to be pondering what Owens was saying. Crenshaw appeared bored. Neither man spoke.

"If that happens, and, by that, I mean not reaching a verdict, it's called a *mistrial*. But, in civil, only nine out of twelve must agree with one another. That's called a *majority decision*. A *verdict. For us? A big-assed loss!*"

Chapter 39

Owens continued his heated tutorial by explaining liability. He described what the law refers to as the *but for* test. As he was attempting to elucidate, Jake inexplicably pulled a small flask from his coat and took a swig, then offered it to each of them. Both declined. But, Baron quickly grabbed it. In doing so, he had fire in his eyes. Although he wasn't particularly short in stature, Reggie reminded Owens of a tough old bantam rooster. And, one with a comb-over. He was also one of the last American cowboys.

"A-a-a-ah," the manager declared. "I needed that. Wanna snort?" Jake asked Owens, gesturing toward his flask, now firmly in Baron's hands.

"No thanks. Clouds my judgment."

Owens paused.

"Clouds yours too, I suspect."

"What's that s'posed to mean?"

"It means…let me ask you a question."

"Yeah?"

"You drinkin' when you hired all these repo men for the same job?"

"No," he lied, failing to further admit the abuse of any Peruvian marching powder.

While Crenshaw enjoyed his daily limit of adult beverages, he needed to keep the spark lit, by snorting lines of at least a half gram of cocaine he was able to nicely spread throughout his work days.

He believed this combination provided him a nice balance, with the booze tempering the rough edges caused by the overuse of such a stimulant. Conversely, the cocaine hydrochloride appeared to neutralize the depressant effects of too much alcohol. What Jake didn't catch was how much all this boozing and doping was now costing him. Were it not for such a business enterprise to easily hide big chunks of cash that he could dip into for his own personal use, without even Reggie catching on that he was doing this, his intoxicant overuse would have long ago been financially out of control.

What he didn't realize was how experienced observers were not fooled. Instead, what they saw was a jumpy drunk, due to his ever-growing addiction. The only people fooled were Crenshaw and people like Baron who didn't drink and had never used drugs.

"I'll bet," Owens challenged.

Now, it was the owner's turn. "You damn well better not be, Jake. You better not be boozin' it up on the job."

He gave Owens a knowing look. He walked over to the sink and emptied the flask. Dropping it on the floor, he smashed it with the heel of his right boot. He then threw the now-bent metal container in the trash. Had he thought to empty Jake's pockets, he'd have found even more to pour down the drain. He actually toyed with firing Crenshaw. Turning toward his manager, he continued his angry invective.

"Let me repeat myself, Jake. You'd better not be boozin' it up on the gul-dang job! I've slowly but surely built this place, from a single used car lot, with three broken-down, tired, old cars for sale, to what I have to show the world today."

Crenshaw began visibly squirming in his seat.

"And, if you think, for a blind second, I'm gonna lose every new and used car lot in my business because you are makin' piss poor decisions, and makin' 'em 'cuz you're drunk, then you are seriously deludin' yourself, boy. And, since I don't want no crazy people workin' for me, you know what that means. This is your one and only chance. I'll send you to the unemployment line faster than American voters fired Jimmy Carter. Just like him, you get one chance."

Jake audibly gulped.

"If I go down in flames, you will personally be ashes, long before that happens. I damn well guarantee it!"

"Reggie, please."

Crenshaw was sweating.

"I would never let you down. You know that. The only reason I took that little belt a bit ago," he fibbed, "is 'cuz I'm nursing a cold. Feed a cold. Starve a fever. I know y'all have heard of that one. And, I knew we wouldn't be dealing with any customers today. Not here at *his* office. I'm not drunk. My breath smells like it from the one tiny nip I just took."

As he said this, he pointed toward Owens with his thumb. I suspect even Stevie Wonder could see they didn't like one another. The lawyer frowned.

"Yeah, it's called *starve* a fever. Not *drown* the damned thing. Jesus, you are such a dolt, Crenshaw!"

The owner held up his right hand, calling for calm. "Boys, let's not bicker. We're here to solve problems, not make new ones."

"Here's the bottom line," said Owens. "If it was me, and a homicide filin' request was sent over from the cops, the kind which I've seen plenty of, I'd personally look for every possible defendant, before I made a filing decision."

"Why?"

"Because I wouldn't want some damned defense attorney tellin' the jury we rushed to judgment. In this here case, possible defendants would be the shooter and anyone else who had a role in the victim's death. Erring on the side of caution, as my old boss says to do, I might even apply the '*but for*' test."

"Huh?"

"The *but for* test."

Charlie made quotations marks with his fingers, as he spoke those two words.

"Here's how that works. But for the actions of certain folks connected to Deals on Wheels, would the victim still be alive? If the answer's *yes*, then another defendant is added. Keep something in mind, though."

"What's that?"

"I never functioned like other prosecutors."

"Hmmm?"

"Too modest?" asked Crenshaw.

Owens ignored him, and continued with his example.

"We all had the same burden of proof to deal with, but…"

"Yeah?"

"This is gonna sound braggadocios."

"So?" said Baron. "You're a good trial attorney, with one powerful ego. Just say it."

"You're right. And, besides, my law school dean once told me *false modesty is hypocrisy*."

He laughed. Neither of the other two men did.

"Okay, the burden of proof I was supposed to meet in every case…"

"Reasonable doubts?" ventured Crenshaw.

"*Reasonable* doubt. *Doubt*. Reasonable *doubt*," he repeated. "Anyhow, I just never found it to be that big of a mountain to climb, unlike some of my colleagues at the DA's office, with one singular exception."

"Yeah? Who?"

"Yeah. Only sumbitch who seemed to agree with me on most of my filing decisions. Decisions to go to trial? Approval of search warrants? Decisions to send cases on to the grand jury? Or, back to the requesting agency for more investigation, rather than taking the easy way out and just summarily rejecting them? The whole enchilada."

"Who's that?"

"I just told you. My old boss at the office. Joshua Travers."

"Who?" asked Crenshaw.

"Joshua Edward Travers, aka *Truth*."

"Truth is," the manager snuffled, "I've never heard of him."

"I remember you talking about him before," said Baron.

"Ever been to California?"

"Why in God's name would I want to go to the People's Republic of Californication?" asked Crenshaw.

Both car men laughed.

"The land of fruits and nuts," the owner remarked.

Both car men started giggling like a couple of school girls.

"San Francisco. Political correctness. Women's lib."

"You can keep the whole damned place," the manager agreed. "I'm a Texan, through and through," he added.

"Tell y'all what, boys," warned Owens. "You can laugh all you want about the left coast. But, if you ever saw Trav in action, you'd never forget him. In fact, be glad he's over in California and not here. You wouldn't want him representin' the other side."

"Why? Is he what you'd call one of them sleazebag attorneys?"

"No, absolutely not. But, let me put it this way. Here's how one of the cops who worked with him once described him. But, before I do that, understand somethin'."

"Huh?"

"Cops are never very generous with their praise...when it comes to anybody. Maybe even more so, when it comes to prosecutors; some of whom they just despise."

"Okay. Have to admit. Hearin' that does surprise me."

"Anyhow, the cop I'm referrin' to said this in a newspaper interview. Here, let me find it," he said as he dug through his wallet. "Here it is. I carry it with me. *Quote: I have always found Mr. Travers without peer when prosecuting criminal suspects. He possesses the unique combination of having the tenacity of an ill-behaved pit bulldog, blended into the expertise of a Supreme Court justice. Unquote.* That, gentlemen, is Solita County DA Joshua Edward Travers."

"That's a strange combination. Liar and a dog."

Owens rolled his eyes, but laughed.

"Sure is, Reg," he said. "But, then again, that's vintage Travers."

"Huh?"

"Trust me on this. You have to meet this guy and watch him in court to fully appreciate what I'm talking about. What that cop was tryin' to say is Trav knows his shit. But, he's kind of like an old street fighter. Let me tell you a story."

Chapter 40

Charlie and I discharged from the military within a few months of each other. But soon, we traveled in separate directions. I was hired by the District Attorney's office, following my two years of private practice hell. Owens, on the other hand, knocked around for a while, traveling, chasing women, just generally decompressing from military life. I heard he even let his hair grow and raised a full beard, but never saw him looking like that.

Thereafter, he was going to hang his own shingle. But, I convinced him life as a DA was great. Like Bennie, he also chose to join me at the DA's office, prior to opening his Austin law office near his alma mater, the University of Texas. It was like the Three Musketeers were riding together all over again. I suspect Owens viewed me like an old mother hen. I continuously encouraged him to become a prosecutor. And, I mean continuously. Actually, I nagged him and I'm not ashamed to admit that. You can never have too many great trial lawyers in the same law firm.

Eventually, Owens succumbed. He gave in. Charlie later told me he wasn't sure if he did this because he really wanted to be a civilian prosecutor. Or, did he do so because he couldn't find any other way to shut me up? In due course, it didn't matter how it happened. The important thing was he did it, joined SCDA, and was a damned good prosecutor. I just wish he'd have stayed in Solita.

Charlie Owens became a Deputy DA, by returning to the southern California high desert near where we were Marines together. But, in due course, we both realized he was far more of a Texan than a Golden Stater. So, back to Texas he went. The Lone Star State was home to Charlie. He was born in this little hole in the wall off U.S. routes 70 and 84 called Muleshoe. Even today, it is barely a wide spot in the road with a population of less than 5,000 residents. And, after a few years as a California prosecutor, upon returning to his native Texas, he entered private practice. But, Charlie knew he needed a much wider population base than his birthplace in Bailey County, so he chose Austin as his new home. Good choice.

He later told me how much he enjoyed prosecution. I knew he would. That was why I wouldn't leave him alone until he agreed to join. By the time he was on our team, I was already part of management. And, I became Owens' direct supervisor. Charlie shared a story with me that actually made me blush. One day, he was telling a friend who had never worked in the legal system about that part of his life. Typical Owens, he tried to paint as clear a picture of it as he could. Somehow, the conversation turned to me. Apparently, he tried to describe what we did for a living. Actually, truth be told, it wasn't Charlie who told me this, but his friend. His identity isn't important right now, so he'll remain anonymous.

I believe the general public needs to know what public servants, especially cops and prosecutors, do for a living. Back then, I regularly reminded subordinates, colleagues, and bosses alike, this was not information constituents would gather on their own.

"Our job," I told them, "is to protect the lives and property of strangers. We have an obligation to inform the citizenry just how hard we work to protect them from the criminal element. Our budgets depend on such edification. And, the media delivers our message for free."

Owens wasn't sure if this was instinctive on my part or if I was already in some sort of a campaign mode. I'm not going to reveal my hand. Either way, it really didn't matter to Charlie. He described me as a natural teacher. Huh? What do I teach?

"Travers," he noted, "almost never walks away from another human being without giving them some sort of lesson."

Informants are great, but this was sure news to me. Even though Charlie moved back to Texas, he and I remain close. For a while, we talked at least once a week. He told me he met Reggie Baron, when he was at his Austin dealership looking at Corvettes.

Charlie was actually browsing, comparing prices and inventory at different dealerships, including Baron's. Little did he initially realize the immense size of Baron's entire organization. Both men are rabid Dallas Cowboys fans. Not me. I like the Packers and the Chargers. But, somehow, they began discussing an upcoming game with the Redskins. Before Charlie left, they traded business cards. One day, Baron invited him to lunch, so he could pick Charlie's brain on a specific legal issue. The rest is history. Baron was losing faith in his existing law firm. He was looking for fresh blood. Reggie didn't remember exactly what Owens said, but something clicked. And soon, Charlie was both Baron's corporate and personal attorney.

In Houston to discuss the Deals on Wheels issue, Charlie and his client were having a business dinner in a local restaurant just outside Houston that specializes in chicken-fried steak. It was in a little place called Tomball. The trip between Austin and Houston was three hours by car. It was quicker by plane. But, Charlie was tired of the hassle of post-9/11 flying. Plus, he enjoyed the independence of the open road. So, he drove and loved every minute of it. Since he was spending the night and Baron was paying for everything, including his travel and lodging expenses, Charlie decided to try some of that local chicken-fried steak he's heard so much about.

I, too, hear Goodson's Café is great, if you don't mind being a heart attack-in-training. Apparently, they don't spend a lot of time concerning themselves with issues like fat and high cholesterol counts. Neither do their many loyal customers. I'm told they keep coming back for more. Baron promised Charlie the chicken gravy-smothered steak was the best he would ever eat. Charlie swears it is. Don't get me wrong. I'm no fanatic. But, even if I didn't believe in following a healthy diet, Molly would only give me so much wiggle room there. Somehow, between mouthfuls and all the attendant chomping and slurping, the conversation turned to me. Owens was describing his life, following his tour of duty in the Marine Corps.

"Whaddya mean?" Baron asked.

"Well, I told you I'd finish the story. Here's how it started. I'd just mustered out of the Corps. I needed to catch my breath. Needed some time to pick lint out of my navel. I wasn't ready to get back into any routines that cramped my style. I didn't even want to shave, at first."

Baron smiled. Owen continued.

"But, damned Travers, my former staff JAG, kept badgering me to join the DA's office. Nag…nag…nag…nag…nag. So, to shut the sonofabitch up, I finally applied. They hired me. Turned out to be a great gig, actually. Had a ball. Travers was not only a great civilian boss, too, but, he was also an outstanding teacher. And, you should've seen him around the cops."

"How so?"

"I swear to God. He was like a friggin' Svengali or something."

"How do you mean?"

"Cops absolutely worshipped the ground the guy walks on. Did then. Still do."

"Why do they put this guy Travers up on some sort of pedestal?"

"That's simple. He's…he's…he's…" Owens dug for the right words.

"He's what?"

"Hold on. I'm tryin' to tell you. He's one of them. He ain't a cop. But, thinks like one. Acts like one. His wife, Molly, calls him *the protector of the protectors*."

"How do you mean?"

"Well, for one thing, he's probably seen the world…what's that expression of his? Trav seems to have an expression for every occasion. He says he's probably seen the world through the windshields of more police cars than some cops have."

"I don't follow. What does that mean?"

"It means he goes on lots and lots of ride-alongs. Patrol. Dope. Helicopters. Fixed-wing aircraft. SWAT vans. Search warrants. High risk entries with SWAT. Low crawlin' with railroad cops in the dead of winter lookin' for train burglars with night vision shit. All that sort of razzmatazz."

"Aside from ridin' around in police cars, you still haven't told me why they like him so much."

"Whatever problem they have, they know they can go to him. And, he's not just helpful. He knows his shit. He writes an advice column. Teaches. Writes books for them. That sort of stuff. Advice on arrests, searches, probable cause, reasonable suspicion. And, they know they can reach him. At the office. At home. Daytime. Nighttime. Drunk. Sober. Sound asleep. Healthy. Sick as a dog. Doesn't matter. He'd take a bullet for any of them and, I suspect, they'd do the same for him. Protective as hell of each of them."

"So, how'd he get the nickname Truth?"

"I told you. That's a topic for another time and place," Owens said as he glanced at his watch.

Chapter 41

Apparently, it just hit Charlie one day that we hadn't spoken to one another in a while. Something jogged his memory. I mentioned earlier that we've been close friends since our days in the Corps. In fact, that's where we met. Bennie Armendariz, Charlie and I met in the Corps and became fast friends. We've been a band of brothers ever since. Like me, Ben's a career prosecutor. Charlie wasn't. According to him, he returned to Texas so he could "make some real money."

Yeah, he's right. A lawyer can make big bucks as a civil litigator. But, I believe I've previously shared that civil cases bore me. Just bore me to tears. I'd be a liar if I said I don't like money. But, if I don't enjoy what I'm doing, what's the point? Same with Bennie. Not Charlie. He was after the money.

But, as things tend to happen when geography gets in the way, we drifted apart. If my memory serves me right, we both had a number of back-to-back trials that consumed us and things sort of slid downhill from there. There was no bad blood between us or anything even close to that. It really wasn't because of any conscious decision making by either of us. This de facto drift just happened. One week we were speaking to each other regularly. The next week we weren't staying in touch that much. Then, we weren't speaking to one another at all.

When people don't communicate with each other regularly, they tend to focus more on what's important in their immediate lives. *Out of sight, out of mind* seems a truism. And, it happens whether or not a person intends it to rear its ugly head. Sadly, neither of us was immune to this particular phenomenon. Sometimes, I'm the one closing the divide by contacting Charlie. Sometimes, he calls me. Anyhow, as I recall it, this time it was Owens who picked up the phone and dialed. He spoke as soon as he heard the voice at the other end. When we talked, he told me he was so disturbed it had been so long since he'd called me that he actually couldn't remember the number he previously had committed to memory. I toyed with teasing him about losing his memory, but for some reason, I didn't. Why, you ask? I don't recall now. Doesn't matter.

"Operator," he said, "I need the number for the Solita County District Attorney's office. I'm sorry. What state? California."

He wrote the number down. Then, he read it back to the operator, just to be sure he heard it correctly. As he dialed the number, he said he couldn't believe how long it had been since he had spoken to me. He was still miffed he had forgotten.

Momentarily, he heard a familiar female voice.

"District Attorney."

Owens smiled. "Travers have a sex change operation? Oh, it's you, Susie Q. So, when'd you get promoted to DA?"

"Oh, I don't believe it. Charlie…Charlie Owens. You old rascal. What are you up to?" she asked.

"Susie, you…sweet…young…thang. How the hell are ya?"

Owens paused between words, emphasizing each of them equally. He could tell from the tone of her voice she was glad to hear him.

"Overworked and underpaid, as usual?"

"So, what are you up to? How is the great state of Texas?"

"I'm doing just fine. Holding vertically. No comment horizontally. I'm in civil practice now. Representing business people. Mostly car dealers. You know Texas. Everything's bigger here. By the way, you sound lovelier than ever."

"Oh, Charlie. Even your line of BS is bigger in Texas," she said, poking good-natured fun at him.

"I thought you said you were in civil practice. How does that jibe with representing car dealers? Shouldn't that be criminal defense?" she teased.

Owens laughed.

"So, do you want to talk to who I think you do?"

"If you're thinking of Travers, then, yes. I do. I see great minds still think alike. Is he in?"

"I'm not sure. Let me ring you through to his office, okay?"

"Works for me, gorgeous."

Even though Susie had heard Owens' flirtatious comments too many times to count, she still blushed, reacting to him just as she always did. She transferred the call to Travers' extension. Susie was easily old enough to be Charlie's mother.

"Travers!" barked the voice.

Charlie told me I always sounded as if every phone call was interrupting me from doing something else…something far more important. Such a perception was generally correct for a couple of reasons. First of all, as a rule of thumb, I absolutely despise phone calls. I hate the damned things. This is multitudinously true. My biggest gripe? I never know who's calling, thanks to our archaic county phone system. It's my own fault. Being a cheapskate, I hate to spend tax dollars on new stuff we don't absolutely need. Maybe someday. Just not this week.

A simple solution would be for me to just ignore the phone's incessant ringing, or ask Susie to take messages. Maybe I should man up and hire a secretary to take my calls. But, any call might also be some cop trying to reach me, stuck in the middle of an incident somewhere, needing immediate guidance on a work-related issue. So, I can't duck them. Those latter calls I gladly field, no matter how busy I am. Always. A cop's job is to protect the public. No matter how much I hate phones, my job is to back their play so they can do just that. That's why I put up with these damnable things. The world needs a more convenient communication device.

It's actually easier when I'm awakened by one of those calls, at home, in the middle of the night. The likelihood of anyone, other than some panicky cop, trying to reach me at one of those odd hours is somewhere between slim and none. I always take such calls. Public safety demands it. If I don't back a cop's play, how can I possibly expect a judge to do the same thing for me or for a cop to help a citizen? Like I learned in the Corps, doo-doo always rolls down hill and gathers speed. If I won't back a cop, in need, how can I ask a judge to back me? My hypocrisy doesn't run real deep. Grumbling as I answer my phone, I hear a familiar voice.

"Ouch, Truth. Damn, did somebody put sand in your Vaseline jar, or what?"

"Charlie Owens. You old sonofabitch. How in hell are you, my brother from another mother?"

"Trav, I am doing great. Just great. So, why are you soundin' a bit grumpy?"

"Oh, you know me, Charlie. I hate these blasted telephones. Frigging antiquated technology. You never know who is calling."

I waited for Owens' reaction, looked up, and saw a couple of dope cops walking into my office. They needed to talk with me. I could tell they were in a hurry. Probably another search warrant. The one by the door was talking into his hand held radio.

"Hey Charlie. I'm going to have to get back to you. A couple of the boys are waiting to bust my balls about something. Probably didn't give some asshole enough community service or something."

I winked and grinned. One of the cops saluted me with an upraised middle finger on his right hand. So nice to feel needed, not to mention feared. Did I remember to include *and respected*? We each said goodbye and hung up.

Chapter 42

The frazzled Harris County prosecutor poured through the meager pages of an incident report. Montgomery debated whether to send it back to the originating detective. It needed additional work. This was clear to him. He was not happy. And, he believed it should be obvious to anyone else with a brain. Could he really send this on to the grand jury, *as is*? If he did, he knew they would no bill the defendant, rather than return an indictment. Would that dispense justice? But, the overworked prosecutor knew he didn't need any more cases to juggle, in order to feel like he was earning his paycheck. Even if the investigation was incomplete, he rationalized it wouldn't change one iota of Texas law that guided his decisions.

Monty enforced laws. He didn't write them. And, he sure as heck knew he didn't write 9.41. Whether he believed or didn't believe a deadbeat had a statutory right to back shoot a repo man was irrelevant. If the repossessor was on the guy's property trying to lawfully take the legal owner's truck at 3:30 in the morning, 9.41 might cover the shooter, *but only if the registered owner believed, in good faith, that his property was being threatened*. Operative words: *his property*. Being legally ancient didn't make 9.41 invalid. That was a question of fact. Sure, his job was to work with the facts. But, he wasn't getting paid to gather them. That was a cop's job. He wasn't a darned babysitter. If they couldn't do their job, that wasn't his problem. He just didn't have the time.

Montgomery knew his job was to enforce the laws, not write them. But, he believed the legislative intent behind 9.41 was quite clear. Texas residents had an absolute right to protect their property. Especially in the nighttime. This meant they could use deadly force. They could lawfully shoot intruders. Under the right circumstances, this included any intruder. Did his state's lawmakers intend to protect repo folks from trigger-happy Texans? If so, then, he reasoned, they should simply say so by amending the law. Doing this would be an easy process.

Of the three branches of state government, the Legislature was by far the most powerful one in Texas. They even had more juice than the Governor. Separate but equal? Not necessarily. And, this appeared to represent the will of Texans near and far. The Legislature merely had to amend the statute and ask the Governor to sign it into law. He didn't see this as anything close to rocket science, by any stretch of the imagination. But, this was the call of legislators, not one for a law enforcer like himself.

They could do it one of two ways. Lawmakers could simply remove the offending language. Or, they could add language specifically exempting repossessors from being used anymore, as convenient targets for armed deadbeats. If the Legislature chose to amend, Monty couldn't think of a compelling reason why the Governor wouldn't sign it. But, whether this did or didn't happen, the issue was of little consequence to him, other than the impact it might have on his workload. What if an amendment meant more work for him? This was simple. If so, he was against it. If it decreased his workload, he would be the first one standing in line waiting to applaud. But, Montgomery also knew he was sympathetic to anyone involved in a shooting.

Riley previously had to shoot someone himself. This made it easier for him to figuratively step into the shoes of any shooter. Granted, in his own case, he was never listed as a defendant, or even as a suspect. Quite the contrary. Far from it, in fact. Every police report and court document Monty read listed him as the victim. Frankly, that made perfect sense, both legally and factually. First of all, he had possessed a concealed carry permit for more than ten years. Many of the local cops knew this.

In the darkened parking lot behind his favorite bar and grill, an armed man tried to carjack him. Monty's permit gave him the unmitigated right to carry a concealed and loaded firearm anywhere in his state.

An attempted armed robbery justified him using his weapon to shoot the addicted felon. He chuckled to himself, in retrospect, as he recalled the shocked look on the crook's face when he was shot.

The thief didn't expect someone looking like Riley and driving into the parking lot in a Mazda Miata convertible to be armed. Ironically, his poor marksmanship saved the robber's worthless life.

He meant to squeeze the trigger of his Smith and Wesson 9 mm, when he aimed, just as he had been trained to do. Monty carefully aimed for the imaginary 10-ring in the middle of the guy's chest. Instead, he jerked his shot, hitting his assailant's forearm. I carry a real gun; a .40 caliber Glock Model 22.

Had the discharged round struck Montgomery's intended target it no doubt would have pierced either a lung or perhaps even the man's aorta or heart. However, the wound merely caused the criminal to drop his stolen hunting knife.

The frightened prosecutor detained him at gunpoint, until the police arrived. Upon their arrival, they arrested and booked this felon, but only after he was treated and cleared for booking at the local hospital's emergency room. None of the officers, on-scene, remarked about Monty's involuntary, trauma-induced release of urine. They saw, but said nothing.

The incident was widely reported, briefly making the white collar shooter something of a local celebrity, and a favorite among many of the local cops, if for no other reason than the mere fact he had shot a bad guy. Many peace officers, despite strapping on a loaded firearm every working day, have never been in a shooting, either on or off duty, with the exception of aiming at artificial targets during required qualifications. Because he was an active duty prosecutor at the time of this caper, his own office declared a conflict of interest. This meant the Texas Attorney General reviewed the shooting and later prosecuted the robber. But, the end result was inevitable.

A robbery victim in Texas, just like anyplace else in America, is legally entitled to utilize self-defense. Use of deadly force by a practicing felon justifies use of deadly return force by their victim. A concealed weapon permit has nothing to do with whether self-defense had been employed. In short, self-defense is self-defense. Such an assailant establishes the rules of engagement for a possible encounter, even if it means they unwittingly bring a humble knife to a gunfight. The victim is allowed to play the hand they are dealt, and to respond accordingly. Monty did just that. Riley decided to speak with the detective before he arrived at a filing decision on the Walker case. He knew the investigation was incomplete and part of his duties required him to tie up such loose ends. Picking up his phone, he dialed and waited for it to ring. Larson was not one of his fans.

"Homicide, Larson," the voice said.

"Carl. It's Montgomery. Calling you about the Walker homicide."

"Yeah? What about it?"

"Well, for starters, I've reviewed every page of every report you've given me. Unless there's more to read to establish the elements, I got bad news. You ain't done with your work yet, bud."

"Which reports have you got? Just list the report writers and the dates of the reports."

Montgomery told him.

"Nope," said the occasionally cantankerous investigator. "You've got everything I've got."

"Any plans to re-interview the shooter?"

"Why?"

"I'm not sure I buy his story about him believing a thief was trying to steal his truck. I think it has holes in it. And, if that's true, he wasn't justified in shooting the guy."

"Whaddya mean?"

"I'm starting to get some rumbles O'Mara wasn't the only repo man trying to get Walker's truck that night. Until we resolve that, frankly, I'm not comfortable with this case. Not by a country mile. And, 'til I am, I ain't movin' forward."

"So, you're tellin' me y'all want me to talk to the car dealer?"

"Bingo."

Larson hung up the phone without saying anything. He was muttering to himself. The senior investigator picked up the phone and called Bob Archer.

Chapter 43

Detective Archer telephoned Deals on Wheels. He scheduled a time and date so he could interview Crenshaw. Among other issues, he wanted to find out exactly how many repo men Jake the Snake had hired to repossess Walker's truck. Once he had that information in hand, he could talk to each of them and reconstruct what happened.

He was not happy that Larson had dumped this part of the investigation on his desk. Archer called it *"another of Larson's little lap-dumpers."* Larson did this frequently to junior detectives. Looming retirement had made him even lazier and more surly than usual. Good riddance to him. The veteran detective had plenty of work to keep himself busy. But, Larson was the case agent with more seniority than Archer. One of his perks, if he chose to do so, was assigning work to his junior partner. And, in this man's opinion, lately, he was doing that far too frequently.

Archer was bound and determined to complete this investigation as expeditiously as he knew how. But, on the bright side, he didn't have to talk to that irritating widow anymore. Fortunately, Larson was dealing with her. She was too pushy for his tastes. He had never enjoyed having to be confrontational, even during suspect interviews. Compound her attitude with the grieving she was doing over her husband's death, and she was more than a handful. He was sure she could drive him to drink. And, he was already doing enough of that on his own.

He wasn't rich enough to even consider affording a liver transplant. Not on his modest cop's salary. He could barely afford his two ex-wives as it was. And, he sure didn't have the connections to get a new liver for free. He wasn't Mickey Mantle. So, his only option was to cut his drinking down. Way down. Amazingly, Archer was skinny as a rail, which shouldn't be the case for a man who drank as much alcohol as he did. In fact, he was so thin, his nickname among his fellow coppers? *The Blade*. He picked that moniker up during his academy and it continued to follow him.

Chapter 44

Once Archer interviewed Crenshaw, he could begin reviewing documents. Hopefully, they would tell him how many repossessors Jake had hired for this debacle he now angrily described as *a major cluster-fuck-and-a-half.*

"Man," he noted. "I had no idea the economy was in such bad shape."

"What's that s'posed to mean?" Crenshaw asked.

"Well, let's look at the facts here, son."

He pointed at some paperwork.

"This guy ain't even quite a week overdue on that missed payment…"

Crenshaw interrupted him. "So?"

"…and," he continued, "you guys, like a bunch of goddamned vultures, send 3 or 4 repo guys after his truck. That many guys? They could have physically carried it away, with their bare hands."

"Pardon me?"

He didn't care if he offended the man. Besides, he didn't like car salesmen. Archer was less than 2 years away from retirement himself. He had also picked up another nickname recently. In fact, so had Larson. It had to do with the fact that both men were short-timers, with retirement looming for each of them. The acronym *ROD*, among cops, stands for *retired on duty.* So, one of their brethren had labeled them the RODETTES, a bit of a play on words using the singing group from the '60's, *Ronnie and The Ronettes.* Ronnie was actually Veronica "Ronnie" Bennett. Neither Larson nor Archer could sing. Fortunately, neither of them tried, even though they were now regularly urged to *sing me a song,* by their fellow detectives.

What if this guy lodged a complaint, Archer wondered? What was the worst the brass could do? Maybe give him some time off without pay? Big deal. He knew he had more than enough paid time on the books so he wouldn't really lose any money. Tally up sick leave, vacation, comp time and holiday leave and he wouldn't even miss a paycheck. Archer wasn't concerned about being disciplined for being rude. But, for some reason, he was absolutely phobic about leaving loose ends hanging around for other cops to tie up. *You catch 'em, you clean 'em.*

While this seemed inconsistent with this near retirement attitude, Archer was what he was. Maybe it was his professional paranoia from being a cop for so many years. Discipline he could handle. Having to deal with the idiots trying to dole it out was a *whole 'nuther story,* as he described it. He understood why Vietnam War *fraggings* occurred. Archer liked to close cases as quickly as possible and just keep moving on.

He didn't need some bleeding heart DA ragging on him because he didn't interview everybody under the sun. He bitterly complained that the prosecutor had his head up his ass on this issue. He didn't like Montgomery, either, calling him *Miss pissy-pants*. The veteran investigator was also ticked that Larson had dumped this work into his lap. He thought Carlton should have had the courage to simply tell the DA he was wrong and be done with it. But, did Larson do that? No. Not Mr. Buckpasser.

Did Montgomery sign their paychecks? Once again, no. A thought suddenly hit Archer. The longer this investigation took, the more likely he'd hear more of the whining and interrogating from that pushy O'Mara broad, as he described her. Was it his fault her husband went out and got himself killed? Did *he* tell Tommy Deen O'Mara to go into the repo business in the first place? Any damned fool should realize skulking around in the dark is also a good way to get shot.

After all, this is Texas. Property rights still mean something. Texas was a place where men could still act like men. This wasn't one of those pinko, commie places like California, the land of fruits and nuts with that cesspool, San Francisco, and all its disgusting bathhouses, and their tatted up gang-bangers. Ironically, it was Montgomery who was in a shooting. Not self-described *real man*, Bob Archer, who had never fired his duty weapon, other than at the range when he had to qualify twice a year.

"Officer, are you even listening?"

"Huh?" he replied. "Sorry. Please repeat that."

Crenshaw was visibly annoyed.

"You haven't responded to my complaint yet. I said I won't be insulted by some damn cop."

"Excuse me?"

Archer was now listening, and listening carefully.

"Namely *you*!"

"Damn cop? Damn cop? Who exactly are you callin' a *damn cop*? You'd better hold on, right there, pardner. Right here and now. This, sir, is a criminal investigation."

Archer's police training kicked in. Mental muscle memory. Old. Rusty. But, still there.

"We can do this the hard way or the easy way. Your call."

"Meaning?"

"Meaning you've already told me you have the records I need to look at. In fact, that looks like them sitting right there on your desk."

"And?"

"And, nothin'. Listen up, my friend. You even consider interfering with my formal investigation? That's called *obstruction of justice*. I'll hook you up so fast your beady little eyeballs will spin. And, I'll do it right here, right now *and* take you to jail. I'm sure there are plenty of folks in there t'would just love to have you as a real close friend. Comprende?"

Crenshaw's face turned red.

"And, while I'm taking you to jail, I'll have another officer come sit here and freeze this place so I can get a search warrant for these same records. That will shut this place completely down, until I say we are done. That could take a day…two days…three days…maybe longer. There's never any telling where a search warrant is gonna lead."

"Huh?"

"It may uncover information that requires the issuance of another warrant. Heck fire, son, I could be here for a month or more," he said as an evil-sounding chuckle escaped his lips. Archer hoped the man wouldn't' really call his bluff.

Crenshaw blanched. First, his face turned red, then white. He feared jail. But, he was far more terrified of Baron's wrath than jail. And, tying up his dealership for a month with a search warrant was a quick way to feel that special fury.

"So, you tell me, and tell me now…right here…right now…how it's gonna be. Okay?"

Jake swallowed. His mouth had suddenly turned dry and the color had drained almost completely out of his face. He feared he was going to wet himself. He'd never been to jail. The stories he'd heard about what went on in such places terrified him.

"H-h-here," he stammered, as he handed over the documents. "Let me know what else you need, officer."

"Well, that's more like it! I didn't think you had it in you." the cynical detective noted, as he slightly puffed out his chest.

A careful review of these documents would give him the information he needed. Later, after he did his repo men interviews, he could complete his report and forward a copy of it to Larson and the DA. Archer hoped this would end his role in this mess once and for all. He was already getting a real headache. And, it wasn't from any hangover. He knew the difference between a hangover headache and one caused by whining widows and lazy partners. This one wasn't from alcohol.

Afterward, he forwarded his supplemental reports and let out a big sigh of relief. From here on out, Larson could deal with all this. He'd try to wrap up his own remaining cases so he could finally get the hell out of Dodge. He had close to a year of accumulated time off on the books. He might even be able to leave before Larson.

Chapter 45

The supplemental reports had *finally* arrived. Montgomery began reading the documents he had just received this morning. And, he was ticked off. Had Larson done his job properly, he would already have sorted through this case and made a decision. If that had happened, he wouldn't be sitting here worried about getting more calls from the O'Mara widow. Most law-abiding people seemed afraid of the DA's office.

Not her. Ms. O'Mara reminded him of a bull in a china shop. She was relentless.

According to the new reports, each of the repo men appeared to play a role in what ultimately happened. He was now almost certain of that. Perhaps, they didn't enter into this equation from a pure criminal law standpoint. But, in order to connect the dots, he needed to know how the pieces fit together.

Hopefully, these reports would adequately enlighten him. Above and beyond anything this case's underlying facts could explain, it irritated this prosecutor, almost beyond comprehension, that he was still dealing with two cops who were wasting his time. Why did he have to show them how to do their damned jobs? Was he paid to be their mentor? What was wrong with these guys? Were they terminally stupid or just plain lazy? He suspected their training was not the underlying culprit. And, it seemed they were always away attending yet another class somewhere. Boondoggles, no doubt.

What was their problem? Cop-after-cop-after-cop he'd dealt with over the years just went out and did their jobs. How difficult was that? He didn't need anyone telling him how to do his own job. So, why couldn't these two just go do theirs? The ones who did their work, unaided by him, did so without whining or complaining. They arrested and booked bad guys. They submitted cases for prosecution. They gathered evidence and testified at trial. They all performed their required duties.

Some of them even knew when to inform a suspect of their Miranda rights, or, when not to do so. Monty disgustedly shook his head. He could feel his blood pressure rising. Good God, this stuff wasn't brain surgery. It required common sense and involved the utilization of a rather elementary process. Cops were supposed to gather facts, apply the right laws and thereafter, make decisions.

If they did that, they would know if a crime had occurred. And, if so, what was it? Was it a misdemeanor? A felony? Or, was it a wobbler that could go either way? If so, should the bad guy be booked? As a misdemeanant? As a felon? Simple and easy stuff. Period. End of conversation.

To Riley Montgomery, this just wasn't that complicated. If the suspect could be booked as a felon, this should be done every single time. Let the DA's office decide what level of criminal prosecution the bad guy should face. What if the cop arrested and booked somebody for a misdemeanor, when he should have done so as a felony? This meant the DA might have to up the ante. Generally, this resulted in criticism from the defense attorney. They might even claim the prosecutor was being vindictive. Or, just as bad, they might claim the DA was *over-filing* the case. However, if the arresting officer did their job and chose the more serious of the two routes, this was generally eliminated as a defense. He wasn't sure who annoyed him more, cops or defense attorneys.

"Heck," he chafed, "even a law student should know basic stuff like this. And, as he knew from having been a law student himself, most of them couldn't find their own fannies with a road map and a tour guide. Hmmm. I couldn't disagree with that. Visions of *Twenty Questions*? *Motor Mouth*?

In any event, Montgomery knew the process of choosing whether to prosecute a defendant, on a misdemeanor or a felony, boiled down to answers to two basic and fundamental questions. First of all, was the victim hurt? If so, how badly? And, what sort of life did the suspect lead, prior to this latest arrest? In other words, are we talking about a career criminal or a person who simply went out and got temporarily stupid?

The first question was easily answered. Did the victim receive any injuries, as a result of the defendant's conduct? If so, were any photos taken? And, was the victim treated by any type of medical professional? If treatment occurred, where did it take place? A medical office? A hospital? If so, was the victim transported by ambulance? If they were, did paramedics treat them at the scene of the crime?

Any of these steps should result in the generation of supporting paperwork. A review of these reports by any experienced prosecutor would determine the first half of the misdemeanor-felony question. Calling any of the report writers to the witness stand would prove those facts to the jury. The other half of this jigsaw picture puzzle, i.e., how the defendant previously lived their life was actually an even easier process than determining the extent of injuries.

Like any other prosecutor, Riley did that by reading rap sheets. He'd done this scores and scores of times. Looking for such answers, Montgomery would review the listed convictions. By doing this, he'd learn the names of arresting agencies, as well as the dates and courts where any conviction had occurred. To any veteran cop or prosecutor, a rap sheet is nothing more than a criminal's resume, written by the government.

A prosecutor should even inspect arrests not leading to convictions. An arrest without a conviction can happen for a number of reasons. First of all, was the case filed? Or, was it later dismissed? Maybe it was reduced to a lesser offense. Some of these have nothing to do with the quality of the case. Sometimes, it boils down to a lazy or an overworked prosecutor. Maybe both. This means an undeserving criminal gets the benefit of the doubt.

Even before he reads anything, the sheer number of pages a rap sheet contains tells a veteran prosecutor if the defendant is an active criminal or just someone who had experienced a momentary lapse of judgment. This can be true, irrespective of whether the crime is a misdemeanor or a felony. The first thing Monty should always review is found in the initial couple of pages. At least, it's the first area I peruse. This tells us if the defendant has any aliases.

As a rule of thumb, a person doesn't need multiple identities, unless they are trying to hide evidence of their own misconduct. A life prisoner once admitted to me at a parole eligibility hearing, if a name is used too much criminally, it gets too hot to use. Montgomery knew legitimate reasons for multiple names do not, in and of themselves, excuse criminal misbehavior. For example, we know why some people go into witness protection.

Riley's professor confided to him one day after his Criminal Law class.

"Son, understand something," he whispered almost conspiratorially. "It takes shit to catch shit."

This particular professor, a former Assistant U.S. Attorney in the district where Houston is located, formerly specialized in prosecuting organized crime cases for the federal government. Riley knew, if anyone could detect fecal matter, it was this guy.

Chapter 46

Dawn O'Mara was worried. Away from the mystifying legal intrigue, and any behind the scenes causation, she was totally in the dark. She'd learned nothing new about TD's murder prosecution, since she last spoke with the prosecutor and the detective. The prosecutor sure seemed more than a bit rigid to her. But, at least, she mused, he took the time to answer most of her questions. However, despite his promise to do so, he had not phoned her. They hadn't spoken in more than a month.

She knew she should phone someone. But who? The DA? The cop? Having heard nothing in so long, she kept trying to convince herself no news was good news. The prospect of bad news was really more than she cared to consider for the moment. The still grieving widow had unhealed emotional wounds. They were deep and excruciatingly painful. After all, she had lost the love of her life. Her rock, Tommy Deen, was gone. And, she didn't know how much more she could carry right now.

Dawn saw that worthless policeman as another story altogether. What was his name? Larkins? Lawrence? Larson? She'd written it down somewhere. Finding the slip of paper, she phoned him and left at least six messages with the female who kept answering his phone. Despite solemn assurances to the contrary, he had not returned her calls. In fact, the bum had not returned a single, solitary one of them. And, on the one occasion when he answered his phone, he might as well have not even been present. All he said was he sent his reports to the DA. Other than that, nothing. Then, he hung up. Dawn didn't realize Larson had not told her the entire truth. It wasn't that he flagrantly lied. His sin was one of omission. The delay was due to his own laziness.

Had he been honest, he would have admitted the DA made him reopen his case to finish work he should have already done without any prosecutorial prompting. He did so only because Montgomery ordered him to do it. He knew this but said nothing. He should have admitted he failed to interview critically important witnesses. And, this would have required him to tell Dawn he would not have spoken to them, until he was forced to do so by the prosecutor. Instead, he wove a tangled web.

If Larson was straightforward with Dawn, he would have admitted his own screw-up had delayed the prosecutor's review by more than a full month. But, because he was nearing retirement, like Archer, the S.S. Carlton wanted no unnecessary waves. In fact, he didn't even want a single ripple on the surface. The fewer people he communicated with, the smoother the sailing would be for him. Fishing magazines posed no stress. He liked them. They were his only friends. And, he already knew where he was moving.

He'd had it with Houston's legendary humidity. He was sick of the smog. He was tired of the traffic. To hell with the ever-growing crowds too. He was also fed up with the criminals, including many whom he'd personally arrested.

Last but not least, he was out of patience with whining crime victims.

"Let someone else deal with all this nonsense. Let them soothe the feelings of whining widows. I'm done. Give me the clear blue skies and white billowy clouds I've seen in the pictures of Montana. Big Sky Country, here I come. Ready or not."

As he daydreamed about escaping from the great state of Texas, the annoying sound of his ringing phone interrupted his mental merriment.

"What now?" he thought, as he picked it up, wishing it were a bottle. A full bottle.

"Homicide, Larson," he moaned. He thought about a medicinal helping of his adult beverage of choice. Jack Daniels and Coke would work just fine. And, he could just as easily skip the damned child's carbonated additive. Too much unneeded sugar. And, too soft. He made a mental note to verify that Kalispell had enough liquor stores. Surprisingly, for such a dedicated drinker, Larson was not terribly overweight. He had a typical paunch that men his age seemed to acquire. But, that was it.

Only those close to him knew how much alcohol he consumed daily. He claimed the red blotches were roseola. But, those in the know realized his cuprous facial coloring indicated chronic alcohol abuse. And, besides, he wasn't fooling anyone. Most adults know what childhood diseases are.

"Detective? Detective Larson?" asked the seemingly annoyed female voice. He immediately recognized the voice. It was Dawn O'Mara. *Please God, not her again*, he thought. He reminded himself to begin keeping a bottle of Jack in his desk again.

"*This*," she emphasized, "is Dawn O'Mara. And, frankly sir, I'm tired of bein' treated like a danged mushroom."

"Yes ma'am?"

"Mr. Carlton," she snapped.

He didn't correct her.

"My husband is already in the ground over in a Tomball cemetery. He and I should be on a fishin' boat somewhere. Maybe even on a cruise ship. Instead, he was murdered by a piece of white trash. But, you don't even care!"

"Now ma'am, I…"

"And, don't y'all be interruptin' me. I will let you know when it's your turn."

Larson said nothing. He opened the current edition of *Field and Stream*.

To himself, he thought "I knew I should have interviewed the repo guys and given her to Archer. Am I getting stupid or what?"

He chided his math skills. Instead, he slowly exhaled and began massaging his temples with his fingertips. He instinctively knew this woman had to vent. That was her. But, it wasn't like he cared about her, or her feelings, as much as one tiny little whit. He quietly set the phone down on his desk and picked up his magazine. She was speaking loudly enough that he could still hear her. He'd pick it up when he needed to speak.

There was only so much of him he could give away before nothing remained. The cop shop was starting to make him bonkers. After this many seemingly endless homicide investigations, he fully grasped how he would cease to exist, had he not erected this sort of barrier to protect his psyche.

He pretended to listen, while she droned on, interjecting an occasional "uh huh" or "yes ma'am," and then would set the phone down again.

But, his mind had already drifted far from any borders contiguous with Texas. Mentally, he was on a small boat, with an outboard motor, somewhere on Echo Lake in Flathead County. He hadn't been there yet, but liked the travel brochures.

The sky looked like…well…*sky*. It was blue. Pure white cumulus clouds floated overhead. They reminded him of big white puffy pieces of cotton. Or marshmallows. As a kid, he loved lying on his lawn in the summer time and trying to guess what animals they resembled.

His Igloo ice chest was mentally full of cold beer packed in ice. It was just big enough. Two six packs. A pint of Jack. Some sandwiches. Just in case he felt like supplementing his liquid diet with so-called comfort food. Frankly, he wouldn't care if he even saw a damned fish, let alone catching any. He couldn't tell a trout from a pike or a perch anyhow. He was mentally sipping from his second can of breakfast beer. Nothing else mattered. Occasionally, he would chase a bubbly brew with a slug of sour mash bourbon. The cool damp air soothed his soul. Larson couldn't even remember how long he had yearned for this most welcome of respites.

The mist was rising off the surface of the water. It reminded him just how good post-retirement life was going to be. Other than birds, he heard nothing else. Off in the distance, he saw a bird cruising over the lake in his general direction. Was it a loon? Maybe he should buy a reference book.

As he tried to identify it, its unusual cry startled him. He heard its call again.

"Detective Larson!" she yelled. "Are you even listening to me?"

Chapter 47

Montgomery asked his secretary to schedule the O'Mara homicide for an appearance before the grand jury. He would present the case to them, but decided he would do so without any charges attached. He really didn't see any other way of offering this matter to them. Montgomery believed he was simply doing his job. He wasn't the one who wrote the blasted laws. He enforced them. As he reminded himself earlier, he was in the Texas executive branch of county government. Same branch as the Governor. Just at a different level was all.

Admittedly, Penal Code §9.41 basically gave every Texas idler a virtual license to use nighttime repo men for target practice, but he hadn't written it. Nor, did he conduct the investigation. All he did was play the piano. And, he'd even made that lazy Larson actually do his job. Critics buzz off. Monty knew he was doing his job. Or, at least he thought so.

"Stinking rod," he scoffed, thinking about him. "R-O-D," he spelled it out. "Retired-on-duty."

Monty was incensed. He actually had to order the man to interview key witnesses who just might shed light on the issue of motive. Why did he even have to waste time doing this? He even threatened to formally complain to Larson's boss. It was true he had not gone with him to do any of the follow-up interviews. But, then again, he reckoned, that wasn't his job either. He didn't get paid enough to babysit cops who would rather read fishing magazines than earn their paychecks. He'd heard the rumors.

As Riley Montgomery sat at his desk organizing the O'Mara file, his thoughts drifted back to how §9.41 became law. His curiosity propelled him to do some historical research so he could better grasp the legislative intent behind it. Important research, Montgomery thought. And, of course, he did it on DA time. He was sure it was work-related, so why should he care if people said he wasn't being paid to do that?

The year was 1888. Times were different back then. Far different, in fact. Montgomery tried to visualize the political environment during those past days in Texas. For starters, raising cattle was a far more prominent part of his state's landscape. Back then, cities like Houston and Dallas didn't have all the fancy glass-faced skyscrapers now standing tall and proud like mirrored edifices. These monuments appeared to exist for the sole purpose of reflecting sunlight somewhere else. Maybe down into the shadows they created by simply being there?

Even though thieves of all sorts remain part of contemporary Texas, they don't occupy the historical role frontier cattle rustlers did. However, one factor was an integral part of the modern Texas political mosaic. It occupied a place of equal importance back then as well. Riley wondered if that was where it got its start.

Today, they are called *special interest groups*. Back then, some simply called them good old boys. As goes Texas, so goes America, they said. Modernly, vehicle and farm implement manufacturers and the vast oil industry expect lawmakers to pay attention to them. In fact, they demand it from both them and the Governor. Generally, they get what they want. Campaign contributions continue to be pretty decent investments. Good bang for the buck.

The same was true of Old West cattle barons. Like any other businessman, their bottom line was their profit margin. Subtracting total expenses from income equaled gross profit. Political donations were merely the cost of doing business. In that regard, Texans were no different than folks in any other state. Then, as now, the object of the exercise was eliminating unneeded expenditures. One such cost back then was herd loss caused by rustlers, aka cattle thieves. Like vampires, these parasites usually practiced their illicit craft under the cover of darkness.

Cattle rustlers to cattlemen were like athlete's foot or jock rash to athletes. Rustlers could claim no socially redeeming value in the eyes of anyone who wasn't interested in buying their stolen cattle. Since most of their stealing took place at night, cattlemen decided they needed to band together to eliminate this problem. Sure, they could create goon squads, stocked with enough sharpshooters to eradicate needless vermin. But, before they could do this, they also needed the imprimatur of their state's lawmakers. Thus, the birth of Texas Penal Code §9.41. Unfortunately, lawmakers who created it also grossly failed to differentiate yesterday's cattle thieves from contemporary lawful repossessors who would subsequently go to work with no connection to the cattle industry or its leeches.

Lawrence Sullivan Ross was born in Bentonsport, Iowa on September 27, 1838. I understand his family migrated to Milam County, Texas the next year. After more or less becoming integrated Texans, this growing clan next moved to Austin. The Sullivan clan ultimately settled in Waco. Unlike other youth, anxious to live elsewhere, "Sul" even attended his home town's Baylor University before transferring to and graduating from Wesleyan University in Florence, Alabama for reasons irrelevant here. Post college, his life took on challenges most other folks barely dream about. After graduation, Ross commanded a company of Texas Rangers. They rescued 34 year old Cynthia

Ann Parker, kidnapped earlier by a Comanche raiding party when she was only nine years old.

Incongruously, following her rescue, she spent much of the rest of her adult life trying to escape back to her original captors. Ross and her other rescuers could only shake their heads in puzzled wonderment. I find no room to disagree.

Later, during the Civil war, Ross fought in 135 separate battles, rising to the rank of Brigadier General. Following the war, he returned to Waco and farmed until he was elected Sheriff of McLennan County in 1873. Continuing his public service, Sul Ross was a delegate to the 1875 Constitutional Convention. From 1881-82, he was a Texas state senator. And, in 1886, he became Governor of Texas, serving for two full four-year terms. One of his appointed tasks was signing 9.41 into law. The Texas Legislature, just like Governor Ross, heard the loud voices of cattle-raising constituents. Lawmakers expeditiously drafted this legislative remedy and sent it on to old Sul for his signature.

No eyebrows rose when the longtime lawman executed the document that spelled it out in sufficient detail. The declared legislative intent was to protect public safety and private property. Privately however, the unspoken legislative intent was to keep moneyed Texas cattlemen happy. Actually, that was secondary. It was really to keep them content and well fed. If the cattlemen were happy and prosperous, they contributed appropriately to reelection campaigns. After all, investments were investments. Cowboys knew a sure thing when they saw it. If you don't have common sense, you aren't a real cowboy.

If the owners of these massive cattle herds perceived rustlers to pose a big enough economic threat to their own wallets, such a concern would be reflected in decreased donations to political war chests. This would specifically impact members of the Texas Legislature and the Governor. So, Texas Penal Code §9.41 was born, with no discernible dissent. Soon thereafter, open season was declared on rustlers, particularly the ones who practiced their pilfering after the sun went down.

As time marched on, the contents of everybody's billfolds continued to grow. Concomitantly, the Texas beef industry diversified its investment portfolios into other engines of economic growth. These included real estate, petroleum and several other commodities of the futures market, stocks, bonds and convertible debentures, among many other items of commerce. Cattle, once their life blood, were now just another aspect of the overall market place.

But, despite many decades zooming past since its birth, §9.41 remains alive and well as the 20th century was greeted by the 21st. Montgomery pondered if it just might be time for change. Or, would §9.41 also greet the 22nd? Only time would answer that.

Chapter 48

Reginald Baron was hopping mad. In fact, he was well-nigh boiling.

"Who in *the* hell does Charles Owens, Esquire think he is already?" he asked himself. He was so angry he didn't want people to even hear him. So, he merely mouthed the words, as he sat with his back to the door of his own office.

"Wants me to pay some damned widow $50,000? Why? Because her husband went out and got killed, skulking around after dark stirrin' up some damned drunk? I don't care if he was doing a repo for one of my car lots or not."

Turning back around, he slammed his fist on his desk, before continuing his outburst. He decided he didn't care who heard him and began yelling. After all, he was the boss and could hire or fire anyone else there.

"Blood-sucking lawyers! They're all alike! Don't matter who they represent; me or some other sap! In my opinion, all any of 'em care about is spendin' other people's money, just as fast as they can get their grubby mitts on it. Write a check…problem solved. Next? How much you need? Lousy leeches, anyhow," he carped to himself. "I need to call Owens and see if he's lost his cotton-pickin' mind."

The more he thought about it, the madder he got. Immediately after reading the investigator's report, he carefully digested his own attorney's opinion. Basically, Owens had determined Baron's dealership committed a number of what he called *torts*. *Civil wrongs*, he called them. According to Charlie, they were almost like crimes, except you didn't go to jail. Instead, you pulled out your wallet. Owens wasn't the one writing any checks. Lawyer's opinion or not, Reggie was sure he'd done no wrong. Owens explained the commission of these torts by a dealership employee made the dealership liable for any damages they caused. What legal sins had they committed, Baron wondered?

First of all, according to Charlie Hustle, they were *negligent*. How did this happen? Per Charlie, "if they did it, you did it," was how he explained things. He said *they* did this by hiring multiple repossessors to seize the same vehicle. Owens legal brief, for his and Reggie's eyes only, described it as *"…a veritable recipe for disaster…"* Reggie saw quotes from both Charlie and some high-fallutin' judges, babbling about something he didn't understand. And, he didn't care to, either.

In doing this, his lawyer claimed the dealership unnecessarily stirred up the debtor because each repo man unsuccessfully tried to acquire Walker's truck. According to Owens, this was akin to turning a spotlight on O'Mara. Like lighting dynamite with a long fuse, he said. TD was generally able to rely on the cover of darkness, combined with his own stealth and experience, to do a quick and safe repossession. Not this time. Per Owens, he backed into an unexpected ambush, resulting in Walker fatally shooting him.

A mortally-wounded O'Mara drove away, only to crash into a ditch where he slowly but surely bled to death. Ironically, according to Reggie's legal beagle, he died right next to Department of Public Safety. Owens called this a *wrongful death*. Actually, all those appellate cases provided this particular labeling. Charlie just shared it with Reggie, saying *but for* their negligence, Tommy Deen O'Mara wouldn't have died *how* he died, wouldn't have died *when* he died and wouldn't have died *where* he died. In other words, he wouldn't have died. But, this wasn't all. Charlie had also said they committed *fraud*. This was what really stuck in Reggie's craw. He could barely contain his ire. His own corporate attorney informing him of this? And, in writing? Baron could feel bile in the back of his own throat.

Owens said RB's own used car manager had lied to O'Mara when he said the repossession, at the center of what was becoming one huge shit storm, was "…a fresh repo…a real clean deal…" All this because they had hired several repo men, instead of just O'Mara? He disagreed. What was the big deal? Baron didn't understand. Dealerships did this all the time, he was told. Especially with a deadbeat like this...this Walker clown.

As he continued reading, he suddenly laughed.

"Who in hell has credit so bad they have to make weekly cash payments anyhow?" Baron asked himself. "Weekly payments? And, in cash? Every Friday by close of business at 5 p.m.? Like clockwork? That meant this bottom feeder had to bring in his cash…his weekly payment…like a good boy or lose his truck."

Johnny had to take his payments to the cashier's window at the very lot where he bought his old beater. And, he had to be there, with cash in hand, no later than the close of the business office, each and every week, until the final payment was made. Like clockwork? Each and every Friday? It was like a public whipping. A full cash payment? Without exception? No excuses? How humiliating!

"Hell," he chuckled. "Nobody likes to be treated like a dog, even an upright dog."

But, then, Reggie frowned, just as quickly as he had smiled. He knew he wasn't like Walker. He was respected because, among other reasons, he had self-respect. And, instead of Johnny finally bringing in that next payment, there was a self-created problem. Walker had breached his contract. He had missed an agreed upon payment. But, that was all it really took. His one misstep. His one sin translated into the loss of his truck. A related irritant? Reggie didn't know why he didn't pay. And, frankly, he just didn't care.

Walker didn't even have the manners to tell the dealership he wasn't going to be able to pay this time. A bum like this should at least have to squirm some. He should have to experience a little discomfort. Repossession would deal with that just fine. But, no. Cowards normally didn't have the guts to confront such situations. And, obviously, neither did this fool. Johnny Walker didn't even have enough class to do this. He was an insult to a good whiskey with the same name, even if Baron was a teetotaler.

Therefore, why in hell should the dealership consider extending him any courtesy, for crying out loud? Once again, Reggie was full of answers. Among other reasons, the answer to that poser was quite simple. They weren't mind readers. They couldn't be expected to know something they didn't know. And, that didn't add up to a tinker's damn anyhow. Walker had missed a payment. If A, then B. Reggie sold cars. He wasn't a social worker. Until the final payment was made, Deals on Wheels still owned the truck. To Reggie, this was open and shut. The confidential brief brought him no comfort. Discomfort instead. Charlie included information he normally wouldn't include in any brief he filed with the court. And, that's because it was a confidential attorney-client brief.

Just as an in-court brief was intended to educate and inform opposing counsel and the court, this one was meant to inform Reggie of his rather dire predicament. And, even though no one else would ever read his moving papers, this one was about to explode right in their faces, if they chose to set it for trial.

This formal-looking document, on numbered pleading paper, even included an actuarial table showing how long a male O'Mara's age should expect to live, under normal circumstances. This also translated into how much he might earn. The paltry sum Owens was suggesting Reggie pay was a mere fraction of what TD might still earn. It discussed legal concepts, such as pain and suffering, and loss of consortium. The latter was referred to in at least one of the cases Charlie cited. Baron noted some bleeding heart judge called it *loss of connubial bliss*.

Reggie couldn't even pronounce the multi-syllabic word. When they spoke, Owens translated it for him. As Baron continued to read, he learned pain and suffering was nothing more than a nice sounding way of describing what it costs to die, especially if you were the car dealer who had to pick up the tab.

Loss of consortium? Reggie read it one more time. All this legal mumbo-jumbo was like a foreign language. Con-nu-bi-al bliss? He sounded the word out. Why in hell didn't they just use real words like everybody else? Words common every day folks understood? Working folks like him.

But, the bottom line here? No matter how he boiled all this down, all Reggie knew was he was looking more and more like old Santa Claus. He was the poor sap who was expected to pull out his checkbook and pick up the tab. And, he didn't even have a beard. Not even a moustache. Charlie's conclusion, after sifting through all this legalese? Baron was supposed to write the widow a check for $50,000. Owens believed the case just might go away, and do so quickly, if Reggie did this.

This sure as hell wasn't what he wanted to do. In fact, he decided, he was *not* going to do this. Instead, he knew what he had to do. He picked up his phone and dialed Owens. He was about to give his lawyer a lesson in cowboy economics and good old-fashioned common sense.

Chapter 49

"**H**ey Charlie," the voice said. Owens immediately knew who it was.

"Yeah Reg? Ya read my PI's report *and* my brief?"

"I think I should change my name."

"Why?"

"Aintcha gonna ask 'to what'? No? Okay, just start callin' me Mr. Moneybags then."

Owens ignored him and just sighed. He was bored with stupidity, was tired and hadn't really eaten anything all day. All he'd had time for was a cup of coffee and half a bagel around 6 a.m. Charlie looked at his watch. It was nearly 7 p.m.

"Listen, Reggie. I'm tired. I'm hungry. And, I'm grumpy. You had dinner?"

"Not yet."

"You like Chinese? You know the one, over on Shepherd?"

"Which one? I don't like that vegetarian crap. I need me some meat."

Charlie agreed they could go to the other one.

"Good. Let's meet there, say, in fifteen minutes?"

"Okay, but give me a half hour."

"Bring the report *and* my brief with you. That way, if you have any questions, you can refer to it while I explain legal issues."

"I made notes."

"Good for you. Bring them too. But, don't forget to bring my P & A's."

"Your what?"

"P & A's…points and authorities…all the appellate shit that's in there. You know? My brief? The one with all the vertical numbers at the left margin, from top to bottom, beginning with 1 at the top and ending with…?"

He heard the click before he could finish his sentence. Baron had already hung up. Owens cussed, then hung up and headed for his car. After a reasonably short drive from his new Houston office, he pulled into the parking lot, parked and walked inside the restaurant. He thought of Baron's chronic tardiness and decided he'd order an appetizer. Even before he entered from the parking lot, he could already smell the delightful aromas wafting through the kitchen's open door at the rear of the building. The hostess greeted him with a smile, just like she always did, at the front door.

"How many tonight, Mr. Owens?"

"Hi Rose. Two. *One adult. One juvenile*," he mumbled under his breath.

"Right this way," she said, as she sashayed toward the booth where he usually sat. He was glad to see it was available. As he waited for his car dealer client to appear, he ordered a carafe of hot sake. And the appetizer. He also ordered a glass of plum wine. Charlie knew his dinner guest had a well-deserved reputation for being late. That's because he usually *was* late. It was almost as if he took pride in personal unpunctuality. So, Owens decided to treat this meeting as if he was solo, until Reggie proved him wrong.

"Damned car dealers," he muttered to himself. "Talk more than goddamned lawyers. Late more often too! I bet if they had to deal with judges, like I do, that shit would change in a hurry."

Looking up from the menu he'd been studying, he was surprised to see Baron actually sauntering toward him. He stopped to glad hand so many people enroute, Charlie wondered if he might be running for public office. As he sat down, the lawyer spoke first.

"Crissakes, Baron. I was afraid I was gonna have to call search-rescue."

The late arrival laughed.

"Sorry," he remarked, still grinning. He seemed to have lost his ire.

As he spoke, Owens could see he was still waving to people scattered throughout the room.

"How 'tis when y'all are as popular as I am."

He laughed some more, then continued.

"But, then again, mebbe you don't. An old sourpuss like you? Damn good thing y'all are such a capable lawyer and all. Otherwise…"

"Otherwise what?" Owens asked, as his eyes narrowed.

"Lemme put it this way. If you was in the car business, you'd be missin' a few meals…quite a few, in fact."

This time Reggie did not laugh.

"Yeah? Well, you're in the *car business*," he said, carefully emphasizing both words. "…And…and…" he repeated, "…you just might be missin' a few future ones yourself."

"Just what in hell is that s'posed to mean?"

Baron's ugly mood returned.

"That's why we're here, remember? By the way, so's you don't think I forgot, your bein' a half hour late ain't a freebee. The meter's still runnin' and the time is bein' billed against my regular twenty hour monthly retainer."

"Why, you cheap sonofa…" Baron began.

"Listen to me. What time were you supposed to be here? You think you're my only client? Be glad I'm here in person this late and that I didn't send an associate to meet with you instead. Try doin' that to a judge. And, you're buying my meal too. And, drinks. Add an appetizer."

"If it wasn't for my damned money and my damned dealerships producin' all the money bein' poured into your one-horse law firm, you wouldn't even have any associates, so don't go gettin' uppity with me! And, to hell with judges. Real men don't wear dresses."

Owens said nothing at first. Then, decided he needed to exercise some good, old-fashioned client control.

"Keep talkin' Meter's still runnin'. I don't mind. Besides, it ain't one. It's several horses now. How do y'all think I'm able to run two offices? And, before you forget, it's my good counsel that allows your business to keep growing. Don't be puttin' the cart before the horse. Ask yourself where your mega-corporation was when we met that day in Dallas."

Charlie glanced at his watch. A very red-faced car dealer took a deep breath and sharply exhaled. In Owens' opinion, his thin face resembled a ripe Roma tomato when he was angry. And, at this point, he didn't care if his noggin flat out exploded. Somehow, the conversation appeared to wind him. Baron normally was a pretty even-tempered individual. But, when he got upset, his face turned bright red, mimicking the top of a thermometer. Baron bore a passing resemblance to a shorter version of Ichabod Crane from *The Legend of Sleepy Hollow*. His forehead and the area above his upper lip now sparkled with beads of sweat that were now succumbing to gravity and running down his face. It wasn't so much the shape of his body, but his head and face.

He ran his fingers through what was left of the hair on his head. Except for the horseshoe-shaped fringe right above his ears, Reggie was smooth as a cue ball on top. He now grew hair on the left side of his head longer so he could comb it over his bald crown. Baron thought it made him appear to have a full head of hair. Others said it looked like a scraggly turban. Owens privately kidded his associates that Reggie's comb-over was so obvious even a mole with a blindfold would be blinded by the glare.

Nonetheless, Baron spent long wasted minutes each morning trying to perfect his hairdo. However, all it did was nearly connect some of the longer left side hairs to those on the right side of his head. But, this only covered part of the top of his head. He didn't realize the peak of his crown was still shiny and pink. If hair was that important to him, Charlie wondered why he didn't invest some of his money in hair transplants. One day, Owens was sharing his view of the car dealer's bare pate with one of his paralegals.

"Jee-zus," he began.

He attempted to control his laughter so he could speak. The subject amused him to the point where he could barely talk. When finally able to regain his composure, his voice was shrill and squeaky-sounding.

"Man, his hair today, if you wanna call it hair, looks like an anorexic spider had crawled up on top of his fucking chrome dome and croaked. Swear ta God, the man would look far better with a toupee. If it were me, I'd just shave my head. And, he dies it, too! I suspect he owns Kiwi shoe polish stock."

Back at the restaurant, however, the car dealer's lawyer almost appeared solicitous, by comparison.

"Baron, you okay? Or, should someone dial 911?" he asked, barely suppressing a laugh. Reggie coughed a couple of times as he attempted to clear his throat, before he was finally able to speak again.

"Funny," he said. "In fact, you're so funny I almost remembered to laugh."

"Look, man, whether you enjoy hearin' what I have to say or not, my job is to protect you *and* your business."

"So why...?" he began.

"Hold on. My job is to prevent you from shooting yourself in the ass."

"But..."

"Hold on...hold on...I ain't done. There's two ways we can do this."

"Yeah?" asked Baron, actually appearing interested in hearing what his lawyer had to say, for a change.

"Yeah. We can be proactive. Or, we can be reactive."

"So, what in Hades do those big words mean?"

Owens explained. And, Baron listened attentively.

Chapter 50

Montgomery began presenting his case to the Harris County grand jury.

"Good morning, ladies and gentlemen."

The eighteen ordinary-looking men and women were gathered together to receive the evidence he would present. They looked like a cross-section from any neighborhood, including yours or mine. Their job was to pay attention, then make a decision.

"As is the case with any other criminal matter, I am privileged to present this evidence to you. I thank you for making your sacrifice to sit as a member of this grand jury. I am bound by the applicable facts and the law, as are you. Personal feelings and emotions can never replace the evidence you receive or the law you must follow."

The roomful of strangers listened with rapt attention. An occasional cough or sneeze could be heard. One or two people would occasionally clear their throats. But, other than these mostly involuntary interruptions, the room was eerily quiet. Even a casual observer could tell those present were listening carefully to what the prosecutor said. Riley was confident they would faithfully follow any directions he gave them. They had no choice. That was their job. They were the grand jury. Making them do it was his. He was the prosecutor. The jurors remained attentive as he methodically presented his case. Unlike unrealistic Hollywood scenes, he anticipated no dramatic Perry Mason-type surprises. Such presentations were normally rather obligatory affairs, much like the occasional coughing he heard. Virtually involuntary.

Grand jurors perform various functions. This includes investigating public entities, such as county agencies. And, they receive and review evidence and law presented them by prosecutors to determine if a criminal indictment is appropriate.

This particular grand jury could do one of two things. They could return an indictment called a *true bill of particulars*, aka a true bill. An indictment commences a criminal prosecution in a courtroom. If so, a petit jury would later hear evidence at any criminal trial thereafter commenced. They could also return a *no bill of particulars*, aka a no bill, terminating the prosecution of a suspected criminal before the matter is ever heard in a court of law as a contested matter. If so, no petit jury would ever be called, selected, or sworn.

Following the unveiling of an indictment, a defendant can generally enter one of four possible pleas: guilty, nolo contendere, also called *no contest*, not guilty, and not guilty by reason of insanity. An indictment means a defendant is expected to enter a plea to a felony charge. With the exception of a not guilty plea, virtually no judge will accept a plea, unless the defendant is represented in court by counsel. Most will insist counsel be present for any and all proceedings. After all, it is a felony.

Even if a judge allows a defendant to plead not guilty, without counsel present, they will advise the defendant of their constitutional rights, including the right to a free lawyer, and will obtain a waiver of those rights, just as they would with their lawyer in court. Trial court judges are painfully aware an appellate court can review anything they do.

If the grand jury returns a no bill, one's defense attorney can be present. But, this is not required. That's because a no bill ends the prosecution of that particular suspect. As a practical matter, however, counsel should be present. Would I be? You bet your ass I would. I believe I've said this before. I err on the side of caution. It's much easier my way. It avoids ambushes, potholes, and pratfalls. The other way encourages them. And, as previously noted, petit juries receive evidence presented during trial. In jury trials, jurors are fact finders, the same way a judge is in a court trial. In a jury trial, a judge's role is to rule on matters of law presented to the court by counsel for either side.

Judges make evidentiary rulings. This means they decide if proffered evidence is admissible. So you don't have to look it up, proffered and offered are synonymous. Don't ask me why, but lawyers like saying proffered. At least, I do. Makes one sound almost erudite, no? Judges rule on motions, i.e., requests for judicial rulings, made by counsel for any party. Additionally, they review agreements of counsel called *stipulations*. If the judge approves them, they are presented to the jury, which can consider them as actual evidence, as if testimony or documents had been presented on that particular point.

Judges also rule on objections made by counsel, on both evidentiary and non-evidentiary issues. Lastly, following the close of evidence by both sides, they instruct juries on what laws must be applied to any evidence received from either counsel.

Irrespective of whether a juror is of the grand or petit variety, they take an oath to be fair and impartial. They cannot participate in any matter, if something exists which would prohibit them from sitting as fair and impartial arbiters. An example of this would be any bias. Bias can be based on a number of factors, whether legal or factual. One such bias is having a preexisting relationship with any of the parties to an action.

Parties in a criminal case can include lawyers, victims, witnesses, Plaintiffs and Defendants. If the nature of the relationship prevents a juror from being fair and impartial, then they must recuse themselves. In other words, they must inform proper authorities they cannot participate and state the reason why.

Chapter 51

One of the grand jurors scheduled to review the killing of Tommy Deen O'Mara by Johnny Walker was biased. This prospective juror had a previous connection with O'Mara. And, it was one that required prompt disclosure. In fact, Billy Ray Fulgerson had more than mere prior experience with TD. He was also one of the grand jurors who heard evidence involving the unfortunate dispute between Tommy and a troublesome neighbor in the not too distant past.

Sadly, this verbal disagreement turned ugly, then physical. Even though Tommy was only trying to protect his own teenage son, it ultimately resulted in criminal charges being filed against each of the two men. That grand jury returned a true bill against TD. In other words, they indicted Tommy. And, they also indicted his neighbor.

Neither party should have been prosecuted, due to 5th Amendment rights. But, both were stubborn men, citizen-arresting each other. When the DA found out about the foolish filing error, he suggested a mutual dismissal. But, neither would agree to that until a court-ordered civil compromise ultimately ended the matter, following the DA's request to reduce each of their charges to misdemeanors was granted by the judge.

Later, TD and Fulgerson traded sharp words. A still heated O'Mara questioned Billy Ray's ancestry. He apparently suggested Billy Ray's mama lived under a porch and bit unsuspecting visitors. Billy Ray didn't forget that encounter. And, he never forgave TD either. In fact, he vowed he never would. But, instead of speaking up and recusing himself, he chose to remain silent. Disappointingly, Fulgerson chose to not absent himself from the instant jury that would decide if the man who killed Tommy Deen should face criminal prosecution. Billy Ray failed to mention this conflict to anyone in a position of authority, violating his oath as a grand juror. In fact, in his role as grand jury foreperson, he became the driving force behind the decision to *not* indict O'Mara's killer. A person selected as a jury foreperson, whether grand or petit, generally can sway other people. That's generally why they're selected.

In grand jury proceedings, defense attorneys are never permitted to be present in the jury room for any reason whatsoever while the grand jury is in session. Therefore, each such event tends to not only be secretive, but very one-sided. In this case, however, the suspect, Johnny Walker, need not spend a penny on legal counsel. Fulgerson was doing it for him and they didn't even know one another.

This grand jury scenario is true, regardless of whether the proceeding is in a U.S. District Court or any county variety of any of our fifty states. In fact, the only lawyer who can be present, *and is present*, is the prosecutor. The advantage this creates speaks for itself. Most jurors expect most prosecutors to do the right thing. Sometimes, they are disappointed. A long standing tongue-in-cheek observation of grand juries helps to explain why prosecutors routinely receive indictments in matters they present to such tribunals. The expression heard, ad nauseum, particularly among defense attorneys?

Grand juries are so prosecution-friendly, they say, *any* prosecutor, irrespective of their level of competence, can indict a ham sandwich. Since ham sandwiches don't commit crimes, this also speaks for itself. Sometimes, defense counsel are correct with their cynical assessments. Therefore, whenever an indictment is *not* returned, there almost always is an explainable reason behind it. The facts of each individual case are usually the reason. Such seemed to be the case with the Walker grand jury. But, such a conclusion assumes the grand jury actually heard all relevant facts.

Chapter 52

After introducing himself to the Walker jurors, Montgomery continued with his preamble. He had done this particular tap dance so many times, it was practically from memory at this point in his long legal career. And, it sounded like it too. Monty was not a stimulating speaker; smart as a whip, hard-working and quite analytical. Just not real comfortable on a stump. One word sums it up: *boring*.

Interesting. He could chew cops up one side and down the other, but was perpetually uncomfortable around any kind of juries. Maybe he should use that old speaker's trick where they visualize the audience all sitting there in their underwear. Monty should pretend all jurors are in police uniforms.

"My job as a member of the executive branch of government is to enforce the law. And, that's true whether I do or don't agree personally with the particular law that determines the outcome of any case."

He paused to measure the jury's reaction, before continuing. One or two heads in the jury box nodded. But, most members simply stared without reacting. This was a pretty typical jury panel. And, Monty was already boring them.

"In their infinite wisdom, our Founding Fathers created three separate but equal branches of government. They did this so each branch could function as a check and balance against the other two. Executive overlooking judicial and legislative. And, those two each oversee the remaining two."

Come on, Monty, I thought. Sell some sizzle with that steak. Someone coughed. Another of the jurors appeared to be in some sort of physical discomfort. She raised her hand. When Montgomery looked her way, he was a bit too slow to acknowledge her.

"Excuse me," she finally said.

"Yes, ma'am?"

"I'm due for back surgery and can only sit for short periods of time. May I stand up and move around? I promise I'll pay very close attention. Same as if I was sittin' down. And, I promise I won't disturb no one."

"Members of this jury, will it bother any of you if Ms. Smythe stands and paces?"

Those who reacted shook their heads from side-to-side, indicating it would not bother them if she did. The prosecutor gauged this as an affirmative response by enough of the panel to qualify. He glanced at each of them, then back at her and smiled.

"Go ahead ma'am. I'm sorry you're in pain. Please do not hesitate to let me know if you need a break. Same with any other jurors. Although I haven't been in there personally," he said, smiling, "I'm told there is a sofa in the women's restroom."

Monty made a funny? Some jurors chuckled. Smythe held her hand up again.

"Ma'am?"

"I'm sorry to have interrupted you, Mr. DA."

"That's quite alright. And, as noted, the break issue is there for every one of you. Not just Ms. Smythe. Additionally, we are all adults, providing it's not done in the middle the testimony of any witness, you are free to address me, without raising your hands first. In other words, all I ask is that you please do not do so in the middle of any of my questions or the answers to them by any witness. Now, having said that, does anyone need a break now? Or, are we ready to continue?"

All indicated they were ready to proceed. Riley glanced at his notes to be sure he hadn't lost his place, as if it would have really made a difference.

"Okay, then let's proceed. As I was saying, there are three branches. Executive. Judicial. Legislative. Executive executes or enforces the law. At the state level, this would include the Governor and staff. Also the Attorney General. Enforcement? That's my job here at county executive level. Legislative branch legislates. That is, they write the laws. Judicial? They judge. That is, among other things, they interpret the laws."

He paused. Then, he frowned. *If I ever talk like that, jurors, please object.*

"Please understand something. My job is not to second guess what the legislators are doing. Judges? They interpret the laws. That's what a judge gets paid to do. And, my job certainly isn't to determine whether a law is constitutional. Again, that's the judiciary's job. Whether I agree or disagree with any given law, just as I alluded to moments ago, my job is to enforce it. And, I'm duty-bound to do so with as much impartiality and fairness as I can find, irrespective of whether I am a huge fan or an unrelenting critic of that same law. Either way, my job is to enforce it. You probably wonder where I am going with this don't you?"

So, why no charges? Pardon my cynicism, Mr. DA. But, you are talking out of both sides of your mouth. As Molly would say, no tiene verguenza. In English, that translates to he has no shame. Negotiable morals, perhaps?

Monty seemed a devoted fan of repetition. As he asked this, he grinned, making eyeball contact with each juror separately. Monty was clearly in control, just as any self-respecting prosecutor is supposed to be, despite his seemingly compromising discomposure. *We don't like disorder. And, we sure* as hell don't like chaos. We need to be in charge. But, this doesn't mean he had to bore his listeners to tears.

"Well," he continued, "I'll tell all y'all where. There's a law on the books, Texas Penal Code section §9.41, et seq. Please understand something. We lawyers use lots of Latin words. We do that so folks think we're smarter than we really are."

Another funny. He grinned again, for the umpteenth time of the morning. Several of the jurors exploded into gales of laughter. I was surprised. Monty actually made another joke? Good for him. When everyone quieted down, he began speaking again.

"*Et seq* is also Latin. It translates into *'and the following'* in English. It generally means there are going to be one or more other code sections that follow the first one. Some folks say this law is controversial. Why is that?" he asked rhetorically, visually polling each of them again, eyeball-to-eyeball, to again weigh any reactions.

"Personally, I don't know if it is and I am not suggesting you believe that to be true, based on what I just told you. Frankly, even if it were, I wouldn't care one way or the other. Here's the crux of the matter."

Montgomery went on to describe in great detail what sort of force this statute permitted and why he believed it permitted any Texan to use deadly force in the nighttime to protect their property. He also explained to them why he believed this further dictated he should bring this case before them without any requested charges against the shooter. In short, he was asking them to not return an indictment.

If they believed Walker was telling the truth when he said he thought he was shooting at a car thief on his property at 3:30 a.m., they should no bill the matter. Conversely, if they didn't believe him, they could return an indictment. Much of this process boiled down to whether Johnny Walker was credible. That is the critical importance of competent and determined criminal investigations. They tend to expose the truth, rather than covering it up or simply burying it, alongside the decedent.

Chapter 53

It was noon recess for the grand jury. Billy Ray Fulgerson was having lunch with one of his longtime cronies; a man he'd known far longer than many of us have been alive. Their friendship began back in their childhoods.

"Can you believe this nonsense?" he asked. His statement sounded more like an answer than a question.

"What nonsense?"

"This damned waste of my time and our tax dollars. Troublin' honest, hard-workin' men like me to *de*-cide if the guy who killed Tommy O'Mara should be prosecuted or not. Damnation. That ain't even worth flippin' a coin over."

His lunch companion appeared surprised, but remained silent, other than to remind Billy Ray he had just returned from a cruise with his wife, and, that they had been well outside any current local informational loops. So, Fulgerson quickly briefed him on the Walker grand jury inquiry. His friend appeared concerned, but said nothing other than to reiterate his absence and the reason for it.

"I've just returned from that cruise. Remember? The Alaska cruise? Me and the missus? Just got back day 'fore yesterday, in fact."

Billy Ray said nothing.

"Sounds to me like your mind's already made up," his friend said.

"Don't like that sumbitch O'Mara. Didn't like 'im when he was alive and, since he's been dead, he hasn't done a damned thing to change my mind."

In fact, Billy Ray hadn't liked TD since O'Mara repossessed his son's car. TD's retort about his mother took things too far for him to ever forgive or forget. Thin skinned folks tend to do that. That influenced his decision-making at TD's prior grand jury matter. He chose to not share any of this with his friend, including his failure to recuse himself in either matter.

"Then," he recalled, "after he gets hisself arrested for fussin' 'n feudin' with his own kid, he wastes my time havin' to sit as a member of *that* grand jury. The things he said to me afterwards. The names he called me. Should've got his assed kicked over that. Well," he crowed, "paybacks are a real bitch. Now, ain't they?"

It didn't matter to Fulgerson that he didn't even have his facts straight. His friend said nothing, at first. But, he wasn't able to remain silent for long.

"It doesn't sound as if you want to see the guy who killed him pay for what he did. You don't think he should hang for that?"

"Onliest thing outta be hangin' on that old boy are his balls."

Fulgerson laughed. His friend simply stared at the top of their table.

"And, 'sides," he continued, "man's got a right to protect his property. 'Specially in the nighttime. I mean, after all, this is Texas. We Texans ain't a bunch a namby-pamby wimps. Not like Californ-eye-ay or those guldanged frogs on the other side of the pond."

"You are right about that," his friend agreed. Disagreements aside, both men were Texans before they were anything else.

Prosecutor Montgomery had directed the jurors to return to the hearing room no later than 1:30 p.m. Fulgerson called out to the waitress for service.

"Hey, Helen Ruth!" he yelled. "We ever gonna get some food here? I got important business today."

"Keep your shirt on, Billy Ray. Like what kind of important?" she asked suspiciously, as she meandered over to their booth. Both ordered lunch.

"Grand jury business," he boasted.

"*Grand* jury, you say? *Taint nothin' grand about any jury you sit on. You crotchety old goat,*" she mumbled under her breath, walking away.

For reasons uncertain, Fulgerson had a knack for hitching his wagon to the right team of horses. Like most other town folks, Helen Ruth had developed an intense dislike of him. He and Bert had been friends since 7th grade. Bert was more forgiving.

"So, Billy Ray," his friend asked, "what makes you think you can be fair enough on this thing?"

"What makes you think I ain't gonna be, Bertie?" he said, as he winked. "Fair doesn't automatically mean returning a true bill, now, *does* it?" A malevolent-looking grin slowly spread across his entire face.

The waitress shook her head, over by the kitchen. She had known Billy Ray Fulgerson for nearly fifty years. She didn't like him any better today than when he tried to be her boyfriend way back in high school. Bert was a nice guy. Why he was still Fulgerson's friend flabbergasted her. His immense wealth meant nothing to her. Even back then, she treated all jerks accordingly. Helen Ruth arrived at the swinging double doors separating the kitchen from the dining room, pushed them open and walked into the kitchen. Once inside, she peered through one of the porthole windows and looked at the two men once again. Her arms, folded underneath her bosom, delivered as loud an unspoken message as the scowl on her face. She placed their orders on the wheel.

Shaking her head, she decided to slip out back and take a cigarette break. Billy Ray had watched her walk toward the kitchen with interest, as he spoke to his friend. She didn't care if his order got cold.

"So, this O'Mara guy's really stuck in your craw, is he?"

"It's more than that. In fact, it's more than just O'Mara. In general terms, I really don't like repo men. But, in specific terms, I don't like O'Mara. Never have. Never will."

"I thought you said he was dead."

Fulgerson merely stared. Another waitress brought their food to them.

"You sure sound like you've had personal experience on the subject."

Fulgerson looked at Bert, but said nothing for a moment or two. He was thinking about the repossession of his son's vehicle. He frowned, then muttered "don't wanna talk about it. All I know is repo men are thieves. All a them. Steal a man's horse? You get caught. You get hung. So, how's a man's truck any different than his horse?"

Bert said nothing, but sat quietly chewing his food. It was obvious Tommy Deen O'Mara didn't even stand a chance with this bigot. First, he drew the short straw during his encounter with the man and his rifle. Now, he was striking out again with a man armed with something even scarier…a grand jury vote. Bert had never personally known Tommy Deen. But, he knew of O'Mara's excellent reputation as a decent, honest, hard-working man. Those who knew him said he was a good family man who very protectively loved his wife and children. TD's reputation spoke for itself by the way he conducted business in what, at times, could be a very ugly trade.

Tom was known to often work seven days a week, providing necessaries for his loved ones. In Bert's mind, this sure sounded like a senseless killing. After all, if the shooter really thought someone was stealing his truck, why didn't he just dial 911? That's what the cops were for. Wasn't it? Nobody was trying to boost the Hope diamond. This was just a silly old pickup truck. And, according to Billy Ray, it was a pretty tired one at that. This grand jury stuff was a completely different situation altogether. Bert felt like he had a ringside seat to a lynching, as he continued to receive firsthand information from Billy Ray. Fulgerson was a man who obviously had already made his mind up.

But, it seemed to go far deeper. From what Billy Ray shared, he obviously intended to influence enough other members of the jury to prevent an indictment. Bert's inherent sense of justice and fair play told him something was clearly not right here. Sure, he wasn't a lawyer and didn't claim to have all the legal ramifications down pat. However, as his mind wandered, he wondered how his friend could so cavalierly prejudge an outcome of an event this important to so many other folks.

He wondered what, if anything, he should do. Bert thought of TD's grieving widow and her sad children. What could he do? After all, Billy Ray was a powerful man. At this point, he still wasn't sure he needed this sort of self-imposed grief in his own life.

Chapter 54

The jurors continued trickling back into the hearing room, following the noon recess. As each person returned, the prosecutor counted them to determine when he could begin their afternoon session. Finally, at 1:38 p.m., the last juror walked in.

"Okay, ladies and gentlemen. Let's get started. And, let's also be a wee bit more punctual, so we can start on time. We have a lot of ground to cover. The sooner we get going, following any recesses, the quicker we can be done with this matter."

Montgomery glanced at his watch. Same time as the wall clock.

"It's now 1:38 p.m. Afternoon sessions begin at 1:30 p.m. Remember, if any of us are not here on time, the rest suffer, waiting for any stragglers. The State will present a number of witnesses. Keep something in mind. In a criminal trial, the burden of proof is beyond a reasonable doubt."

Monty paused and looked around at the jurors, both for dramatic effect and to make sure he had their attention. Once he was satisfied he did, he continued.

"Here, however, all that's required is *probable cause*. Why? That's because this is the *pre-indictment* part of the case. In other words, your job is to decide if an indictment should issue. If you find probable cause supports the evidence, then and only then may you return a true bill of particulars. If not, you must return a no bill."

He looked around to see if there were any questions pending.

"That's why grand jury proceedings are far more abbreviated than a trial. We only have to establish something in the neighborhood of a *scintilla* of evidence. Basically, this amounts to what is called a *prima facie* case. In other words, the evidence we'll present is rather superficial. Almost skeletal. That's the law. Any questions?"

His question was met with a number of head shakes from side-to-side. Some of the jurors actually went so far as to audibly say *no*. However, a couple of hands went up. In response to the inquiries, he explained what scintilla and prima facie meant.

"Okay, let's get this thing started, then. Our first witness is…"

Montgomery described each and every witness he intended to present, including their names and their role in the case. Since no defense counsel was in his way to interrupt, his latitude was practically unlimited.

"Now," he said, "do any of the parties to this action cause any of you to believe you cannot sit fairly and impartially as a juror?"

Monty looked around before continuing, but there were no replies.

"Does anyone have any information as to any other prospective juror whom you believe may not be fair and impartial, including yourself?"

He again waited for a response and even went so far as to visually poll each of the jurors in the room again, including Billy Ray, who had a neutral expression on his face. His only reaction was to shake his head, indicating he could be fair and impartial. The prosecutor observed no one had answered in the affirmative. So, he continued.

"When I say parties, just so there is no confusion here, I mean the victim, Tommy Deen O'Mara, the defendant Johnny Walker, and anyone I've already told you is a witness in this matter. That even includes me. Anyone?" he prodded.

Montgomery mentally confirmed he hadn't missed any responses. Fulgerson swallowed nervously, but said nothing. Rather than make eyeball to eyeball contact with the prosecutor, he glanced around to see how other members were reacting. He made a faux show of pretending to clean his glasses. But, as he did, he could feel perspiration beginning to drip slowly down his sides, inside his shirt. It had already reached his beltline. He was glad he wore a dark shirt today.

"Hearing no objections from any of you," observed the DA, "let's call our first witness, State Trooper DJ Timothy from the Texas Department of Public Safety."

Montgomery chose to not present an Opening Statement. The witness came forward when called by the bailiff. He was wearing what appeared to be a standard issue tan patrol uniform with long sleeves, a light blue tie and red shoulder patches. His Sam Browne belt holding his duty sidearm, its holster, and his other accoutrements was black leather, in what is generally described as a basket weave pattern. His shoes were also black leather with rubber soles. As he approached, the clerk spoke.

"Sir, please raise your right hand."

The witness complied.

"Do you solemnly swear to tell the truth, the whole truth, and nothing but the truth?"

"I do."

"Please state your full name and spell your last name."

"Name is DJ, uh…Daniel John…Timothy. T-I-M-O-T-H-Y."

The clerk nodded to the prosecutor and said "your witness, counsel."

"Thank you, madam clerk. Sir, by whom are you employed?"

"Department of Public Safety, Texas Highway Patrol."

"In what capacity?"

"State trooper."

"How long have you been so employed?"

"Nearly sixteen years."

"And, on Saturday, February 26, 1994 were you so employed?"

"Yes."

"On that date, at approximately 9:30 a.m., were you on duty, wearing a distinctive uniform, like the one you are now wearing, and driving a distinctively marked police vehicle?"

"I was."

"Did you observe something unusual on that date and at that time?"

"I did."

"Please describe that?"

Timothy answered the question with a narrative answer. But, his testimony failed to include this was actually his second trip past the immediate area that morning. He actually drove by the first time at approximately 8 a.m., but didn't stop. Had he taken the time to do so, he would have realized the engine to Morris' wrecker was running, just as it was still doing when he finally stopped to inspect it at 0930 hours. Montgomery failed to ask why, even though it was in Timothy's incident report.

In Riley's opinion, it added nothing to his case. He believed the THP Trooper's role was to merely identify the crime scene and relay the chain of its custody to the first HPD officer on scene.

"I was working routine patrol in the 400 block of West Canino, just inside Houston city limits, and observed a dull red over black 1982 Chevrolet pickup truck sitting nose up in a ditch on the north side of, and at a 45 degree angle to, the roadway."

"License plate?"

"Texas plate number 6865TC."

"Can you give us a landmark, so the jurors know where the 400 block of West Canino is?"

"Certainly. That's basically just south of DPS. I'm sorry. That's the Department of Public Safety office."

"Once you made this observation, what did you do next?"

"I parked, got out of my patrol car and walked over to the truck to investigate."

"Describe those observations."

"Sure. As I approached the vehicle from its rear, I noticed it wasn't just a pickup truck, but one of those wreckers. You know? It looked like a repo wrecker. A sling wrecker. Had a whatchamacallit? A winch and other equipment that folds down out of sight into its bed when they aren't in use? It's what I'd call one of those low profile rigs."

"Anything else?"

"Yes, upon closer inspection, I observed what appeared to be a Caucasian adult male, maybe mid-50's, dark hair, clean shaven, lying partially across the bench seat, partially on the floor, in a pool of what appeared to be blood. His head was near the passenger door. It appeared he had fallen from behind the steering wheel. I also observed a number of what appeared to be 8&1/2 x 11 inch sheets of paper. Official looking types of documents. They appeared to be partially covered with dried blood. It was a single vehicle traffic collision."

"Have you seen blood before?"

"Yes sir. As I mentioned already, I've been with DPS for nearly 16 years. I've cleaned up more than my fair share of fatal traffic collisions. Frankly, more than any man deserves. So, yeah, I've seen blood before. Lots of it."

"Were you able to determine the condition of this person?"

"You mean if he was still alive?"

"Yes."

"Yes sir. As I reached in to turn off the ignition…"

"You mean the engine was still running?"

"Yes sir."

"Go on."

"I noticed the man in the truck was not moving. I couldn't see any breathing. No pulse. Skin cold to the touch. I was able to see what appeared to be at least one gunshot wound on his upper right side, in between his chest and back, near his right lung.

"What did you do next?"

"First I contacted my supervisor. Then, I had dispatch notify Houston PD because this was their jurisdiction for such calls."

"For clarity, why them?"

"My job is to patrol the highways and byways of my assigned jurisdiction within the state of Texas, primarily attempting to help motorists in need of assistance. Since this man was obviously dead and there was nothing more I could do to assist, I contacted the law enforcement agency with jurisdictions over dead bod…I mean deceased persons who appear to be homicide victims."

"Homicide?"

"People who die at the hands of others; as opposed to suicides. Since I didn't know what we had at this point, I chose to err on the side of caution."

The trooper failed to mention he might have arrived ninety minutes too late.

"Did you find any firearms inside the vehicle?"

"No sir."

"Thank you. You're excused."

Montgomery next called Houston PD officer JD Beaverton to the stand. He was wearing his patrol uniform, with a light blue short sleeved shirt and navy blue trousers. The trim at the top of each shirt pocket and the epaulets across the top of each shoulder matched the color of his dark uniform pants.

Like Timothy, his Sam Browne and shoes were also black leather. The officer stated his name and was sworn in. He sat at the witness stand, awaiting any questions.

After establishing he was employed and on duty as a Houston police officer the morning of the incident, Riley continued with his questioning.

"And, officer, after you were briefed by Trooper Timothy, what did you do next?"

"I pronounced the victim."

"Please continue."

"Yes sir. I opened the passenger door and attempted to locate a pulse, but could not find one."

"What did you do at this point?"

"I pronounced him."

"When you say you *pronounced him*, please tell the jury what this means."

"I'm sorry. It means I pronounced him dead…determined him to no longer be alive…at the scene where his vehicle had obviously come to rest."

"Why do you say obviously?"

"No skid marks. And, you could see where its front bumper was somewhat augured into the bank on the north side of the ditch. Plus, there were no other tire marks indicating it had left that location."

"Other than what you've already told us, did you make any other observations about the victim?"

"Yes sir. He appeared to have some sort of wound in his upper right chest. I later learned a projectile entered the side of his right chest and exited through the side of his left chest. Basically through both lungs, from right side to left side and exited."

"Please explain."

"I say this because, from that point heading toward his waistline, there appeared to be lots of blood on his back. It was as if that was the area of entry, and blood exited, pouring down his torso. Gravity, you know? Oh, and I didn't notice any blood on him above that area. The only other blood I saw appeared to be because he was lying in it on the floorboard."

"Anything else?"

The question actually called for a narrative answer. However, since this was a grand jury proceeding, no defense counsel was there to object. Montgomery was trying to move as quickly as he could, just as he did with Timothy. He had other work to do.

"Yes. The entry wound appeared to be consistent with the height of the bullet holes I observed in the left rear sheet metal of his truck's cab, just below the rear window. My immediate impression? He was shot, got weak, lost consciousness, crashed into the ditch. Impact threw him onto the floorboard where he lay, as he bled to death."

"How'd you do that?

"With a tape measure, measuring from the bottom of his right buttock to the location of the wounds I observed. Then, I measured from the driver's seat cushion to the location of the bullet hole in the rear window."

"Okay."

"I'm sorry. Let me add one more thing. I want to be clear. The entry wound didn't appear to be in his upper back. It appears he was backing up. You know? Turning around to look out his rear window, when he was shot. In other words, rather than an entry wound in his back and exit wound in his chest, entry was his right side, exiting out the other."

Beaverton's answer also was conclusionary and speculative. Monty had not laid any foundation to establish the expertise of Beaverton, prior to asking his question, and before the officer answered it. But, no defense attorney present meant no objections.

Beaverton's last answer was gratuitous. Montgomery considered striking it from the record. However, since he expected the jury to return a no bill, he didn't expect any defense counsel would scrutinize it, deciding to not waste his time. A mistake?

"Did you learn the identity of the victim?"

"Yes sir. Tommy Deen O'Mara, owner of E&A Recovery located up in Spring."

"Do you know what the definition of a homicide is, officer, say as opposed to a suicide?"

This question called for a legal opinion. An objection to it in court would normally have been sustained, thus preventing the jury from hearing it. But, as with the previous objectionable question, or with Timothy, no one was in the room to object.

"Yes sir. The killing of one person by another, as opposed to one dying at one's own hands."

"Did anything lead you to believe it was anything other than a homicide?"

"No sir. I found no weapons consistent with the sort of injuries I observed about the person of Mr. O'Mara. And, what appeared to be at least one bullet hole was a pretty good clue."

"Did you remain at the scene until detectives from your department arrived?"

"I did."

"And, did you give a statement to one of them?"

"I did."

"Who would that be?"

"Detective CL Larson."

"Thank you sir. Nothing further. Next witness, Investigator CL Larson of the Houston Police Department."

After eliciting his testimony, the prosecutor also thanked and excused him, then proceeded to other witnesses. HPD detective Carlton Larson testified he notified O'Mara's widow of his death.

The prosecutor next asked the detective if he had spoken with the shooter, Johnny Walker. Larson testified Walker told him he only shot *at* O'Mara and did so because he believed the victim was trying to steal his truck.

He further testified Walker told him he attempted to shoot over the repo man's head and only meant to scare him away so he wouldn't steal his truck, thus preventing a theft of his property.

Next witness was Walker's wife. She testified she was awakened by the sound of what she believed was a gunshot around 3:30 a.m. She further testified she made two phone calls to the Harris County Sheriff's Office to report the shooting.

Elaine Walker testified she first went next door, after she woke up to use Johnny's grandmother's phone. When Montgomery asked why she called the Sheriff instead of HPD, she said it was because they lived in Harris County, as opposed to Houston proper. She couldn't remember who told her that.

She didn't realize the prosecutor already knew she hadn't made either call, including the one she claimed to make at 6:30 a.m. from work.

Larson had already reviewed the phone records of HCSO and HPD. He determined neither call was made. He knew this. So did Montgomery. The only player left out of this particular loop was Elaine Walker.

Little did she realize this misstep would soon earn her another trip to the courthouse. This time, however, she'd be the defendant, following the grand jury delivering a true bill and the ensuing indictment against her.

In due course, each witness completed their testimony. After summation, the prosecutor directed the jurors to retire to the jury room so they could deliberate. He cautioned them they now had the case and must return timely with their decision. Because he was the subject of this proceeding, Johnny Walker did not testify. Montgomery knew, if called, he would simply assert his 5th Amendment right to not testify against himself.

De minimus non curat lex.

Chapter 55

The grand jury returned to the hearing room. Predictably, their verdict did not include an indictment, despite Dawn O'Mara's heart-wrenching testimony. It was a no bill, just as Montgomery knew it would be. But, this was not terribly surprising. The prosecutor asked them for a no bill, before they left to deliberate. Could they really do anything else? Monty and Billy Ray's one-two punch was devastatingly accurate.

The jury obediently delivered, just like grand juries tend to do. A no bill was requested. A no bill was delivered and received. He soullessly shifted gears and moved on to the next case on his legal assembly line. As soon as Montgomery knew this, he returned to his office and spoke with his secretary.

"Grace, schedule a grand jury for Elaine Walker. The charge? Perjury. Seemingly, her equivocation outranked TD's murder. We need a reporter's transcript of hers and Larson's testimony before the Johnny Walker grand jury I just completed. I'll contact HPD and HCSO myself and make sure each department prepares a report. They each need to expedite them, to my attention. So, once I contact them, please follow up in a couple of days."

As he spoke, she scrambled in order to capture everything with some quick notes. Apparently, Monty didn't waste words like *please* with support staff.

"Remember, be sure to follow up. As soon as the RT is ready, send each a copy. Tell them to include the transcript with any reports they submit."

Grace rolled her eyes at Monty's serious lack of people skills. While she was used to being talked to like she was an idiot, she sure wasn't very close to liking it. After talking to her, he walked into his office to phone each of the detectives he needed to speak with. He dialed the first number and waited for it to ring. As soon as he heard the open line, he spoke.

"Larson," he began, "that Walker woman committed perjury. I'm pissed. I don't want her getting off on a misdemeanor for making a false police report. Her lies made the guys at HCSO look like Keystone cops for more than a week."

The vehemence of this comment surprised Larson. Montgomery continued.

"The media told the general public they blew off two 911 calls. You guys had to waste time proving you did nothing wrong too. She *will* be held accountable," he emphasized. "Let's bury the bitch!"

Chapter 56

The still-livid widow paced in and out of her kitchen, fitfully moving back and forth between rooms. She walked from kitchen to den, and back again. The angry woman was trying to calm herself. But, she remained so irate she could feel her head pounding. Dawn feared she might have a heart attack. Maybe even a stroke.

Her best friend, Janie, held her right hand in both of hers, trying valiantly to keep pace with her. She also rubbed Dawn's arm, as she tried to stay abreast.

"There, there, darlin'," she cooed. "Don't y'all worry none. We are gonna search and search until we find the justice y'all need. All the justice. I mean, after all, y'all are gettin' a lawyer, right?" she finally asked.

"Are you serious? After this so-called prosecutor? Mr. Do-o-o-nothing? Might as well have had a car salesman doing the work. They'd be more honest, no doubt. After this, Janie, I'm just uncomfortable with lawyers."

Wells seemed puzzled.

"Here's what I mean, girl. If I were to get stuck with a lawyer like that…that…that spineless, lazy, *girly-man* prosecutor who wouldn't even try to indict TD's murderer, much less do it…"

She sputtered, as she tried to finish her sentence.

"We both know what good *he* did! Absolutely nothin'! That's what!"

"No darlin'. Y'all know we ain't just talkin' about some ordinary prosecutor. I know lawyers who are real heck raisers. We sure ain't talkin' about no Montgomery. We're talkin' about a real prosecutor. This one comes to us hand-picked by none other than Charlie Owens himself. You know? Like I said, a real one. One who can come here locally, who can review your case, can go into court and kick somebody's rear end, if it deserves some serious kickin'."

"What are you talkin' about, Janie?"

"I told you a few days ago why you needed a lawyer. Remember?"

"Yeah."

"And, I gave you a name too, didn't I?"

"I'm not sure. Tell me again."

"Joshua Travers."

"Who?"

"Joshua Travers. He's a California DA."

"Janie, why would I want to go to California to hire a lawyer? And, a prosecutor, at that? After the experience we've just had with that big pile of horse doody here in Harris County not doing his job and really goin' after TD's murderer, like he should have?"

Dawn appeared distracted. She suddenly whipped her head in Janie's direction.

"Wait a minute. Charlie who?"

"Funny you should ask. I've got a friend. He does nothin' but civil stuff now and…"

Dawn interrupted. "What's civil?"

"That's where people sue each other. You know? One side, maybe both, askin' for the court to award money?"

"Okay?"

"Anyhow, let me give him a call and see if he's interested in helpin'."

"What did y'all say his name was?"

"The one here?"

"Yeah."

"Charlie. Charlie Owens. He used to be a prosecutor out there in Cal…"

"Prosecutor? Wait just a doggoned minute. I thought I heard you say prosecutor a bit ago. But, I thought y'all said we were talkin' about a real lawyer? I thought y'all said we weren't gonna get another prosecutor involved? Now, you're talkin' about two?"

"No, I didn't say no prosecutor. But, y'all are right. I did say we're gonna get y'all a real lawyer. Sometimes you just gotta rely on the input of friends. Girlfriend, keep something in mind. Y'all know how some doctors are far better than others? Same with preachers? Same with auto mechanics? Same with…" she paused for effect. "… repo men?"

Dawn raised one eyebrow.

"Yeah?"

Janie knew she'd struck a nerve. Although he had always been an inherently humble and modest man, TD prided himself on the quality of his work and the energy he poured into their E&A Recovery business. His widow knew this. Dawn viewed TD far superior to other folks in the repo business. In her mind, it wasn't a subject even worthy of wasting time discussing with others. And, that was also the reputation O'Mara had among the locals who understood the repo business. TD was viewed by both of them to be as good as a repo professional could be.

"Well, like I said, it's the same thing. Doctors? Lawyers? The whole bunch. Some are average. Some are plain bad. And, some are just far better than the others."

"As I said, Charlie used to be a prosecutor. Joshua Travers was his boss. But, he quit that job. Now, he represents clients privately here in our state. He sues other folks for his clients and defends his clients when other folks sue them. And, he and Travers stay in touch."

"Really?" she asked.

"*Dawn*, darlin', know what we need to do?"

"What's that?"

"Y'all need to meet Charlie. Talk to him yourself, so you can convince him to convince Joshua to represent you. And, if he will, to convince you to hire Travers? Why don't you let me arrange a lunch for the three of us? That way, you can meet each other."

Dawn merely stared.

"According to Charlie, if any lawyer on planet Earth can get you the justice you deserve, it's Travers. Owens can't represent you because he's the lawyer for the car dealership that hired TD to do the repo that killed him. And, even on those rare occasions when Travers loses, he says the other guy is always a bit bloodier than himself."

Chapter 57

When I was sure my office door was closed, I spoke again.

"Okay, Owens. Speak to me. This had better be good. You interrupted my tutorial for a couple of the newer kids. What's that? Feedin' 'em some raw meat, of course. Getting them in the right frame of mind for battle. Now, they probably forgot everything and I'll have to start at the very beginning. You know how these rookies are."

I chuckled. Owens didn't. He was pausing before speaking. He appeared to be collecting his thoughts. I know Charlie. I know his M.O. Sometimes he has to slowly mull things over before he speaks. Don't get me wrong. He's not dumb, just deliberate.

Let's be honest. Patience is not my universal strong suit. Mine generally ranges from little to none whatsoever. For one thing, I always seem to have far more work to do than I have available time in which to do it. I know. My choice. My fault. Mea culpa. Don't get me wrong. I'm not whining. Just stating facts. But, I also know it isn't like my former protégé to call just to chew the fat. We're both too busy for that. So, I listen. But, once I know what Owens wants, his call immediately causes me ambivalence.

Charlie and I also have a longtime understanding. Unless we say otherwise, anything we discuss is akin to the 10-35 discussions California coppers have with one another or me. They don't have to worry about getting bit on their ass. He already knew Dawn wanted to hire me. And, even though I hadn't told him yet, so did I. The last thing in the world I needed was to juggle yet another proverbial ball. To say I was a bit flummoxed was like calling the Sears Tower a bit tall.

But, since I knew at least as much as Owens did, I decided to have a little fun. Before I spoke again, I signaled the cops I was almost done.

"So, whoa…whoa, Charlie. Stop. Let me see if I've got this right. You represent a car dealer. Correct?"

"Well, I represent many vehicle dealers. This one in particular is my biggest client. He owns a whole slew of dealerships around Houston. Actually, has a number of them in several states. Without him, I probably wouldn't represent the rest. He's that influential. And, he's also that rich and powerful."

"Okay. And, you're telling me this one's fu…" My thoughts quickly flashed to Molly. I was still trying to clean up my verbal act. She'd sure like that. I continued. "…uh…fouling up big time, right?"

"Yep. It's more than that. They *keep* screwin' up. It's not like they messed up once and learned their lesson. The owner is one of those west Texas cowboys who has great difficulty following directions…from his lawyer or from anyone else, for that matter. Plain ornery and stubborn. Smart but Muleshoe mule-stubborn. His Deals on Wheels manager is even worse."

"How's that?"

"My client has me on a $10,000 monthly retainer. Twenty hours max, at $500 an hour. Anything over twenty, I charge him my usual $600 an hour, plus any expenses I incur."

"Why the difference?"

"I asked. He agreed. I bill him. He pays me. Supply and demand. I supply him with legal guidance and demand he pays me. He supplies me with cash flow and demands I guide him. Remember law school contracts? Mutuality of obligation and all that crap?"

I laughed. This time, so did Charlie.

"You know I know the repo man's widow wants to hire you, right?"

I did. He was obviously referring to Dawn O'Mara. Now, I was curious how he and she had even connected with one another. After all, Texas is one big state. He explained. I paused to catch my breath.

"Don't care, dammit. Last time I checked, Charlie, Houston's still in Harris County. And, Harris County's still in the great state of Texas. In fact, I just had a brain storm. If she does what I'm suggesting, she'll be doing just like one of my constituents here in Solita County would do. They rely on *their* DA…*me*…to prosecute their own criminal cases. As we both know, DA's change their minds. Even on filing decisions."

"Stand by on that, Trav. Grand jury's already no billed the guy who killed her hubby. DA says he had no choice, thanks to the controlling Penal Code section."

"Yeah? Well, as we both know, beauty is in the eye of the beholder, too. One man's ceiling is another man's floor. One man's trash is…"

"Yeah, yeah…*another man's treasure*. Listen, I'll explain everything, as I know it, before we get off the horn. So, in the meantime, just stay with me on this issue, okay?"

"Okay. I'll keep my powder dry. But, not for long. This woman wants me to represent the surviving family members of the repo man that the stupidity of this dealer…*your client*…killed? And do it as both a prosecutor and a civil lawyer? On the same case? Does she really understand what I do for a paycheck? Or, what jurisdiction means?" I asked somewhat rhetorically.

He didn't respond. Apparently, I didn't give him enough time to answer.

"I don't think so," I said, answering my own question.

"She does, Trav. And, two hats are involved here. Special prosecutor *and* plaintiff's counsel."

"That's nice to hear. But, I sure as hell haven't told you I'm interested in representing anyone yet, have I? Dammit, Charlie, I'm a prosecutor. A California prosecutor at that. Specifically, a Solita County prosecutor. Even more specifically, *the Solita County District Attorney*. Remember? I feed exclusively at the public dining table."

I didn't realize I was holding my breath. So, I exhaled.

"How in hell do you expect me to sell this line of bullshit to my constituents?"

He laughed. I could see the cops were beginning to fidget.

"Charlie, I'm serious. And, I'm *not* a civil lawyer either. You know that. But for law school Torts, I wouldn't know a civil wrong from a hedgehog."

This heart-to-heart went on far longer than I preferred. I kept telling Charlie I had a ton of work to do. But, Mr. Persistent would have none of that. He explained stuff like the preponderance of the evidence standard for civil cases being far, far lower than beyond a reasonable doubt, how I'd only need to convince 9 jurors instead of all 12…blah...blah…blah. By now, I was fidgeting. I'd finally reached my limit and asked Owens to get to the point. So, he did. Convincingly so. We are talking Charlie Owens, at his best, closing argument-precise, convincingly so. He explained he believed Dawn O'Mara deserved zealous representation. Charlie, the great persuader.

As Baron's lawyer, he didn't want someone leading interference for her that was going to "slime my client and me," as he put it. He reminded me he'd worked for me long enough to know he could trust me on both counts.

"And," he added. "I don't want this thing tied up in the appellate courts for decades, costing my client a ton of money. Besides, I hate appellate work. It's absolutely B-O-R-I-N-G!!!"

Then, he paused to ask a question. "Any appellate court ever accuse you of not adequately representing your client? I'm talking about either as a defense attorney or as a DA."

"Well, one appellate court said I committed prosecutorial misconduct in an unreported opinion. Said the trial court's error in not spanking me for telling a joke during closing was harmless beyond a reasonable doubt, due to the strength of our case. But, no, they didn't reverse."

"Who wrote the opinion?"

I told him. He laughed, then cursed a bit, finally calling the judge a pantywaist and a backstabber, plus a word I won't use here. And, if I won't use it…well, you get the general idea. I laughed. We both knew the current Presiding Justice. I certainly agreed with the backstabber label. Pantywaist?

Could have fooled me. I kiddingly asked Charlie if he knew something I didn't. I won't repeat his vulgar retort either. It included a personal pronoun and a clear, unambiguous verb. Let's leave it at that.

Years earlier, I'd sat Pro Tem for his Honor, when he was still a trial judge and I was in private practice. Looking back now, it seems like several lifetimes ago. I privately shared an idea with him about substituting community service for jail, on minor offenses, to save tax dollars. He told me it would never fly, due to possible liability. Then, six months later, the sonofabitch publicly presented my plan, claiming the idea was his. Predictably, I opened up my big mouth and criticized him. He didn't forget. Vengeance is mine, sayeth the Lord? Try an appellate jurist for size too, while you're considering that particular issue.

Charlie said he'd already indirectly spoken with Dawn through one Janie Wells. He reiterated what she had already told me. She was pissed off and was ready, as Charlie put it, "...to sue the whole fucking world. My words, not hers," he emphasized.

I finally admitted she and I had spoken to each other. He wasn't surprised. But, I reminded Owens again I wasn't licensed to practice law in Texas. Charlie explained I could appear *pro hac vice*, by going to court under the license of a Texas lawyer. He already had someone in mind and said the guy was a decent civil lawyer. Real decent, in fact, according to Charlie, who reminded me, since my law school was ABA-approved, I could even apply for a Texas license, under the doctrine of reciprocity. I had no need for a second bar license and told him so.

Charlie took a moment to brief me on the area of Texas law that authorizes special prosecutors. These can be licensed Texas lawyers who essentially step into the shoes of a government prosecutor, but only with prior proper legal authorization. They can do this when something untoward happens, such as *official corruption*. The added requirement, he said? The prosecutorial office with jurisdiction over such an issue must also choose to do nothing to right the perceived wrong.

For some reason, Richard Nixon and special prosecutor Archibald Cox sprang to mind, as did Bill Clinton and Ken Starr. I can't articulate it. But, something about those recovered memories seemed to set me off. Suddenly, I could really feel Dawn's pain. And, I mean, I could really feel it. Damned Owens now had my attention. *Sonofabitch!*

"Tell me more," I asked, as I released a big overdue sigh.

Charlie talked about the rules of Texas civil discovery, using words like interrogatories, depositions, and so on. After we hung up, I found myself looking at the brief on my desk once again. Before we did so, however, he rescued me by pointing out support staff, such as paralegals and law clerks, would basically take care of all the heavy lifting on the case. That sounded good, as law and motion stuff generally bores me to tears. I like court. Period. Especially if it includes the words *jury trial*.

"Charlie, I gotta run. But answer two questions for me. One, how do I have jurisdiction to prosecute a Texas case? Secondly, why should I do this in the first place?"

Owens meticulously explained both points. I looked up and saw another cop. She knocked and walked into my office, waiting somewhat patiently for me to hang up. Finally, I shook my head up and down, as if Charlie could see me through the telephone.

"I see," I said. "Makes sense, CO, kind of, anyway. Gotcha. Okay, Charlie. I'll call you."

When I hung up, I apologized profusely to the two ever-patient dope cops. Truth be told? They really weren't rookies. Each of the longtime lab rats smiled, but only after pretending to choke me out, like you play an air guitar. Just arms squeezing a pretend neck. We have enjoyed many memorable choir practices, including one up in Monterey at the annual California Narcotic Officers Association conference several years ago.

I pretty much hate tattoos. Seen way too many prison tats. But, stumbling around up there, at 0200 one night, the Task Force guys and I decided we'd each get a scorpion tat on our ass. Seriously. Fortunately, we were sober, by the time any so-called *body art shops* were open for business, later that same morning. Our hilarious idea no longer seemed so funny, with hangovers. Tryin' to recall if the statute on that particular caper run yet. I counted mentally. That story is good for at least two six packs of ice cold Negra Modelo, con vasos frios, y stogies, y some of Molly's mouth-watering carnitas. Add her amazing arroz, sizzling salsa y chips, and you're set.

"By the way," I joked, "your civil procedure class is on the house."

I held my hands up, like a priest does at a Catholic Church altar, while saying Mass. They smiled again, and each made the sign of the cross. Then, each of these knuckleheads bowed. In unison with each other, no less. I pretended to bless them, as I intoned *dominus vobiscum*. The late-arriving female genuflected, and blew me a kiss. I mock caught it. Cop humor. Where do they get this stuff? You gotta love it! And, them! God bless cops!

Chapter 58

Dawn was absolutely incensed when she received the news. For a woman who generally didn't swear, she was more than a bit over the top. As some Texans might say, she appeared to be teaching herself a whole 'nuther vocabulary.

"No bill? No bill?!" she screamed. "How in goddamned hell can they no bill that piece of white trash? He murdered my husband. My ever lovin' husband! And, you know what really pisses me off, Janie?" she wailed.

"What's that, darlin'?" ever patient Janie asked.

"I had to learn about this from the TV news, no less. TV!" she shouted. "That candy-assed, lily-livered prosecutor didn't even have the guts, or the manners, to call me up. He should've told me this himself. And," she continued, "he knew about this as early as yesterday. Yesterday!"

"Tch...tch..." Janie replied.

"What can I do? I can't just sit back and do nothin'. I can't accept this."

"I don't know darlin'. I just don't know."

"I can't take this lyin' down. I've gotta do somethin'. Harris County needs a prosecutor with some cajones!"

Janie asked what *cajones* were. Dawn explained. Janie blushed. She simply wasn't used to hearing such language coming out of Dawn's normally proper mouth.

Chapter 59

Charlie Owens and I were on the phone again. He was briefing me about the no bill just handed down by the Harris County grand jury. Predictably, he was on a tear. I didn't realize Dawn had given Janie an earful and she, in turn, had done so with Charlie.

"Frankly T, this one sounds like a no-brainer. The shooter should have been indicted. Walker admitted shooting *at* the victim. He claimed he thought the guy was a car thief trying to steal his truck. Said he was just trying to scare him off. Car thief? Ha! I mean, give me a break. If nothing else, how about at least a negligent homicide filing? Felony murder rule?"

I started to ask a question. Instead, I got steamrolled.

"He knows he's in arrears," he continued, "and he thinks a guy backing a wrecker down his driveway is a car thief? I realize you haven't done an investigation yet, but it sounds to me like HPD did a real weak-assed investigation. Pedantic piece of shit. Definitely not the kind I was used to seeing the cops do out there in *"liberal"* SoCal. Haven't worked with the coppers here in the same fashion, but, I wouldn't expect anything different here either."

I tried, without success, to interrupt again. I decided to just let Charlie wear himself out. And, curiously, he is also the guy representing the dealer.

"In fact, even before HPD got on scene, a THP trooper drove by the vic's wrecker around ninety minutes before he even got out to investigate. Can you believe that? He didn't even stop his first time by! That time of the morning, he sees steam coming from the tailpipe, but doesn't realize the engine is running? Any shooting aside, has he ever heard of medical aid calls? What do you think? Does that create a problem, proving the cause of death? Shooting trauma vs. bled to death, due to lack of timely medical care?"

"Well, if I were the prosecutor, I'd consider that a possible causation issue. Might be an issue. Maybe not. Don't know at this point. Keep going."

Owens next explained why he believed the HPD investigation was deficient. The more he spoke, the less convinced I was I didn't agree with him. The presence of other repo men certainly couldn't be ignored, even if it had no actual bearing criminally. It just didn't feel right. Why had the cops apparently ignored that issue? Charlie also talked about the visit to the dealership, prior to O'Mara's murder, when his killer threatened to shoot anyone he caught trying to repossess his truck. Sure didn't sound like a valid car thief defense to me, either. No competent trial lawyer ever ignores common sense. *Uh, Charlie, you realize you're provin' my case, right?*

A new cashier had lectured Walker about a prior late payment. She explained the consequences of any more late payments. And, she embarrassed him by saying this in front of another customer, apparently prompting him to make his threat. Talk about notice of an inherently dangerous condition. If Deals on Wheels knew about it, then they had a legal duty to share this with O'Mara or any other repo man they hired to seize Walker's truck. I asked Owens to tie this together with other possible evidence. We continued speaking confidentially.

He tied things up, and, quite convincingly, if I do say.

"Although this bimbo was dumber than a cucumber salad," he said, "she did make herself a reminder note. And, even though Crenshaw also heard it, she informed the finance manager, after Walker left. Wanna hear how he avoided payin' the piper?"

"You mean Walker? Talk to me, W. Charles"

"Trav, it's worse than you can imagine. He wasn't arrested either."

"How come?"

"You mean other than because of a less than vigorous investigation and a limp dick prosecution?"

"Yeah."

"Penal Code 9.41, et seq."

"9.41? I'm familiar with it."

"That's our *deadly force* statute. Basically," he chuckled, "it's a Texas hunting license to kill people you don't like."

"Charlie, I thought you were one of those silk-stocking lawyers now. Didn't dirty your hands with criminal stuff anymore? I've researched 9.41. But, how in hell do you know about it? All you do now is civil, remember?"

"T, I'm still a prosecutor before I'm anything else. I keep my ear to the trail. This one goes way the hell back to the 1880's. Basically, it gives any Texan the right to smoke someone they catch on their property, in the nighttime, *if* they can establish the guy was tryin' to *steal, vandalize, break-in, commit a violent crime,* and so on. Also gives Texans the same right, if the guy is tryin' to leave the scene, after committing such crimes."

Charlie returned to Dawn O'Mara.

"Question is, assume she asks? Will you accept her offer?"

"Charlie! I've already told you twice. Texas isn't the only place where people are inconveniently dying!"

"Can't your second-in-command handle things while you're gone doing an errand of mercy like this?"

"Charlie, here's my concern. Let me just come straight at you on this. Even if I decide to become the white knight in shining armor for some poor out-of-state damsel in distress, assuming I could even get up to speed quickly enough as a special prosecutor *and* as a Texas civil lawyer, for God's sake…"

"Yeah?"

"Well, how would this sit with my constituents…with the Board?"

"Huh?"

"Well, goddammit, Charlie. Think about it. Brand new *official* DA. I say to them 'oops, 'scuse me for a few months folks. I have a job to do that has nothing to do with what you're paying me to do here. And, I still need you to pay me my salary while I'm gone, 'cuz I'm doin' the other one for free'."

At the time, I didn't know it. But, Owens failed to disclose to me his true motivation for getting me into the middle of this homicide. Sure, he knew I was honest and ethical, and all that crap, just like I knew he was. Well, sort of, anyhow. He knew he wouldn't have to worry about my pulling any sleazy shenanigans. However, it had nothing to do with not getting slimed or dealing with appellate courts. He was actually looking for something to direct attention elsewhere.

His biggest concern was being able to get the focus of attention away from his client. Charlie wanted to be able to at least suggest other defendants were as liable on civil issues as Reggie Baron and his dealership were. If he could suggest they were more liable, even better. A grand jury no billing a guy like Johnny Walker immediately shifted a lot of unneeded attention from Reggie Baron's direction. Frankly, if I were him, I'd do the same damned thing.

An indictment of Walker, on the other hand, tended to keep the spot light more on the guy who squeezed the trigger. Baron might be a sonofabitch. But, at least he was Charlie's own sonofabitch.

There had already been one unnecessary death. Owens wasn't about to let anybody kill the goose that had already laid so many golden eggs for him.

Chapter 60

Acouple thousand miles away from Houston, I was stubbornly trying to dig my heels in. Owens, however, seemed bound and determined to convince me I should come to Texas and practice law for a few weeks. Or, more. No offense, compadre. I'm busy. Charlie is no dummy. It was quickly obvious to him why he was not doing a very stellar job convincing me. So, he shifted gears and tried a little flattery. I'm a sucker for compliments, just like any other idiot. He knows it. But, my naivety does have limits.

"Thanks, Trav. Know what my biggest professional regret to date has been?"

"Nope."

"I've never been able to be your second chair in a courtroom," said a somewhat dissembling Owens. "We've never tried a case together. I know this sounds a bit corny. But, even with all our kiddin' around, there is no other lawyer…*anywhere*…I respect as much as you. I'd love to work with you in court on the same case, in front of the same judge and the same jury. Even as opponents."

The statement caught me by surprise. Although we had been professional associates, and were longtime friends, I could not recall Owens ever paying me such a compliment. Or, anyone else for that matter. What was going on? Was he really being sincere?

"Thanks, Charlie. Your kind words flatter me. I know I bust my ass trying to be the best trial lawyer I can be. But, the reason I succeed is because I work and work and work. Just like you. That's why you're a success. I certainly don't view myself as any flaming genius or anything even close to that."

"I do," was his reply. I could feel my face turning red.

This was followed by silence. *Aw geez.* Then, Owens spoke again.

"Remember the death penalty case you tried, shortly after I left SCDA?"

I hadn't thought about that one in a long, long time. In short order, Owens refreshed my recollection, as we lawyers like to say. We lawyers have lots of other odd expressions. A layperson would simply say "now, I remember."

My junior associate and I ultimately convicted all three surviving cop-killers of first degree murder. Two of their associates made the mistake of getting into a gunfight with arriving cops. They both bled to death up in the cold and rugged San Bernardino Mountains. The five had murdered an innocent cop who was just trying to do his job. I didn't care which of these dirt bags actually pulled the trigger. They deserved to fry. All of them. I didn't care if the actual killer was one of the two my warriors-in-arms had capped up in the mountains. They were all dead to me.

We convinced the jury to find three special allegations true. We argued they murdered a peace officer, and, did so during an ambush and a robbery. Per California law, a robbery is a continuing crime until the perpetrator gets to a place of apparent safety. These three maggots didn't, killing one of my LEO brothers trying to reach shelter. That turned the former robbery into a murder. And, that paved the way to hell for each of them.

Each of these allegations qualified it as a capital case. I was pleasantly surprised how quickly the jury voted for the death penalty. Next, we had to convince the judge at sentencing a month later that factors in aggravation outweighed factors in mitigation. By doing this, we could legally justify imposition of the death penalty by the jury. Actually, sentencing was continued a few times. It finally happened nearly four months later. But, this caused me no heartburn whatsoever. They weren't going anywhere, except eventually to hell. A defense team trying to save a cold-blooded killer's life is supposed to pull all the stops. And, did these guys. Failure to do this subjects a lawyer to possible professional charges that they lacked adequate zeal. Big enough lack? Loss of license to practice law. A delay wouldn't change any of the underlying facts in any fashion whatsoever.

Life in prison without the possibility of parole was not an adequate punishment for these three bastards. I didn't care how damned long it took the appellate courts to approve their executions. Two of their associates were dead. They, too, deserved death. These mutts had no socially redeeming qualities. When a pursuing officer rounds the blind corner of a mountainous dirt road and is instantly met by fatal gun fire, I have zero interest in feeding and clothing his killers for the rest of their worthless lives. If I could, I'd pull the lever myself. They are lower than vermin. Lower than insects.

I wasn't concerned about convincing the judge this was a legitimate capital case. But, I had to establish an adequate record to justify the death penalty's imposition. Some judges are known as sentencing hammers. This particular guy was a sledgehammer. Even better? He'd never been overturned on appeal. The judge, known informally as *Chino Charlie*, had a well-deserved reputation for sending lots of defendants to prison, even following convictions in routine felony cases. Old Charlie didn't give many felons probation. My kind of judge.

Chino became part of his moniker because the California Institution for Men, Reception Center Central, aka CIM-RCC, is located among the many cow pastures and strawberry fields in rural Chino. Therefore, many insiders simply call it Chino or CIM. Convicted felons with prison sentences from throughout southern California are transported to CIM-RCC, in order to be evaluated to determine which prison will ultimately house them. Anyhow, Chino Charlie sounds better than CIM Charlie.

Charlie is merely an abbreviated version of this judge's first name, Charles. His surname isn't terribly important. If you know the judge, you know who I'm describing. And, if you don't, frankly, it tends to lose something in the translation.

In any event, the man was legendary. Apparently, the trial took a lot out of him. He's now in heaven. Rest in peace, Charlie. You did your time here. We requested death sentences. We got them. Their trip to Chino? Nope. They went directly to the Bay Area where San Quentin's Death Row awaited them. They now face execution. Somehow, all this made me think about duty and honor and all that stuff all over again. That made me ponder what Owens had shared with me. And, in turn, that made me ask myself if I should represent Dawn.

This would be one dangerously delicate dance.

Chapter 61

I won't bore you with all the details. But, let's agree that W. Charles Owens, Esquire, is good at networking. He's also a master of the art of persuasion. So is Dawn O'Mara. Somehow, she had convinced Charlie to talk to me. And, he did so quite convincingly. Charlie and I agreed Dawn deserved zealous representation. He talked to her about his perceived role for me, in both a civil and prosecutorial capacity. He explained that his review of the known facts convinced him his client was indefensible.

I realize some folks particularly other lawyers, will find it odd to an extreme that an opposing counsel helps select the very lawyer who ends up representing the other side. But, I found no ethical breaches. Charlie was merely exercising his free speech rights and being opinionated to an extreme, just like me. He knew she had already communicated with me. But, he wanted to make sure she was sure. She was. And, she told him so. Rather than merely focus on whether he could beat the case, his motivation was to control damages for Baron. Charlie was that skilled as a trial lawyer.

Therefore, after obtaining appropriate waivers, he talked to Dawn several times.

"I've already told you it would be a fair interpretation to conclude my client is dead on the facts. I mean fried…cooked…SOL, liability-wise. With his permission, I'm now talking to you."

"You did say that. Uh, SOL?"

Charlie explained. Dawn blushed.

"And, therefore, the last thing I need is for my client and me to be tripping and stumbling over some doofus representing you who don't know what they're doin'. We will not see this case tied up for years in an appellate court. There's no need for that."

"Huh?"

"Visualize you're playing baseball. Who would you rather face, when you're at bat…a pitcher who can control where they put the ball? Or, some guy who is more likely to hit you in the head because they can't do that? Facts are gonna come out. The law's the law. Those are both givens. I can't change either one of them. Neither can my client. Nor, can you."

Chapter 62

Dawn's meeting with Owens proved to be quite instructive. Among other things, he brought her up to speed on my time in courtrooms as a trial lawyer. He called it *"Travers' battle record as a courtroom brawler."* I had to laugh. What was he smoking? We had spoken. But, she wondered if he was exaggerating. Dawn was cautious by nature. TD's murder and the failure of Harris County to prosecute his killer made her even more skeptical. She was willing to listen, but would do so with one eye open. Good for her.

While Charlie, Dawn and Janie Wells were meeting, I was being interviewed by a local TV reporter following sentencing on one of my dope cases. She was young and good-looking. She appeared to have just stepped off some runway as a model. Apparently she was also aiming for a Pulitzer or something. Some dope cops were waiting for me to review their search warrants. I was getting antsy. I didn't realize those three Texans were watching me in Owens' conference room on his wide screen TV.

Let's hear it for national news. Dawn later told me what really caught her attention were my comments at the end of the interview. Big deal. Part of my job. It's called occasional posturing. This reporter was wearing me out with her silly questions. I decided to take things to a new level and end the interview.

"Look, I'm out of time. Gotta get ready for my next case," I said while still on camera. "Go talk to the cartels. They can probably tell you to the penny what a ton of their cocaine is worth."

The reporter blanched. She appeared to have lost her composure for a moment. But, being a proud professional, she quickly regained her self-control and soldiered on with the rest of our interview.

"Which cartel?" she asked.

"Arellano Felix. Same SOB's that're so damned generous with bounties...on heads of folks they don't like."

"Like who?"

"Like me," I replied.

My eyes shot daggers at the camera. By now, I wasn't even looking at her. I was in the zone. The reporter appeared at a loss for words, so I decided to help her...sort of. So, I glanced at her and spoke again.

"Try Tijuana. See if they're listed in the phone book. First names are Benjamin and Eduardo. Brothers from the same mother."

This skirt just wasn't giving up. And, I was now long out of patience.

"And, Mr. Travers," she queried, "do you believe this case should deliver a specific message to this particular cartel?"

"Yeah," I said, chewing on my unlit cigar.

"And, sir, what would that be?"

I stood up and stared straight into the camera. I was no amateur. This was not my first rodeo. I'd already been down this particular media highway many times before. She was now just wasting my time. I made sure I was going to get my money's worth.

"Stay the hell out of Solita County!" I growled, as I pointed at the camera with my stogie. "Listen to me, you godless thugs. You are murderous cowards. If my cops catch your drivers, they'll arrest 'em and seize every single bit of dope and money they find. And, if they arrest 'em, I'll send 'em to prison. Next, we'll be looking for each of you losers. This ain't Mexico. Comprende?"

Chapter 63

Owens phoned me again. I didn't realize he and the other two had just seen me on television. Nor, was I particularly interested. I was just finishing my review of yet another search warrant. The interview had put a serious dent in my schedule.

"Okay, Trav," he began. "We are reaching the point where the rubber needs to start meetin' the road."

"Charlie, I don't mean to sound unsociable. But, I'm trying to review a search warrant. Got a copper on the other side of my desk. And, it looks like he's ready to shoot me if there are any more delays. I feel like an air traffic controller today."

For added effect, the narcotics officers looked at me, grinned, got real close to the phone, then unfastened and fastened his holster repeatedly, saying nothing. When he was satisfied Owens understood what he was doing, he bowed at the waist and sat back down.

"And, you know the drill, Charlie. We ain't got time to burn. We still need to get a judge to sign off on this, so me 'n the boys can go serve it."

Owens regrouped. Once again, he tried to convince me to represent Dawn O'Mara, but first had to get a quick dig in. My fellow Gyrene plain wasn't giving up. Just like a damned leatherneck. Charlie made me so proud sometimes, even when he pissed me off.

"So, still playin' cops and robbers are we?"

I said nothing. Charlie waited for a reply. Hearing none, he continued.

"Truth, I don't mean to beat this to death. But, we have to discuss your role in Dawn O'Mara's life. The three of us just saw your latest TV interview. Nice touch. Tossin' the gauntlet down to the cartels. Have you considered just painting a bulls-eye on your back and bein' done with it? Or, are you just going completely nuts on me?"

I decided to ignore his teasing, so I could ask a question.

"What three?"

"Dawn O'Mara, Janie Wells and me."

"Okay. Hey, as to the cartels? Screw 'em, Charlie! Screw 'em and the burros they rode in on. Bunch of low life pussies, anyhow. I was just doin' my job. Same as always."

"Yeah, right," he jibed.

"What have I been saying for the past twenty-five years? Among other things, we should've offered dope cartel eradication services to Mexico, instead of goin' to Iraq or Kuwait."

"I know what your idea of cartel eradication services is, JT."

"That's right, Charlie. The POTUS should have issued an ultimatum a long time ago. Something like this: *'You've got 180 days, Mr. President of Mexico, to get rid of your cartels. If they ain't gone by our drop dead date, some U.S. Marines with a few really special tools will visit. Some air support will participate.'* You'd quickly say adios to some assholes. Right?"

"I know. I know. You've said that before."

"Is not a threat at our southern border more immediate than one from halfway around the world?"

"Of course."

"And, can we forget the torture-murder of *Kiki* on February 9, 1985? That should have been when we drew the line in the sand. A U.S. Marine...*a federal dope cop*...gets murdered by thugs, for just doin' his job down there, and, not just killed, but tortured to death? Yet, cartels still aren't eradicated? Somethin' wrong with that picture. This country is goin' to hell in a hand basket. I'll say it again, Charlie. Dutch didn't make many mistakes during his time in the White House. But, allowing cartels to watch '86 arrive was not a good way to start the New Year. Not in my book, at least. Kill 'em all! Mexico must learn how to do some serious ass-kicking and we should be their teacher. This is not a criminal problem. It mandates a military solution."

DEA Special Agent Enrique "Kiki" Camarena was murdered during a special assignment in Mexico. I honor him. May he rest in peace. Owens knew I was venting. He heard me say the same basic thing many times before, so he didn't reply. I didn't care. He didn't need to say anything. Camarena's murder delivered a message to American law enforcement. Plata o plomo. Silver or lead. Cartels knew they wasted their time offering the man a bribe. So, they just kidnapped and physically tormented him until his life left him. The sick, twisted bastards. I changed subjects and asked Owens another question.

"Hey, CO, are we facing any statute of limitations problems? We both know murder has no deadlines. So, we shouldn't be concerned with it impacting any criminal charges in your state, right?"

"Nope. No statute. Same as in Cali."

I hate it when people call California *Cali*. It sounds so damned yuppie-like. Charlie knows how I feel about that. In my opinion, he lived in California too long to call it Cali. But, I said nothing, although I almost had to bite my tongue to keep quiet.

"How about civil? I assume fraud and wrongful death have statutes. What's Texas law on that issue? What sorta time frame we lookin' at in your state? Are both torts the same? Same statutes of limitations, I mean?"

Owens explained. I listened. His answer assured me we had adequate time to deal competently with both issues. Yet, more immediately, I still needed to deal with this search warrant. The cop in question was chomping at the bit to get it to a judge and go search for the usual stuff dope cops with warrants look for, namely dope, U.S. currency, packaging material, dominion and control items, and documents such as utility bills to establish residency at the place where the contraband is found.

I know that particular drill. Time is of the essence. Evidence disappears. I toyed with what Charlie just said. Then, it hit me. Although it's been consuming my thoughts, until now, I haven't fully comprehended what my fascination is with the O'Mara matter.

However, there are still issues I need to be sure I've adequately addressed before I decide. First of all, I'm a criminal prosecutor. That's all I've ever done as a lawyer, with the exception of a very brief, almost negligible, stint as a private practitioner. I'm a trial lawyer. But, I'm not a civil litigator or whatever those guys call themselves. Yeah, I handled a couple of personal injury cases. But, each of them settled. That's really not litigation. It's what Monty Hall does. It's called *let's make a deal*.

Besides, my physical turf is the wild and dry southern California desert, not some megalopolis like humid Houston. Sure, there are possible issues I'll have to resolve with the Board of Supervisors. But, I truly feel bad for the O'Mara widow and the loss she and her entire remaining family may suffer from for a long time to come. I can help them and know it. This isn't novel. This is how any caring prosecutor should feel about crime victims. Especially if the crime is cold-blooded murder. Not just DA's. We should all be touched emotionally. But, Texas isn't my turf. Like I said, I'm a desert rat. So, I continue to rotate back and forth, trying to do the right thing.

Please grasp something. I am married to criminal law just as much as I am married to my beloved soulmate, Molly. I still recall what they said during our first week in law school. Orientation. Our Dean described *lady law* as a jealous mistress. That may sound sexist. It may even be sexist. But, it's also a truism. Those were different times back then. There were almost no female lawyers or law students. So, law school was much more of a good old boys club. And, I learned about it the hard way on more than one occasion. I've been a prosecutor for a long time. I don't know who's really the more jealous mistress, the law or my wife. Probably the former.

Back to civil law. Civil is like a foreign language to me. While I don't mind learning foreign languages, and generally take to them like a duck takes to water, competing in this particular arena is something I haven't done before.

Civil is also something I have zero interest in, if you want the truth of the matter. Yeah, sure I'm a quick study. And, I have no hesitancy whatsoever getting up to speed on something I've previously known nothing about. I've done it before and I can do it again.

But, how much time will it take me to get up to speed on the O'Mara matter, if I say yes? Considering how tight my schedule is, I won't have any extra moments to begin with. And, here's an even more basic problem. Criminal law tends to be quick and action-filled, akin to a one night stand, at the risk of sounding crass. That's what I love about it. Please pardon my vulgarity, but, in a matter of speaking, it's sort of a *wham-bam-thank you-ma'am* experience.

Civil law, on the other hand, reminds me why normal people do not look forward to kissing their cousins. There's just no spark. A couple of the private attorneys I've spoken to freely admit civil cases tend to drag on forever. However, that appears to not be a concern for this particular one. That is, *if* I am getting the straight scoop from Owens. And, I already know Charlie has a hidden agenda he thinks I don't know about. That's what is really driving him to get me involved.

During previous discussions about civil law, I learned these are deliberate, ponderous affairs. They consume mountains of paperwork. I'm a tree hugger, not a tree killer. That is *not* synonymous with *liberal*. And, I prefer moving slightly faster than your garden variety glacier, unlike civil, which appears to slowly compete for last place.

Discovery in California criminal cases, by comparison, is simple. The defense needs to see the prosecution's evidence and vice-versa. In other words, you show me yours, I'll show you mine. Each side prepares and files a short boilerplate written request. Civil, on the other hand, breaks discovery down into a whole bunch of separate and specific components. Some of this is referred to as *paper* discovery. It includes a shopping list of individual discovery methods.

What do these include? There are General Interrogatories, Special Interrogatories, Requests for Admissions, and Requests for Production of Documents. In case you're wondering, these are not typos. Each one is capitalized because that is its official name. This also means lots of paper and lots of dead trees. Thoughts of this are not tickling my funny bone. Let's put it that way. When I say I'm a tree hugger, I am *not* kidding. Old farm boys tend to gravitate in that direction. I love trees. In addition, there's also *oral* discovery. This stuff also has its own name. They call it *Depositions*. Both sides attempt to learn the other side's strengths and weaknesses by employing each and every one of these ponderous discovery tools, as lawyers for all parties bill, and then bill some more, by the hour.

To me, it seems like much ado over nothing. With criminal cases, you always have a judge lurking nearby, just in case you need to settle a fight. But, in civil? You have to calendar any spat so a judge can resolve it later. Why? Simple. Lawyers like to argue.

As I contemplate what my former student is suggesting, I find myself unexpectedly amused. First of all, I don't see myself hauling boxes and boxes of documents into a courtroom, like a damned pack mule in a monkey suit. Frankly, I've always thought civil lawyers look a bit silly going to court lugging their large, boxy briefcases. But, beyond that, I can't logically explain why. Maybe I think mere preponderance of the evidence is just too easy a burden of proof.

Like any other self-respecting prosecutor, there's a perverse sense of pride in knowing the burden of proof we must meet is as tough as it gets. I have yet to try a case where a defense attorney doesn't remind jurors how high our burden of proof is, hoping the jury will agree and decide it's too high for any lawyer to meet; sort of like climbing whatever that really tall one is in the Himalayas. I think it's called Mt. Everest. They obviously do that because they mistakenly think jurors won't or can't reach that high. However, if that be true, then can any defense attorney please explain why they also whine about our prisons are bursting at the seams? Can't have their cake and eat it too, can they?

Nor, does the idea of having to convince only nine out of twelve jurors enthrall me in the slightest. No challenge. Sure, this is arbitrary. But, it's how I feel. Why would a major league baseball player choose to play Triple A, instead of being in the majors? What is this preponderance of the evidence nonsense all about anyhow? *More likely the allegations are true, rather than not true?* What in *the* hell does this mean? You prove your case if you convince the jury by any fraction beyond 50%? Not very compelling.

As a prosecutor, I'm used to dealing with more absolute borders. *Guilt beyond a reasonable doubt.* Twelve unanimous jurors reaching a guilty verdict. Beyond a reasonable doubt approaches a near stratospheric bar we are expected to hop over. This means each juror has to determine they feel *an abiding conviction to the truth of the charges* the defendant faces. A unanimous verdict means no wiggle room. No shades of gray permitted here. You can have any color you want as long as they are bright, bold swatches of black or white. The entire jury believes the defendant did the crime? If so, they convict. If not? The bad guy doesn't have to pay the piper. Period.

I pride myself on the quality of each case I present to each and every jury. The defense attorneys I battle in the courtroom, week after week? They remind me just how solid my cases must be, in order for my side to prevail. According to the opposition, in order to win, a prosecutor must meet the highest standard of proof in the civilized world. At least, that's what defense counsel tells jurors during closing argument, and at any other time they can sneak these words in. Why do I love hearing a defendant's mouthpiece say this? Here's why. Here is what they are saying. The standard of excellence we must meet is higher than their own miniscule courtroom burden.

To win, a defendant must create reasonable doubt. This means they must confuse at least one juror into not believing their client is guilty. Why is this such an amusing notion? And, what's with this highest standard of proof in the civilized world nonsense? Hell, if the standard is really *that* high, could these same armchair Generals please explain why there is so much prison overcrowding? Does this mean the USA has a bumper crop of great prosecutors? You tell me. I'll invoke the Fifth on this one.

What does proof of guilt beyond a reasonable doubt really mean? It means a juror who votes guilty must be able to say, hypothetically, on the morning right after the verdict, that they still believe the defendant committed any crime for which they were found guilty by that same jury of twelve former strangers. And, ditto for years later.

As I weigh this thought, an idea suddenly pops into my head. And, it makes me laugh. I've told you before I rarely lose jury trials. This isn't being braggadocios. I'm merely stating facts. It merely means I have an established track record for exceeding this lofty burden of proof elucidated by opposing attorneys in nearly each and every jury trial I've ever handled. They're the ones who bring this up, ad nauseum, during every trial, not me. So, if they're right, it means I've convinced each and every juror, in each and every winning case, my side has met our burden of proof. Therefore, if I've tasted success this frequently in this bare-knuckle arena, what does it also mean?

I suspect you've already figured this out yourself. It means proving a case by a mere preponderance of the evidence to only three quarters of the same number of jurors should be a far easier task than the one I am used to meeting, trial after trial, no? Arriving at this momentary epiphany, I more fully appreciate the need to listen to Owens' suggestion that I represent Dawn. Sure I love challenges. But, as I age, I also better appreciate the need to work smart, not hard.

Among other issues, I now understand something far more profound. Successfully representing a plaintiff should be much easier than what I do as a prosecutor, even if I've never handled a single, solitary civil matter in front of a jury.

My lack of prior civil experience now appears to be a wholly irrelevant thought. As the old saying goes, *parts is parts*. I'm confident failure in this new arena is not a serious option. I've won too many times meeting a far more strenuous burden of proof. I take a moment to ponder Charlie's promised tutorial. But, first, I must focus on a couple of other concerns.

First of all, Owens is right. Dawn deserves a good lawyer. Her husband's murder has irrevocably disrupted her entire family's life, and has done so completely. She will never again be permitted to return to how things were, no matter how hard she tries. She will still be a good person and a great mom. But, she'll never again be TD O'Mara's wife. Next, even though Charlie's client appears clearly liable, he nonetheless deserves an opposing attorney who is not some unethical dirt bag. If he's going to be found liable, it needs to happen, based on relevant law and facts.

I already know, from first-hand experience, you can win and do so handily, without oozing slime all over the courtroom. Lastly, as I try to objectively evaluate the situation, maybe, just maybe, I can convince the Board this trip is a true errand of mercy. If I can't do that, it's all over but the shouting.

Chapter 64

Her house was eerily quiet. Midnight was approaching and Dawn was getting ready for bed. As she brushed her teeth, she couldn't remove a punishing thought from her mind. TD was gone. He was *really* gone. She stared into her bathroom mirror, and started to cry again. Her eyes were welling up with tears. Slowly but surely they filled up. The salty discharge began running down both cheeks. First, as a trickle, it morphed into a steady flow. Dawn dipped her hands into the flowing water and began gently patting her face.

Looking into the mirror again, she saw a pitifully sad façade assessing her through its own pair of red, watery eyes she almost didn't recognize, even though the face she saw was unmistakably her own. She finished brushing her teeth between nearly suffocating sobs. She angrily asked God why He was doing this to her.

Dawn's crying jag lasted almost five minutes and filled her sinuses with mucus. She blew her nose and dropped the tissue into the waste basket. After changing into her pajamas, she knelt down beside her bed to say her evening prayers, as she always did. Yes, she was more than a little upset with her Creator. But, akin to a marriage, she was having a spat that wasn't going to lead to any divorce.

As she spoke, her upper lip trembled. She began weeping again, quietly at first, but increasing in both volume and intensity. Dawn beseeched the Almighty for help. Suddenly, she sensed a presence in her room. A hand placed ever so lightly on her shoulder startled her, even though intellectually she knew there was only one other person in the house. She wiped her face on her sleeve and tried to be brave. It was her youngest daughter Cecelia. Dawn had called her CeCe for as long as she could remember. So did any other people who really knew her.

"Oh Mommy. I'm so sorry," she began, as she joined her mother in what had been her private moment of grief. "You miss Daddy too, don't you?" Cecelia asked softly. She, too, was crying, but not as hard as Dawn had been. She tried to not cry, but started again. She scolded herself for not being a better role model for CeCe at a time like this.

"Oh CeCe, baby. I'm so sorry you have to see me like this. I'm supposed to be the strong one now," said Dawn, wiping her eyes on her now wet pajama sleeves. "I shouldn't be this weak. Should I now?"

"Mom, you're not being weak. We just both miss Daddy. He was our rock."

"Yes he was, baby. Yes, he was."

CeCe knelt down beside her mother and rested her head on Dawn's shoulder.

"Mommy?"

Cecelia only called Dawn that when she was feeling particular vulnerable. Mother reached around daughter to give her a reassuring hug. CeCe snuggled closer to her. Dawn hugged her even tighter, and Cecelia, which she now preferred, scooted even closer.

"Yeah, honey?"

"Are we gonna be alright?"

"What do y'all mean?" Dawn asked, as she got up and sat on the edge of her bed, allowing Cecelia to rest her head on her momma's knees. She began stroking her hair. Doing so was soothing, almost therapeutic.

"I mean what's going to happen to us...*without* Daddy?"

"You mean how exactly?"

"*Financially?*"

Dawn paused before answering.

"We'll be fine, CeCe...just fine," she lied.

In truth and fact, Dawn didn't have a clue what the real answer to CeCe's question was or even should be. After all, she'd never been a widow before. This part of her life's journey was on totally foreign soil. She'd have to just feel her way along.

She would continue praying to God for guidance before going to sleep tonight, and hope that He would provide her the answers she so desperately needed, but knew she didn't have right now. In fact, Dawn had never felt this lost, even as a teenager. She instinctively understood what her daughter was feeling.

CeCe gave her Mom a hug and a kiss, thanked her, and went to her own room. Dawn tried to pray again, sliding off her bed and back onto her knees. After contemplating for a moment or two, she began to pray.

"Lord," she said, "help me to do the right thing here. My life, at the moment, is a complete and total mess. The man I love more than life itself has been murdered...gunned down...like he was some kind of stray dog. I am nothing but a big pile of shambles."

She took a deep breath.

"But, I don't know why I'm telling y'all that. You already know all of it, don't you? So, why *am* I telling you all this? You, who are all-seeing and all-knowing, don't need little old me tellin' y'all stuff you already know. Do you?

Why did you do this to me? Please tell me what I have ever done to deserve this?"

Dawn cried some more, then got up and wandered around her big house. She wasn't done praying. But she needed to just be able to do something at the moment, other than conversing with her Deity. Seeking a mental distraction, she walked down to their den and turned on the TV, almost hoping she'd find TD in there watching some late night weather show. She caught herself, suddenly remembering what had turned her life upside down so violently.

She wasn't really interested in watching it. But, she needed something to get her mind off issues for a moment or two. She didn't even want to think about TD. And, she certainly didn't feel like talking to God, at the moment, either. She still felt betrayed. It wasn't that she didn't want to pray. She did. Dawn just couldn't decide how to properly organize her thoughts. And, she didn't know if this was the time to try having such a conversation. Right now, Mrs. O'Mara felt mentally vapor-locked. She also felt like her God had let her down by permitting TD's death.

Although she desperately needed the intervention of her one and only Lord and Savior, she also wasn't sure how to go about this. Dawn had talked to God daily for a long time. Right now, however, doing so seemed akin to learning a new language, for some reason she couldn't explain. Dawn didn't even know where to begin. Sitting in her recliner, she absent-mindedly thumbed her way through the channels, not even realizing when she had turned the set on. After going through every available channel, at least three times, she looked at one she'd seen before. Then, she looked again.

She decided there was a reason why God had brought her to the television, and to this specific lawyer's infomercial, in particular. A few fleeting moments ago, she had felt angry and sad, empty and adrift. Now, she had a purpose, and, once again, knew why she was supposed to wake up each and every morning again. This was not the time to be with TD again. Sure, nothing was ever going to bring her husband back to life. One day, they would be reunited in paradise. Just not yet. As the good book reminded, there was a time and a place for every purpose under heaven. To that sad end, she was becoming reconciled. But, a profound realization told her the Lord was now expecting her to do something…something *positive*…something *significant*…something *else*, and, to do that particular something *now*.

Up until that very moment, Dawn had vacillated back and forth on the subject of whether she should sue the dealership. She was positively certain they had killed her TD. Before, however, she wasn't sure what to do or how to do it. Previously, she really knew nothing about the legal system. Now, she was warming to the idea of suing the dealer for money. Lots of it. After all, they set the stage that got TD shot to death by the man she called *that loser piece of white trash.*

But, she wasn't sure if there was a meaningful point behind it, other than receiving the extra money it represented. She really didn't need the dealer's money. First of all, their repossession business had been very good to them financially. TD had wisely invested those proceeds by creating a totally diversified portfolio. Thanks to his advisor, this included real estate, stocks, tax-free municipal bonds and T-bills. Plus, his various insurance policies had a cash value totaling seven figures.

Dawn had never been superstitious. But, she was a devoutly religious woman. For a long time, she had also believed in omens. And now, she was convinced her stumbling across the commercial was not mere happenstance. No, it was not coincidence. She knew in her heart of hearts, everything in life happened for a reason. And, it was becoming clearer and clearer the reason she was going to do this was because it was time. In the meantime, she had to make a phone call. First, she said a short prayer.

"Meanwhile, in California, I was mulling things over."

Chapter 65

My eyebrows rose sharply, as I began reading the unexpected letter. I had just extracted it from an envelope with no return address and no sender's name. Normally, such a delivery would end its journey in my wastebasket, rather than on my desk. In the black and white world of impatient people, if a message is that important, I believe the sender should have the manners and take the time to say who they are on the envelope. If not, on my watch, it's instant round file time.

However, for reasons unknown, my curiosity somehow got the best of me. Maybe it was the postage. I could tell by looking at it that it hadn't originated in the United States. At first, I asked myself if it was one of those ongoing scams from Nigeria that are way too common. The lowlife bastards who do that crap have absolutely no shame or conscience. I opened the envelope, unfolding the cover letter, before I set it face up on my desk. I ironed out its creases with the heel of my right hand, so I could read it more easily. I may be perpetually busy. But, truth be told, nosy wins out, for me at least, quite easily.

"Dear Mr. Travers:" it began.

As I started to absorb this, I began to smile. What in *the* hell is going on this week? First, Dawn O'Mara tries to suck me into her case two thousand miles away. Then, Charlie teams up with her to do the same thing. Now this? The phone rang. I fumbled, dropped it and lost the connection, in the face of serious cursing.

I continued reading. In the meantime, however, my job is to work with the cops, so we can protect our community's public safety. But, instead, what's going on? Suddenly, people are coming at me like I'm some sort of damned mercenary?

What's next? I read the sender's name again, which was on the enclosed business card I was now staring at. Where did this guy come from and who was he? My immediate impulse was to wonder if he was some cartel kingpin. Please don't' get me wrong. I'm not suggesting that every person of Mexican ancestry is in the dope business, any more than those of Italian ancestry are in the Mafia.

But, I also know the problems the Republic of Mexico is having with drug cartels. As an editorial aside, that pisses me off. I love Mexico and it rips at my heart to think I may never see the place again, at least as long as its cartels haven't been exterminated, like cockroaches need to be. I glanced at Spanish words. As I said, I know Mexico is the home base of the cartels we're fighting here in the USA. This keeps getting curiouser and curiouser. If the cartels aren't calling on me, then who? The card read:

Pablo Francisco Gomez-Ayon

Secretaria de Comunicaciones y Transportes

Eje Central y Eje 4 Sur (Xola)

Ciudad Mexico

Republico de Mexico

Republic of Mexico? Secretary of Communications and Transportation? Mexico City? What in *the* hell is going on here? The letter writer invited me to telephone him. The stranger wanted to discuss two issues. Telephone him? Me? The guy who hates phones? Well, we'll just have to see about that, won't we? He said these concerns were important to each of us, and to our respective countries. Our respective countries? Wow! This guy suddenly had my attention. Apparently, he mistook me for a USA goodwill ambassador. And, who gave him my name in the first place? I could practically feel my radar quivering.

One issue immediately caught my attention. It dealt with the obscene profits being reaped by the murderous bastards running the drug cartels operating in Ayon's country. And, they have been doing that with seeming impunity for way too long.

I knew all about those jokers and thought of my own bounty. The message was quite cryptic. It referred to narcotics, and, in part, included the following partial line: "the narcotics slowly, but surely, threatening to destroy both of our great countries." The other topics were *illegal immigration* and *firearms*, the former from the Republic of Mexico to the north; the latter from the USA into Mexico. The wording made it appear the writer saw linkage between the three. I had to agree.

Today, I'm no longer able to separate dope and weapon smugglers from those with human cargo. Ayon appears to rely on impeccable sources of information. I've been in this business too long to not see that. His missive didn't include more details. But, Gomez-Ayon, or whoever he actually was, appeared to see the same linkage. He hinted a mutual meeting would be instructive. Assuming this guy really was the Secretary of Communication and Transportation, he appeared to be a man on a mission.

Impulsively, I grabbed my telephone. Yes, I hate phones. You know that. I know that. Why I did this is beyond me. But, this guy had my attention. My curiosity overwhelmed my will power. The spirit is willing and all that good stuff. And, I had no other way to reach him. Besides, I've already told you I am nosy.

So, I dialed. The phone began ringing. I heard a voice. And, it was a pleasant one.

"Secretariat de Comunicaciones y Transportes."

It sounded virtually melodious. Lyrical even. The cheerful female voice apparently had spoken these same words untold previous times. She sounded like she was on autopilot. Polite, professional and methodical. A woman in charge of something?

"Bueno. Habla Abogado Joshua Travers. Que siera communicarme con Secretaria Ayon, por favor."

(Thank you, Molly. Thank you. Thank you. Thank you.)

"Un momento, señor."

After a brief pause, another voice came on the line.

"Señor Travers? This is Pablo Francisco Gomez-Ayon," he said in perfect, unaccented English. "But, that's a mouthful, isn't it? Perhaps, that's why my friends call me *Pancho*."

He laughed, as he said this. Pancho is Spanish for Frank. Hopefully, our conversation would also be frank.

"Sir, your English is impeccable. I only wish my Spanish was even a fraction as good."

"It must be. You got past Maribela, didn't you?"

Ayon had a hearty laugh. He appeared to be a rather jovial sort. And, very self-confident. I didn't know him. But, I instantly liked the guy. I mean, really liked him.

"My English better be passable. Mater Dei High School, UCLA undergrad, and law school at Boalt Hall. Frankly, I'm still shocked I passed your bar examination. First try, no less. Pardon my French, but it was one gigantic bitch."

I laughed, declining to tell him, at this point, what I had called it myself.

"I hear you," I replied. "My former law school classmates still joke that a man named Joshua Travers is wandering around America somewhere, mumbling *'I could have sworn I passed the bar exam.'* The reference being, of course, that I…"

"…stole the poor man's identity?" He finished my sentence. "That is priceless."

Ayon roared again, seemingly overflowing with merriment. After a few moments, he got serious and spoke.

"Sounds like you had a bit of a fan base at your law school."

Ayon appeared amused. His glee sure seemed genuine.

"More of a lynch mob. Just some wise-ass friends of mine. That subject requires at least a couple of Negra Modelos. Maybe even a shot or two of

Herradura añejo. Maybe more. And, add a couple of Excaliburs. Not a conversation for a non-secure telephone line."

"So, you are an aficionado of Mexican adult beverages?"

"Shouldn't every adult be?"

We both laughed. I didn't even know this guy, but found myself really taking a shine to him. Interestingly, he completely ignored my comment about secure telephones.

"So, Mr. Ayon, to what do I owe this honor?"

"You mean my letter? And, yes, before I forget, this line is a very secure line, in case you're concerned. Yours?"

"It is. Yes," I added, referring to his missive.

"Joshua…I'm sorry…may I call you by your first name? By nature, I'm a very informal man. And, please, call me Pancho. Just never call me late for dinner…or adult beverages," he joked.

I laughed again, as did he.

"Sure you can. Joshua…Josh…Trav…JT…and, believe it or not, some of my really clever dope cops actually nicknamed me *Truth* a while back. And, there's a couple more from a defense attorney or two. All that is probably worth at least a six pack. Amazingly, some of those nicknames have actually stuck. So, take your pick, Pancho."

Ayon chortled again.

"Obviously, your officers know you. I'm told American cops are some of the more cynical people on the planet. Even more than our own officers here in Mexico. I actually saw that when I interned at the Alameda County DA's office during law school."

"Really? You worked at a DA's office?"

"Yes. Showering you with such monikers is both a sign of respect and love. And, to answer your question, as to why I sent you the letter…I'm assuming that's what you're referring to. How can I say this? Your reputation precedes you. It appears some of…"

Ayon paused. I wondered where he was going with this.

"Before we go further, I must have your assurances everything we discuss from this point forward is…how do your officers call it? I forget. 10-39, isn't it? 10-38?"

I laughed. He was wrong. But, he had also done his leg work.

"10-35? Sounds to me, jefe, like you have more than done your homework. Sure, 10-35, it is. Hell, us bein' lawyers and all, we could even label this *attorney-client* stuff."

Ayon got serious. He let a momentary pause hang in the air before he spoke more.

"Let me cut to the chase, as you Norte Americanos say. I know you to be a man of impeccable honor. Normally, I would not be satisfied with mere telephonic confirmation. Instead, I'd require a notarized affidavit attesting to what you have just orally promised."

"Wow, I am truly humbled, Pancho. You flatter me. I won't disappoint you."

"I know that. Yes, you are correct. I do my homework. My friends confirm a man with so many nicknames is not only loved by his friends but is also paid attention to by his enemies, no? Unlike you, I have but one modest nickname. And, I probably wouldn't even have it had I not been named after my Gran Tio Francisco. So, this tells me you are far more loved...*and noticed*...than I."

"My favorite uncle was also named Frank, may he rest in peace. His first name was actually Francis, I think. Named his only son Francis. Everybody calls my cousin Franny."

"Interesting."

I understood Pancho was probably referring to the bounties, rather than our respective late uncles. But, I wasn't sure. Since I could think of nothing to say, I replied "really?" That wasn't profound. But, he truly caught me off guard.

"Really, Joshua. You know I'm specifically referring to the bounty the Arellano Felix cartel placed, not only on your head, but on those of each of your drug interdiction officers and your beloved K-9's."

I listened, but said nothing.

"Keep in mind, I, too, have trusted informants. In other words, I'm talking about your entire team. That tells me you put the, how do you say that...put the hurt on them...on the cartels...the big *financial* hurt?"

I laughed.

"Yeah, we learned those guys take their profits very seriously and have zero sense of humor about it. *Plomo o plata* speaks volumes."

"You mean plata o plomo. Yes, doesn't it?"

"Got that ass-backwards, did I? What you just said might also explain why the ACLU filed their bogus racial profiling lawsuit against the California Highway Patrol."

"Hmmm...sounds like we both have been doing our homework."

We both chuckled again. I felt like Pancho and I were connecting.

"Joshua, you are a bright man. There are things I simply could not include in my letter to you. But, please understand something. I'm not a loose cannon indiscriminately firing balls here and there. I contacted you on behalf of my nation's President. Upon his own orders. The issue is of great, no *grave*, importance to both of our sovereign nations."

"Dope, illegal weapons and illegal immigration?"

"And, corruption. You know? Las mordidas. And, since we are flying below the radar, I trust you grasp the role your criminal street gangs play in this scenario?"

"You're singing to the choir, Pancho. Don't get me started on those two evil handmaidens...gangs and dope. Like ham and eggs. Or, green eggs and ham. FYI, I'm also aware our same American gangs, profiting from the illegal dope trade, are the route salesmen for your country's cartels. And, I believe they are beginning to factor illegal immigration into the equation, as well. It appears you also believe this."

"Si, como no! My sources make me proud, Joshua. You do your homework."

"So, how do I fit into this picture you envision?"

"There's a reason the cartel in question chose to not offer you la mordida, in order to make you go away. They, too, do their homework. They know it would be a monumental waste of their time."

"Excuse me?"

"That's why you have the bounty. Others, unfortunately, including many of our own law enforcement and military, even some in the prosecution and judiciary, have been bought off to look the other way. This rampant and growing corruption not only is tearing apart the very fabric of a county I love very much. It is also threatening to do the same with los Estados Unidos."

I paused before responding. Holy shit! Was this guy actually saying what I just heard?

"On this plomo o plata...I mean, plata o plomo...scenario, am I to draw any inferences about the ACLU lawsuit?"

"Well, let me put it this way...and, we can talk in more depth when we are not on the telephone...who do you think stands to profit the most, if your state kills its drug interdiction program?"

"My guess? Your cartels."

"But of course. And, remember, California tends to lead the way. If interdiction falls in the Golden State, it will eventually fall throughout all of your country."

"Plata o plomo, eh Pancho?"

"Precisely, my friend. Please understand something. Mexico not only views your country as a friend. We also count on America's inherent strength and integrity to function as a balance…*a counterweight*…to the cancerous corruption slowly threatening to absolutely destroy our magnificent land."

"I have to admit I am more than proud of how clean American law enforcement remains. Las mordidas are not part of the USA way of life."

"Not yet at least. The key word," Ayon noted, "is *remains*. The bad guys call their sinister plot *Operation Silent Border*."

Chapter 66

I vacillated. I was leaning toward agreeing to represent Dawn O'Mara. But, first, I had to talk to Molly and take her temperature on this issue. If she isn't behind something I am trying to do, it isn't going to happen. Happy wife? Happy life. Like I've observed before, period, end of conversation. I had two loose ends that needed tying. One was making a decision on the O'Mara matter. The other was convincing the Board of Supervisors I could comfortably leave the office in Stealth's hands for a few short weeks, if that was what I decided. To me, the latter was a non-issue.

The Board needed to understand this could be done, without destroying the office. Sometimes elected officials are short on personal courage. Also, I had to know I could do this without destroying my own career. The latter trumped the former. I don't mean to sound like a wimp. But, I have worked too hard for too long to become the DA to screw that up. In short, that wasn't going to happen. I would never throw that away.

It wasn't that I didn't have complete confidence in ADA Armendariz to step in. My concern was whether I could count on certain members of the Board to not use this as an opportunity to torpedo me. Not all of them were in my corner. I'll explain. One or two of them had the motive to do just that. Let's just say that memories of unpleasant events tend to linger longer in the minds of some folks than they should. And, some folks don't appreciate how seriously I take my law enforcement duties.

Both steps required Molly's involvement. We had just spoken by phone. I packed up any work I needed to bring home and stuffed it into my briefcase. I can't recall the last time I haven't brought at least one pending piece of prosecution home with me. Frankly, this job, this calling, is almost like a second skin. Even though mi corazon and I were going to engage in a potentially involved discussion, I saw no reason why today should be any different. As a rule of thumb, I've never found the need to bounce any ideas off other people, with the exception of Molly. Well, okay. Sometimes with Bennie. It isn't so much that I'm too arrogant to do so. I am simply very comfortable in my own hide and have never found decision making to be a tremendously involved event. Therefore, I choose to not overcomplicate my life.

With Molly, however, things are different. From day one, I've seen her as a person separate and apart, at the risk of repeating myself, from what I view as the rest of the thundering herd. Sure, I am still light years ahead of her in terms of formal education. But, this is never a reason for me to ever doubt the solidity and strength of her guidance and counsel. Molly has never steered me wrong, so my confidence in her is well placed. She has several honorary doctorates from the University of Common Sense.

As I explained to her one day, "never confuse post-graduate *classroom knowledge* with *raw intelligence*. The former you give yourself. The latter God gives you." And, He had given her that in spades, as well as a suffocating amount of horse sense.

My arrival at home was followed by my departure from the Porsche. In other words, I stopped and climbed out. Unlike my usual arrival home, our dogs didn't waylay me this time. I assumed they were on the other side of the property, probably chasing a rabbit or something.

Hopefully, they were eating the damned thing. Those cute-looking rodents with the lovable floppy ears caused so much damage to our cacti I have really grown to dislike them. There. I said it. The fuzzy little creatures I was so taken with, at first, I insisted we buy them rabbit pellets to eat, every time I bought bird seed for our flying friends, stabbed us in the back by beginning to devour our planted flora. Fauna was clearly winning that particular war. I am not pleased, to say the least.

Olfactory delights were already wafting from our kitchen. The aromas promised sufficient gustatory satisfaction. Experience is a reliable instructor, as is memory. I entered the kitchen through the garage and saw her in front of the stove. My bride was stirring something in a large frying pan. I smiled as I gave her my customary hug and kiss telling her I was home. I'd hang up my firearm in a bit. Later, after a discussion which lasted more than two hours, I finally felt prepared to make the right decision.

The decision wasn't particularly difficult. I'm sure I could have done it myself. But, Molly's thoughts and, more importantly, her underlying reasons she relied on, assured me I had chosen the right fork in the road.

"Prioritize," was the last word I recalled her saying. My call to Owens could wait 'til mañana. In the meantime, I needed to find a nice shady spot and do some air pollution with a cigar, while I supped an adult beverage. Maybe a Negra. Maybe not.

Chapter 67

As the maneuvering continued, I spoke with Charlie, he spoke with Dawn and, in turn, she spoke with me. Don't ask me how it happened, but the next thing I knew, I was deplaning at William P. Hobby airport in Houston. To some, life is a bowl of cherries. To others, it's a whirlwind; more like a sorbet, perhaps.

I looked for a familiar face. I saw Owens. He, in turn, spotted me. As some sort of a weird joke, he was holding what appeared to be a handmade sign in big block letters that read: "**THE *TRUTH* SHALL SET YOU, BUT *NOT* FOR FREE!**" And, he had purposely printed all the R's backwards. At least, I hope he did that intentionally.

Huh? To this day, I swear to God, I just don't understand Charlie's sense of humor half the time. I asked him to explain. He wouldn't. I asked again, in the car. The dumb-ass only smiled. I begged. He laughed. We drove to his office where I met Dawn.

On the way, finally giving up on getting an answer to my question, I explained my discussion with the California Attorney General's office. I asked him one more time to explain his goofy sign. He gave me one of his patented looks that suggested I do something anatomically difficult with myself. I've seen that look before. I gave up.

I told Charlie I obtained the AG's legal opinion concerning whether they believed any ethical issues prevented me from representing Dawn. Charlie told me he'd done the same thing with his own state's AG. Good man. He was on top of things, as usual. Both offices said they found no ethical impediment to my doing this. I was safe on that issue. Who in their right mind is going to argue with opinions from The Attorney Generals of two states as big as ours? He was just as concerned about his role, vis-à-vis me, as he was with mine. Each AG said a written conflict of interest waiver from all parties should adequately deal with any issues.

The meeting with Dawn went smoothly. Charlie was kind enough to allow us to use his conference room. We did so because I knew I could trust him to not do something underhanded, like hiding listening devices inside the room. Even so, we nonetheless swept the room electronically, in Owens' presence, to make sure Dawn was comfortable. I did that purposely, with Charlie right there, so she would better appreciate our level of longtime mutual trust. Once clear, he left us alone so we could talk privately, hypothetical attorney to client.

Dawn answered my questions and I answered hers. I reminded her I'd made no decision yet. And, I promised to let her know as soon as I did. Dawn already knew my work history as a trial prosecutor but not the sheer volume of cases it entailed. In spite of her independent research, she was quite surprised to learn my actual quantity of cases. When you've been doing this as long as I have, the numbers just keep piling up. Seemingly impossible goals quickly become very reachable ones.

She learned how much more difficult it is for a criminal prosecutor to obtain a favorable verdict than it is for a civil litigator. We discussed the burdens of proof and the number of jurors one is required to persuade in each setting. I explained my envisioned role for each team member: two lawyers, an investigator, a paralegal and a law clerk. Lawyers would supplement one another. Each of us fulfilled a separate function. And, I would be the first courtroom chair, even though I was working through the Texas lawyer's license. Dawn was a bit taken aback. Apparently, she expected me to do all the work myself. I explained the division of labor for any legal team. Each of whom was also present. I added I didn't have a Texas license. Once the lesson plan was over, Dawn seemed satisfied. I explained I would utilize Gilbert's Texas bar license because I didn't expect to practice law in Texas again, other than for this one particular case.

She received a cram course in civil procedure, thanks to Owens quick seminar during our drive from the airport. Included subjects? Discovery. Law and Motion. In Limine Motions. Trial. Voir Dire. Evidence. Jury Instructions. And, last but certainly not least, Opening and Closing Arguments.

"So, people" asked Dawn, feeling practically buoyant. "Where do we go from here?"

I promised I'd be in touch soon.

Chapter 68

By the time I returned to California, I had already met with my tentative trial team, thanks to Charlie. As noted, Owens didn't attend our meeting. Doing so would have violated the attorney-client confidentiality privilege. Not on my watch. Or his, either. But, his conference room was sure convenient. Civil practitioner Harvey Gilbert, our other lawyer, attended my meeting with Dawn, as did the rest of the team. Harvey would be what's called second chair. I was first chair because…*well*…I insisted I be.

Retired cop Buck Masters was our investigator. Norma Melendrez was our paralegal. Our law clerk was a fresh-faced kid named Jennifer Walling. Seeing her innocent glow almost took me back to law school. It was like another lifetime ago. *Déjà vu all over again*, as Yogi Berra once observed.

I asked each of them to provide me with a written breakdown of their legal experience. I did the same for them. We traded contact information so we could communicate. The meeting turned out to be even more productive than I had hoped. And, I explained to them how much I valued punctuality and candor, both for me and my employees, as well as any clients. As a hypothetical example, I explained 8 am meant eight o'clock in the morning. It didn't mean 8:02 or even 8:01. USMC…hoorah!

After saying this, I methodically asked each proposed member if this created any problems for them. This was the time to lodge any objections and we could go our separate ways with no hurt feelings. There were no dissenters. I liked this group. Dawn also attended the meeting and raised no objection to anyone who was to be part of our tentative plaintiff's team, including me. Essentially, this meant the only remaining issue was for me to make a decision.

Without any warning, Dawn ambushed me with a sharp-edged question.

"Joshua, don't you think you're being a bit tough on everyone?"

"No, I don't," I said. "If we come into court screwed up, where we can't even agree on the correct time, I can guaran-damn-tee you the jury and the judge are gonna be far tougher on everybody than I am. Anybody know what a defense verdict is?" I asked.

"What's that?" she asked.

"Snake eyes," I said. "Nada Zip. Zilch. Zero…it means we've just gotten our asses handed to us. That's what it means. Same is true, whether we are talking about a criminal case or a civil case. It means we lost. And, the real loser is the client. That's you!"

I knew Dawn was religious and didn't like profanity. But, I had a point to make, early on, and wasn't there to sugar-coat anything. This was the time and place where any neoprene would need to meet the highway. I carefully explained everyone's role and followed that up with written job descriptions. No one had any questions. I explained the chain of command, i.e., Harvey reported to me. The rest of the team reported directly to him. I made sure everyone knew I also had responsibilities in Solita County. If I accepted Dawn's offer, this meant Harvey would have to fill more of my shoes than he otherwise might. Sgt. Buck said he had no issue with *not* having anyone to supervise.

"Oh, and one more thing, boys and girls," I added.

"What's that?" asked Norma.

On a scale of 1-10, I had already privately rated her as a nine-plus, beauty-wise, without giving it more than a single second's thought. But, I kept my thoughts to myself. Purely a clinical observation. I was quite happily married and planned to keep it that way.

"Norma, I haven't chosen a second in command after Harvey. It's not that I don't think you, or Buck, is up to the task. It's just a cleaner chain of command if all of you report to him. It's a small enough team. It should work fine. Otherwise, it's just too vertical."

I addressed the entire group.

"Norma and Buck both have different jobs. And, frankly, this will keep you more than busy enough. You don't need the added complications of supervising someone else. And, your work needs oversight by a lawyer. So, Harvey's the logical choice."

"I understand," said Norma, with a grin on her face. "No problema."

"No grumbles from me, either," said Buck. "I chose to not seek any promotions as a cop beyond sergeant because I enjoyed working the streets far more than I'd enjoyed being someone's behind a desk boss. Besides, I had to get direction from a DA on the legal issues back then. Same difference here. A lawyer's a lawyer's a lawyer."

I nodded. "And, Jennifer," I said. "Both Harvey and I have been where you now are. You're still in law school. Someday, I suspect you'll be a damned good lawyer. But, you're where we were, when we were where you are. So, I suspect you're hanging on by your fingernails. This ain't criticism. Just an observation. Been there, done that."

Jennifer blushed, but said nothing. I laughed. Harvey nodded and smiled.

"Hey kid, don't be intimidated by my comments. We learn to walk long before we learn to run. That's all I'm trying to say. Nobody expects you to be making any appearances before the U.S. Supreme Court this week."

I smiled. This time, so did Jennifer. The rest of the group laughed. She did too. Dawn smiled but had no comment.

"One more thing," I added.

Everyone quickly quieted down.

"Harvey and I have already researched this next issue. Special prosecutor."

"Which is what?" asked Dawn.

"Special prosecutor? Texas law permits the appointment of a private attorney to be a special prosecutor in cases where misconduct by government officials is suspected."

"How does that impact us here?" she asked.

"Simple. A confidential informant has already been interviewed by Buck who claims he has knowledge that one of the grand jurors committed misconduct by not recusing himself from the Walker prosecution."

"I know who that dirty bird is!" Dawn spat.

I merely smiled, but said nothing. I could see Ms. Prim and Proper had a temper. Clearing my throat, I continued. Her outburst of near profanity was unexpected, at least by me. Perhaps we'd struck a raw nerve.

"Harvey Gilbert is a longtime private attorney in the Lone Star state. As such, he qualifies to be a special prosecutor. This would allow us to investigate whether the former grand jury was allowed to render an illegal no bill. It's my position the misconduct of one of those jurors and the outcome of the Walker investigation are inexorably intertwined. And, tainted."

I explained this meant they were so closely connected they couldn't be separated. If a grand juror corrupted the outcome, and a special prosecutor was appointed, we might show the investigation was so totally contaminated, we deserve a new grand jury.

"But, how can we trust this DA's office to do the same job the second time they messed up the first time?" Dawn asked.

"We can't," I said. "That's why we either go through the Texas Attorney General's office or the U.S. Attorney for the Southern District of Texas, where Houston sits. We ask them to appoint Harvey as special prosecutor. And…"

I grinned from ear-to-ear.

"…under his license, Harv appoints me as his *assistant special prosecutor.* We try to show malfeasance by the Walker grand jury resulted in a miscarriage of justice. If we do, then we ask the Harris County DA's office to recuse themselves and we seek a second indictment of Walker. If they don't do that, we ask a judge to boot them."

"How do we do that?"

"We show the investigation was shoddy and the prosecution wasn't any better because Billy Ray Fulgerson wasn't kicked off the jury before he was able to poison the whole damned thing."

Dawn smiled.

"Why in tarnation aren't you working for Harris County, instead of So...So...?"

"Solita County?" I asked.

"Dawn, you understand this is not a guarantee? And, I'm talking about the whole enchilada. Special prosecutor? New grand jury? Second criminal prosecution? Civil case? None of it's etched in granite. This is the nature of the beast called the legal system."

"Oh, I know. But, Lord, it's so refreshin' to have a prosecutor who appears more interested in findin' justice, than just shufflin' paper work."

"As long as you understand this," I cautioned.

Mrs. O'Mara said nothing. She merely patted her heart with the fingertips of her right hand. My guess is that she understood where I'm coming from.

Chapter 69

Once I returned home, I assessed which issue needed my immediate attention the most. Even though I hadn't made a decision on Dawn's request, I had already given Gilbert what he needed to begin the process of requesting special prosecutor status, just in case. I also knew I was in one of those not-so-rare time frames where I was triaging and simply doing the best I could do. Nothing would be gained, if I unduly stressed myself out on that particular issue. Mentally, I shifted into a more leisurely overdrive.

"So, Mol," I began. "Give me your read."

"You do mean on the DA issue?"

"Well, yeah. That and how a sabbatical in Texas would impact my professional life here, including present and future."

Molly thought about this for a bit.

"Pro bono," she said finally.

"Huh?"

"Pro bono. Don't big civil firms allow their junior associates to volunteer time for worthy causes? DA's office is the biggest law firm in Solita County. And, you're top cop. You can set a great example!"

"Yeah. I think so. But, how would I know? I'm just a dumb old county prosecutor."

Molly shot me a withering look. This would be a good time to say nothing.

"Well, you brag about being a pioneer. Be one then," she instructed.

I started to interrupt, but that only merited her famous wave of the hand. Little gal. Little but intimidating. She continued without missing a beat. I decided to applaud discretion, not valor. When it comes to research, no one is better than Molly. I was curious where this was heading.

"What better way to set an example for the rest of the public sector than to do something no other public attorney has ever done?"

I mulled that over. She suggested I go directly to Chairman of the Board Irving Baker and see what he thought. She explained what she meant. I should try to convince the Board to somehow designate this as an official function for Solita County. The ace I held was a straightforward quid pro quo trade. The Board would approve the trip, cover my expenses, and pay me my salary. In return, any attorney fees I earned would go directly into the Solita County General Fund, upon my return from trial.

As was her style, Molly merely looked at me after speaking, both waiting for and gauging my reaction. Her jet black eyes, sparkling in the sunlight, peered into my very soul. I momentarily contemplated what she said. Molly was absolutely right, even though she was proposing something audacious. She was telling me to do more than merely enter the lion's den. Her idea could put pubescent Solita County on the map.

She was directing me to beard the alpha lion of the entire pride. After all, Baker had been Chairman for more than seven consecutive years. He had been a fixture on the Board for nearly twenty. He'd done this long enough to practically be iconic.

If I could persuade Irv to support me, then the newcomers, Marquez and Jefferson, most likely would follow suit as well. Both had well deserved reputations for being political fence sitters. I suspected this was due to their political inexperience and attendant insecurity. Both should easily be swayed by Baker. In this regard, this just might be the double-edged sword I'd been looking for. Leave it to Molly. On the one hand, their inexperience would cause them to be cautious. Up to this point, any decisions by either of them smacked of this. But, it was also quite likely this would force them to rely on the voice of experience, to wit: one Irving Baker.

I decided to grab the bull by the horns. I picked up the phone and dialed Baker. I invited him and his wife up to our place for a barbeque. It turned out to be a very productive get-together. He and I enjoyed nice cigars with single malt scotch. By the time they left, Buck had assured me I had his vote too.

Since I had just rolled the dice successfully, I decided to push my luck one more time. I explained why I thought it was a good thing, PR-wise for Solita County, if I represented Dawn O'Mara. Baker surprised me again and said he agreed with my financial reasoning. Irv knew Charlie Owens and this, no doubt, contributed to his agreeability. The Chair was the Board's lynch pin. Whatever direction he leaned, a majority should follow.

I methodically explained my proposed role. I would function as a civil litigator and attempt to also be a special prosecutor. He somehow saw the visibility the case would give us, as a way of obtaining hard to get grant monies. He said it would put us on the map. It sounded to me like Irv wasn't against the idea of doing some chest thumping. Good man.

I wasn't sure I agreed, but decided this was not the time to argue the point. Doing so would not gain my position a single inch of turf. Besides being cheap, like me, Irving was also an inherently fair man. That part of it seemed to appeal to him strongly. He surprised me too, with the depth of his knowledge of the legal system. I didn't even have to explain what pro bono or pro hac vice meant. He knew I would have to practice behind the shield of Harvey Gilbert's Texas bar license. What really twanged his heartstrings as much as anything was my promise to donate all the attorney fees I earned to our county's General

Fund. Like me, Irv Baker didn't waste money. Now, I could make my decision with no loose ends.

Therefore, planning ahead, I went to speak with Assistant DA Armendariz. Like I've previously mentioned, Bennie and I go back to our early days in the Corps, same as with Charlie. I hired both of them as Solita County prosecutors. Excellent decisions. Because Ben had the good sense to stick around, he was the one who continued getting promoted, until he only reported to me, now that I was the actual District Attorney. So, in addition to taking Molly's temperature, I had to be sure we were in sync.

In case you're wondering who would have become the Assistant DA, had Charlie stuck around, frankly, I don't know the answer to that hypothetical. And, since I don't waste my time responding to hypothetical questions, you're wasting your time asking. I couldn't assume Benjamin was reading my mind. Therefore, if I did this Houston gig, I had to be sure he was ready, willing and able to take the reins while I was away. This wasn't going to take a lot of fine-tuning, as we each knew what the other did.

I didn't set any specific amount of time aside to talk with him. All I needed to do was to make sure we both were able to set enough time aside at the same time so we could discuss the important issues needed to insure the office continued operating properly.

This included stuff like who would fill in for Ben so he could fill in for me; who would fill in for that guy, and so on. Some folks would certainly have to wear more than one hat in my absence. Not too surprisingly, BA and I were both on the same page, in terms of who we believed needed to fill the various roles, if I did this.

God bless chains of command. I suggested…no, actually, let me correct that…*Stealth* suggested…we each write a list of how this should be done so we could literally compare notes. Anticipating this, I handed him my own list I brought with me and told him I wanted to see his the next day.

Like a Timex wristwatch, he gave me his as requested. Right on schedule. Some might think I'd be concerned that Armendariz would see my notes and simply copy them as his own. If anyone believes this, then all I can say is that they don't know Bennie.

Nor, do they know me either. First of all, like me, my second in command is his own man. He's a Marine, first and foremost. And, no one, including me, tells him how to think. Sure, he has to follow orders from me that he may not agree with. But, this doesn't mean he isn't capable of engaging in independent thinking. He does that daily. Trust me on this. Take that straight to the bank. When two people have known each other as long as we have, they tend to be on the same mental wave length.

So, when Bennie told me he wrote his own list, without even first glancing at the one I handed him, I had no reason to question his veracity. Yes, we agreed. But, as the old saying goes, great minds tend to do that on occasion. Modest ones too. Just not ours.

The important thing? We agreed on the major issues. And, I now knew I could take on this O'Mara project without ruining the Solita County District Attorney's office in the process. Public safety would remain intact during my absence. As would my peace of mind. From the halls of Montezuma to the shores of Tripoli, and all that good stuff. The few. The proud. The Marines. Yeah, yeah. I know. I digress. But, you get the picture. More importantly, Bennie got the picture too, so I knew the office would be in good hands during my absence.

Chapter 70

Shifting gears, I phoned Harvey Gilbert to see how things were progressing. Of course, I had official duties I couldn't ignore. So, please don't infer I was giving them short shrift. But, I needed to know what was happening on the Texas legal front. My curiosity was getting the best of me, and I needed to be briefed.

"Hey Harv. Josh Travers. What's going on with the O'Mara case?"

He explained.

"Shouldn't we hold off on the civil suit, until we see what happens criminally?"

"I'm not sure," he said. "We've got plenty of time to bring the civil matter to trial, if we file to toll the statute of limitations. Then, we can see what happens criminally. Once we know that, we proceed civilly. It's like separate sides of the same blade. Unless, that is, you see this differently."

For the uninitiated, the statute of limitations is a deadline within which a case must get to court. This includes doing things like filing a criminal complaint, commencing a preliminary hearing, beginning a jury trial, and so on. Its length depends on the type of matter and whether it is a civil or criminal case. To my knowledge, the only type of case with no such limiting statute is murder. If there is another one, I sure haven't found it. And, I have looked. If you know of any, I'd appreciate a heads-up. Call me. We're in the book. On second thought, ask for Bennie Armendariz.

"Huh? If we accomplish our objectives with the criminal case, and convict that jerk, then all we have to do civilly is prove Baron and company helped cause TD O'Mara's death, and how big a check they should write. Right, Harv? Maybe we should mull that over."

"Not really."

"Huh?"

"No, that's not what I mean."

Harv explained how far work on our civil case had progressed. We shifted topics from civil to criminal.

"So, Harv. Any word yet on the special prosecutor request?"

"Actually, yes, but let's deal with these, one-by-one, okay?"

I sighed. "Okay. Talk."

"First of all, as we've already discussed, the AG denied our request for appointment of a special prosecutor. I sought review of that denial and they denied our request to review their denial of our request."

"Yeah…yeah," I said. "I know what we've already discussed. What I need to know, dammit, is what's going on. Do I need to pack my bags and head to Houston?"

"Well, that's what I'm trying to explain, Trav. The good news? U.S. Attorney has granted us special prosecutor status. In that approval, they will even deputize me as a special Assistant U.S. Attorney…"

I interrupted. "And?"

"If you'd quit interruptin', maybe I could explain all this in a day or less."

"Sorry, I'm just on a tight schedule at the moment. Just jacked up a bit."

"Josh, you are always on a tight schedule. Take a pill," he joked. "After all, you are the same guy a Presiding Judge once threatened to hold in contempt if you didn't quit *overbooking* your act, right? You told me about that yourself. Like you, I, too, have good sources of information."

I laughed. "Hollow threat. He didn't even have the balls to tell me that to my face. I was still handling court-appointed defense cases at the time. He used the prosecutor as his messenger boy. But, we're off track."

"Okay. We won the battle. Now, we must decide if we go to war."

"Huh?"

"Josh, we have to decide if we first prosecute Johnny Walker. I don't think we should."

"Why? If we win, wouldn't that be *res judicata*?"

"First of all, the burden of proof is far less civilly. And, if we nail Baron on the issue of liability, we'll have to present evidence of Walker's shooting of O'Mara. That'll give us two bites of the same apple."

"Huh?"

"I'm painfully aware of your repeated admonitions that you don't try cases in the media. But, it sure wouldn't hurt to have a nice civil verdict behind us before we convene a grand jury."

"Lemme think about that, Harv. But, what you're sayin' does make sense."

I had another thought.

"Harv, should we file a federal lawsuit and consolidate both actions into it?"

"Dunno. Let me research that and get back to you. Pros and cons either way. Federal would be fast-tracked because it involves civil rights. But, it also means convincing ten jurors unanimously. In Superior Court, it's only nine of twelve."

"You've already filed the lawsuit in Harris County Super, right? Should we decide to go federal, we can always file there and dismiss our Superior

Court action. Now, assuming we stay in state court, all we need to do is commence discovery, so we get this to trial before we run out of time, right?"

"True.

"How much time we got?"

Gilbert updated me. After agreeing on a timeline, we said goodbye, then hung up. Suddenly, an idea hit me. I quickly called him back.

"Harvey. Just had a brain storm. Send out a press release."

"Huh?"

"Send a press release."

"For what?"

"I'll bang one out and fax it to you. Basically, it'll do two things: (a) announce your appointment as special prosecutor, and, (b) say *why* you've been appointed. When you get what I send, put it on your letterhead and send it out verbatim. I'll even format it for you. At least doing this will set the record straight on what should happen to Walker criminally."

I hung up. Then, I called Baker.

"Irv. Looks like my potential time in Texas is going to be a much shorter stay than we previously believed."

"What's that supposed to mean?"

I explained. After I hung up, the smile from Gilbert's phone call was still plastered across my face. Following a brief interlude, unless something from left field hit me right in the kisser, it looked like I should have pretty smooth sailing.

Chapter 71

Harvey Gilbert and I spoke again. We decided tactically to try the civil case first, and do it in Harris County Superior Court. Although I thought we had a fair shot at getting it into federal court, if the end result would be the same, and would require more work, why waste time and energy contesting unnecessary jurisdictional issues?

Taking the path of least resistance didn't mean taking the easy way out. It just meant working smart, not hard, as I've said before. However, we did send out the press release announcing Harvey's appointment as special prosecutor and our intention to reopen the TD O'Mara slaying. We purposely didn't use the word murder to avoid being accused by any lawyer representing Johnny Walker of prejudicing prospective jurors. After him beating the rap the first time around, we were taking no chances on letting him skate on another technicality. He sure as hell wasn't getting two bites of that same apple.

The morning of trial was still a few weeks away. Chairman Baker remained true to his word. He spoke rather convincingly to fellow Board members Julian Marquez and Aretha Jefferson. Even my personal nemesis on the Board decided to not fight this. Irv also spoke to him, mindful I had previously convicted him of driving under the influence. I don't know what Baker said, but the guy was meek as a lamb. The Board would pay my full salary and cover my expenses, while I was so engaged in Texas. Amazing.

Jefferson, usually reticent, made the motion. I would be there on official business.

It was time for public discussion. An unethical defense attorney I've battled for years publically called me a Nazi. He called my trip a boondoggle. Marquez surprisingly declared him out of order and demanded he sit down.

"Sit down, sir. You are out of order!" bellowed a normally quiet Marquez, overstepping Baker's role as Chair. A smiling Irv said nothing.

Surprisingly, the normally obstreperous attorney meekly sat, amid a chorus of boos. He appeared stunned. He wasn't used to even senior judges speaking to him that way. After he sat, he rose and quietly left, soon thereafter. The Board was asked to vote. They voted. Marquez moved. Jefferson seconded. The Board unanimously approved. Soon, I would be on my way to Texas.

Chapter 72

arris County Superior Court Judge Clancy N. Henderson took the bench to call our case. His bailiff had just given his customary formal opening, requiring all in the courtroom to rise. The man in uniform intoned:

"…all rise and face the flag, the emblem of our Constitution, and remembering the principles for which it stands. The Superior Court of the State of Texas is now in order. The Honorable Clancy N. Henderson, Judge Presiding. Be seated and come to order."

After all assembled took our seats, Judge Henderson spoke.

"Calling the matter of Dawn O'Mara, et al, Plaintiffs, v. Lone Star Motorcars Inc., dba Deals on Wheels, Reginald Baron, et al, Defendants. Counsel, please state your names and make your appearances for the record."

I spoke first.

"Morning, your Honor. Joshua Edward Travers for Plaintiffs and each of them."

"Harvey Stuart Gilbert for Plaintiffs."

"W. Charles Owens for Defendants."

"Thank you counsel," said the judge. "Time estimate?"

"Ten days."

"Concur," said Gilbert.

"Stipulate," agreed Owens.

"Any preliminary matters?"

A shake of our heads was accompanied by the word *none* from each of us.

After a pause, Owens spoke again.

"Actually, I do have one motion."

"Counsel?"

"I just read an article in the Chronicle," he said holding up a newspaper. "An article says Mr. Gilbert just got appointed as special prosecutor. Says he might convene a grand jury to investigate possible juror misconduct concerning the no billing of Johnny Walker in the death of Tommy Deen O'Mara. He's the decedent at the center of this case."

"And?"

"I don't want any mention of this to get to our jury."

"So, what exactly are you asking me to do, Mr. Owens?"

"Three things. First, preclude them," he said, pointing at Gilbert and me, "from telling the jury anything about that, by way of jury selection, opening remarks, evidence, closing, and so on. Two, we need to know if the jury has read anything about this. Three, if so, has it prejudiced them in any fashion?"

"Counsel?" asked Henderson, looking at me.

I shrugged, as did Gilbert.

But, I added gratuitously, "polling the jury might stir up more than it's worth."

"Okay, here's what we are going to do. I'll grant the motion and poll the jury. But, before I do so, counsel is welcome to provide me with how you believe such an inquiry should be worded. Might this be a good time for a chambers conference?" asked Henderson.

"Can't hurt," I replied.

"Sure," said Owens.

"Okay," shared Gilbert.

Once we were in chambers, Henderson took off his judicial robes and hung them on the hook behind his door. He sat down behind his desk, motioning for all of us to sit. His baritone voice commanded respect. He was authoritative, but he seemed to be a gentle man. The judge was an African American male who appeared to be in his mid-to-late 50's. He reminded me of a cross between actors James Earl Jones and Morgan Freeman. Except for his graying salt and pepper hair, he still looked every bit as imposing as he did during his linebacker days at Grambling, where he earned second team All-America honors. And, yes, I research more than mere legal issues.

"Mr. Travers," he began. "Damn, you're a bit of a rock star, it appears," he said chuckling. "Let me see if I've got this right. You're an elected DA from California, but somehow you are here getting paid your salary, as if you were here on official business? Representing a client in a civil matter? And, you got a 5-0 vote on that from your Board of Supervisors, no less? Pray tell, how'd you pull that off?"

I blushed. "First of all, your Honor, I see you do your homework."

He laughed again. "That's called staying abreast of current events."

"If I did that, it would be called gathering intel on opposing counsel."

Everyone laughed. Just a bunch of good old boys enjoying one another's company. He waited for my answer. Nice focus. I like that in a judge. It means some defense counsel isn't likely to get away with blowing smoke up his ass. I answered.

"Yes and no, judge. First of all, I was appointed, not elected, to fill the slot our recently deceased incumbent held for many years. His unexpired term has two years left. So, I will face election then. But, yes, I'm here and getting paid to do so. Long story. Too long for this time slot."

"I'll bet," said Henderson, laughing again.

He was still unaware of the request of Harvey Gilbert to be appointed special prosecutor and the recent approval of that request by the U.S. Attorney's office. For tactical reasons, Harvey and I had decided to keep that information confidential, appropriately treating it as attorney work product. Now, it was out, thanks to the press release. Following some obligatory haggling, the four of us, lawyers and court, agreed on the wording the jury should hear regarding Harvey's appointment as special prosecutor.

"So, Charlie," asked the judge. "Why hasn't this case settled? You do realize the horrendous exposure your client is facing, don't you?"

We were off the record. This meant the court reporter wasn't present, by mutual agreement. This allowed everyone to speak far more informally than attorneys and judges usually speak, even in chambers. If we needed the reporter, the judge could summon her.

"Clancy, you're singin' to the choir on that one. It's a sore subject, to say the least."

It was obvious from the casual way Henderson and Owens spoke to one another, they were well acquainted. I decided to not even attempt to gain that level of familiarity in the short two weeks this trial was expected to last. I honestly didn't know the man. To be that informal would be disrespectful. This wasn't about fear. It was all about manners. I knew the facts and the law would more than speak for themselves. I didn't need to do any apple polishing.

Plus, Harvey was also a local. So, I wasn't real concerned about getting home-courted. Especially by Owens. Charlie hit hard, but never below the belt. He didn't have to foul. His legal punches were generally lethal for opposing counsel. Gilbert had already assured me we were on solid legal ground and could expect the judge to make tight, crisp decisions, based on what the law required him to do. I'd already carefully reviewed Harv's legal research and agreed.

Buck Masters had also assured us the case was factually healthy. We didn't see any visible land mines we needed to avoid. I had plenty of confidence in our assembled team. This made me more than comfortable delegating needed work to each member of it. I liked the way everything and everyone meshed together. So did Harv.

"So, Mr. Travers, I've read your complaint. The first allegation: DPS, specifically by and through its Department of Motor Vehicles, administratively sustained the complaint you guys filed, posthumously, on behalf of the late Tommy Deen O'Mara. You claim Deals on Wheels committed fraud in connection with certain representations they allegedly made when they hired him?"

"That's right. Fraud in the inducement. We believe the finding by an official state government agency charged with the responsibility of regulating that type of occupational license adds credence to our allegations. And, it's also res judicata," I added, almost as an afterthought. Henderson's eyebrows rose.

"They on your witness list?"

"Yes sir."

I pointed to their name, and number, on our list. Charlie frowned.

"Thanks. Okay, give me your Readers Digest version on all this, Charlie," asked Henderson.

"Since we are off the record, let me be candid. My client is stubborn. He's penny-wise and pound-foolish."

"So," said the judge, "Reggie thinks he knows more than you, does he? Thinks he can't lose? And, on top of everything else, he's too damned cheap to settle?"

I was beginning to understand that the Houston legal community has that same small town feel that I was used to back home. The population numbers might be far higher. But, the relevant players all seemed to know one another.

"Basically," replied Owens.

"Mr. Travers," Henderson asked. "Y'all agree?"

"He speaks the truth, judge."

"Got no choice, but to do that," laughed Owens. "This cantankerous SOB trained me," he said gesturing toward me with his thumb.

I also laughed. Henderson merely looked at us. He appeared to be studying both of us, like he wasn't sure what Charlie was talking about or why.

"You as big a pain in the neck as this guy?" Henderson asked, hooking his own thumb in Owens' direction.

"Bigger," I said.

We all laughed.

"Here's what we need to do," said Henderson. "Charlie, I don't want to see you getting sued by your dumb-assed client when he loses. So, before we start pickin' a jury, I'm gonna question him, on the record, as to what, if anything's, been done to try and settle this case. I'm also gonna find out why he won't budge and let him tell all of us. Also, on the record. So please be specific."

Picking up his phone, he asked the bailiff to bring Reggie Baron, his court clerk, and the court reporter into chambers. As soon as everyone was seated,

Henderson called the session to order and had each lawyer again identify ourselves for the record.

"Also, let the record reflect Reginald Baron is present. Here's what we are going to do. First of all, it's my understanding we aren't going to settle this matter and will proceed to a jury trial. I need to hear from everyone, including Mr. Owens and Mr. Baron, as well as Plaintiffs, as to why this hasn't settled. That's assuming, of course, I have my facts right. The record should further reflect lead counsel for Plaintiffs, Mr. Travers, has represented to the court that he'd be willing to discuss a settlement, as long as any such conversation isn't unilateral."

I nodded, then added "that's correct, your Honor."

Baron pretty much reiterated what Owens told the judge. In short order, we could all see spending more time on this issue was a waste of time and energy for court and counsel alike.

"Mr. Owens?" asked Henderson.

"You heard my client, judge. Frankly, there's nothing more I can say."

"Okay then," said the judge. "Let's be back in court at 1:30 today to begin Voir Dire. Any in Limine motions, counsel?"

A shake of the heads by each counsel.

"Nothing, other than what we've already filed," I said. "Unless your Honor has any questions, I believe our moving papers speak for themselves."

"Same as to any of our filed motions," said Owens.

"None? We're off the record."

Chapter 73

As soon as those present in Henderson's courtroom sat, the judge spoke. Looking around, he noted prospective jurors appeared to fill his entire courtroom. Nearly every seat in the spectator gallery was occupied. And, on trial days, jurors sat in those seats, as members of the jury panel, so the lawyers and judge could select twelve regular jurors and however many alternates court and counsel decided to add as a backup, in case any regulars had to be excused from jury service, once the trial commenced.

That was good, the judge observed. It meant we were likely to select an entire jury, plus alternates, without having to bring in more prospective jurors from another panel. He quietly conferred with his clerk to determine how many jurors were here. She counted, then told him 86 were confirmed. The clerk further informed him 98 summonses were mailed by the Jury Commissioner. He directed her to talk to him later about the possible issuance of arrest warrants for those who failed to appear.

"Ladies and gentlemen," he began. He ran his fingers over the top of his thick wooly shock of closely clipped hair. "I'm Judge Henderson and this is a civil matter entitled Dawn O'Mara, et al, Plaintiffs, vs. Lone Star Motorcars, Inc., dba Deals on Wheels and Reginald Baron, et al, Defendants."

He also read the case number. Why did this really matter to the prospective jurors? It didn't. Henderson was just making sure he was keeping the record clean, just in case any appellate court was asked to review his work. Meticulous judges rarely get reversed. As Henderson spoke, four more people entered the courtroom and sat down. Henderson stopped talking, turned to his clerk and nodded. She asked the remaining jurors to identify themselves. One by one, they stood, gave their names and sat down.

"Madam Clerk, please call the first eighteen names," he directed.

Henderson told us he was glad we had previously agreed to a six-pack method of selecting alternate jurors. Doing so speeded up the selection process considerably. The selected twelve in the rear two rows of seats in the jury box would be designated regular jurors and the chosen six sitting in front of them, or the *six-pack*, would be our alternates.

They would join the regulars to deliberate the outcome of this case, but only if any of the regulars were excused, once they were empanelled. As the clerk began calling names, she continued reaching into the wire mesh rotating cylinder, which almost resembled a symmetrical colander with a hinged door. It contained slips of papers with names of each prospective juror. Eventually, eighteen names would be called. We would choose twelve regular and six alternate jurors from this group.

"Ladies and gentlemen; I mentioned earlier this is a civil matter. Mrs. O'Mara and the other Plaintiffs are suing Mr. Baron and the other Defendants. The allegations are Defendants and the agents for Defendants caused the death of Mrs. O'Mara's late husband, Tommy Deen O'Mara. It is also alleged they committed fraud in their hiring of him to do a repossession. Plaintiffs further claim this resulted in his ultimate death."

Henderson read the caption of the complaint, verbatim. Next, he read the charges.

"Plaintiffs are asking for both compensatory damages and punitive damages. I'll instruct you on the relevant law defining what those are later in the trial. My job is to tell you what the law is and to rule on any evidentiary issues.

Henderson paused and peered around to see if the jurors appeared to be absorbing this. They seemed attentive. He then continued.

"Your job, as judges of the facts, will be to receive evidence and apply the law I give you, in order to decide this case's outcome. This will require you to listen carefully to testimony, and review anything else I tell you is evidence. You must follow the law as I instruct you. Note taking is *strongly* encouraged," he emphasized.

He gave one of his rare courtroom smiles, took a sip of water and continued.

"The next part of the trial is jury selection. It goes by a pair of French words: *Voir Dire*. They mean *to speak the truth.*

Henderson explained the purpose of Voir Dire, telling them this meant picking a fair and impartial jury. Next, he asked general questions to determine if anyone felt they could not be fair and impartial to all listed parties.

He carefully listed the names of each of the parties and all witnesses provided him by counsel. When he asked if any of them knew anyone connected to the case, one of the jurors raised their hand. He acknowledged her.

"Juror number 11. Yes ma'am?"

"I don't *know* him. But I know *of* him?"

Her answer sounded like a question. Her voice rose at the end of the sentence.

"Who's that?" he asked.

"That attorney over there."

She pointed toward me. I began to feel discomfort.

"The good lookin' one with the curly salt and pepper hair," she said.

She began to blush. I did too, quickly pretending to be reading a document.

"And, how do you know him?"

"Seen him on TV. He's that California DA representin' the Plaintiffs."

I looked up, displaying a poker face.

"Any reason why you can't be fair and impartial to both sides, in view of that apparent knowledge?"

"No. Just thought I should mention it."

"Thank you. Any others?"

Two more hands went up. Both Owens and I made notes. Henderson carefully questioned both jurors until he was satisfied they could be fair and impartial. I leaned over and whispered to Gilbert who nodded and wrote something on his own legal pad.

"Okay," said Henderson. "Plaintiffs get to go first, so, Mr. Travers? Mr. Gilbert?"

"Thank you, your Honor," said Gilbert, as he rose and walked toward the podium.

The judge was very informal, away from his courtroom. But, Harv already knew he ran his public domain with an iron fist, deftly secreted in a velvet glove. He knew the consequences of venturing too far away from the podium. Harvey promised me he wouldn't even try. Not in Henderson's courtroom, he said. He told me the story of the young lawyer who did that, without first obtaining permission. He made that mistake only once. Gilbert witnessed the carnage first hand. Without judicial fiat, you didn't do this, while addressing jurors or questioning witnesses. Doing so was strictly verboten, without prior judicial imprimatur. Outside the courtroom, they might be Harv and Clancy, even over a couple of beers. Inside was a different story altogether.

We believed we had a failsafe system in place. Harvey was to follow the basic outline we had prepared whenever he questioned jurors. Harv was a civil whiz. He wasn't a trial machine. Not yet, anyhow. Prior to determining if we would excuse anyone, following each round of questioning by him, we would confer and decide who stayed.

"Ladies and gentlemen," he began, "as Judge Henderson has already said, this is the portion of the trial we call Voir Dire. It's also called jury selection. Whether you hear any of the lawyers pronounce it *voor dyer*, *vwah deer*, or some other way, the end result is the same."

A juror nodded in agreement. Harvey smiled and nodded back. He was smooth. Gilbert was an inexperienced trial lawyer, but he sure had potential. That was obvious.

"This is jury selection. The object of the exercise is for all of us to search for the truth. We need twelve people who will be fair and impartial regular jurors. We also need an as-yet undetermined number of alternate jurors who can do the same thing, if called to replace any regulars."

Gilbert paused and looked at the first juror who said she saw me on TV.

"Mrs. Reynolds," he said, "you told us a bit ago that you saw Mr. Travers on television."

"Yes sir," said the grinning juror.

She appeared to be immensely enjoying the sudden attention. Was this her personal fifteen minutes of fame? People who enjoy jury duty too much tend to make me uncomfortable. Are they just friendly? Or, do they have a hidden agenda?

"And, you promised the judge you can be fair and impartial to both sides, right?"

"Yes?" she answered, looking a bit confused. Once again, her answer sounded like an inquiry. I was beginning to wonder if she was mentally challenged.

"You won't give our side any more or any less credibility, just because he's a DA, will you?"

"No sir."

Suddenly, a rogue thought hit me. This was bizarre. Here I am, practically a brand new county DA in California. And, I'm lead counsel in a civil case in Houston, even doing so with no Texas bar license. It made me wonder if I should write a book about it. But, I was woolgathering. This wasn't the time and place. I needed to concentrate. So, I pushed any stray notions out of my head, returning my full attention to the ongoing exchanges between Gilbert and this prospective juror.

"If you had to choose sides, right here and now, which side, if any, would you find it difficult to be fair and impartial for?"

"I don't follow," she said, slightly furrowing her forehead.

"Let's see if it helps if we do this numerically, on a 1-10 scale. The number *one* will represent being totally fair and impartial. You with me so far?"

"Yes?" she said, again with an inappropriately upward tilt at the end of her one word reply.

"And, the number ten signifies being totally unfair and partial. In other words, just the opposite. Okay?"

"Sure," she said.

"Like Judge Henderson already said, our side of the case is called Plaintiffs. The other side are Defendants. So far, so good?"

"Uh huh."

The court reporter spoke up. "Excuse me, your Honor. I need an understandable response."

The judge interrupted.

"Good point, Madam Reporter. Thank you. Mrs. Reynolds," Henderson began, "the court reporter is absolutely right. I should have mentioned this earlier. Questions calling for a *yes* or *no* answer need to be answered with a *yes* or a *no*. Saying *uh huh* or *uh-uh* is very confusing to the reporter, and to the typist who later has to transcribe what has been said here. So, your answer is...?"

"I'm sorry," the juror repeated. "*Yes*?"

Dammit, she did it again. But, the judge didn't call her on it.

"Thank you. Same rules apply to everyone who speaks in this courtroom. Is that clear to everyone?" he asked, as he surveyed his courtroom. "Mr. Gilbert?" he directed.

"Clear to me, your Honor," kidded Harvey.

Henderson said nothing. He didn't have to. His frown and narrowed eyes spoke volumes. No absolution, despite them knowing each other way prior to Clancy getting his judgeship.

"Sorry, your Honor," he said, somewhat chastised, as he respectfully nodded toward the judge. "Mrs. Reynolds. Where would you place Defendants?"

"I dunno," she said. "Maybe a two or a three."

"Really?" he said. "And, Plaintiffs?"

"A four...maybe a five."

"Why?"

"Don't you guys have the burden of proving your case?"

"Yes, but..."

Henderson interrupted, as I gritted my teeth. This dullard would *not* be a juror. She is out of here!

"Sorry, Mr. Gilbert. Let me intervene, if you don't mind."

Gilbert merely gestured to the bench, as if to say *go ahead, do my job, too.*

"Ma'am, you are confusing burden of proof...which is Plaintiffs' job...with your duty as a juror to be fair and impartial to both sides. Both sides have an absolute right to expect your unconditional impartiality. Got it?"

I made a note on my own legal pad in large bold block letters. **DUMBER THAN A DAMNED BRICK! DUMP HER!!** As Voir Dire continued, the first juror was excused, at Plaintiffs' request. It was number eleven, Marcie Reynolds.

After her removal, jury selection continued, akin to a tennis match. Both sides alternately excused jurors, or, declined to do so, as our respective turns arrived. After a little more than a day, the judge had sworn in twelve regulars and six alternates. Is quick jury selection better or worse than doing it slower? I don't know. I'm not really sure if there is a difference. I'm sure that jury consultants will have differing opinions on this. But, that's what they do for a living. For me? I'm not sure if it makes any difference.

Meanwhile, both groups took their separate oaths to do their respective jobs.

Chapter 74

Henderson looked right at me. We previously told him I would deliver Plaintiffs' opening.

"Opening Statement, Plaintiffs? Mr. Travers?"

I stood, but said nothing. Henderson turned to address the jury again.

"Jury members, this is the part of the trial where lawyers for both sides can give their Opening Statements. I say *can give* because they may or may not do so. This is where they can tell you what they believe the evidence will establish. This isn't the time for argument. What any lawyer says is not evidence, unless I say it is. Mr. Travers?"

I picked up my legal pad and walked to the podium, turning toward the bench before addressing the jury, as I routinely do. Lawyers learn quickly to not ignore the judge. This includes making sure to get their permission to enter *no-man's land*.

"Permission to enter the well, your Honor? I think better when I'm moving."

I grinned. Henderson didn't. Instead, he frowned and scratched his head. The judge seemed to be pondering something. He paused an inordinately long aggregate of time, before speaking again.

"Normally, Mr. Travers, I insist counsel remain at the podium. However, as long as you confine your movement to the area right in front of the jury box, I doubt this will disturb the conduct of our trial. If it appears to do so, I'll tell you. Immediately. Otherwise, you're on safe ground. Same goes for all counsel. Proceed, sir."

"Thank you," I replied, before turning my attention elsewhere.

"Your Honor," I began again, "Madam Reporter, Madam Clerk, Mister Bailiff, esteemed opposing counsel and members of the jury. On behalf of my clients, the estate of Tommy Deen O'Mara, Dawn O'Mara and any other survivors of Mr. O'Mara, I thank you all… or, should I say y'all?"…for the opportunity to present our case." I said, breaking into a somewhat mischievous grin.

A voice from the spectator gallery said "all y'all. Plural." Henderson remained impassive, but quickly addressed the unsolicited speaker. Owens rolled his eyes. Some people laughed.

"Sir," he began. I will admonish you, but one time. Don't do this again. If you do, I will hold you in contempt of court. You can spend the next five days in jail. Understand?"

I didn't turn around to look, and frankly, since I didn't recognize the voice, I didn't care who said what they said. I wasn't alone. Neither did any other the other lawyers in the courtroom. Participation from the peanut gallery is never encouraged. A courtroom is more akin to a formal Broadway theater or an opera, than a night club with stand-up comics and boozed up patrons that like to heckle the guy at the microphone.

The meek voice replied "yes sir, your Honor. Sorry sir."

As soon as Henderson nodded to me, I continued without missing a beat. I was on a roll and needed to maintain my momentum. An entertainer can't afford the luxury of permitting the audience to dictate performance.

"As his Honor has already said, this is Opening Statement. What I say now is not argument. Nor, is it to be viewed by any of you as evidence. This portion of the trial allows me to tell you what I believe Plaintiffs' evidence will prove.

I paused and stroked my chin with the middle knuckle of a forefinger.

"Think of this portion of the trial as a roadmap."

Some of the jurors noticed my legal pad was still at the podium. I could tell. They were looking at it, not me. I pretended to not notice. I had not picked it up or even glanced at it. Some old habits are harder to break than others.

"And," I continued, "this is what I believe the evidence will tell you."

As I spoke, Dawn had begun to quietly cry, as she sat at her place at counsel table.

"On approximately February 26, 1994, Tommy Deen O'Mara was co-owner of E&A Recovery with his wife Dawn O'Mara, seated over there."

I gestured toward her.

"He was hired by Deals on Wheels to do what should have been a very simple repossession; the kind Mr. O'Mara had previously done hundreds of times, and quite successfully, I might add."

I paused and cleared my throat, taking a small sip of water from the paper cup I'd set at the edge of counsel table when I stood up. I drank not so much because I was thirsty but from years of doing this. Force of habit? No, it was more like a prop.

"But," I continued, "this turned out to not be the clean deal...*the fresh one*...Jake Crenshaw promised him. Crenshaw was manager of that used car lot. In his role, he functioned as agent for Reginald Baron and Lone Star Motorcars, Inc., at Deals on Wheels, a small part of Mr. Baron's *vast* auto empire," I emphasized.

Owens fidgeted in his seat. He didn't object, although I expected he would.

"And," I continued, "this all happened a few short days before Mr. O'Mara's needlessly tragic death. Crenshaw hired him to repossess a vehicle, with an overdue note, from one Johnny Walker. This debtor lives over on Berwyn, right here in Harris County. Witnesses will tell you that residence is right outside of Houston city limits. They will give you its precise address."

Pausing to take another sip of water, I glanced at the jurors before resuming my presentation.

"Here's the problem. That so-called fresh deal wasn't fresh at all. Crenshaw failed to tell Mr. O'Mara the truth. In fact, he flat-out lied to him. And, the truth was simple. Crenshaw had hired at least three other repossessors to do the same repossession of the very same truck, without telling anyone there would be other repo men involved trying to repossess the same exact pickup truck."

I paused a moment, to collect my thoughts. I was also studying the jury to see how they were reacting to what I was saying. One or two appeared to be casting unhappy-looking glances toward Baron who was sitting where he was supposed to be, right next to Charlie at counsel table. Satisfied by that reaction, I continued.

"Unfortunately, by the time the late Mr. O'Mara arrived at the Walker residence around 3:30 a.m., at least two other repo men had already stirred Walker up. Was it two? Three? The witnesses don't agree 100% on that. But, regardless, by that time, an angry Johnny Walker was hiding in the shadows with his high-powered rifle, like a Mafia hit man."

Owens jumped to his feet. "Objection. Improper Opening Statement."

Henderson shook his finger at me. "Mr. Travers, you know better. Sustained. The jury is admonished to disregard the reference to any Mafia hit men."

I continued.

"Sorry, your Honor. He shot our victim in the back, doing so as Mr. O'Mara was lawfully backing up to tow away Walker's truck he was there to repossess. A mortally wounded Tommy Deen O'Mara drove off, crashed into a nearby ditch, in front of the local DPS office over on West Canino. And, there, he slowly bled to death."

A gasp was heard from one of the female jurors. I glanced in her direction. She appeared to be crying. At counsel table, Dawn was now actively sobbing inconsolably. The judge glanced down at her.

"Counsel," he asked generically, although I knew the question was directed at me, "would this be a convenient time for our evening recess?"

Chapter 75

Once we returned to our reserved conference room at the Hilton Houston Post Oak, Dawn began profusely apologizing to me for the third time. I had assured her earlier she had done nothing wrong. But, this didn't stop her from asking for forgiveness again.

"I am so-o-o sorry," she said. "I didn't mean to make the judge stop court early."

"Don't worry about it. Your emotions are genuine. Anyone with a brain can see that. And, if it ends up causing some delays, that's the way the cookie crumbles. Judges get paid to deal with the pain of victims. And, if some of the jurors feel your pain, that's all the better for us. If they all feel the way you do, far be it from me to stop them. Be respectful, but be real. You are being very real, Mrs. O'Mara. I know what I'm saying. I've been doing this a while."

"So," asked Norma who wasn't in court, "other than that, how is the trial going?"

"Well," I said, "we're only in my Opening. I was probably somewhere between one-third to one-half way done. It was a good time for a recess. While I certainly wouldn't wish Dawn's grief on anyone, the timing was perfect."

I grinned.

"How do you mean?" asked Jennifer.

"I was tired. I'm dragging my ass, Jen. I'm in trial mode. So, that means I'm burning up energy 24-7. When I'm in trial, I don't sleep worth a damn. I'm up before the chickens and I'm out of energy long before the night owls are even beginning to leave their roosts, even though I keep tryin' to work. This means I can hopefully get a fresh start in the morning. Finish Opening and begin presenting our case. Hey Harv!" I yelled.

"Yeah?"

"How we doin' on jury instructions?"

"You mean considering you're not even done with Opening yet?"

For some reason, that made me smile. So, I smiled.

"Yeah. Considering."

"Well, keeping in mind any unexpected evidentiary considerations that could pop up and force us to change everything…"

I crossed my arms in front of my chest and began tapping my foot on the floor.

"Yeah?"

Gilbert paused. Only then did he allow a sly smile to sneak out.

"They're done."

"Done?"

"Done, subject to any required last minute modifications to conform to any unexpected facts."

"Let's see," I said, as I opened my book on Texas civil jury instructions. These ones are the ones I found in the Texas Civil Practice & Remedies Code.

I began comparing the ones Gilbert and Melendrez drafted to the ones in that book. I mentally compared them with what they would look like had I done them myself. They waited expectantly, as I read. I took my time. This wasn't a speed contest.

"Well?" an impatient Jennifer finally asked. She was the one who actually did the legal research and most of the writing.

"Not bad…for a bunch of amateurs," I finally said.

Those assembled looked disappointed. Norma looked devastated. Law clerk Jennifer was near tears.

"Hey," I said, "lighten up, you guys. I'm just kidding. Good work. In fact, excellent job. Absolutely perfect. I wouldn't have done them any differently."

"No differently?" asked Norma.

"Nope. Hey, have you folks had dinner yet?"

They hesitated, apparently waiting for someone to respond, or for me to say more. I said nothing for a moment, merely looking at everyone.

"C'mon," I urged. "I'm starvin'. Oh, did I remember to tell *all y'all*? I'm buying," I added, placing particular emphasis on the colloquial words I learned in court today. Now, I knew what a southerner meant when they were trying to address a group, as opposed to an individual.

"Well," laughed Buck. "Why in hell didn't *y'all* just say so, in the first place?"

Everyone laughed again. Dawn and CeCe also agreed to join us. When we got to the restaurant, I treated each member of the team and Dawn and Cecelia to whatever they wanted to eat and drink, including dessert.

The meal cost a bundle, but I slept like a baby that night, waking up refreshed and alert at 3:15 the next morning, just raring to go. Solita County picked up the tab. The Grey Goose martinis may have played a minor role. Since it was Saturday, I debated going home for the weekend.

But, I knew I had a lot of reading to do and elected to stay right where I was.

Chapter 76

We were back in court on Monday morning. As usual, I was seated at counsel table reviewing my notes, just as soon as the courtroom was opened. While doing this, I felt someone tap my right shoulder. Glancing up, I saw a grinning Buck Masters. He looked a lot like the proverbial cat that just ate the canary. Initially annoyed at having my concentration interrupted, I realized there probably was a very good reason why he and Jennifer were in the courtroom; especially this early. And, especially on a Monday.

"Morning Travers," said Buck. Typical cop, addressing others by their surname.

"Sarge, Jennifer," I acknowledged. "To what do I owe this honor?"

I forgot to mention earlier we sometimes called Buck *Sarge*. He was a sergeant at time of retirement from law enforcement. We liked calling him that. He liked hearing it. Hell, he'd earned his uniform's chevrons, so I saw no legitimate reason to not give him the respect he deserved. Like his stripes and hash marks, he'd earned that title.

"Here," whispered the investigator. "Read this."

"What is it?"

"As you California boys say, this is 10-35. Just read it, okay?"

I took the document from Buck, smiling at the reference to that section in our 10-Codes. Actually, I believe the correct one is 10-36. Immediately, I knew it was an investigative report. In fact, it was one of Buck's.

"Buck," I started to chastise. "I've already got everything."

He said nothing. Instead, he merely pointed to the name in the subject line. I immediately realized this was a new name. It was not one I had seen previously. Instinctively, I set it face down and looked up at him again.

Masters had his right forefinger to his own lips.

"Just read it, okay?" he whispered.

He spoke so quietly, even with his gravelly voice, I still had to strain to hear him.

Chapter 77

s Sarge and Jennifer were leaving, the judge took the bench to begin Monday's session. The bailiff directed all present to stand while he completed the formal opening, just as he did every morning. For afternoon sessions, he generally just asked everyone to come to order and remain seated. SOP for my county too.

When his uniformed deputy finished, Judge Henderson sat down. As soon as he did this, everyone else, beginning with courtroom personnel and all us lawyers, followed suit. Only after everyone was seated, did he speak.

"Ladies and gentlemen, I trust everyone had a good weekend. Mr. Travers was giving us his Opening Statement when we recessed at the end of last week. So," he said as he nodded in my direction, "sir, if you would continue."

As I expected, Henderson purposely failed to mention why we unexpectedly recessed. It's not considered good judicial manners to bring to everyone's attention the fact that the recess was called because a plaintiff was inconsolable.

The reason is two-fold. On the one hand, the judge doesn't want an appellate court to reverse a judgment because the jury may have felt undue sympathy for the Plaintiff. And, conversely, he doesn't want an appellate court reversing the outcome because the Defendant complains that the jury became prejudiced, due to an emotional outburst. This is sort of in line with the old expression "damned if you do, and damned if you don't." So, a thoughtful judge won't say anything either way.

"Thank you, your Honor," I said, as I stood and walked toward the podium.

Without thinking, I set my legal pad on top of it, before arching and stretching my back. A loud popping sound was heard. Like the judge, I, too, ignored that. One of the female jurors slightly grimaced at the sound. Approaching the jury box, I grinned.

"Apparently, mortality doesn't like being tested. Combination of too much football and motocross, but not enough mental horsepower. Stepping onto too many playing fields; stepping off too many motorcycles at speed."

I smiled and once again paused.

"Some cynics might call the latter exercise *crashing*."

Several jurors laughed. Henderson frowned. At first, he said nothing. However, some people in the spectator gallery laughed too. As noted, this area is privately referred to by some courtroom regulars as the *peanut gallery*. Henderson cleared his throat. Without looking at me, he spoke.

"Mr. Travers, your Opening, please? If you would indulge us, sir?"

This is how judges politely tell lawyers to knock it the hell off and get to work. Only his voice was smiling. I nodded toward the bench, cleared my own throat, interlaced my fingers and turned my palms outward, stretching my hands and fingers before continuing. I knew I'd found his funny bone and would remember that.

"Certainly. Sorry, your Honor. I digress. Okay, where was I?" I asked rhetorically.

Following a momentary delay, one of the jurors tentatively raised his hand.

"The victim had just died?" they volunteered.

"Ah, yes. Thank you," I replied. He was answering my rhetorical question. As a trial lawyer, you gotta love that, especially when it's the right one.

Although I had my back to him, I could practically feel Owens grimacing. Privately, I was pleased for two reasons…three actually. First, it meant some of the jurors were already paying attention to what I was saying. That is *muy importante*. For you non-Spanish speakers, that means *very important*. Sure, this isn't evidence, but it nonetheless meant they were soaking in what *I* was telling them. Secondly, this particular juror was calling TD *the victim*, and not merely some amorphous name appended to the case. That told me where his head was. And, lastly, they were interacting with *me*. The latter factor had a double-edge to it. It told me the jury seemed receptive. And, it might put Owens on the defensive, for reasons separate from the party he was representing.

This tends to throw a lawyer off balance, forcing them to mentally stay ahead of opposing counsel, rather than merely following their carefully scripted game plan. If so, this was just fine with me. As a trial lawyer, I'd be more than happy to gain an advantage. Somewhat imperceptively, it's like forcing an actor to abandon lines they had invested so much time perfecting. For a stage performer, it's akin to hiding their floor marks. And, trial lawyers tend to be interchangeable with actors in a bigger way than many folks realize. Smiling to myself, I maintained a poker-face and continued apace.

Meanwhile, as opposing counsel silently grumbled to himself, Charlie was doing his best to look nonchalant. Trial lawyers make good poker players. To untrained eyes, he appeared stoic. But, I could almost smell his discomfort. And, it was downright fragrant.

"Ladies and gentlemen, Tommy Deen O'Mara's young widow, Dawn, will tell us about the route this case has taken, following her late husband's murder, when she testifies. She'll explain why it sure wasn't quite what she expected," I began.

Owens was on his feet like he had a spring up his fanny. His face was beet red.

"Objection. I don't recall any court labeling Mr. O'Mara's death a *murder*."

Henderson nodded his head.

"The sentence is stricken. Jury is admonished to disregard it and counsel is directed to rephrase," ordered Henderson.

"Very well, your Honor," I remarked, suggesting I didn't agree with the ruling.

After a minor pause, I continued from the exact spot where Owens' objection had interrupted my flow. I rephrased the sentence, by replacing the word murder with homicide when I restated it. However, it was my perception that either Owens or the judge asking the jury to disregard my purported miscue was akin to asking them to un-ring a tolling bell. I wanted them to mull this over a few times. The seed was planted. Now, it just needed nurturing.

I continued my Opening as if I hadn't even been interrupted.

"For one thing, even after Johnny Walker admitted to both his wife and the police he had pointed his high-powered rifle in Mr. O'Mara's direction and squeezed the trigger, for all intents and purposes, nothing happened remedially on the decedent's behalf."

I heard one juror clucking her tongue. And, I knew it wasn't directed at me.

"In other words, ladies and gentlemen, we're talking no arrest…no prosecution…no jail…no conviction. Court documents we later will introduce will corroborate Mrs. O'Mara's contention that this sad scenario occurred."

I described the antediluvian law, originating in the 1880's, that gives any Texas resident the lawful right to use deadly force to protect their property in the nighttime. I chose to not talk about its history. My concern? It might help Owens' case.

Technically, I knew I was intruding onto the judge's turf and was also arguing, rather than simply giving an Opening Statement, but there was a method to my madness. It was worth a shot. I told the jurors why our evidence would show the investigation was inadequate, including the failure of authorities to really dig for information. This should have been done, I pointed out, but, somehow it wasn't. I described this as particularly egregious, especially considering Walker claimed the only reason he fired was because he thought TD was trying to steal his pickup truck. Why didn't he just run next door to his grandma's house and dial 911? This left too many unexplained holes. Too many unanswered questions. Next, I attacked the filing decision by the District Attorney's office, which resulted in the case being sent to the grand jury with no charges requested. Isn't this why there are jury trials? I compared it to a leading question that begs the very answer it elicits.

"You simply don't leave these loose threads hanging. Not in a murder investigation. I mean, come on, someone has just lost their life. This is a slap in the face to both Tommy Deen's memory and all his loved ones. Furthermore, if…"

"Objection, your Honor!"

Owens was on his feet again. His face was as red as a stop sign. The judge looked at him, as if he was expecting an objection, but hadn't decided how he would rule.

"Improper Opening, *again*," Owens pointedly insisted.

"Sir?" asked Henderson.

"Counsel is using the word *murder* again."

"Well," weighed Henderson.

I spoke up. Interestingly, Charlie didn't complain that I was also arguing, rather than making an Opening Statement.

"Judge, I am saying murder *investigation*. That's what these things are called. If anyone should know that, Mr. Owens should."

He hesitated and appeared to be contemplating it, by rotating his hand, palm down, fingers and thumb spread; turning it back and forth from side to side.

"No. I'll sustain it. It's stricken. Jury will disregard. Counsel will rephrase."

My calculated gamble had worked, both tactically and strategically, I did this for a couple of reasons. First, I wanted the jury to develop a mindset favoring our clients and, simultaneously, to be critical of a criminal justice system that didn't do its job.

Although it might not make sense to a layperson why I would cause an objection I didn't expect to win, doing so was never my goal. I was simply trying to get the jury into the right frame of mind as soon as possible. And, if I won the objection, that would be icing on the cake. By forcing Owens to either remain mute or to object, it put him in the untenable position of interrupting my Opening Statement yet again. Doing so might cause at least some of the jurors to feel sympathy towards Plaintiffs and be critical of the defense. I was testing him and Charlie certainly understood what I was doing and why. I knew he didn't like it one single bit. Oh well. All's fair in love and war.

Owens' objections needed to be the equivalent of telling the jury to think about any color, but blue. With the drama underlying Charlie's protests, my hope was that the word *murder* would override either untimely death or homicide. We needed outrage. Plus, any future objections I made to anything either Owens or his witnesses said might be blunted. Once again, I had forced Charlie to draw first blood.

"Thank you, your Honor," I replied, prior to continuing. And, I could now employ another tactic, by asking the judge to have the reporter reread back what I just said.

"I'm sorry, your Honor. Could the reporter read my last remark?"

I actually did this so the jury could hear what I said twice, by claiming lack of recollection. Charlie rolled his eyes, but said nothing. He knew he could object. But, he wisely chose to not draw undue attention to it by objecting again. Smart man. Henderson nodded. The reporter was already attempting to locate my statement. Having done so, she read it out loud, verbatim. Then, she prepared to continue recording.

"Thank you, your Honor…Madam Reporter. As I was saying, certified court documents will prove the grand jury not only listened to, but faithfully followed the prosecutor's Pavlovian directions, by returning a no bill. Talk about manifest destiny."

I stopped to visually poll any juror reaction. Then, and only then, did I resume my Opening.

"In other words, even though other evidence we will present will convince you conclusively that Johnny Walker fatally shot Tommy Deen O'Mara, nothing happened that should have brought a cold-blooded killer to the bar of justice. Absolutely nothing, until now, that is. Apparently, having an abandoned and malignant heart was irrelevant."

I looked at the floor, saying nothing for a few seconds, awaiting an objection. I glanced up at the jury and could see several pairs of angry eyes shooting proverbial daggers at no one in particular. I knew I'd just hit the ball with the solid part of the bat.

"No arrest…no booking…no indictment…no prosecution…no conviction…no punishment for killing an innocent man who was just trying to do his job. We will prove Walker's contention he believed O'Mara was a truck thief is stuff you could quickly green your up lawn with. And, I submit, justice delayed is justice denied."

Shifting gears, I next described the role the dealership played in the O'Mara homicide. I said the catalyst setting all the machinery into gear, leading to Tommy's death, was his being hired by Deals on Wheels to repossess Walker's truck.

While I conceded Walker pulled the trigger of the firearm that caused the mortal wound which ended his life, I said the evidence focused on causation. Yes, Elaine Walker prevaricated, when she said she had phoned the police to promptly report the shooting, possibly delaying, or even preventing, the arrival of emergency personnel.

However, the lie was ex-post facto, or after the fact of the shooting. So, I argued it really added nothing to this equation. Although I didn't say this, when someone is judgment-proof, why waste your time suing them? Both Walkers were penniless. They were financially irrelevant. And, even if she failed to report the shooting, did it add anything to the case legally? Therefore, the fact she lied was practically immaterial because it had somewhere between zero to de minimus impact on the victim's longevity. TD was probably dead, or near death, when his truck left the West Canino pavement, before plowing nose first into the ditch.

The dealership, however, was a whole different situation. First of all, I explained, no evidence would be produced he would have died on February 26, 1994, *but for* the fact they hired him. Had they not hired him, he wouldn't have died. Not as he did, or when, anyhow. Simple logic.

The jurors were listening with rapt attention. I explained to them, in painstaking detail, the distinction between wrongful death and fraud. As I spoke, I noticed at least a handful of jurors taking notes. This was a good sign to see them scribbling away.

The first allegation merely required proof by a preponderance of the evidence that O'Mara would not have died, but for their actions. In addition to the wrongful death allegation, we accused the Defendants of fraud. And, I was now telling the jury the same burden of proof, preponderance, must be met to establish fraud.

"Members of this jury, I'm not trying to usurp Judge Henderson's job by telling you the law. First of all, that's his job, not mine. And, frankly, at the risk of sounding like a consummate apple polisher, he does that just fine."

Some laughter was heard from the box and the spectator gallery. Henderson pretended to not hear what I had just said. I smiled back at the jurors before continuing with my Opening, trying to build on the developing rapport.

"However, in order for the rest of my Opening Statement to make sense, I need to give you the basic elements of fraud. That's one of the wrongs we accuse Defendants of committing. Fraud, also known as *intentional misrepresentation*, requires an intentional misrepresentation…to a material fact…causing someone else…damages."

"I'll talk more about fraud at the end of this trial. At that time, I'll tell you more about its financial significance. For now, however, I'll only tell you it's tied to something called *punitive damages*. More on that later. I promise."

As I neared the conclusion of my Opening remarks, I reminded the jury the remedy our clients sought was monetary. Good, old-fashioned All-

American dollars. U.S. currency. Greenbacks. I promised to be more specific, after they heard all the evidence.

Upon doing so, I did what I always do. I thanked them for their service as jurors and for the attention they had given my Opening remarks. Then, without further ado, I returned to my place at counsel table and sat down.

As I did this, Gilbert slipped me a note. It read: **THIS IS GOLD!!!** Harvey even accentuated it with big exclamation points. At first, I thought he was complimenting my Opening Statement. It turned out he hadn't even been listening. Being a typical lawyer, he was simply running full tilt with his blinders on. As Harvey handed me the note, he pointed toward the investigative report Buck had dispensed earlier the same morning. Henderson spoke again. I'd have to read it later.

I desperately wanted to accept Harv's opinion at face value. My personally optimistic side practically begged me to do that. But, my professional side reminded me to proceed cautiously. It would be a far easier path to follow. And, that's the one I chose.

"Ladies and gentlemen. We'll be in recess until tomorrow morning. I have other court business. Please remember the admonition I've given previously. Do not discuss this case with anyone, including other jurors, until I say you can do so. Remember to immediately report any attempt by anyone to talk to you about this case to the bailiff. Please be here by 9:30 tomorrow morning."

I welcomed the recess for a couple of reasons. First, it would leave the jurors with *my* words still floating in their heads for the evening, rather than Owens'. And, I was anxious to learn what Buck had apparently uncovered.

Chapter 78

Back at my hotel room, I quickly peeled off my suit, and replaced it with a T-shirt and a pair of sweat pants. I poured myself an ice cold Grey Goose, and placed some pillows in front of the headboard so I could comfortably read while lying in bed. I already knew I would order my meal from room service, so I could continue working. I wasn't going anywhere, and began reading Masters' report. It carefully and comprehensively documented his interview of a witness that wasn't on Charlie's witness list. Immediately, I had to ask myself why they weren't included.

It wasn't like Owens to miss anything this significant. I know his work.

Yes, I insist on meticulous preparation. You already know I'm obsessive-compulsive. I've told you that. Whatever. But, be that as it may, I don't recall seeing this person's name before, with the exception of seeing it in Sarge's investigative report. To be sure I hadn't misread anything, I reviewed both witness lists again. Nope, he hadn't enumerated such a name. If the defense had chosen to hide this from us, I wasn't alarmed. None of the discovery provided by them listed her. Not a problem.

Therefore, failure to disclose was a major violation. Our remedy would be to ask the court to bar Owens from calling her as a witness. As I continued reading, it was soon quite obvious why he didn't list her, assuming he even knew about her. And, maybe he didn't. She was so damaging to them, she was virtually radioactive. If not hot from that perspective, she certainly would at least qualify as another type of weapon of mass destruction: *toxic*. I smiled, as I sipped my favorite ice cold elixir.

"Well, Charlie," I mused to myself, "Here's the proverbial smoking gun. Buck found it and I'm the guy who's gonna pull the trigger."

Either way, I was more than pleased. Buck discovered some good stuff. Jake Crenshaw knew Walker publicly threatened he would kill anyone trying to repossess his truck. Walker said this, months prior to Tommy Deen O'Mara's death. And, Crenshaw knew it. This could be nothing, if not obvious to any reasonable person. I could plainly see this. In the law, this is referred to as *prior knowledge of a dangerous condition*. And, he did this in the presence of at least one independent witness, providing corroboration.

Two wits, if you counted the cashier. Three, if you included Jake. And, it also taught me an immediate advantage civil cases have over criminal. Even if Crenshaw was being sued, he could still become a witness against himself. I could hardly wait.

In a criminal matter, any defendant has absolute 5th Amendment protection to not testify. Unless he voluntarily agrees to take the witness stand, no prosecutor can even lay a glove on him. Civil, fortunately, isn't so hyper-technical. In fact, if I chose to do so, I could even call Jake as a hostile witness, when it was my turn to present my own case. If he wasn't facing criminal sanctions, he wouldn't be able to hide behind the cladding of the 5th. Therefore, I might be able to hoist Crenshaw on his own petard. And, he would take Charlie along for the ride.

At the time of Johnny's threat, the Snake was hard at work trying to convince the buxom young blonde he was worthy of her heart, or at least some interior/exterior portions of her nubile body. He did this at the exact point in time Johnny arrived to make a payment. Walker's tirade upset Jake. It interfered with his flirting. Buck's private note, *for Travers' eyes only*, accompanied his investigative report and covered every juicy morsel of this, in great detail. Men employ lots of gyrations to woo women, as women already know. But, I cannot recall ever seeing anyone else go to the extent Jake did to bed this particular fair damsel. That's why I was satisfied the event was one Crenshaw would not be likely to honestly forget.

As I continued reading, I further learned a guy named Rupert Lawson was also at the dealership the same day. Lawson was there to lodge a complaint, when Walker made his threat. For different reasons, Johnny interrupted two men trying to persuade someone else to do something. Interestingly, Jake played contrasting roles in each scenario.

Johnny spoke the threat directly to Crenshaw. But, Jake never provided this information to anyone else, including his immediate boss. Later, he would claim he believed Walker was simply blowing off steam because he was drunk. Jake insisted he unintentionally mentally suppressed this information. He said it was inconsequential. Inconsequential? Where in the world did he learn such a big word?

Aside from that, he also didn't know Lawson filed a formal complaint with DPS. That's because Texas DPS wears several hats. In addition to providing peace officers of the Texas Highway Patrol, they also regulate auto dealerships. I learned the latter portion of DPS fulfills the same role as my own state's Department of Motor Vehicles.

Today, CHP is a legal entity, separate and apart from DMV, except for the receipt of fees humble DMV produces to keep mighty CHP afloat. It even had its own TV show called CHiPS, starring Eric Estrada and Larry Wilcox. Texas DPS, however, still maintains the big tent approach. One size fits all. Lawson's written complaint alleged that Crenshaw lied to him, in connection with the sale of the car he purchased from Deals on Wheels a few months earlier. In the law, we call that fraud. I could tell Rupert was genuinely irate from merely reading it.

The reason for Lawson's trip to the lot was to persuade Crenshaw to resolve his complaint, so he didn't have to waste his time complaining to DPS. But, since Jake rather unceremoniously told him to *go blow it out your ass* from behind the safety of the cashier's window, this failed to rectify things, at least as far as Rupert was concerned.

In order to adequately explain his predicament to DPS, Lawson's complaint included what Jake said, word for word. For good measure, he even described Crenshaw's attempts to hit on the cashier in his presence. Once again, nice corroboration.

Buck cautioned me to treat the information confidentially, or 10-35 in California cop jargon. The reason was not to protect the identity of Lawson. Rather, it was to conceal the manner in which he obtained the information in the first place. When I spoke with Masters later, I discovered Sarge's confidential DPS source was none other than his former beat partner, before both retired from Dallas PD. He was now a DPS investigator, assigned to their motor vehicle division. Rebirth for cops is not unusual. Buck's former partner unveiled the information, but only after Masters promised he would never divulge how he learned this. The purposely vague manner in which Masters wrote his report allowed him to allude to the complaint lodged, without revealing how he obtained this information.

Using standard police argot, he simply referred to him as a *confidential reliable informant*, or CRI. And, since Buck shared this with me, it was protected attorney work product. Nice touch, Buck! This allowed us to lawfully and ethically keep the person's identity safely concealed. We could not be forced by anyone to reveal this to anyone else, including the judge.

In the meantime, Buck still needed to interview the remaining witnesses. All of this was more than merely damaging to the defense. It was the very sort of impeachment evidence that would blow Owens' case right out of the water. And, I couldn't wait to do that in front of God and everyone else in the courtroom. Lawyers are *not* required to provide the opposition any advance notice they intend to present impeachment evidence. I relished the prospect of ethically ambushing Charlie. And, I vowed, I would do just that. The score would soon become Travers-3; Owens-0.

While my preference would have been for all interviews to begin prior to trial, sometimes you have to do what you have to do. This was one of them.

Chapter 79

Next morning, we were all back in court. I had to avoid alerting Owens to this mystery witness. We couldn't afford to get caught waving any unintended red flags. I needed to keep her under wraps. If ever there was a time to wear a poker face, this was it. The cards we now guarded were too valuable to lose; not this late in the game. If we lost this edge, there was no way we could regain our momentum. Trials are strange animals. Once momentum shifts, it's gone. Like a leaf blowing in the autumn wind.

I didn't want Charlie to spot any sort of smugness, either facially or in my overall demeanor. Harv didn't even know about this yet. My concern was that we might arouse suspicion, if I appeared to be suddenly avoiding him. I opted for business as usual.

"Morning, Charlie. Ready for battle today?"

"I'm loaded for bear," he replied.

"Good. That should put us on some semblance of even footing with one another," I replied, chuckling, practically feeling like I was whistling while walking past a cemetery. I wished him good luck, taking a playful poke at his shoulder. As soon as I did this, I immediately asked myself why I did it. A quick glance at Owens told me Charlie had a strange look on his face. Did he know? I wasn't sure. Yet, my opponent said nothing. Could he know what I knew? Or, was it just my imagination?

Suddenly, Henderson appeared. His bailiff brought everyone to order with his now familiar soliloquy. When he was done, we all sat down. I surreptitiously glanced at Owens again but wasn't able to pick up any meaningful clues.

"Morning everyone. Are we ready to proceed? I take it there are no preliminary matters this morning?" he asked.

Hearing no reply, he turned to Charlie.

"Mr. Owens," he inquired. "Defense Opening?"

Owens scratched his head. He appeared to be considering the issue. He cleared his throat. Before answering, he lifted his legal pad and looked at it. Charlie appeared to read something before he answered.

"Thanks, your Honor. Defense reserves Opening."

Now, my mind raced. Did he know? If so, what did he know? Did he know about the Rupert Lawson complaint to DPS? What about his witnessing Walker's threat? Had Jake shared this with anyone else? Was the Snake really as arrogantly stupid as he appeared to me? If so, this could be a whole new ball game.

"Jury members," said Henderson. "Mr. Owens just told us he is reserving. That means he is exercising the same right any defense attorney has to not make an Opening Statement until later in their case. This means he isn't doing so at this time, but may choose to do so later, once Plaintiffs have rested. That is, after the moving side presents all their evidence. Or, maybe not."

He turned toward the jurors again.

"Ladies and gentlemen, we are at that part of the case where Plaintiffs can begin presenting their case…their evidence. That's because they have the burden of proof. They must do so by what's called a preponderance of the evidence. Appellate courts tell us meeting this burden means it's more likely the proponent has convinced you the allegations in their complaint are true, than that they are not true. Having said that, Mr. Travers, you may call your first witness."

"Thank you, your Honor. It goes without saying that Plaintiffs won't reserve anything."

Henderson normally would greet such a wise crack with a scowl. But, for some inexplicable reason, he didn't. Instead, he smiled. This nearly left me speechless. But, I couldn't let the jury, or anyone else in the courtroom, know that a judge or anyone else was having such an effect on me. I had to maintain a poker face. Any more surprises? Owens didn't react. His face carried the countenance of a statue.

"He knows, dammit. I know he knows!" I silently scolded myself.

But, if he knew, it was too late to do anything about it. So, I immediately shifted gears and focused my attention on what I needed to do, as Plaintiffs' lead counsel. I previously decided to set the tone for the case early, by calling Dawn as our first witness. The order of witnesses a lawyer calls is basically a crap shoot. You make this decision after evaluating your witnesses. You want to end on a strong note. But, if you can, you also begin robustly. I chose to blast out of the starting blocks, with lots of smoke billowing. If we built up enough momentum early, that could well set the tone for the entire trial. Nothing ventured, nothing gained.

"Plaintiffs call Dawn O'Mara."

"Dawn O'Mara, this way please," requested the bailiff.

He led her to the witness stand, like a stern but kindly uncle, even though she was mere feet from him when he addressed her. Before she was able to sit, the clerk stood and instructed her to raise her right hand.

"Do you swear to tell the truth, the whole truth, and, nothing but the truth?"

"Yes, ma'am," Dawn replied.

"Please be seated," said the clerk, who also sat.

Again, Dawn did as I had previously instructed her. Upon doing this, she adjusted her chair's location. Next, she adjusted the microphone, just as I'd shown her to do, when we went through a mock presentation days earlier, in preparation for today.

It's important to make any witness feel more at ease with their role. And, Dawn was as important a witness as we would have. I waited for her to be completely settled, before I spoke. Once I was satisfied she was comfortable, I began her direct examination.

"Good morning, Mrs. O'Mara. Do you reside in Harris County?"

"I do."

"And, for how long?"

She answered. Although she wasn't crying, I detected a slight quiver in her lip.

"Are you familiar with a business known as E&A Recovery?

"I am."

"How so?"

"That was our business."

"You said *our*?"

"My late husband and me."

Dawn's lip trembled more. She began to tear up. I waited for the dam to burst, knowing it would happen.

"You also said *was*. Does it no longer exist?"

"I'm closin' it. Sellin' it. One way or the other, I'm gettin' rid of it."

"How come?"

"My husband's…dead."

I had cautioned her to not use the word *murder*, to avoid sanctions by the court. She complied. Her lips now almost appeared to vibrate. And, she started to cry.

"You okay to continue, Mrs. O'Mara?"

She took a sip of water, but said nothing. I said nothing and merely waited. She took another sip of water, but still said nothing. Judge Henderson looked at her, but also remained silent. She cleared her throat. I waited and the court waited.

"I…I…I'm sorry," she began. "Yes," she said, "I'll be okay."

"What was your husband's name?"

"Tommy…" She paused. "…Deen…" She halted again. "…O'Mara…" She began to cry again, much more so than before. She was really weeping now. Even her shoulders shook, as tears streamed down her face. She even appeared having difficulty being able to catch her breath at first.

"Let's take a short recess," said the judge, facing the jury. "Folks, we'll be in recess until 10:05. Remember the standard admonition I've given you each time we've recessed. Do not discuss this case with anyone until I instruct you otherwise. Okay?"

Chapter 80

ourt reconvened on schedule. Dawn seemed composed enough to resume her testimony. While I continued her direct examination, Buck was elsewhere interviewing Rupert Lawson. His DPS complaint stated he heard Walker make his threat at the dealership. Rupert noted that he heard Walker's intimidating gobbledygook, even though it wasn't the actual basis of his complaint. He believed surrounding details corroborated his complaint. The big man correctly decided such attention to detail helped establish his own credibility. It did.

Masters decided he would speak with Lawson, before interviewing any remaining dealership witnesses. His reasoning made perfect sense to me. Lawson didn't work at the dealership. Therefore, his independence, as a witness, spoke for itself. Taking his statement first would allow Buck to measure his perception against those of the other two witnesses, and vice-versa. Once Lawson gave his statement, Sarge could interview Crenshaw and the yet unnamed cashier listed in Rupert's complaint.

Knocking on Lawson's front door, Buck saw a doorbell button. But, he nonetheless chose to knock. Years of contacting people at their residences, as a cop, conditioned him to instinctively mistrust doorbells. He had yet to forget what he and other officers dubbed "the dumb doorbell caper." They were attempting to serve a search warrant on a dope dealer. The defendant lied at the suppression hearing, claiming his doorbell didn't work.

The judge appallingly accepted his testimony over that of four veteran officers. They each heard it loud and clear. The target of the warrant used the fabricated malfunction as proof he didn't have adequate time to open his front door for officers. In the meantime, however, instead of opening it. He made use of the time to flush most of his stash of narcotics down his toilet. Officers were only able to seize a mere fraction of his dope. The case agent estimated the crook had flushed nearly 2.2 pounds of cocaine. The case's dismissal was like feeling salt being rubbed into open wounds.

The perp claimed he would have welcomed the officers into his abode with open arms, had he known they were at his front door. In his own words, *what law-abiding citizen wouldn't welcome police officers into their own home?* Instead, frustrated officers were forced to break his front door down, to begin their judicially authorized search of his premises.

The judge who granted the motion to suppress evidence ignored officers' testimony they caught him flushing cocaine hydrochloride down his toilet. They were fortunate to salvage a mere couple grams of the kilo he was flushing. If it wasn't for the other indicia that supported their belief he was selling dope, such as scales, pay-owe sheets and packaging material, the DA told them he wouldn't have even filed the case.

The lucky dope dealer asserted he only knew officers were present because they splintered his front door with a battering ram, when he failed to answer his door. Officers affectionately called it *the key to the city*. The judge ruled the officers violated the dealer's privacy rights with their violent entry because they failed to comply with knock-notice requirements. Several officers testified they heard the doorbell functioning. The man testified otherwise. The judge agreed with him.

This was all the justification the well-known liberal judge needed to suppress the seized evidence. If that were my case, I'd have made a formal request, in my written opposition to the defense motion to suppress evidence, that the judge and counsel visit the crime scene to confirm the doorbell was operational. My added request would be to freeze the scene with uniformed officers, until such inspection occurred. And, if the judge denied that request, I'd have appealed the denial. One kilo of cocaine is enough to get more than 40,000 addicts high simultaneously, not to mention all the crimes committed to obtain their drug of choice. To be precise, that is 44,000 addicts. This is serious stuff, with major public safety ramifications.

Anyhow, from that moment forward, young officer Masters always knocked. His gut told him there was a reason why this judge was easy on dope cases. He was right. Other cops had shared their suspicions about this same judge. Lawyers and courtroom personnel said he took far too many recesses. In fact, he took far more recesses than any other judges did. He also tended to disappear during most of them. He claimed he was exercising by climbing interior stairwells of the courthouse.

Whenever he returned to his courtroom, he always seemed peppier than before he called yet another a recess. He even talked faster. Rumors swirling throughout the community strongly hinted the judge was fond of a certain white crystalline substance. And, these swirling anecdotes were indeed correct. The judge naively failed to realize how many folks were paying attention to his escalating drug habit.

A bailiff once observed white powder on the edge of one of his nostrils. The judge claimed he got messy eating a donut covered with confectioner's sugar during a recess. But, curiously, no one recalled seeing any donuts that morning, either in the judge's chambers or in any of the other usual places court staff generally kept them. And, the judge wasn't reputed to be a donut eater, in the first place. Plus, would that make sense for someone so committed to being in shape that he climbed stairs during recesses?

Clanging bells began sounding. These reports suggested that the freed dealer was actually the judge's own illegal drug supplier. Ultimately, several complaints found their way to the State Commission on Judicial Conduct. A lengthy hearing before the Commission ultimately resulted in his removal from office. His lawyer tried to convince him to enter a proposed substance abuse rehabilitation program. The errant judge adamantly denied using drugs. The Commission found no mitigating factors, and voted unanimously to remove him from the bench. Buck was glad he didn't have to put up with such frustrations anymore.

After a brief pause, the door he was knocking on opened. An adult male dwarfing Masters stood in the open doorway. This was no easy feat. Sarge was nearly six feet three inches tall himself. But, he immediately felt quite small.

He estimating the stranger's height to be at least six feet nine inches. The man's weight easily topped three hundred fifty pounds. Three hundred fifty very solid pounds. The man's bushy beard, combined with his sheer size, gave him a fierce appearance. However, he had a surprisingly nonthreatening voice. It sounded much higher pitched than what Buck expected to hear. It didn't sound the least bit feminine. But, it was certainly not bass or baritone either. The best way to describe this man's vocal sound was to call him a *high talker*.

"Yes?" the man asked, in a fairly neutral tone. His tone was neither friendly nor hostile.

"Mr. Lawson? Rupert Lawson?"

"Yes?" he repeated, slightly frowning, making Buck understandably uncomfortable.

"I'm Buck Masters. I'm a PI, uh private investigator, working for the Plaintiff who is suing Deals on Wheels," he added, as he handed the man a business card.

Lawson instantly displayed a wide smile. He invited Buck inside, and was completely candid with the information he provided. He pulled no punches regarding his dislike of Jake Crenshaw. Rupert called him *a low-down venomous snake in the grass*. Masters took Lawson's complaint against Deals on Wheels from his briefcase, but didn't show it to Lawson. He began asking questions.

Rupert confirmed everything he accused Crenshaw of doing was true. He agreed to testify under oath to the event. Lawson pulled out his own copy of the complaint, handed it to Sarge and told him he could keep it. Masters' host further agreed the interview could be tape recorded. In addition to freely discussing what Crenshaw did, he repeated nearly verbatim the threats he heard a drunken Johnny Walker utter about what he would do to any repossessors.

Even though Rupert was a big man, what he heard Walker say made him shudder. He repeated it to Masters. Did he believe Walker's threat was real? Of course. That was why he still was on edge, as he talked about it. Guns scared him. The big man described the pert blonde cashier in great detail. He particularly remembered her well. He said Crenshaw appeared far more interested in getting up close and personal with her, than obtaining a solution for his complaint.

By the time Masters left, Lawson had provided him a treasure trove of information. Thanking him for his cooperation, Buck handed him a subpoena. This was standard operating procedure for a veteran like Masters.

Chapter 81

Following the Lawson interview, Buck decided to speak with the cashier next. His interview of Crenshaw would have to wait. He believed the lot manager might not be cooperative, just based on the kind of liar he was rumored to be. And, he didn't want to queer his chances of talking to the employee, if Crenshaw got goosey on him.

If Jake went sideways, Buck didn't think he would let him interview the mystery female. So, erring on the side of caution, he decided that being able to question two of three witnesses was far better than just one. Masters believed this route was more likely to be productive. But, if Crenshaw surprised him and agreed to talk, he gave up nothing in the process with this approach.

Granted, he didn't even know the cashier's name yet. But, he'd remedied far bigger obstacles. Buck was not the least bit daunted. He'd find her. Rupert's description of her was more than adequate. Obtaining the cashier's name wouldn't require Crenshaw's blessing or his involvement anyhow. Buck was not going to miss this opportunity. He kept his investigative options open as usual. According to Lawson, she was a *young, tall, leggy blonde* with *blue eyes deep enough to swim in*, *bodacious tatas* and *a killer ass*. Soon, Buck would find out if he agreed. If nothing else, Buck was a discerning man.

When he learned Crenshaw was off the lot running an errand somewhere, Buck wasted no time getting to Deals on Wheels. His cop instincts told him the man was probably out trying to score dope or get laid. If there was one thing he understood, it was human nature, especially the allegedly human nature of grease balls. He didn't care if the errand was some romantic dalliance, an illegitimate one, or even an unlikely legitimate one. All he knew was that he needed to hurry over there and stay ahead of that particular curve.

As soon as Buck walked onto the dealership's floor, he spotted her, quickly making a beeline for the cashier's window. A quick glance at the lissome blonde with D-cup breasts told him he need look no further. He had hopefully found his validating witness. Rupert Lawson didn't exaggerate. This had to be the same woman the man described.

Once he was at her window, she looked up. Buck introduced himself, handed her his business card, and asked if he could speak with her. His many years of interviewing strangers were the only reason he didn't get tongue-tied. *She was that beautiful!*

He glanced downward from her eyes to the place where her hips disappeared behind her counter. Slowly but surely, he worked his way back up to her absolutely riveting deep blue orbs. Everything about her practically mesmerized him, including her protruding nipples. Sarge couldn't believe his good luck. She wasn't wearing a bra. And, he was wearing his glasses. He tried hard to not stare. The woman introduced herself as Annalee Rutherford. She was both smart and engaging. Annalee was not the dumb bimbo he and Travers had previously envisioned, based on the wholly incorrect description they had been given. Despite her youth, she actually seemed overqualified for her job.

Buck asked her about the Johnny Walker incident. Like Lawson, she remembered it clearly. *An astonishing event*, she said. *Not as astonishing as you are*, Buck silently pined. When he asked her why it was so memorable, she gave a number of reasons. She said none of them were pleasant reminders. First of all, she said *he smelled like a cheap brewery*. On top of that, *he generally just smelled bad.* His breath oozed unmistakable odoriferous evidence of halitosis. And, it appeared to be fighting with stale tobacco for bragging rights. He was disheveled. His shirt wasn't completely buttoned, and was partially untucked. Except for no visible evidence of physical injuries, she noted, he looked almost as if he had recently been in a fight.

Annalee found it difficult to even get close enough to her window to deal with him, due to his stench. Even though the opening was only a small slot at the bottom of its protective glass, he nonetheless physically overwhelmed her. Walker was also loud, obnoxious, and rude. She couldn't recall the last time another customer had so badly misbehaved, or swore so much. And, she was more than used to dealing with unhappy people. After all, she worked at an iron lot that carried its own paper for the worn out old beaters they sold.

Buck asked her to describe the threat. Like Larson, it still upset her. *What was it about his intimidation that bothered you the most*, he asked? She thought for a moment. She appeared to be searching for the right words.

"You mean, aside from Jake's latest sexual harassment of me?"

He blushed. "Yeah," he said.

"It wasn't what he said that was so disturbing. It was that wild look in his eyes, when he said it. He had the eyes of a killer!" she remarked.

Had she not seen Walker's cold, soulless expression, she might have assumed he was merely trying to be braggadocios for her benefit. Due to her amazing good looks, Miss Rutherford was used to strange men showing off around her.

But, she told Buck, Walker was more than a mere drunkard trying to impress her with his toughness. Annalee called him *crazy*. Not just garden variety crazy, but out of control, stark-raving-nuts crazy.

"No," she observed. "It was more than that. Far more, in fact. When he said this, he wasn't even looking at me. At that precise moment, it was as if I didn't even exist."

"Really?" asked the curious investigator. "What did he say?"

"I'll never forget his words."

"What did he say?"

"He said: 'anybody ever takes my truck…papers or no papers…I'll blow their…' Can I say that? I don't want people to think I'm a lowlife or something. It's obscene."

Buck laughed.

"Can you say what?"

"You know. The F-word?"

"Ms. Rutherford. That's done in courtrooms all the time. If you're quoting someone, the judge is not only *not* going to complain. He's going to expect you to do exactly that. You're quoting someone exactly. It's evidence. Think of it as taking a verbal picture, okay? Go ahead. You can say the F-word. I'm just gathering facts."

She smiled.

"Okay, then," she said. "He said '…I'll blow their…their…*fucking* head off.' Whew! My Lord. That was difficult!"

"And, you're sure he wasn't talking about thieves?"

"Absolutely. Two reasons. Want me to explain?"

"Sure."

"First of all, he mentioned papers. Anybody who goes out to repo a vehicle for Deals on Wheels always gets repossession paperwork, so they can prove they're lawfully taking the vehicle. That's in case they have to explain why they're there…to the owner…to the police…whomever."

"Okay."

"Secondly, he made that comment almost as soon as I said something to him."

"What's that?"

"I told him he was lucky. I reminded him I should have closed five minutes earlier. Had I done so, I'd have been gone. He wouldn't have been able to make his payment for the week. His loan would have been in default then, instead of a week later. That would have subjected him to immediate repossession. Maybe the next day. That's how he said it."

Buck repeated to Annalee what she told him Walker said, in order to confirm he heard it right.

"Uh huh, that's right," she ratified.

"Anyone else hear this?"

"Of course. I know for sure two other people did."

"Really? Who?"

Buck intentionally omitted what Lawson just told him He wanted her unvarnished version, and didn't want to taint her perception.

"Yes. One was Jake Crenshaw," she said.

Masters tried to hide his delight in hearing this. Now, two independent witnesses confirmed he heard Walker make the threat, or made one he should have heard. As she said this, she rolled her big blue eyes. He knew what the answer was going to be, but asked anyhow. Looking at her eyes, he realized they were probably closer to the color of turquoise. Buck was beginning to feel positively smitten, very grateful he was single, even though he was sure he didn't have a prayer with someone this beautiful. She had to have a boyfriend. Maybe even a fiancé, although he saw no engagement ring.

"Would Crenshaw admit he heard this?"

"No, I don't believe so."

"Why?"

"Two reasons. First of all, he'd have to admit he was right there violating federal law, by harassing me, again, just as Mr. Walker was making his threat. Second? He'd have to admit he knew how dangerous that psycho was."

"How about the other witness?"

"He was this big old guy. He sorta looked like a cross between Hoss Cartwright and Grizzly Adams."

Buck showed her the picture he took of Lawson during his interview.

"This him?"

"Yes," she exclaimed. That's the man! I'm positive."

Masters shifted gears.

"I couldn't help notice the way you rolled your eyes when you mentioned Jake Crenshaw. Was there a reason for that?"

She sighed, and rolled her eyes again, folding her arms over her tantalizing breasts, as she appeared to collect her thoughts, in order to say what she had to say precisely.

"Yes, he's such a pig. He's always trying to hit on me. I have zero interest in him. First of all, he's my boss and I don't...*pardon my expression*...poop that close to my own food bowl. And, for goodness sake, he's married. Call me old-fashioned, but I don't date married guys. Plus, he's just...he's...oh, yuck!"

"So, what's a nice kid like you doing working in a place like this?" Buck asked good-naturedly.

"Are you hitting on me, now, Mr. Masters? Are you single?"

"Nope," Buck stammered. "Uh, just doing my job. Trying to find out what makes you tick. And, yes, I am single."

Annalee smiled, before she answered him.

"I'm in school. College, actually, I'm taking a year off. Ran out of money. I'm saving so I can return and get my degree. Hopefully, I can start again this fall."

"Pretty, bright, and motivated. You are off to a good start in life, Ms. Rutherford."

"And, you're off to a good start, too, Mr. Masters."

Rutherford smiled demurely, as she said this, subtly glancing at the bare ring finger on Buck's left hand, noticing it had no tan line, like that on the men who remove their wedding bands to pretend they are single. He knew she was now the one flirting, but ignored her. The wily investigator wasn't done with this interview. And, he had to concentrate. Her good looks alone were distracting enough.

"You mentioned two others heard Walker. What were they doing?"

"Big guy was mostly complaining about something. He said Crenshaw lied to him about the vehicle he bought from us."

"And, Crenshaw?"

"You know…the usual…"

"What do you mean?"

"Trying to unsuccessfully sweet-talk me into bed…*again*. The man just doesn't give up! It's like he's on automatic pilot, or something."

"I know you witnessed all this. You just told me so. But, what was it that told you Crenshaw heard Walker's threat?"

"Words and actions," she swiftly replied.

"Excuse me?"

"Words and actions," she repeated, without any hesitation whatsoever.

"No, I heard what you said. Please explain."

"Walker pretended to hold a rifle, as he spoke. He looked right at Jake and pulled an imaginary trigger. As he did this, he yelled *bang*!"

"Anything else?"

"Yes. Do you need my home number?"

Masters smiled.

"And, it is?"

"281…"

As she spoke, he began to write it down.

Chapter 82

Masters learned Crenshaw had returned to the lot. He quickly located him. The Snake was walking toward the office. This was indeed fortuitous. Sarge hoped Jake didn't put his defenses up. He already had a game plan. Buck would pretend to be a potential customer.

The PI decided to play this card. He'd try to finagle a test drive. His police instincts told him he might need a subterfuge. Ruses worked well for cops trying to bag criminals. Jake appeared to walk on common ground with them. Nothing ventured, nothing gained. He decided he'd have more luck talking to Crenshaw, or more importantly, getting Crenshaw to talk to him, if the car man was a captive audience, in a moving vehicle, with a lawman. That settled it. Buck was going on a test drive.

Predictably, Crenshaw quickly spotted Masters. He made a beeline in his direction, like a heat-seeking missile. Buck feigned interest in a vehicle he was looking at. He was glad the recorder he used for interviews was small enough to hide in his coat pocket. He remembered to turn it on, right before Crenshaw saw him.

"So," Jake began, "ain't she a beauty?"

"Yeah. She looks okay, but how's she run?"

"Perfect. Want me to start 'er up for you?"

"Don't bother, unless that includes a test drive."

"I'll be right back with the keys," Jake promised. He headed toward the office to retrieve them. When he returned, he handed Buck the keys.

"Here y'all go."

"Why don't you hop in too?" Masters asked. "I'm sure I'll have some questions. If I like it, that'll speed things up, just in case you're interested in making a sale, and, more importantly, I'm interested in making a purchase."

Buck could tell Crenshaw was ambivalent. When Jake first spotted Masters, he was heading toward the office. Sarge thought it was because of a customer. He didn't realize Jake was trying to convince Annalee, once again, to have dinner with him, after he did a line or two. Crenshaw thought he finally detected some softening of her armor, even if it was really nothing more than the cocaine beginning to soften up his own brain. But, if so, he wasn't going to pass up the opportunity to tap that. However, it was duty first. That was how he got paid.

He thought this one seemed eager to buy. Buck had already inserted the key Crenshaw had given him into the ignition, and started the motor. He reluctantly climbed into the passenger side of the vehicle, trying to prime the pump with a big phony smile. After all, a dollar was still a dollar. If he made the sale all by himself, he didn't have to share his commission with any covetous salesmen. But, as he shut the door, he glanced around the lot to make sure there weren't any other prospective sales he might lose. To hell with the salesmen. If he had his way, they wouldn't even have any. But, Baron obviously had other thoughts.

As they were pulling onto the street, Crenshaw suddenly instructed Buck to stop.

"Slow down," he said as he opened his window, and handed a man and woman one of his business cards. "Jake Crenshaw," he remarked. "Lot manager. Test drive. Look around. Check out our quality inventory. Don't go away. I'll be right back, if you have any questions."

As they drove away, Buck decided tactically to ask mundane questions about the vehicle to kill time, and, in order to be able to question Crenshaw about the Walker incident. Plus, doing so would lower Jake's defenses, so it wouldn't appear the investigative questions were just jumping out at him from nowhere. Since his own hands were on the steering wheel, at the moment, time was his best friend. He wisely anticipated the possibility of reluctance by Crenshaw to talk about Walker's threat. Owens or Baron, maybe both, had probably already cautioned him to keep his mouth shut about anything concerning the lawsuit.

In fact, not only might Jake refuse to talk, he might even react with hostility. However, if they were far enough away from the lot, Buck figured he might acquire helpful information by employing divergent tactics. The worst he could be told was no.

Following a meaningless string of vehicular questions, Buck shifted gears, rather than answer Crenshaw's "what'll it take to sell you this one?" inquiry.

"So," he began, "bet you deal with all sorts of folks, huh?"

"Everybody's different. That's for sure. People are people."

"I imagine they range from calm to crazy, huh?"

"I don't follow."

Buck shifted his mental and verbal gears, deciding to go for broke.

"For example, I heard about that Walker guy. What about him?"

"Huh? Who?"

"Johnny Walker."

"Don't ring no bells."

"Bought a truck from you."

"Nope."

"Weekly payments? Payments late? The promise of immediate repossession, if late? Default time? Threats to kill any repossessors?"

Buck paused, and looked directly at him before returning his view to the surrounding traffic.

"Killed a repossessor? One *you* hired?"

He looked at Crenshaw again, who appeared to be sweating. Beads of moisture were already forming on several areas of his face, in particular, between his upper lip and nose.

"Pull over," Jake demanded.

"Huh?"

"Pull over. Don't know who in hell you are, mister. But, this here test drive's over. I'm driving now."

Chapter 83

Allow me to explain something seemingly incompatible. I am a personal optimist. The glass is always half full; never half empty. But, professionally, I must be a pessimist. That's just the nature of the legal arena where I toil.

I'd just completed Dawn's direct examination. I've seen lots of tears gushing from witness stands over the years. But, this was the most tear-soaked testimony I've ever experienced. She couldn't have appeared more emotional, even if she was a trained actor. And, she wasn't. This was the real deal. Any observer could see why she was crying. Her heart was broken. And, it might be broken irrevocably. Hey, I'm not a shrink. I merely had to see the top of the witness stand. It was a used Kleenex display. Could've been a TV commercial. Mountainous barely describes it. And, this wasn't for show. I've seen shows. This was not a show. Dawn's grief was the real McCoy. Just like her.

Prior to presenting our case, I debated how I wanted to do the order of witnesses. Depending on the sort of case, this can be crucial to the outcome. In other words, based on the batting order, it can be a win or lose proposition. I routinely spend a fair amount of time on this particular issue, no matter what sort of case I'm trying. It ties directly into my attention to detail I've previously talked to you about. This isn't just me and my cases. Trial lawyers do this. It's how we must function. We have to do it or we get our hats handed to us, in front of God and everyone else in the courtroom.

That's embarrassing. And, depending on whether it puts you on the winning or the losing side, it can also be a career-maker, or breaker. Therefore, it's a good idea to get this nailed down l-o-n-g before you ever go to court. Law school is a good place to start. The phrase, *practicing law*, isn't just an expression. And, yes, practice can make perfect, assuming you are practicing doing things the right way, and doing it long enough.

Calling Dawn, as our first witness, could set the tone for the entire trial. But, that also could be a mixed bag. If the jurors bond with her, that's a good thing. However, it's also a gamble. Here's why. On the plus side, it allows the jury to see the devastation a small, fast-moving piece of lead can cause a potentially limitless number of people. It sets the tenor. However, by not making her our last witness I was tactically taking a big risk.

Doing this could completely diminish the impact of her testimony and resonate throughout our case-in-chief. If we started off hot as a fire cracker, but fizzled at the end, every ounce of energy the entire team poured into this case was for naught. If that was the end result, our client would suffer. Nothing else mattered. We needed balance. And, thanks to Sgt. Masters' investigative work, it appeared we had that, and then some. If my assumption was correct, it meant our case was basically a steak sandwich. Strength on both sides, with solid evidence in the middle. Now, that's a real meal.

By now, I was also convinced a civil case was certainly no more difficult than a criminal case. In fact, so far, it seemed far easier. While this may be true, there are always at least a couple of exceptions to any general rule. To begin with, the burden of proof is far less in a civil case, than a criminal one.

Whenever I have to describe burdens of proof to laypeople, my hypothetical measuring stick is an adult human body, standing tall. Proof of guilt, beyond a reasonable doubt, is the highest one. You know this. We've already talked about it. Using my measuring stick, this one reaches the top of your forehead, right above your eyebrows. That's not some textbook criminal standard. It's mine, a practical one I created.

It's the example I use whenever I explain it to people who aren't in the courtroom every day like I am. And, remember, we also need to convince the entire jury to vote guilty, if it's a criminal matter. That's unanimous. All twelve members. If I don't erase reasonable doubt in every mind in the jury box, as to each and every element of every charged crime, I don't win. It's that simple. This means the unproven crime is gone.

Written jury instructions caution us that we aren't dealing with all possible or imaginary doubt, because everything related to human affairs has doubt. These originate in the appellate courts. And sadly, appellate cases tend to be too damned esoteric. Perhaps too many appellate justices are overly concerned other folks won't find them intellectual enough. Ergo, the use of such big words. I mean, come on. That's not how people talk. Or, maybe it's because they rely on their law clerks to write opinions. Law clerks need to impress strangers. Been there, done that. In reality, we are simply talking about being sure the prosecutor proved that the bad guy did the crime. No rocket science required. Just plenty of hard work.

The appellate cases don't quantify reasonable doubt in numerical terms. And, no one talks about it in the courtroom, mainly because no one really knows. That's because appellate courts find comfort in tossing around *glittering generalities*. Call me cynical. But, personally, I'd have to say reasonable doubt is as close to 100% as you can get, and still leave room for some doubt. You need to be able to wake up a decade from now, and still feel content you correctly voted guilty, instead of letting a bad guy walk free.

Preponderance, on the other hand, when using my own example, barely hits above one's beltline. And, I'm not talking about your garden variety seven foot professional basketball player either. This is a big difference! It's a little more than 50%! In fact, it's anything above fifty percent. And here, I only have to convince nine civil jurors…*nine*…rather than the usual unanimous twelve. *That* is extra comfort! Like wearing stretch pants. Let me be perfectly candid.

We are talking about the difference between day and night. And, more importantly, Buck has uncovered some solid impeachment evidence. This gives our case added strength it normally wouldn't possess.

Impeachment evidence is never a given. But, if you have some, it is an absolutely unexpected bonus. Use of impeachment evidence allows us to have a case that begins on a strong note. In this case, as noted, we first offer Dawn's own testimony. And, because of our impeachment evidence, I know we can also finish far stronger. We can do this, using witnesses who have no reason to be biased in favor of anyone, especially Plaintiffs. So, we start stout and end even more resilient.

In retrospect, I was delighted with our decision to call Dawn first. She truly set the mood for the entire trial. First of all, she was a grieving widow. Her genuine grief was still so raw, so near the surface, any member of the jury could virtually taste it. Each juror could share her pain. They can even feel her pain. And, she bonds with them. She is one of those rare witnesses who simply radiates credibility. I know many cops with lots of time on the witness stand who don't come across nearly as naturally as she does up there. By the time she left the witness stand, at least five of the jurors were visibly crying. One or two were audibly sobbing. Another two periodically rubbed wetness from their eyes. Owens wisely declined to cross-examine Dawn. Charlie wasn't going to antagonize them. Smart man.

Charlie, you've learned your lessons well, my brother. Meanwhile, Henderson was wasting no time.

"Next witness for Plaintiffs?"

"Thank you, you Honor. Plaintiffs call State Trooper DJ Timothy."

As with Mrs. O'Mara, the bailiff summoned Timothy to the stand. The clerk administered the same oath. And, the officer also promised to tell the truth, the whole truth, and nothing but the truth. So far, evidence was unfolding smoothly. No land mines in sight. This didn't mean I could let my guard down. But, it was nonetheless comforting.

After the oath, he gave his full name, spelling his surname, as instructed. Then, he sat, adjusted the microphone to suit him, and calmly waited for me to commence my examination. I could tell he'd done this dance before.

"Good morning, Officer Timothy."

He smiled.

"By whom are you employed?"

"Good morning, sir. Texas Department of Public Safety. Highway Patrol Division."

"Were you so employed and on duty on…"

By the time I completed my last question, I was able to obtain Timothy's observations at the crime scene, or, at least, at the part where TD O'Mara breathed his last breath. Timothy described his particular role in the investigation.

I knew the testimony of HPD investigator Larson was not going to be terribly helpful. I had read both of his reports, including his initial and supplemental. Buck and I both agreed this had not been a terribly spirited investigation. Why did we believe Larson seemed almost pre-programmed to conclude the shooting was legally justified? The answer: Texas Penal Code 9.41, a most convenient scapegoat.

However, Buck's own dogged investigation uncovered Larson's personal bias against people in the repo business. Larson had been a repossession target many years earlier, during a particularly contentious divorce that had sucked the financial wind out of his sails. Surprisingly, he still had not completely recovered from that, despite the passage of nearly twenty intervening years.

Larson's less than friendly attitude was not fatal to our chances of success. We could establish his bias by introducing relevant paperwork. It would explain his negative personal experience with repossessions, and more importantly, his attitude about them. We needed to do that and work around him. It might even help us show his own bias had warped an investigation, poisoning any chance Walker would ever be prosecuted.

I'd be a liar, if I said I didn't feel discomfort impeaching a police officer, even if it was someone I had never worked with professionally. My respect for most cops was ingrained, at this point in my life. But, I had a job to do. And, do it, I would. I also had a client who was counting on me to obtain justice. So far, it had eluded her. Don't misunderstand me. And, I mean *please* don't. I'm not saying I respect someone just because they're a cop. People earn my respect. The professionalism and dedication of most of the LEO's I have served exceeds that, and then some. Proof of the pudding and all that stuff. Here's what I'm trying to say. Generally, cops must convince me they *don't* deserve my respect. Larson was doing exactly that, sans effort. I've served alongside enough cops to know the good ones from the slugs. Larson was a proven Cornu aspersum.

Buck had worked with Larson. In fact, Masters was Carlton's first field training officer, aka FTO, when Larson was fresh out of the academy. FTO Masters evaluated him. It turned out to be nearly fatal to the rookie officer's budding career. Buck recommended termination. After Larson was sacked by Dallas PD, he was hired by a few smaller departments. Working his way back up, Houston PD eventually hired him. Fortuitously, he was assigned a kinder training officer. She didn't see him through Buck's critical eyes.

This one chose to forgive the errors that caused his first FTO to hold Larson's feet to the fire. This time, he completed his HPD field training and probation. But, none of it changed Buck's professional opinion of him. Stupid, plus lazy, did not thrill Sarge. He mumbled something about leopards not changing spots. Maybe, he said leprechauns. He mumbles, remember?

In fact, Buck's evaluation of Larson still resonated nearly as loudly today as the fact of his own repossession. Buck was comfortable with his decision. He wasn't going to amend it. He didn't mince any words, when I asked him to describe Larson.

"Worthless as tits on a…"

Laughing, I interrupted him.

"10-4. Not exactly a ball of fire, is he?"

"Hardly. If I had my way, he'd be lucky to be pushing a golf cart at some mall."

Nonetheless, we were able to elicit some helpful testimony from Larson. Walker admitted to him he shot at O'Mara, even though he initially claimed he merely shot his high-powered rifle over him, saying he thought the noise would scare him off. Larson said Walker told him he thought TD was trying to steal his truck.

Pardon my cynicism. But, this was a ludicrous statement and I wasn't going to let him get away with describing it any way, other than how it really happened.

"With a wrecker, sir? A sling truck?" I asked. "How does one confuse that with a vehicle thief? And, you've been a cop how long?" I expected an objection, but got none.

Larson sat there with his mouth open for a moment or two, before finally saying "I don't know. I'm not sure," failing to say how long he'd been a cop.

"Was the area around Johnny Walker's truck examined for any evidence?"

"Yes."

"Do you know what burglar tools are?"

"Yes."

"Please explain."

He did.

"Did you find any burglar tools anywhere near Walker's truck?"

"No."

"Was the area where Mr. O'Mara bled to death also examined?"

"Yes."

"Find any burglar tools there, in his wrecker?"

"No."

"Any in the area around it?"

"No."

"Sometimes criminals throw contraband items from the vehicle they are driving so they can't be connected to them, when they are being pursued by police officers. Did you find a trail of such bread crumbs leading up to where the victim's truck was wedged into the ditch in front of DPS?"

Owens objection was sustained, which allowed me to ask the same question a second time, but using the words *burglar tools*, instead of *bread crumbs*.

"No sir," he replied this time. Two bites of the same apple…again.

I heard chuckles from the jury box. As I stole a peek at them, one or two had big smirks on their faces. Undoubtedly, we scored the most points when Larson testified he initially was satisfied Walker believed he was scaring away a car thief. He said he interviewed dealership employees, but admitted he did so only after the prosecutor ordered him to do that. I toyed with adding the prosecutor to our witness list. However, I felt somewhat at odds with doing that. My reasoning was practical. First of all, it was redundant.

The judge most likely would not have granted our request. More importantly, I believed Montgomery's testimony wouldn't add anything to our case. Frankly, he seemed no more interested in dispensing justice than Larson. On the one hand, sure, he had forced Larson to complete the investigation. But, he inexplicably sent the case to the grand jury, without charges requested. A thorough investigation, no doubt, would have sent the case to the grand jury, *with* charges, resulting in an indictment.

I read the same investigative reports Montgomery reviewed. I had questions that were not answered by anything I read. The issue wasn't Penal Code 9.41. It was failing to answer why Walker was allowed to get away with falsely saying he shot at an alleged thief. If I pressed Montgomery for an explanation, his cryptic answer, as with Larson, would no doubt have been "…it's the law…" Pardon my cynicism, but bullshit!

After belaboring the point for a while, I decided to abandon this issue so I didn't lose the jury to boredom in the process. I still had more ground to cover. We needed our jury to stay alert. An interested jury is a happy jury. I wasn't going to rock that particular boat. As I prepared to ask another question, my delivery was interrupted by the sound of the judge's voice.

"Mr. Travers, would this be a good time for our evening recess?"

Chapter 84

My pager vibrated, just as I stood up. On its digital display was a cryptic note from Buck. It read: "97, Hilton. 87?" This was his cop-speak way of telling me he was at the hotel and wanted to know if I could meet him there.

As we gathered our files, I asked Harvey to wait outside the courtroom.

"Charlie, buddy? Mañana," I said as I was leaving the courtroom.

Outside, I asked Harvey if he could meet us at the hotel.

"Buck is waiting for us. Hopefully, he's interviewed the wits listed in his report."

Harvey promised to go there too. I figured I'd find Buck in the bar. Sure enough, he was there. When we arrived, Buck was waiting for us in a booth near the main bar. He was nursing a dark beverage. It looked like either a whiskey or iced tea, on the rocks. I assumed it was Scotch. Its color was dark. And, it's Buck's beverage of choice. I doubted they served iced tea in a highball glass. Even if they did, I couldn't picture Sarge drinking tea any more than I could picture W.C. Fields sipping water. Buck Masters and iced tea went together like I'm told Hatfield's and McCoy's used to get along with one another. Masters signaled the waitress to get her attention.

"Another one a these," he said, with no detectable slurring, as he held up his glass. "And, for my friends here, let me see if I remember this. Grey Goose, shaken, not stirred straight up, ice cold but no ice, with two BIG olives for him," gesturing toward me. "Rum and diet Coke for him," he pointed at Gilbert, enunciating everything, without as much as even a tiny hint of any speech impairment. Buck did a good job of holding his booze. That's good. I despise sloppy drunks, just as much as the next guy. If you can't stand the heat, get out of the kitchen. And, if you can't handle adult beverages…well, you get the idea.

"You, sir," I noted, "remain a trained observer."

"Old habits die hard," a grinning Buck replied.

"Good memory, too," said Harvey.

Buck beamed again. Our drinks arrived. The waitress gave each of us our drinks. I was impressed. Each got the right one. And, she didn't spill a drop. I'm not used to paying for tavern-provided Grey Goose I don't get to drink. I always bitch about it, insisting they bring an unspilled replacement. I'm cheap. But, I don't lick tables. So, if more than a wee drop is spilled, I demand they take it back and bring me a full one.

"So, any luck contacting the wits?"

"Yep, all three, Josh. In fact, here's my report. And, in case you care to listen to them, here's the interview tapes. Even taped Crenshaw. But, let's just say he was a bit uncooperative. Had to use a different tactic. But, it's obvious, if he denies it happened, he's lyin' through his teeth. Two independent wits will both contradict him, as will his taped interview. I was able to legally justify that, without his consent, on the premise that I was investigating a possible felony. And, the other two will testify to that. You'll have fun with him on the witness stand. This, I guarantee."

"So, tell me about your tactic with old *Jake the Snake*."

Masters explained everything to us, including how Crenshaw terminated the conversation, and the sham test drive. Jake was so angry, he even banned Buck from the lot, as soon as they returned. I applauded Buck's decision to interview Annalee first.

"So, any other interviews needed? Re-interviews, maybe?"

"Nope and nope."

"Just stand by and be available to come to court, in case I need you to impeach Crenshaw, or any other hostile witnesses. Okay?"

"Copy," said Buck.

After our meeting, I took everything Buck gave me to my room. Once there, I reviewed the dinner menu and called room service for food again. It didn't look like I was going to see the inside of another Houston restaurant for a while. Let me be real blunt here. Molly's cooking has spoiled me for restaurants. She's that good, or they are generally that bad. Probably a little of both. But, it's also been my experience that restaurants trump hotel room service any day of the week. I wasn't looking forward to eating. But, I was hungry, and really had no other choice.

I also knew this was going to be another late work night. Once I hung up, I phoned home. I needed to update Molly, as the trial continued to unfold. Hearing her voice would be a plus. I truly needed that. But, unlike confidential client communication, courtroom stuff was fair game. I could share it all with her without any ethical breaches.

Chapter 85

It was 3 a.m. I was already awake. Wide awake. Rather than simply toss and turn in a strange bed, I decided to get up and make some coffee. Besides, witnesses would be waiting in the on-deck circle, and I needed to be sure we were all ready for court. Marine Corps training. Best on the planet. *'Ten hut.*

Early morning cogitation has always worked best for me. This goes back as far as college. Actually even earlier. I'm a morning lark. This is when my energy level is highest. I not only am a farm boy, but, in junior high, I threw a morning paper route. Old habits. You have to do that early in order to get to school on time, come rain or shine. So, while the rest of the thundering herd is still snoozing, I'm up and already hard at work. I try to do this daily. I maintain a tight schedule. And, it's important to keep my witnesses on some semblance of a schedule, too, both for them and my case.

But, this is no easy feat for a number of reasons. Part of this high-wire act includes not only estimating the length of my own direct examination for each of my own witnesses, but also guessing how long their cross-examination might last. The latter I have zero control over. Nor, does the judge, if you really want to know the truth. Judges tend to shy away from being accused of interfering with a defendant's 6th Amendment right to counsel, and being able to present their defense. Any experienced trial counsel knows this. Trying to guesstimate what an opposing counsel is going to do is just about as predictable as herding cats, especially if you are a humble prosecutor second guessing the defense.

It can't be done. And, I'm telling you that right now, with no hesitancy. Some defense attorneys purposely try to mess with prosecutorial composition. This is done to upset prosecution witnesses and prosecutors. I know how long trials *should* last. I've given enough time estimates to legitimately make that claim. But, this doesn't mean it's an accurate predictor of how long they actually will last. In addition to defense strategy, the courtroom itself somehow presents unexpected surprises, tending to pull judges and others involved away from jury trials for a variety of reasons.

A judge who is in trial may have other matters on their calendar they must deal with; same with any trials lawyers. And, witnesses, whether they are officers, other experts, or civilians may face issues that interfere with their role as witnesses. Telling a witness to appear for a morning session generally isn't good enough. Such an instruction can translate into way too much potential down time. Therefore, an early morning appearance may even result in a witness finally leaving court in late afternoon, or worse.

Some lawyers believe they have the right to unduly inconvenience other people. They can. We all can. It's enforceable by a judge's contempt powers, which can translate to time in jail. Some lawyers routinely inconvenience witnesses because they can. But, don't you find it inappropriate to presumptuously force witnesses to waste their precious time simply because a lawyer has the legal power to do this?

Witnesses deserve to be treated courteously. If an attorney doesn't grasp this, then they are nothing more, nothing less, than an arrogant hooligan. There, I said it. And, I mean it. I prefer to use the frightening power allotted to me as sparingly as possible. Never use more than is ever necessary. The success of our cases depends on the cooperation of our witnesses. Yes, we have the power to issue subpoenas. And, with rare exception, it matters not who that certain someone is.

The power of a subpoena outranks both the powerful and the weak. There are consequences for not obeying a subpoena. For those who don't obey? We have the power to obtain an arrest warrant. Recalcitrant witnesses can be forced to take the witness stand, in handcuffs. I've done it. Trust me. It's not that difficult. But, doing this must be very selective. Any chest-beating aside, first and foremost, witnesses are human beings. I know I am inconveniencing you in some fashion, by merely asking you to show up, testify, and help me meet my burden of proof, with or without a subpoena.

So, whether I am required to do so, I always allow myself a maximum fifteen minute window of flexibility for each witness. Anything beyond that, in my humble opinion, is nothing short of professional arrogance, and undue inconvenience to witnesses. Besides, as a constitutional officer, neither my deputies, nor I, work *for* the court. As executive officers, we have a constitutional duty to work *with* the judicial branch of government to dispense justice. We are equal partners with one another. Let the judge be pissed. I have big enough shoulders to handle judicial temper tantrums. And, I have done exactly that, more than once.

Part of dispensing justice also means being fair and just to witnesses. Therefore, I will not inconvenience people simply to feed my own ego, or the one belonging to the person sitting up at the bench. Sure, courtroom lawyers call judges *your Honor*. But, that doesn't mean DA's and judges are not legal equals. We are. This is not me hypothesizing. Like anything lawyers do, I rely on law, when I make such a declaration. And, the U.S. Constitution is as good as it gets for American law.

I've began practicing this approach, long before I was the Solita County District Attorney, and am not going to change that methodology just to get along with yet another elected official. If it ain't broke, I don't fix it. Thank you, Founding Fathers.

Chapter 86

As the final witness for Plaintiffs stepped down from the witness stand, I remained standing next to counsel table. Unless Gilbert had more evidence I wasn't aware of, we had just completed the presentation of our entire case, including testimony from all our witnesses, and the introduction of each and every planned document. This was a pivotal moment.

"One second, your Honor," I advised, as I quickly conferred with Harvey.

"So, Harv," I whispered, "I have we remembered to introduce all of our exhibits?"

"Yep," Gilbert replied. "All one hundred thirty-nine of them."

Many were photographs. Some, which I wanted the jury to see, wouldn't be admitted. Henderson had already determined their probative value was outweighed by their prejudicial effect. Damned lawmakers and all their nit-picking.

"All wits testify?"

"Yep."

"Have we left anything out?"

"Nope."

"You're positive?"

"Yes, I am."

I gave him one additional glance. He simply raised his eyebrows up and down, but said nothing more. I nodded, before turning back toward the bench.

"Your Honor, Plaintiffs move all their exhibits, previously marked for identification, into evidence."

"Mr. Owens?" inquired Henderson.

"May counsel approach?" asked Owens.

Up at side bar, out of ear shot of the jury, Charlie told the court which photographs he didn't want admitted. For the record, he objected to each of them as possible items of evidence.

"Only twelve through fourteen and fifty-seven through sixty-three."

"You're objecting to 12, 13 and 14? The autopsy photos? And, 57, 58, 59, 60, 61, 62 and 63? The crime scene pictures?" asked the judge.

"Yes."

"Basis?"

Predictably, Owens claimed the prejudicial effect outweighed any probative value for all the photographs, same as I would have done, were I in his shoes. Typical boilerplate stuff. The first three were autopsy photos. Henderson overruled Charlie, with the exception of number thirteen, which was probably the most graphic picture.

As to numbers 57-63, Henderson noted they were simply pictures of the decedent, with either Dawn identifying him, or crime scene photographs. He found no undue prejudice. I didn't either. But, I understood Owens had a job to do. Once we returned to counsel table, the judge explained his ruling to the jury.

"Ladies and gentlemen, with the exception of number 13, the court is ordering the rest of Plaintiffs' exhibits into evidence. The court finds all, except number 13, legally relevant and probative. I realize you haven't seen that one. And, you never will, due to the ruling the court just made. But, the weight you attach to any evidence is exclusively your decision, including any photographs. Not my call. When you retire to the jury room to deliberate, all items of evidence can go with you. Or none. That's your call."

He looked at me.

"Anything further, Mr. Travers?"

"Plaintiffs rest," I said, feeling the typical relief that occurs, whenever I am done presenting a case. For some reason, this part of a trial always reminds me of hearing proctors, calling time at the end of my bar exams. Never elation. Just relief.

I quickly double-checked everything mentally. I had to be sure. Harvey Gilbert is becoming a damned good trial lawyer. He's a very quick study. Excellent civil lawyer. But, first and foremost, I always rely on my own instincts. Today was no exception. Not this trial. It never is with any of my cases. But, this one? Especially so. Today was today. Only the present matters.

"Defendants?" asked the judge. "Opening Statement?"

W. Charles Owens, Esq., stood and thanked the court, prior to giving his Opening remarks which took approximately ten minutes. After he finished, the judge asked him to call his first witness.

Charlie knew we had come very close to inflicting mortal wounds on Jake Crenshaw's credibility. Just as we had planned, this was done primarily through evidence of Johnny Walker's threat at the car lot to kill any repossessors he caught on his property. We presented that through the combined testimony of Lawson and Annalee. We pooled this incriminating evidence, with the car man pretending to not know anything about the threat. Disclaimers to that effect appeared to zigzag throughout his entire testimony, both on direct and cross-examination.

He might have gotten away with it but for their combined testimony. Their effective tag team quickly disposed of that contention. That is the crucial significance of impeachment evidence. The truth shall set you free. And, it generally does.

Owens knew he had to rehabilitate him on that issue, in particular, and do it expeditiously. If he didn't, his case was toast. Charlie knew it. That was essential to their being able to defeat the fraud allegation. Even though impeachment knowledge was more relevant to the negligence count, credibility is credibility.

If the jury found Crenshaw unbelievable on any issue, they could disregard the entirety of his testimony. Did the jury believe Jake lied about his knowledge of Walker's propensity for violence? If they did, they could completely discredit him. In other words, the jury was either going to believe Crenshaw, or not believe him. Just like the bar exam, this one would be pass or fail. And, this wasn't just lofty lawyerly supposition. It's right there in the jury instructions Henderson would read to the jury. This wasn't legally unique to our case. This is part of standard jury instructions that are read to juries throughout America, trial after trial after trial. If you recall from our earlier discussion about Voir Dire, it's a search for the truth.

As a veteran litigator, Charlie knew how much this particular count increased the odds of a huge verdict for us. Sure, he understood the wrongful death charge was potentially going to be a painful pill to swallow for his client. But that sort of damage can be numerically calculated. It paled greatly, when compared to fraud. Wrongful death awards are primarily based on the simple crunching of numbers. Lawyers introduce actuarial tables, establish earnings by a decedent over their working life, and project future earnings. In somewhat abbreviated terms, a jury is asked to make a decision, based on what the decedent would have earned, during the rest of their working life, but for their untimely death.

Fraud, on the other hand, is like the proverbial elephant in the room. Make that one rogue bull in musth. And, like an elephant, the penalty it carries is much weightier, should a plaintiff prevail. And, we are talking about one big healthy adult pachyderm. Unlike wrongful death, which sounds particularly egregious to a layperson, fraud is not limited by the same restrictive compensatory damages rules. Basically, the very sky can be the limit. Perhaps beyond.

Compensatory damages, as the name implies, are meant to compensate a party for damages they can prove to have actually suffered. Destruction of a ten thousand dollar car merits compensatory damages of ten thousand dollars, not ten thousand and one dollars. Add any other incidental damages permitted by law and, voila, you have compensatory damages for the loss of that vehicle.

Properly arriving at the right figures tends to be a rather mechanical process. If it's proven by a preponderance of the evidence that the decedent would have earned $100,000 during the remainder of their interrupted working life, then the amount a jury should award is $100,000. Not a penny more and not a penny less.

Not so with fraud, however. And, that is because of punitive damages, also known as *exemplary damages*. Recovery by plaintiffs for proven fraud is essentially limited to how ticked off the jury is about what they believe the evidence shows the defendant did. Sure, such beliefs need to be supported by evidence presented at the trial. But, if they are, then the jury tends to pretty much have free reign. We lawyers and judges privately refer to punitive damages as *smart money*. This has nothing to do with anyone's IQ, nor their personal brain power. It does not denote intelligence or knowledge.

Smart money is so labeled because payment of such an award is expected to hurt or *smart*. Charlie knew this jury would pretty much have unlimited independence, within reason, in awarding punitive damages. For this reason, he actually preferred they would make an exorbitant award. If they did this, it increased the likelihood he could successfully convince the trial judge, or an appellate court, to grant his request for relief, should he lose.

Such absolution could reduce the amount, set it aside or, even grant a new trial. Owens' endeavor to rehabilitate Crenshaw, with the testimony of Deals on Wheels cashier Annalee Rutherford actually made sense. It did in theory, at least. In theory, this was nothing short of brilliant tactics by a skilled trial counsel. But, what looks good on paper doesn't necessarily match up in practice.

He made me curious. Doing this allowed Charlie to revitalize Jake, *without* subjecting him to potentially brutal cross-examination by me. But, anytime any witness takes the stand to testify, there are never any guarantees. Such would soon be the case here.

Jake already did enough damage to their defense, as one of Owens' own witnesses. When long-limbed beauty Annalee Rutherford took the stand, her testimony didn't even come close to bearing the rich fruit Charlie hoped it would produce. Instead, it far more resembled fruit from the proverbial *poisonous tree*. Charlie was about to violate a cardinal rule of examining witnesses.

Never ask a question if you don't know the answer.

Owens should have known better. I taught him that myself. And, I really drilled that into his head. Yes, there are limited exceptions to that, but I won't get into them here. We don't need to turn this into a primer on Evidence.

"So, Ms. Rutherford," he began. "You seem to have a rather high opinion of yourself, don't you?"

"Just exactly what do you mean, sir?" she asked deferentially, sounding almost meek.

"According to your earlier testimony, you claim Mr. Crenshaw was *hitting on me again*, as you put it, when you say Mr. Walker was also making his *purported* threat to kill any repo men he ever found on his property, correct?" he said, carefully emphasizing selected words.

"There's no *purported* to it, Mr. Owens."

"I beg your pardon? Did you not say Mr. Crenshaw was hitting on you?"

"Yes. That's nothing new.

Owens elected to not have the gratuitous part of her answer stricken. His question called for a yes or no answer from her. Legally, her answer, after the word *yes* was non-responsive. But, Charlie ignored it. This meant the jury was at liberty to consider it as evidence. I'd have gotten that struck in a blind second.

"And, did you hear everything he said?"

"Yes."

"You're saying you comprehended two simultaneous conversations?"

"They weren't conversations, sir. They were two simultaneous monologues. But yes, I heard them both. And, quite clearly, in fact. I can still recite them nearly letter-perfect."

Owens paused a moment, as if to collect his thoughts. He said nothing at first. If I were him, I would have asked the judge to strike her unrequested remark. Doing this would regain control. But, I sure as hell wasn't going to tell Charlie how to beat us. I could tell he was taken aback by Annalee's mental sharpness. I knew she was one sharp cookie. Charlie was painfully learning this too. One of the jurors laughed. A second one tried to not smile. I bit my lip and pretended to study my notes. Sometimes, self-control is more difficult than it is otherwise. This was one of those times. I bit down even harder, distractingly massaging my temples. Watching opposing counsel getting their ears boxed is both educational and entertaining.

"So, doesn't it make sense to you that Mr. Crenshaw was more interested in you than in Mr. Walker?"

"You mean do I believe Mr. Crenshaw is heterosexual? Oh, very much so."

Members of the jury and the spectator gallery exploded with gales of laughter. Owens ignored the answer. His face reddened. I couldn't help but smile. So, I did. Henderson chastised Annalee, and gaveled the court to order. She meekly apologized. But, I could tell she wasn't chastened. The lady was clearly enjoying this.

"Let me ask you this," said Owens. "If Mr. Crenshaw was that enamored with you, how can you be sure he even knew Walker was there?"

"Oh, he knew," she said.

Owens continued to violate the cardinal rule for trial lawyers. It shocked me that Charlie hadn't done his homework. He knew better. I'd taught him. This was now starting to reflect on me. He had just asked yet another question, even though he didn't know that answer either. It appeared he was not giving Ms. Rutherford credit for the mental acuity she clearly possessed. A bit of latent chauvinism, perhaps? My initial assessment of her was sure wrong. She was one bright human being. She continued. Owens didn't see the land mine until it was too late. She continued to gain even more traction.

"As that obnoxious drunk made his threat, he was pretending to hold a rifle, pointing it right at Jake's head."

Frankly, part of me wanted to ask for a recess, so I could bitch slap some common sense into his thick head. Any foolishness displayed by one's student reflects poorly on the professor. Talk about ambivalence. Half of me wanted to laugh. The other half wanted to cry. Owens seemed distracted, in thought. He attempted to display his best poker face. He moved documents around at the podium. But, Annalee was far from done.

"Don't you want to know what he did?"

"No ma'am. No question pending. I ask the questions. That's my job. You provide the answers. That's yours."

Owens paused, rubbed his own forehead, and spoke to Henderson.

"No further questions, your Honor."

When it was my turn for re-direct examination of Annalee, I wasted no time getting her to provide the very answer Charlie had struggled to avoid.

"Ms. Rutherford, what did Mr. Crenshaw do, when he saw Mr. Walker simulating holding a rifle?"

"Objection," said Owens. Assumes facts not in evidence."

"Sustained," said the judge.

I purposely asked the question the way I did so there was no confusion on the part of the witness as to what answer I wanted. Unlike Charlie, I planned ahead. I knew it would be sustained. No harm, no foul.

"Let me re-ask that. Did Mr. Crenshaw see Mr. Walker at this time?"

"Yes."

"How do you know this?"

"I was watching both of them. Mr. Walker was right in front of my window. Mr. Crenshaw was to his side, but inside the glass. They were inches apart from one another. No more than two feet or so. Jake was closer to Walker than I was. And, I heard everything he said crystal clear. I also saw his entire pantomime with the simulated weapon. Plus, Crenshaw was looking right at him."

Wow, I thought. She was good! Better than a lot of cops I've seen in action. I glanced over at Owens, who appeared as if he was going to object. Instead, he minimally shrugged, and said nothing.

"What did Crenshaw do?"

"You mean when Walker pointed his make believe long gun at him?"

"Yes."

"Objection."

Owens was on his feet again, fighting for the very life of his case.

"Basis, counsel?"

Owens started to speak. "I…"

Henderson interrupted him and turned toward the witness.

"Ms. Rutherford, did you see Mr. Walker do this yourself?"

"Yes sir."

"Do you know what a rifle is?"

"Absolutely."

She explained, even contrasting a rifle to a shotgun and each to a handgun.

"No foundation. Lack of expertise."

"Overruled, Mr. Owens. Ms. Rutherford, you may answer."

"Do you remember the question, Ms. Rutherford?"

She smiled.

"I do, Mr. Travers."

"And, what did Crenshaw do?"

"Apparently, Mr. Crenshaw is skilled at multi-tasking."

"Objection. Non-responsive."

"Sustained."

"What do you mean, when you say Crenshaw is skilled at multi-tasking?" I asked.

"He turned white," she said. "He looked like he'd just gotten shot. He turned and stared at me. I could see the fear in his eyes."

"And, so there's no confusion, when you say Mr. Crenshaw, to whom are you referring?"

"Jake Crenshaw. Deals on Wheels lot manager."

"Nothing further."

Owens continued to appear outwardly indifferent, despite the beating he'd just taken. He was absolutely dying inside. I was sure of it. Like any veteran trial lawyer, he learned a long time ago to never show others how much any punch hurts. It's a lesson many of us trial lawyers learn. I know. I sure have.

However, just as Charlie was discovering, attitude was not altering the composition of his case. Just like me, he was stuck with the same facts. He knew the futility of attempting to apply lipstick to a pig. Irrespective of shade or quantity, the basic product was still pork.

Nothing Charlie could do would ever make it taste like giant prawns, sautéed with garlic, in extra virgin olive oil. It wouldn't mimic a beauty queen. Nor, would it ever smell like rose petals. Best case scenario? Charlie understood his client had better belly up to the bar. Prepare to pay an award for the wrongful death of Tommy Deen O'Mara. He still hoped against hope he could beat the fraud count. I wouldn't bet money on that. Not anymore. That appeared to be very wishful thinking, at the moment.

Annalee's testimony had nothing directly to do with the fraud committed, in the hiring of TD to repo Walker's truck. Her testimony had nothing to do with the number of assigned repo men. However, she damaged Crenshaw's overall credibility so badly, it was unlikely the jury would believe anything he told them. Owens still had a job to do. Within the bounds of law and ethics, he had to regain the jury's trust. The real question? Could he?

The job of any civil trier of facts is to crunch numbers. First of all, this jury had to determine if an award should be made. If so, how much would compensate the survivors of Tommy Deen O'Mara, for his loss? As a husband? A father? A provider? As for Charlie preventing them from awarding punitive damages, their case appeared to be in a non-recoverable free fall. If we proved fraud, oppression, or malice, the jury could award punitive damages. And, probably would. We understood our mission well. But, did he?

Once a jury makes this determination, the sky is practically the limit. As plaintiffs, we didn't have to prove a correlation even existed between the amount of actual damages, and what they believe they should award for punitive damages. At this point, the jury would simply decide how badly to hurt Reggie Baron, Jake Crenshaw and Deals on Wheels. Owens informed the judge he had no further witnesses. Henderson turned to me.

"Rebuttal, Mr. Travers?"

"None. Thank you."

I didn't even bother to ask Harvey this time. Instinctively, I knew we were better off just stopping while we were ahead. And, ahead we were. Yes, we thoroughly prepared each witness for their time on the stand. Those chickens were coming home to roost. But, I also knew how unpredictable witnesses could be. The defense had not produced any evidence to dispute what our case-in-chief established. Thus, I saw no reason whatsoever to continue presenting evidence. As the old songs urges, *you've got to know when to hold 'em, know when to fold 'em, know when to walk away, know when to run.*

Why risk rolling dice we didn't need to even touch? Henderson inquired if both sides rested. We each said yes. The end was near. The only remaining tasks, before this case went to the jury for deliberation were jury instructions, and final arguments.

"Okay, then let's do this," said Henderson, turning toward the jury box. "Counsel have rested their respective cases. This concludes the presentation of evidence. That means we are almost done."

One of the jurors clapped lightly. Another said "yay."

He looked at the jury, paused, frowned, and then continued.

"No talking, please," he reminded them.

"There are two remaining portions of this trial. One is jury instructions. The other is closing arguments. Court and counsel need to meet to discuss instructions. It's one of those behind closed doors things you hear about. We'll do that at 9:30 tomorrow morning. So, jurors, you are excused for the rest of the day, including alternates. You will receive different instructions, once we are done with these two remaining portions."

Henderson gave one of his rare courtroom smiles.

"Please be back here no later than 1:30 tomorrow afternoon. At that time, counsel will each have the opportunity to argue what they believe the evidence has established. Remember the admonition. Do not discuss the case with anyone, including each other. Court's in recess."

The bailiff stood to direct the jury from the courtroom. Once they were gone, Henderson rose, and left the courtroom. Others began leaving. Harvey smiled, as he gave me a playful punch on the shoulder. I felt good. Was my optimism premature?

Chapter 87

The next morning, Owens, Gilbert and I met with the judge to select jury instructions. This process is rather simple and straightforward. Attorneys on each side give the judge our requested written instructions. The court either approves them or doesn't. Some fighting is bound to occur. That's because lawyers are involved. If the court approves them, these legal recitations are read to the jury. These are the laws jurors are duty bound to apply to the facts, in order to make a decision. Once they do this, the jury can arrive at an appropriate conclusion. If the court authorizes them, these instructions are the ones the jury applies to the evidence they receive during the trial. These, and only these, instructions, as applied to the facts, determine the outcome of any trial, whether criminal or civil, if the jurors are being true to their oaths as jurors.

Most instructions proffered by counsel are what lawyers refer to as *standard* instructions. In this particular trial, they are found in the Texas Civil Practice & Remedies Code. Any other instructions are known as *special* instructions. Special instructions are custom ones lawyers draft, based on relevant statutes and/or appellate cases.

Specials are drafted if either counsel can't find a needed instruction from the packet of standard instructions, and believes the jury needs to focus on some issue the trial's evidence has established. Creating specials isn't mandatory. But, if the standard ones don't cover a factual scenario from evidence presented during your trial, and you want to convince a jury such evidence is significant, you cannot do it without an instruction covering that. Failure to do so amounts to malpractice, in my humble opinion.

If a standard one cannot be found, then a special instruction is prepared, including the legal principal you rely on. Next, you ask the judge to add it to the proposed packet of instructions, in one of these off-the-record sessions. Like any enterprising trial lawyer, I've drafted my share of specials. It helps bolster my own case. And, it gives opposing counsel something else they need to wrestle with.

It isn't what I'd call a terribly complex procedure. But, it is time consuming. Like anything else a trial lawyer does in their pursuit of victory, it's tedious and work-intensive. For any courtroom warrior, it boils down to rolling up our sleeves and doing the work. Irrespective of whether the instructions are standard or special ones, they are the law. The jury is duty bound to follow them, in order to arrive at a proper verdict. In most trials, the lion's share of instructions is presented with minimal fanfare or strife.

Let's dwell on one point for just a moment. When I say a jury is duty bound to follow the law bundled up in the instructions, I am not saying they have to automatically agree with either lawyer's interpretation of presented evidence. In other words, while no juror can disregard the law, a juror can disregard presented facts. In fact, that's a jury's job, i.e., to determine what the evidence presented to them really means. Jurors are triers of the presented facts, akin to a judge in a court trial. In the informal skirmishes between lawyers to persuade the judge which directives should be used, some present more of a challenge than others. Generally, special instructions are finagled over far more than standard instructions.

In the instant trial, an almost incendiary instruction is the one dealing with *agency*. We requested this one. Actually, I did, directing Harvey to prepare it. Initially, he told me I was wrong. But, I knew I wasn't, so I insisted he use my suggested case. That's part of the turf of being first chair. You get to make final decisions. And, that's also why I insisted I have the last word, when I agreed to represent Dawn in the first place. I need to be the guy who has concluding call on anything.

Harv thoroughly researched this area. Both Jennifer and Norma assisted him with this momentously important task. And, they did great. Gilbert relied on both statutory authority and case law in our written briefs. I carefully reviewed all their work. Ultimately, he agreed with my position, even becoming quite passionate about it. He contended the law of agency meant Lone Star Motorcars, Inc., dba Deals on Wheels Used Cars, was responsible for the sins of its authorized agents. That's precisely why I insisted he build the instruction around the case I selected. Go get 'em, Harv!

Interestingly, we relied exclusively on a California case, *Feather River Trailer Sales, Inc. v. Sillas,* rather than one from Texas, since I found none that fit our facts quite as nicely. I'd used this particular case many times before in my own state. It was even helpful, whenever I prosecuted defendants for theft by false pretenses in conspiracies where I was able to show agency situations existed. After some debate between us, I finally had to insist Harvey include this case. At first, he disagreed. At one point, our discussion even got quite heated. As you might surmise, the big bone of contention was the fact it was a California case. We were here in Texas relying on it to win this trial.

Lawyers are required to take an entire semester of Legal Research at the beginning of law school. I won't bore you with the details, since it continues to bore me to death, other than to say there are cases that fall under the rubric of *persuasive* authority and ones that are called *mandatory* authority. Judicial appellate courts are broken down geographically throughout America, with each having authority for their own piece of turf. And, there is also a pecking order, with trial courts required to do what their own appellate courts tell them to do, in their written opinions, on legal issues. Certain appellate courts outrank all the others. The U.S. Supreme Court is at the very top.

Like lawyers, judges rarely agree on anything. Therefore, neighboring jurisdictions may review a similar factual situation, but arrive at two totally different conclusions. An old lawyer joke asks how to quickly obtain thirteen different judicial opinions. Just place twelve judges in the same room. The decisions rendered by the appellate courts, in your physical area, are the ones you mandatorily must follow, if you're a trial judge. Those from other areas can be followed but don't have to be because they are persuasive, rather than mandatory.

In fact, if the appellate court in your locale renders a decision at odds with one from a neighboring jurisdiction, whether you like it or not, you must follow the law, as interpreted by your own appeals court. Again, mandatory versus persuasive. I admit I've oversimplified this basic issue. And, for sake of brevity, I won't get into more esoteric stuff, like state versus federal questions, or foreign courts. Fortunately, I found no Texas appellate case that contravened *Feather River*, nor any contrary federal cases.

Therefore, what should have been a merely persuasive case became the only relevant law on the issue of agency. This meant Henderson had little choice, but to follow its legal reasoning, almost as if it was mandatory authority. My reliance on this California case to prove civil fraud came from an established track record. I personally believe it describes the law of agency better than any other case I've found, irrespective of its situs.

After he completed his own research, not terribly surprisingly, Harvey did a complete one-eighty. He now strongly agreed with my interpretation, and for the very same reasons I did. That's like observing appellate justices do their own legal weighing, beginning by leaning east, then finally resting at west, or vice-versa. Understandably, it's not common for lawyers to use cases from other jurisdictions as mere persuasive authority. You are essentially trying to label them mandatory, by default.

The named defendant in *Feather River* is Herman Sillas. At the time, Herman was the Director of Motor Vehicles for California DMV and was sued by the owners of Feather River Trailer Sales, Inc. It wasn't that Sillas did anything wrong. But, as Director, they sued him to convince the court DMV was wrong on a licensing decision. Because Sillas was in charge of DMV, he was the named defendant. They sued because DMV revoked their occupational license, after finding Feather River's employees had defrauded customers. The dealer claimed Feather River was not responsible for lies their employees told customers. As Molly would say, *no tienen verguenza.* Trial court reversed DMV. The appellate court disagreed. They upheld the revocation. Harvey and associates did 99% of the work on this particular instruction, as I was in trial. So, even though I was the reason we even knew about the true significance of

Feather River, I asked Gilbert to address the court, rather than myself. I thought it only fair that he, not me, be the lawyer to argue this point for us.

A seemingly nervous Gilbert cleared his throat. He began to speak.

"Judge, *respondeat superior* binds the principal. Makes the principal liable for any damages caused. In this case, Lone Star is liable because Mr. Crenshaw intentionally misrepresented relevant facts, when he hired Mr. O'Mara to repossess Walker's truck. *Feather River* is absolutely clear on this issue."

"Nonsense," said Owens. "When Crenshaw acted, even assuming he *lied through his teeth*, as counsel contends, he overstepped his bounds. He exceeded the limits of his authority. Is counsel actually contending my client hired him, so he could lie to the general public doing business with Lone Star? Or, specifically to Deals on Wheels customers, for that matter?"

As is standard practice, these informal discussions were not on the record. Not at this point in time, at least. Henderson assured us everything would be reported later, once we all agreed which instructions the court should approve. When we did this, he would be put everything on the record. He would direct the court reporter to record everything, including any argument of counsel. Harvey would get to make the same basic argument, a second time, even though everyone knew what the ruling was going to be. Henderson would tell us before he summoned the court reporter.

"I need some quiet time to review your P and A's. I'm going to my chambers to do this. I'm particularly interested in reading *Feather River*. Must confess. I've never read that one before. California case, counsel? You realize it's merely persuasive authority?"

"Yes sir."

"Anyhow, let's reconvene at...say...10:15?"

When Henderson returned to court, all three of us were eagerly awaiting his decision. He informed us Plaintiffs' Points and Authorities, particularly *Feather River*, correctly stated the law governing agency.

Owens had lost again. Everyone was excused until 1:30.

Chapter 88

A standing room only crowd began quickly filling up the courtroom for the afternoon session. The crush of media made it claustrophobic. Many had followed the case, from the very day Tommy Deen O'Mara bled to death. Everyone was back in court to hear arguments of counsel. Present were field reporters from TV, radio, and newspapers. They jockeyed for position. Gilbert even pointed out a couple of local TV anchors he recognized. Unlike when I'm at home, I recognized no local talking heads. Only the nationally visible ones.

I thought I saw Geraldo, but wasn't sure, and, frankly, didn't really care. I had a job to do. It took priority over any media. I glanced, but could only see it was some short guy, with a big moustache. He was holding a microphone, and appeared to be talking non-stop. I could tell he was with a TV station. Another guy was pointing one of those big cameras on top of a tripod at him. A station identifier and logo were attached to his microphone. I was moving too fast to confirm. Frankly, it didn't matter. I was working. Someone was calling my name, but I kept walking. I pretended to not hear them.

We entered the courthouse. Both Harvey and I were repeatedly asked for a statement about the case. Remaining true to my word, every inquiry was met with a simple "no comment" from me, or words to that effect. Harv said nothing whatsoever, giving me the distinct impression he was a bit rattled by all the media attention. Some media members appeared fascinated by the unique facts surrounding the case. Others were curious about the California lawyer who was lead trial counsel. And, still others wanted to know why any prosecutor was trying this civil case in Houston. They could keep guessin'.

"Sorry folks," I said, as we weaved our way through the crowd. "I've already told you I won't comment on this matter, until the trial is over. Once that happens, I promise you'll have my undivided attention. I'll answer each and every relevant question. But, not before the jury finishes their work on our case. I don't try cases on the six o'clock news. If you knew me, you'd know that."

Owens was walking past us, when I said this. He snorted, but said nothing. One of the reporters turned, and looked at him. The media knew Charlie represented the Defendants. Little did the closest muckraker know Owens' impetus. Charlie, on the other hand, remembered how I regularly utilized the media in Solita County, when he was still on my team. But, I've always believed my methodology makes sense. Why? 'Cuz it does. The media is the sole entity to keep our constituents informed about the quantity and quality of our work. I dealt with the media so much it has become common for TV reporters to smile, by the end of an interview, and remark "…there's our sound bite…"

Charlie used to tease. He said I needed a press agent. He should have known I'm eclectic. Politely phrased, it's never been beneath my dignity to *borrow* a good idea. None of us are that original. Shortly after he said that, Solita County had its own media liaison. *Thank you, Charlie!*

Henderson took the bench. He seemed in a hurry. The bailiff was still calling the afternoon session to order. Even though it was today's second half of court, the uniformed deputy gave the formal opening he normally reserved for morning sessions. He deferred to the court.

"Ladies and gentlemen," Henderson began. "We are now at that part of the trial where the court reads jury instructions to you. Once I do that, counsel can argue."

He paused and smiled. I couldn't believe it. Was Henderson actually making a joke in his own courtroom? Due to his usual seriousness, people didn't know whether they should laugh. Most didn't. I did. I knew he was being jocular. Been doing this too long to not get it.

"I don't mean debate with each other," he clarified. "I mean argue their cases to you. In other words, they will tell you what they believe the evidence proves, or doesn't prove. Before I begin, I need to remind media present of the court's previous caveat."

His smile vanished. He looked sternly in the direction of the first few rows in the spectator gallery where most media were seated, as well as the back wall where the television cameras stood silently.

"My granting your request to be here is a bit novel. Frankly, I haven't permitted this, prior to this trial. I'm still uncomfortable with the notion that cameras are here in my courtroom. Madam Reporter, please mark this portion of the transcript," he directed, then returned his attention to the jury.

"Please. No one misunderstand me. I took an oath to protect and defend the Constitution. This includes the First Amendment. I gladly accept your contention. The public does have a right to know about newsworthy cases. Your lawyers have convinced me you have a First Amendment right to so inform them. But," he said, wagging an index finger, "I will order all of you to leave, if there is any interruption of this trial. I will not have a tug of war between free speech and a party's right to Due Process. Not in my courtroom, anyhow. A sin by one of you is a sin by all. Interruption means the abuse of free speech. Not its exercise. Is everyone clear on this?"

The judge scanned the courtroom, as he spoke. Some heads nodded. Film in cameras was already rolling. Henderson began reading the jury instructions he had already approved, including the special instruction dealing with agency. *Respondeat Superior*. Reading the instructions took more than fifty minutes.

Henderson purposely did this slowly and deliberately, so the jurors would more likely absorb them. He finished, and addressed the jury once more, before turning toward counsel table.

"Okay, jurors, now it's time for counsel to do their closing arguments. First will be Mr. Travers or Mr. Gilbert, since Plaintiffs have the burden of proof. Then, it'll be Mr. Owens. And finally, Plaintiffs will have what's known as *final* argument or *rebuttal*. Mr. Travers?"

He addressed me. I was first chair. I waited a moment, before slowly standing up. Doing this gave me time to collect my thoughts. Next, I picked up my yellow legal pad. I bent over to say something to Gilbert. Harvey nodded. He gave me a sheet of paper. My routine did not vary. But, this time it wasn't an investigating officer riding shotgun at counsel table. It was Harvey Gilbert. The jurors couldn't tell what document he handed me. But, any regular courtroom participant should instantly recognize it. An exhibit list. This one was Plaintiffs'. It was ours, numbering each of our exhibits chronologically. Defendants' exhibits, on the other hand, were alphabetically designated. Don't ask me why it's done like this. I don't know why, other than it helps keep clerks from assigning exhibits to the wrong party. How did this begin? Your guess is as good as mine. No offense, but don't know and don't care.

I needed to have this list, in my own hands, for quick reference. Harvey needed to know what I needed, during my argument. I could refer to a particular item of evidence. He had an identical list at counsel table. We had to function as more than a mere team. During closing, we had to be one and the same person.

Before the jurors entered the courtroom for closing, I had already obtained our evidence from the clerk, so we could keep it at counsel table. Harvey could quickly hand me any evidence. Like most experienced courtroom clerks I've dealt with, this one kept everything in a big cardboard box. Certainly not fancy. But, it was quite functional. Function always trumps form during any jury trial. Especially during argument. Harvey placed the entire box right in front of himself on counsel table. As long as he could see me, and vice-versa, we were fine.

"I trust permission to enter the well still remains, your Honor?" I inquired.

Henderson nodded.

"Thank you, your Honor. Ladies and gentlemen of the jury, your Honor, court staff, distinguished opposing counsel, and members of the media. On behalf of my clients, Dawn O'Mara, Cecilia O'Mara, and the other surviving members of the O'Mara family, I thank each of you for this opportunity. What we seek is simple: long-awaited, yet long-denied, justice for a long-suffering family. Each of them deserves far better."

I described the events depicted by the evidence. This included testimony and documents establishing how Defendants negligently caused the wrongful death of Tommy Deen O'Mara. I also argued Defendants committed the fraud which led to his death. Since this was closing argument, the judge allowed additional latitude than usual, for all counsel. In other words, we could talk about law, even though it is the sole province of the court to tell the jury what the law is. Therefore, I referred to *Feather River*. I described in great detail why we proved Defendants were liable, under what is known as the law of agency.

"Folks, none of us should be here today, except for one person. Dawn O'Mara shouldn't be here. Neither should her minor child. Nor, her adult children. Mr. Owens shouldn't be here. Nor, the Defendants. Mr. Gilbert shouldn't be here. I shouldn't be here. Nor, the judge or court staff. Neither should you. Especially, not the media. *You* know who *should* be here: *Tommy Deen O'Mara*. Unfortunately, the only one who should be here, isn't here. Ironically, that is why we are here, to explain why TD isn't. Defendants killed him. The cops, the DA, and the Texas Legislature don't even give a rip."

"He's D-E-A-D! So, what's the remedy? We'll talk about that, in a bit."

I paused, sipped, and studied the jury again. I swallowed.

"I don't mean he should be here in court, of course. I'm talking about being here in the same physical plane as the rest of us. It's one we no doubt take for granted. What should he be doing? Working? Goofing off? Having fun with his lovely wife Dawn? Making love with her? Spoiling their children? Being a husband? Being a dad? He should be doing anything other than what he happens to be doing, thanks to the fraud and negligence of Defendants."

I could feel my eyes closing to narrow slits, as I glanced from one end of the jury box to the other. I paced. I stopped. I pounded the air with my fist.

"We all know what he is doing, don't we? Tommy Deen O'Mara's cold, lifeless body lies motionless in the dank ground over at a cemetery in Tomball. All this is due to the deception of Jake Crenshaw, and the greed of an auto dealer who cares more about money than human life."

I glanced toward the jury. One or two of the women were wiping their eyes. I continued. After completing my opening argument, I thanked everyone and sat down, without referring even once to what I had written on my legal pad. I purposely left it at the podium. It was for Charlie's benefit and simply read: *if you don't know the answer, don't ask the damned question!*

When it comes from the heart, it seems to flow more easily. As I passed the podium, I should have slowed to pick up my oft-neglected legal pad and carried it to counsel table. Once I was there, I should have set it down gently, as if it were a Ming vase. But, Owens would soon learn why I left it there. All's fair in love and war. And, the courtroom is a known battle zone.

I try to be aware of my surroundings. This includes the courtroom. I was satisfied we had emotionally touched the jurors. Had we probed deeply enough? Would Owens' comments now fall on deaf ears? I decided I'd settle for some hearing-impairment.

Charlie stood up to give his closing argument. He walked toward the podium. He surreptitiously peeked at my legal pad. Owens thought I had erroneously left it behind. I gauged his reaction. I could tell his emotions were running wild. But, being the trooper he is, he shifted gears, pretending to not have even read anything and began to argue. Considering what he had to work with, he actually did a pretty decent job.

I could tell I'd messed up his concentration a wee bit. I didn't do anything illegal or unethical. I was just having some private fun with an old Marine buddy, pushing his buttons; teasing him for his mistake made while cross-examining Annalee.

After his closing, I stood up again. As the judge had just explained, I had an opportunity to rebut what Charlie had contended in his argument to the jury. I visually polled them, the spectator gallery, and the media, as I rose. Everywhere I looked, I saw what appeared to be faces of stone. Since Owens had just addressed the jurors, I took this as a good sign. My hope was that either his recitation, or our evidence, was responsible for their demeanor. After all, a good man should still be alive and well. But, he was dead and buried. Moving my notepad to the side on the podium, I spoke again.

My rebuttal argument was relatively brief. I have never subscribed to the idea that longer is better. Not in the courtroom, anyhow. I try to think like a juror. If it bores me, I assume it'll bore them. I believe most people get jaded quickly. I've always believed a lawyer does their job best by simply presenting convincing evidence. What's the point of flagellating a moribund equine? Too much attorney-speak is a fast way to do just that.

Owens' own argument lasted nearly three hours. I was sure I heard someone snoring. By comparison, our opening was less than an hour, even though we had the burden of proof. Why would I tell you I believe in brevity if I don't practice it?

One of my long-practiced trial tactics has been to purposely leave out little tidbits, here and there, during any argument. The reason I do this is to give jurors the opportunity to play amateur sleuths, as long as I remember to present the evidence I need to meet my burden of proof. I do this so they can connect the dots. Today was no exception. My final argument was less than ten minutes. As I wound down rebuttal, I shifted into high gear.

"Okay," I said to myself, "time to twang heartstrings. Let's win this epic battle."

I paused and took a sip of water. I did this, not because I was thirsty, but purely for dramatic impact. Sometimes, silence is golden. I swallowed, and began to speak.

"Folks, the evidence clearly establishes that Defendants are responsible for the horrible, painful, premature death of a loving husband and father. A proud lifelong Texan. A longtime member of this very community. His widow, Dawn, can't bring him back, even though she will love him with all her heart 'til her dying day."

I paused, sipped and studied the jury again. I swallowed.

"Neither can the judge. I sure can't. Neither can you. Folks, this isn't rocket science. No one can make Tommy Deen O'Mara experience the sweet taste of life-sustaining air again. All any of you can do is to reach into the bottoms of each of your hearts and award Mrs. O'Mara and their children a monetary award that doesn't insult the memory of this decent, loving man."

I stopped and folded my arms. Then, I continued.

"I'm not even going to tell you what that number should be. I'm confident TD and family can count on you to do your jobs properly, and honestly, *unlike some other folks.*"

I paused to measure the jury's reaction, and then, wrapped up my rebuttal. The targets of my remarks included Crenshaw, Larson, Montgomery, and the rest of the hyena pack. It didn't matter that the latter two weren't parties to this lawsuit. Heads nodding told me the jury understood.

"All I'll say on that point is this. Punitive damages are meant to punish Defendants for what they did. Jake Crenshaw lied to TD about the repo. That killed him. What did he call it? Let's see: *...a clean one...a fresh one.* These lies caused TD's murder. When the neighborhood drunk, Johnny Walker, wasn't arrested or prosecuted for murdering Tommy Deen O'Mara, justice was denied. A case sent to the grand jury, *without charges*, isn't my idea of honest prosecution. Justice was *not* dispensed."

I paused a final time, slowly inhaled, and exhaled, then spoke.

"Frankly, there's no way you can ever give TD justice, no matter what you do. However, Plaintiffs deserve justice. From his grave, Tommy Deen O'Mara cries out. Do you hear him?"

I paused, cupped a hand to my right ear, paused and continued.

"He beseeches you to provide his loved ones with just that. Remember. Justice delayed is justice denied. Please," I said, with my voice cracking, "don't deny them a second time. Thank you."

Chapter 89

Following three days of deliberations, the jury finally returned to the courtroom. This meant they had reached a verdict. How did I know? The clerk told me. This is standard fare. If you want to know anything about what is going on in any courtroom, ask the clerk assigned to that particular court.

Frankly, I was concerned they might be deadlocked. They weren't. The alternates were excused following closing arguments. But, per standard operating procedure, they were admonished by the judge to remain available, just in case a regular juror was excused. That is the exercise of sound judgment. Trust me, it happens. The judge also admonished them to not talk about the case to anyone, unless they were otherwise instructed by the court. Again, standard instructions. The alternates left the courtroom, shortly after the regular jurors went to the jury room to deliberate.

I don't get nervous. But, I do occasionally get concerned, depending on what sort of issue has chosen to bury itself deep beneath my skin. And, now, I was getting very concerned. So was our entire legal team. We had the burden of proof. I couldn't let Dawn down. So, why had the jury taken so damned long to reach a verdict?

A lengthy period of deliberation could be significant. Each of us was concerned it could possibly mean no verdict. Or worse? A defense verdict. During our team meetings, I explained this to everyone, including Dawn. All were prepared, but each was antsy. However, as we pondered the delay, we also knew our collective conscience was clear. We prepared this matter as thoroughly as any case I've ever touched. To say I'd missed a few hours of sleep would be an understatement. In fact, I was burned out and looked forward to returning home and recharging my batteries.

Harvey Gilbert's expertise on civil matters more than made up for my own lack of prior practical experience in this arena. Harv was my mentor. He turned out to be an outstanding teacher. And, he prepared me on civil issues, just as I had prepared him for trial. In short, we had done everything we could do.

Civil cases were still hugely boring to me, compared to criminal. But, thanks to Harvey Gilbert, I had gotten up to speed rather quickly. So had the rest of our team. We functioned as a cohesive unit. Mere weeks earlier, we were complete strangers. Even though I had absolutely no interest in doing so, I was confident I now could try another civil case all by myself. Harv and I tried to read faces. Had we won or lost? All we saw were poker faces. None of the jurors would even look toward counsel table. *Sonofa…*

Frankly, aside from any of the fertilizer so-called experts toss around, jurors are not real predictable. They are hard to read. The juror who smiles at you, and appears to be engaged with you throughout the trial, may be the very one who torpedoes your case. Conversely, the one who sits there, and does nothing but sulk and scowl, may end up being selected foreperson. That same guy may even be the driving force that convinces the rest of the jury to agree with your interpretation of the evidence.

People are fickle. So, sitting there, even after this many previous jury trials, I didn't feel I knew a bit more about the human nature of juries than I did as a brand new, squeaky-clean courtroom rookie who could barely find the jury box; let alone the water carafe. I silently exhaled. The judge addressed the jury. It was time for a reckoning.

"Ladies and gentlemen. I understand we have a verdict?"

I saw a number of heads nod.

"Okay, who's the foreperson?"

Juror number seven raised her hand. I wasn't surprised. Neither was Gilbert.

"Have you completed and signed the verdict forms?"

She nodded, indicating she had done so on behalf of the entire jury.

"Please hand them to the bailiff."

She complied. The bailiff took the paperwork from her. Without any further direction, he handed them directly to the judge. He'd done this before. I could tell. Henderson reviewed them. He gave them to the clerk to read.

However, as the judge silently read the still secret verdict, I noticed one of his eyebrows curiously rise. Although it was almost imperceptible, Gilbert and I both saw him do this. We silently exchanged glances. More butterflies. Old poker-faced Clancy had given away something, with his quirky gesticulation. But, what did this mean? Once again, I was in the dark. Like Dawn, I was feeling a helluva lot like a mushroom. And, I didn't like the menu.

"Madam Clerk," he said. "Please read the verdicts."

She stood, adjusting her glasses, before speaking. She read it verbatim.

"In the District Court of Harris County, Texas, 269th Judicial District. Dawn Lee O'Mara, et al, Plaintiffs, vs. Lone Star Motorcars, Inc., et al, Defendants, Case No. 96-06621, verdict, Count I…"

After the verdict was read, Dawn was initially standing. Then, she sat down, placing her head on counsel table. I feared she had fainted. Next, she got up. She wildly began jumping up and down. She looked around excitedly. Her pupils appeared dilated. She started hugging people. She hugged me. She hugged Harvey. Then, she snared Norma, Buck, and Jennifer, fiercely hugging each of us, practically squeezing the air out of our lungs. Next, she gave each of us a kiss on our cheeks. But, she wasn't done. She was nowhere close to being done. She sought even more targets.

Dawn continued hugging everyone within arm's reach; anyone who would stand still long enough for her to do so. She reminded me of Pac-Man gobbling up pac-dots. Apparently, she wanted to be sure her hugs didn't miss anyone. They almost didn't. Somehow, she even hugged Charlie Owens. This was a first. I never remember a plaintiff hugging a defense attorney. Pardon me, but this civil stuff is strange shit. He probably wanted to die. Owens' face turned bright red. Dawn looked around for other bull's eyes. I've never seen a sane person this close to being delirious.

She spotted Baron, quickly moving out of hugging reach. He scrambled for the door, barely escaping. Apparently hugged out, Dawn replaced hugs with words. Lots of words. Lots of loud words. She was practically screaming.

"Oh my God…oh my God…oh my God!" She repeated this, over and over. "I can't believe it. We won! We won! This is finally over. Thank you Lord." She looked up toward the ceiling, though a waterfall of tears, remarking "We did it, TD. We did it, baby!"

The jury had already left the courtroom. So had Judge Henderson. I urged caution. Owens quickly gathered up his belongings, and left the courtroom. Smudges of Dawn's lipstick were still on his cheek. He looked dazed. Reggie Baron was already outside, presumably running for his car.

I stood in front of her, holding her shoulders with both hands.

"Dawn," I began, "you understand we ain't done yet. Right?"

"What do y'all mean?" she asked.

"Defendants have remedies. And, these ones do, too."

"What can they do?"

"We've talked about this several times. Remember? They can ask Judge Henderson to reduce the punitive damages amount. They can ask him to throw it out altogether. They can even ask him to order a new trial."

"Wha…" she began. "You mean the hundred million dollars isn't ours?"

I held up both hands to calm her down. I found her hands, and held them in mine.

"No. Not yet, anyhow. Right now, those figures are just numbers."

"Huh?"

"Let's assume we continue litigating this case to a successful conclusion. That could take us through appellate courts for at least the next ten years. Probably more. This is a whole lot of moola."

"So, what do we do?"

"Charlie Owens is a fair man. And, he's a smart man. But, his client is an idiot. Let me talk with Charlie. I'll see if he and I can arrive at a meeting of the minds. We need to find a figure both sides can live with. A reduced figure, of course. Maybe greatly reduced, but, one you should find more than acceptable."

"Okay."

"Keep something in mind, Dawn. The law is on our side. Yes, we won. Yes, case law is clear on the issue of liability. Both the judge and the jury made all the right calls. The only variable? Can Charlie convince his client to be reasonable, and end this? Otherwise, they file an appeal. That could make us both old long before we need to be."

"What do you suggest?"

I had anticipated this. And, I'd already spoken with Gilbert, earlier in the day. I gave her a figure we believed would work. So, I guess I wasn't surprised, when Dawn accepted what I said without a fight.

"Joshua, I've told you from day one, you're in charge here. I'm not a lawyer. I know repos, not law. And, I rely on you to tell me what we should do on stuff like this. You've obviously been right on everything so far. Why in the world would I begin disagreeing with y'all now?"

I promised to let her know the results of any discussions with Owens. But, first things first. I had to phone Molly, and give her the good news. In doing so, I also gave her an estimate of when I'd be home again.

As I hung up the pay phone in the hallway of the courthouse, I spotted Owens.

"Charlie," I yelled, sprinting in his direction. When I got close enough to talk, without yelling, I spoke to him again.

"Let's talk. Neither of us needs this case to drag on for the next decade, or more. I need to get back to California."

"I agree," said Owens. "Reggie is driving me nuts. What do you suggest?"

"Let me put it this way. You're the only one with client control issues. Dawn will do whatever I recommend. Here's what I suggest. File your post-trial motions, and calendar them. Harv and the rest of the team can bang out our responsive pleadings. Then, I can come back to Houston, and we can argue them in court."

He nodded his head, side-to-side, like a metronome, weighing my words.

"Makes sense, so far."

"Once we do that, I'm confident the judge will deny all your motions, based on his prior rulings, on the same issues. Assuming he does that, we can sit down and settle this, by arriving at a figure both sides can live with. Then, we can obtain judicial approval."

"And, that would be?"

I told him. Owens appeared to weigh what I said a second time, nodded, and smiled.

He didn't say yes. But, more importantly, he didn't say no. Then, he frowned.

"Of course," he added, "that's assuming I have my dumb-assed client on board."

My normally bullet-proof stomach suddenly got a shooting pain.

"But, of course," I noted, surreptitiously rubbing my gut.

Chapter 90

I was back Houston. Motions and responsive pleadings were prepared, and filed. The usual cast of suspects was present. Predictably, Judge Henderson denied all of Owens' post-trial motions, with the exception of one. Charlie's request to decrease the punitive damages award by the jury wasn't denied. The judge said he would take it under advisement. This made me a bit edgy. I knew it couldn't increase. But, it could sure drop all the way down to zero. All three lawyers thought we knew why he did this. He was simply keeping a bargaining chip on the sidelines to assist counsel, as we attempted to conclude this matter, without a trip to an appellate court. At least, that was why I hoped he did it.

Owens and I had spoken to Henderson privately about a possible post-trial deal. He was receptive. This opened the door for both sides to take this case to the next step. That would allow us to give the matter permanent closure. An order from him would do just that. Anticipating the court's ruling, we had already instructed our team to prepare a motion. Filing it would put the matter back on calendar, so we could have a chambers conference with el juez, before I left Houston to return home again.

If this maneuver worked, we might settle the matter. Baron was present in court. Owens told him this was a mandatory appearance. He explained this meant Reggie had to be present, and why he had to be there. Once Baron had calmed down sufficiently, Charlie explained this was a golden opportunity to get Plaintiffs to agree to lower the amount of the verdict to a figure the billionaire could actually afford to pay.

"I'm trying to save your business empire, Reggie," he insisted.

Owens added that this wouldn't be out of pocket. The judgment would be paid by his errors and omissions carrier. That explained the appearance of the new lawyer in the courtroom today. A lower payment meant lower future insurance rates, than he'd have, with a hundred million dollar payout. The insurer's counsel had filed a motion for *Interpleader*. Technically, this was not the correct procedural vehicle. Nonetheless, it permitted the insurance company, and any of its lawyers, to have standing in court to participate, like the rest of us were already doing.

This allowed the insurer to fully participate in any settlement. Owens and I quickly explained what we sought to accomplish. She objectively soaked up this information. Predictably, as soon as all of us were back in chambers, Baron began his tirade.

"Judge," he said, "I ain't done nothin' wrong. I've fired Crenshaw. I'm firin' Owens. Hell, I might as well go bankrupt."

Henderson held up his hand.

"Sir, you can't do that."

"Do what? Fire my lawyer? Why not?"

"Go bankrupt. Actually, both. Your case is still before this court, as a post-trial matter. The only way you can fire your lawyer, or he can fire you, is with the court's permission. That, sir, isn't happening. Not at this 11th hour! We're not done. So please, just be quiet."

Henderson took a moment to glare at Baron. He gestured to Charlie.

"Mr. Owens, can you please explain why he can't go bankrupt?"

"May I, judge?" asked Charlie.

Henderson nodded, as if to silently indicate that was what he just said.

"Bankruptcy won't erase an award of punitive damages. You're on the hook for that. Every penny. Or, should I say, your insurance carrier?"

"I'm not giving legal advice, sir. But, I know the law. Your lawyer is absolutely right," added Henderson.

This led to more off the record discussions between Baron and Owens, Owens and insurance counsel. Both of them talked with Gilbert and me. And, all of us spoke with the judge. It was fast becoming a ride on a merry-go-round. I was getting dizzy. The negotiations went on for the remainder of the morning. They resumed again, right after the noon recess. Finally, near 11:30 p.m., an agreement was finally, but firmly, reached. I was exhausted, hungry and grumpy.

All parties agreed to resolve the matter, with the additional understanding any settlement would be permanently sealed. It would remain confidential. It's so hush-hush, I can't even share the details with you. Everyone was relieved, but each appeared to be exhausted and testy. All this jaw-jacking made each of us tired and raw. I knew the settlement still had enough zeroes in it to keep the O'Mara clan more than comfortable for the rest of their natural lives. And, then some.

In case you're wondering, the top secret nature of this stipulated agreement means I can't even tell you how much it is. But, let me suggest something. If you were Dawn, you would have to win more than a few lottery jackpots to feel this good.

As this, slowly but surely, wound down, I couldn't ignore the beeping only I could hear. Was my radar telling me it might not be over yet? The suspense was really starting to get under my skin. This I didn't' need. It was now time to deal with a certain state senator who opined that TD died because he wasn't quick enough. Sonofabitch will regret that.

EPILOGUE

The brief, but authorized, truancy of Solita County's one and own DA had ended. Their beloved top cop was home again, just as quickly as I'd disappeared. Assistant DA Armendariz assured me there were no brush fires to extinguish. It felt good to be back in the saddle. In fact, it felt nothing short of wonderful.

A series of official acts now awaited my decision making. First, as part of my office's planned reorganization, I created a brand new position. The title? *Chief* Assistant District Attorney. I originally came up with this particular idea years earlier. Brent Marvin stole it. Now, I was implementing it properly. The Chief ADA would run our day-to-day operations. That freed me up to work more closely with the other two branches of government. Now, I could pursue grants, and be more hands-on with greatly needed public safety legislation.

After Three Strikes became law, legislative energy, and mental acuity, seemed to wane. I had some fresh ideas. The CADA had to be someone I could trust implicitly. They had to seamlessly step into my shoes, when I was otherwise occupied. This would be an at-will position. I chose to not waste time interviewing strangers. I knew who I wanted, and why I wanted them.

Bennie was picked for two reasons: (a) I could. (b) He was a perfect fit. I didn't have the luxury of dwelling on this for long. Question: who would you elect? Correct. People rest, your Honor.

Needless to say, I was delighted he accepted. We didn't need the rigmarole of interviewing a parade of candidates. Too much dead wood aboard. Critics would claim I wasn't being objective. But, none of them had walked in Bennie's loafers. Or, my own. Stealth didn't even know I was doing this, until I did it. I like the right kind of surprises. He's known me long enough. Mr. Armendariz should know I am just as capable of selectively sneaking up on folks, as he takes great pride in doing.

Human Resources even liked my suggestion. Not that it mattered. They quickly got to work. HR drew up the job description for the new position. This included duties, minimum qualifications, and total benefit package, including salary. They knew what I wanted. I put it in writing.

Before I contacted them, mainly as a courtesy, I first contacted Irv Baker to make sure the Board would support this. They overwhelmingly approved. I didn't really need their blessing. But, I believe in transparency. Whenever possible, I also salute cooperation. Serving is a privilege, not a right. Baker assured me he spoke for the entire Board. My third official homecoming duty?

Deliver the promised check to Chairman Baker. I phoned him, making arrangements to meet. I could kill two birds with one stone.

The bank draft represented the entire portion of my attorney fees from the O'Mara lawsuit. Before delivering it, I endorsed its back side. The amount far exceeded what Solita County taxpayers spent to send, feed, house, and retrieve me. In fact, their total expenditure was a mere fraction of what I gave them. This included my salary, and all my expenses. On the front of the check, in the lower left hand corner, I added **SOLITA COUNTY GENERAL FUND**.

After meeting with Baker, I addressed the Board, *en banc*. I presented the eight-figure check to them at a special ceremony in our county's Administrative Center. We invited the media to witness this unique event. And, show up, they did. You still curious as to how much? Here's a hint. The California Public Records Act will allow you to learn, to-the-penny, the amount. It's forty per cent of the full settlement amount.

Following too many interviews, I returned to my office. I attacked a formidable stack of paperwork. No sooner did I slide behind my desk, than my damned phone began ringing. Naturally. The first call was from Harvey Gilbert. I wasn't surprised to hear his voice. We had previously discussed our special prosecutor role. This case had been anything but static. No sooner was one decision made, than it was quickly replaced with another issue to solve. In other words, it was what trial lawyers do for a living.

Stated another way, it was just another trial. I expected Harvey to tell me he was ready to convene a grand jury to prosecute TD O'Mara's murderer. Consistent with this entire journey, yet another surprise awaited me. I couldn't have been more wrong.

"Trav, you ain't gonna believe this," he began breathlessly.

This wasn't at all like Harvey. He's normally very calm, cool, and collected. Gilbert is one of those truly consummate professionals. But, he sounded like he was hyperventilating. I also couldn't remember him ever saying *ain't* before.

Unlike me, he was too prim and proper to fracture English like I occasionally do, on purpose

"Believe what?"

"Remember the late Johnny Walker?"

"How could I not? I…wait a minute. What do you mean *the late* Johnny Walker?"

"I'm holding the October 4 edition of the Houston Chronicle. Guess what the headline says?"

"Dammit, Harv. I'm busier than a one-legged man in a butt-kicking contest here."

He read the headline.

"MAN WHO FATALLY SHOT WRECKER DRIVER KILLS SELF."

"Holy Hanna! You…you…you mean Johnny Walker? *Our* Johnny Walker?" I was stuttering.

"That's what I just said. Deader 'n a door nail. Keep in mind. All I have, at the moment, is the newspaper article. But, it's him. Right name. Right victim. Chronicle even has Walker's picture. It's him. The same guy we've been planning to prosecute."

"Sonofabitch!" I spat. "Motherfu….." I interrupted myself. "Now what?"

"Well, we can still empanel a grand jury to investigate the violation of TD O'Mara's civil rights. Posthumously, of course. As a part of that, we could also ask them to determine Walker's cause of death, right?"

"How'd he die? Newspaper say?"

"Suicide. Gunshot to the heart."

"Hmmm," I mulled that over. "What kind of firearm?"

"Shotgun."

"Shotgun?"

"Yep. Standard length barrel and stock."

"Shotgun? Standard length?" I repeated. "He'd have to be part gorilla to have arms that long. How in hell does somebody shoot themselves in the heart with a full size shotgun?"

"Painfully. Lots of grimacing, I'd guess."

Harvey let loose with an unusually wicked-sounding laugh. Again, it didn't sound like him. Not even close. I wondered if he might be nipping some of grandma's cold medicine. But, I detected no slurred speech. I ignored his wise crack, and briefed the G-man on what to expect next.

"A Coroner's inquest will determine if it's a homicide, or a suicide. Harv, we need to decide if we even want to summon a new grand jury. If Walker's dead, is there really a point in us going down that road? I don't give a rat's ass how TD's murderer died. Besides, I'm here on my home turf again. I've got plenty to keep me busy, right here in Solita County. Lemme call Dawn. See what she wants to do. Then, I'll get back to you, okay?"

"Makes sense to me."

We hung, up. After dealing with a couple more unexpected calls, I hung up again, and made some notes. I thanked that caller, and hung up yet one more time. I quickly dialed, before another ringing phone could interrupt me. I impatiently waited for it to ring.

A pleasant female voice answered. At first, I thought I'd misdialed. I failed to identify myself.

"I'm sorry. I'm trying to reach Buck Masters."

"One moment," said the satiny voice. I pictured silk, slathered with pure raw honey. She sounded familiar. In the background, I could hear the muffled sound of a brief conversation. I instantly recognized the other person. The gruff voice belonged Sarge.

"Hello?" asked the male voice.

"Buck? It's Travers. Who does the lovely voice belong to, that just answered your phone?"

"You mean *our* phone? That's my new roommate…and *fiancé*…"

He paused. I could hear a quiet chuckle at his end.

"…Annalee Rutherford…"

"You dog. You sly dog. You sly, sly dog. Way to go, you crafty old cradle robber! Practically makes you a pedophile, no? How many decades older are you, than she? What'd you do? Kidnap her? You holding her hostage? Fess up, buddy boy. Or, maybe you better just invoke your 5th Amendment rights."

He laughed, then directed a good-natured invective at me.

"Anyhow, congrats. Hey, Sgt. Gumshoe, let's shift gears for a sec. Here's something new. I just learned this. You know our mad triggerman has expired, right?"

Masters laughed again. I could tell Annalee had improved his normally dour disposition. I blamed this on him looking through the windshields of too many police cars, over the span of too many years; doing so while generally divorced.

"You mean Johnny Walker? You beat me to the punch. I was just preparing to call you. Yeah, he's expired alright. Like curdled milk. Good riddance, I say. Talk about a complete misuse of oxygen!"

"Tell me about it. Hey, I need some info, Bucko."

"Yeah?"

"Harv says the Chronicle claims he killed himself. But, the pieces ain't fittin' together real well. Not for my poor little pea brain."

"Doesn't make sense to me either."

"Really? Why?"

He explained. Buck and I were still on the same wave length.

"Buck, I need a favor. Can you send me the incident reports and any crime scene photos?"

"Sure. When y'all need 'em?"

"Yesterday?"

"Aw Lord. Same old Travers," he laughed. "Want me to E-mail them to you?"

"Huh?" I asked. "What's E-mail?"

"Never mind. I'll explain some other time. I'll snail mail them."

We both laughed. He assured me he'd help. We ended our conversation, only after we discussed that certain blasé Texas lawmaker that needed to be spanked. *Vengeance is mine*, sayith the drug czar. Buck, Harvey, and I had already formulated a game plan. We will send him to the unemployment line, if it works. Let's save that discussion for another time, okay?

What the hell was E-mail? Snail mail? I envisioned a greased slide. Obviously, both were something new. I sure as hell wasn't staying up with some of this new technological stuff. I'm way too young to be a damned dinosaur. Help!

Two days later, a thick manila envelope arrived. The return address said Masters Investigative Services. Two names were in the letter's masthead. Both had private investigator licenses, accompanied by their own individual numbers. I recognized them as the types of numbers assigned to state-licensed private investigators, by their own regulatory agency. One was Buck. The other? Annalee Rutherford. There was also something in the letterhead I hadn't seen before. It read MIS@compuserve.com.

I wondered what that meant. When I spoke with Buck later, he said it was something he called his E-mail address. News to me. He explained that E-mail was some new technological thing. It was part of something even bigger. The World Wide Web? What in the hell? I promised myself I'd explore all that later, when I had time. I like new stuff, but I was still learning how to use my damned fax machine, for crying out loud. Now I had even more electronic crap to deal with? When will it end?

As I contemplated all this, I removed the envelope's other contents. I found a five page incident report by the Harris County Sheriff's Office. It had several color photographs, from various angles of a reposing Johnny Walker. A couple of cops stood nearby. One was Larson. Johnny was face-up. He sure looked dead.

His shirt was spattered with what appeared to be blood. Stippling was present. The gun's muzzle probably made contact. The shot pattern was tight. A piece of wadding from the shell partially protruded from his chest wound. It wasn't a pretty sight.

As I studied the pictures, I re-read the report a few more times, perusing it more slowly each time I read it. Then, I studied the photos again. I read the report one more time. Suddenly, it hit me like a ton of bricks.

"No way. No way, Jose," I said to no one in particular. No one was in my office, but me. But, as usual, that wasn't going to stop me from talking out loud. Old habits and all that good stuff.

"This guy didn't kill himself. He *did not* kill himself. Not like this. Old dumb-assed Johnny was never smart enough to bend the laws of physics this far. Not by himself. And, if he didn't off himself, who did?"

As I said this, I had already picked up my detested telephone and begun dialing. Will I never learn? Autopilot seemed to be orchestrating my next moves…

About the Author

artin C. Brhel, Jr., is a man of many parts, as *Tombstone's* Doc Holliday might observe. Marty insists he's *been there, done that* so many times, he feels more like Walter Mitty, than Walter Mitty.

Put another way? He's worn a few fedoras during his adventurous journey. Beginning with *Deadly Duty*, every *Joshua Travers, DA Adventure Series* novel will be replete with clues. Some true. Some false.

Correct interpretation of the aforesaid intimations could well cause you, the reader, to discern the plot of the next tome the author is already writing. Or, is it plots? But, then again, maybe they won't. Maybe they are all false.

Truth Travers knows. But, does he know you well enough yet to share? It's not that Travers doesn't like you. He's just a cautious lad. His tours of duty as a USMC JAG and as the Solita County DA further restrains him.

During law school, Marty clerked for both public and private law firms. He guest-lectured Con Law I students on search & seizure issues, while he was still a Con Law II student. After taking the grueling California bar exam, he was sworn in. And, as a private attorney, he was soon representing accused criminals.

But, grasping that his ethical duty to zealously represent his more dedicated felony clients created an occasional conflict with what he saw as a higher calling, i.e., being a good neighbor, he joined the Riverside County District Attorney's office in 1987. He has three reported appellate opinions.

Following a four-year stint as Staff Counsel in charge of Department of Motor Vehicles' Los Angeles legal office, he relocated to the multi-city Coachella Valley, incorrectly labeled Palm Springs by tourists. Could he now dispense justice, in quantities proportional to proven wrongdoing?

During his fun run in the sun, the *drug czar of the desert* held many challenging positions: Deputy-in-Charge of Indio Municipal Court, Deputy-in-Charge of the Palm Springs office, Deputy-in-Charge of Misdemeanor Pre-Trials, and Deputy-in-Charge of Major Narcotic Violator Program for the county's seemingly infinite Eastern Division, finally stopping at the Arizona border.

Following DA retirement, he got serious about writing books, and even created his own website, www.CourtroomSurvival.com. Brhel also accepted an invitation to teach cops at the academy level throughout southern California, eventually doing that from coast to coast.

His DA days also found Marty with his own talk radio show, *Crimefighters*, after he created two non-profits: the Crime Control Education Foundation and the Crime Control Foundation of America. These allowed him to write public safety legislation and testify before the California Legislature.

Post-DA-retirement, he appeared in state and federal courts. Many of his civil rights clients were cops he served with, maltreated in the workplace. As Legal Defense Trust Administrator for the Riverside Sheriffs' Association, he oversaw work-related legal representation of more than 3,000 RSA members.

Next, he did a 3-year hitch with Board of Parole Hearings, conducting parole violator and life prisoner eligibility hearings, before joining their Strike Team. They implemented newly enacted Penal Code §3000.03, reviewing legislatively-mandated early release requests of more 40,000 prison inmates and formal parolees.

Trying to focus on his writing, he was soon appointed to the San Diego Superior Court as a Judge Pro Tem, continuing what he started in Riverside County courts back in 1978. He finally returned to Orange County last fall. His esposa bonita, Mary, is a fellow writer, inventor, and gifted photographer.

Columbo displays her distinctive work at www.fineartamerica.com, while she edits her first novel. You can ask her about it, and her moniker. Meanwhile, Marty just accepted a 2-year appointment to the City of Laguna Niguel's Traffic & Transportation Commission.

The award winning former DA's next escapade, you ask? Maybe Truth Travers knows. He claims it involves some Texas lawmakers and what apparently is a bad Texas law...